Dukes & Deke's

a novel

Torie Jean

SC
Creative

This book is a work of fiction. Names, characters, places, and incidents either are products of the author's imagination or used fictitiously. Any resemblance to actual events or, places, persons, living or dead, is entirely coincidental and not intended by the author.

DUKES AND DEKES

TORIE JEAN

SUNSET AND CAMDEN CREATIVE

www.toriejean.com

Copyright © 2023 by Torie Jean

All rights reserved. No portion of this book may be reproduced, distributed, or transmitted in any form, or by any means, including information storage and retrieval systems, without prior written permission from the publisher or author, except for the use of brief quotations in a book review or post.

Cover Art: Claudia Bonet, @clauins_ on Instagram

Previous Cover Art: Anna Silka

Typography: Brenna Jones, @brennajonesdesign on Instagram

Title Page Art: Kelsey Bowman, Let's Get Lit Design Studio

Editing: Jax McQueen, Starry Eyed Scribbles

Copyediting: Sonja Kaye

Formatting: Torie Jean

For information on subsidiary rights, please contact Laura Crockett at Triada US

ISBN: 979-8-218-30791-2

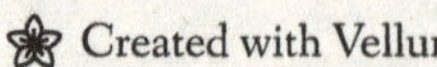 Created with Vellum

For Memere

There's not enough space in a dedication to tell you how much I miss you, so I wrote you a book instead (except the naughty bits, please disregard those.)

Thank you for showing me how strong soft girls really are.
Thank you for never letting anything in life dim your brilliant spirit.
Thank you for teaching me how to love selflessly and fearlessly, even when it hurts like hell when people pass.

Tu me manques, toujours.

Je vous aime beaucoup

Author's Note and Content/Trigger Warnings:

Hi, there! Just a quick note to say—hey! Thank you so much for picking up my book! That was so very kind of you.

Before you start reading, I would like this to serve as a final warning, that while my writing is naturally humorous (I hope) DUKE AND DEKES is not a rom-com. It's a contemporary romance that deals with heavy topics that may be triggering for some. If that's you, it's okay if you use this book as a paperweight or doorstop. Put it on a shelf with its friends, and open it when you're good and ready, or never at all. Be kind to yourself first and foremost!

And just an extra special note to those of you with endometriosis or other chronic illnesses. While this book isn't as heavy-handed on certain aspects of endometriosis as perhaps FINDING GENE KELLY was, it's still a realistic portrayal of navigating life with an undiagnosed disease, and the transition after diagnosis. Please, please, please be gentle. It's okay if you can't handle a book with that journey. Using books to escape is one of my favorite coping mechanisms. I'll understand, promise!

While this list may not cover every aspect of this book that could be heavy or triggering for some, here are some topics of note:

- Heavy discussion of grief and mourning loved ones as a central theme
- Family member whose death was a result of battling cancer
- Accurate Endometriosis rep (chronic pain, on pain vomiting, blacking out, and other aspects of living with the disease—Aulie will use narcotics on page as well)
- Medical gaslighting – Chapter two is particularly heavy, including a rough pelvic exam, please proceed with caution.
- Incorrect internal dialogue as a direct result of ableism and gaslighting
- Emergency surgery

(I promise there is so much joy and romance in these pages too!)

Content Warnings: This book has many instances of adult language and two open-door intimate scenes, one oral and one with a vibrator. Because this book has accurate endometriosis rep there will be no penetration. Please be kind and mindful that this is a reality for a lot of people battling this disease, and other pelvic dysfunctions.

Factual Note: Apropos of nothing, when I started writing this book in 2019, licking a player wasn't illegal in the NHL, it is now (thanks, Marchy!) Also, Jack's suspension is way longer than is realistic, but I needed that length for reasons so please forgive the artistic liberty there.

Final note: The chronic illness rep in this book is...well... chronic. It will be present in almost every chapter. Use that knowledge to proceed according to your personal tastes.

P.S If you don't have poutine at the ready, you may want to gather some before starting this journey. You have been warned.

Prologue

Jack Parker

Five Years Earlier

Play: *I've Just Seen a Face by the Beatles*

*J*ack Parker, handsome, broody, and rich, with a chaotic party home and miserable disposition, seemed to unite some of the worst qualities of existence and had lived nearly twenty-two years in the world with very little to comfort or appease him.

"Hey, Parker...get your ass under the funnel." Grady O'Callaghan, chaos personified, shook the tired frame of the hockey house—a colonial on the edge of Wentworth University's campus—with his booming voice.

Dammit. Jack was usually outside by the time Grady tried this shit.

He had his sore muscles to blame for this slow exit. He swore his face had met with the boards more times in today's Finals game than it had the rest of the season combined.

"I'll pass. If you assholes burn the house down, save Gus—he's in his room," Jack said before he zipped up his sweatshirt, grabbed his literature assignment, a book of poems, and headed out the door.

There was no way in hell Jack was funneling anything.

Not when he'd seen that long tube in far too many orifices the past few years but never in the sink.

Outside, fresh salt air wafted in from the nearby bay and cooled Jack's lungs. His breath crystallized on the exhale. Winter's last laugh as April blinked alive.

Without a destination in mind beyond "far" and "away," he strolled down the dimly lit walkway. A full moon hung overhead, casting an ethereal glow near the church at the end of the path.

Don't wait for the sun to rise, Jack. Tomorrow holds no promise to be bright, his dad, the amateur philosopher, used to say. *Learn to appreciate the moonbeams and starlight that shine through the darkest nights, and a different peace will find you.*

He snorted to himself, shaking his head. If Jack had known the endless nights he would face, he might have heeded his dad's advice. But it was too late to wander for light now.

What the hell was wrong with him? He should have been partying with the rest of his team. He should have been celebrating his game-winning goal. Celebrating their *championship*.

But instead, he was aimlessly roaming his campus close to midnight, wallowing in the hollow feeling that had consumed his chest for the past five years.

What was the point of any of this if his dad wasn't there to see it?

His dad should have seen the deke. He should have been there to celebrate it.

The never-ending earworm of *but he wasn't there, and he never will be* followed him around like a second shadow.

He wished he could say it was because his dad, as the Boston Brawling Badgers legend and two-time Stanley Cup Champion, was just too busy to make it to his son's games. That John Parker wasn't a family man, like his best friend Gus's father who was the scum of the earth.

But none of that was true. John Parker was the best father, husband, and hockey player Jack had ever known, and he was gone—not on a trip, but from the earth. Cancer had taken him at the age of forty-eight, stealing him from Jack when he still desperately needed him.

I don't know how to pick myself up out of this, Dad. Give me a shot in the arm—something—to stop feeling this fucking miserable.

A white blur stood illuminated under the halo of a streetlamp ahead. Jack's steps slowed. Was there an angel in the fountain?

"Oh, *F—ernGully—*" the figure exclaimed.

He laughed at the creative censoring and stepped back on his heels. The point of this walk was to be alone.

"Son of a biscuit. Why did I do that?" Water sloshed under the angel's searching hands. Her foot caught on something as she flailed, and she flopped into the bottom of the basin with a yelp. "You just had to be dramatic, didn't you? Well, see what you've done now?"

Gathering herself, she continued her frantic patting and shifted further into the light. Jack halted his already half-hearted retreat, held arrested by the cascading moonbeams that danced over her large pair of downcast eyes.

She walks in beauty, like the night.

The poem by Lord Byron he memorized for English called to him.

Of cloudless climes and starry skies;
And all that's best of dark and bright
Meet in her aspect and her eyes;

Here, near this fountain, Jack understood starry-eyed for what it should be. Not naïve enthusiasm and boundless idealism, but someone, he sensed from the way sadness hugged her like a cloak, who knew the raw pain of life and loss and shone through with a smoldering brilliance regardless.

A heart he assumed had long since died drummed against his

chest as he pulled closer to the fountain—as if it was coming home for the first time in years. A devout skeptic in fate, narwhals, love at first sight, and other such fantastical notions, he couldn't explain the sudden change—but something in his core hummed at an unfamiliar frequency, saying *this is it, this is the day you met the one.*

April Seventh.

Four-seven.

Forty-seven.

"Need any help?" The words leaped out of him, avoiding the filter that all too often over-analyzed his speech to silence.

"Sandra Bullock, you're a quiet one." The young woman in the fountain jumped with a turn. Her face lit with recognition. "Oh, hi, Jack. You know I'm actually glad it's you," she laughed, steadying her breath. "Don't suppose you have a metal detector handy?"

Jack cocked his head to the side. He didn't remember meeting those eyes before, but the woman certainly knew him. Maybe she was at the game or something. Patting his pockets, the edge of his lips curled up. "Oh, dammit. Seems I left it in my other sweatshirt."

Wait, was that a joke?

"Ha. Ha." She wiped at the beads of water trickling down her forehead after her impromptu swim. "I don't know why I'm bothering. There's no way the ring Tyler bought me was a genuine diamond. This is what I get for ignoring my brother and falling for a bad boy. He was right—please don't tell him I said that." Her eyes sliced to Jack, and he put his hands up in surrender.

"Our secret," he said, since he hadn't a freaking clue who her brother was or what she was talking about anyway.

"But what can I say? The heart wants what it wants, and I've always had a thing for the reformed rake trope, you know? Like, I even think Wickham could be redeemable if he tried. Can you believe that? Wickham! A-ha! I found it."

She bent down and retrieved something in the water, rising again with a triumphant fist to the sky.

Jack stood by, dry and amused.

"I know, I know, always the dramatic silly little thing—that's still me. But I swear this time my dramatics were justified," she said, showcasing a ring in her palm.

"No judgment."

"Never with you." Her lips twitched as if she knew judgment was his entire personality.

No, that wasn't the best thing for her to know about him. Maybe he could show he had a charming side, too.

Well, first, he'd have to develop a charming side, but he could, for her.

He beamed warmly down at her, still perplexed by her familiarity.

Maybe they'd shared a class together? Anthropology?

He'd dozed through that one.

Attempting to exit the fountain, the woman's soaked dress hung heavy around her legs, causing her to trip. Jack wrapped his arms around her as her hand fell firmly on his bicep and the night sky held captive within her gaze collided with his own wandering eyes.

His heart jolted awake from its heavy slumber. *Hello there. I've been waiting for you.*

"You're going to get your book wet!" she shrieked.

"It's just a book of poems, nothing to worry about."

A couple of soggy pages were the very last thing he was worried about when he had a thousand tiny sparks shooting from where her hand rested on his arm. He flexed his hand at his side, hoping to get rid of the unsettling tingling sensation.

To be fair, he had asked for a shot in the arm, but this —this was—

Unnecessary? Disgusting? Horrific?

All those things, to be sure, but it was also oddly...*intoxicating?*

"Just a book of poems," the woman scoffed, swiping at a strand of hair sticking to her forehead. "I'm sure Wordsworth would be delighted to hear that."

No retort was offered as Jack's head cleared itself of all things nineteenth-century poetry. The translucent garment that clung to every inch of her revealed her bold decision to forgo a bra with her dress.

Don't stare.

"Thank you, by the way," the woman said.

"Huh?" *No, seriously, look away.*

"I said, thank you?" She followed his gaze, wrapping her arms around herself. "Oh hell, I can't let my brother see me like this. He's already going to murder me as is. Although I guess he can't kill me twice."

"You probably shouldn't be walking around campus like that either." Jack scratched his head, stuffing his free hand in the pocket of his sweatshirt. His sweatshirt! In a fluster, he ripped it off and wrapped it around the woman's shivering shoulders.

"Much appreciated," she sighed, pulling it tight against herself.

Jack started multiple sentences in his head, all but one dying on his tongue. "I don't live too far from here. I can lend you some dry clothes. Maybe walk you to your dorm or where your brother is."

"I don't—" Whatever sentence she started floated away in the evening breeze. Her eyes widened, and she quirked her brow in amusement. "You don't recognize me, do you?"

Busted.

"N-no. Sorry. Did we have a class together or something?"

"Or something, yeah." A mischievous smirk slowly bloomed across her face.

"Cool. Cool. So," Jack bounced on his toes, "since you already know my name, I feel like it's only fair..."

"Just call me Lydia Bennet since I certainly feel like her tonight." She extended her hand out.

Jack recognized the Bennet name from a book he was supposed to read for his British Literature class but didn't. Apparently, whoever this woman really was, she wasn't going to help him rediscover her identity.

Jack reached out with hesitation, recalling the pricking sensation that rooted and wound its way to his heart like a thorny vine the last time they touched. His calloused hand engulfed her long, dainty fingers, which fell like ice against his skin and lingered longer than necessary.

"We should get you warmed up." He cleared his throat, finally releasing her hand. "If you feel comfortable coming to my house."

"That should be fine." Lydia trudged ahead with no directions needed. "I'm pretty sure I could take you in a fight anyway."

"I don't know. After watching you take on that fountain, you'll need to work on you balance to keep up with me." He hurried his steps to keep pace.

"Oh, he's got jokes suddenly!"

"Don't get used to that." He flashed her a faux-stern look, the ghost of a smile tracing his lips.

The opening riff of *"Old Time Rock and Roll"* greeted them as they crossed the threshold of his house a few moments later. Uh-oh. His teammate Grady charged down the hall, sliding along the wooden floor sans pants. Jack yanked Lydia out of Grady's path a fraction of a second before the defenseman accidentally slammed her into the wall.

With a small gasp, Lydia pulled tighter into Jack. Lilacs and rosewater accosted his nostrils and sped up his already racing pulse. Whomever this woman was, he needed to get her warm and dry and out of his house and life as quickly as possible, or else he was going to die of cardiac arrest.

"Oh my god, is he okay?" Lydia asked.

"Hey, pretty lady." Grady flashed a cheesy, woozy grin before crumbling to the ground.

"He's fine." Jack stepped over Grady's limp body. "I'm going to get you some clothes; you can follow me if you want or stay here. Wherever you're comfortable."

"I think it might be safer in there," she whispered.

"Wise choice," he said, hesitating before turning the knob to his door and allowing Lydia entrance.

An apology for his unmade bed danced on the tip of his

tongue, but Grady's voice bellowed in from the living room with an ominous "Cowboy it up!" and took priority.

Jack shot his head around. "Grady, don't you fucking dare. Cowboy broke a wall last time. And a defenseman."

Frozen mid-squat, the golden retriever of a man unleashed his puppy-dog stare, weakening Jack's resolve. "Tiny cowboy?"

"No, absolutely not." He crossed his arms. "No cowboying in the house."

"Let's take this party outside, people!" Grady managed through an onslaught of belches. The party followed his march out to the backyard, and a welcomed hush fell inside the house.

"What's cowboying?" Lydia whispered through the fragile silence.

"They jump on each other's back—" Jack explained, shuffling through his drawer. "And the person they jumped on tries to buck them off." He glanced at his shirts, reaching for a comfortable long-sleeve one and a pair of flannel pants. "It usually ends with someone injured. He flashed her a sheepish smile, handing her the stack of clothes.

"That sounds like a terrible idea."

"Most of what happens in this house is." He shrugged. "I'll leave you to it."

At that, Jack *should* have left the room, but his brain, fully engulfed in "What the fuck is happening? We're feeling things, and I don't like it, buddy" flames, had very little energy left to dictate movement.

Lydia stared at him with a tilted head. "Well...okay, then."

"Right!" His eyes widened before he forced himself out of the room. A tiny fit of delicate giggles accompanied his departure. Leaning against the closed door, he ignored the strange feeling in his gut. "Do you want something to drink? We have...beer."

"Is hot water a possibility?"

"I could microwave some."

"A bit sacrilegious, but that would be serviceable, given the situation."

The door creaked open. "Sorry, Jack. Do you mind?" She

motioned to the zipper on her back and gathered her long caramel hair to one side. "Apparently, I'm useless."

Jack swallowed down a ball of nerves.

All the times Grady said, "Bro, let me teach you what chicks want—" and he cut him off with, "Grady, shut up, you're drunk," taunted him at that moment.

He must have picked something up through osmosis, though, right?

He grasped the cool metal of the zipper. Goosebumps raised on Lydia's neck as his fingers grazed her soft skin.

"You have a... you're... your..." A coughing fit seized his tightened chest. "You have a nice neck."

Yeah—so that was a hard no on the osmosis theory, then.

"You think so?" Lydia peeked over her shoulder, and her long, black eyelashes fluttered, falling to rest across her cheek. "I've always appreciated its functionality, but I hadn't given it much thought otherwise." She raised her gaze to meet Jack's. His breath caught as a twinkle passed through the warm chocolate and flecks of gold that danced along her iris, like an actual starburst flaring from within.

Frozen, he stood, arrested by a simple glance, and tried to form some witty response to save the conversation. But complimenting a neck didn't lead to much follow-up beyond maybe the mention of giraffes. And thinking about how an animal could exist in such a state as ridiculous as that long-necked freak sent Jack's thoughts in a spiral. Oh, fucking hell, why was he thinking about giraffes? And what was that awful noise coming out of his throat?

"Jack, are you okay?" Again, a small, syrupy-sweet giggle shook Jack out of his giraffe-filled spiral. He met her stare, cheeks burning hot, and realized in that instant something egregious.

That look she flashed him was *intentional*. She was *enjoying* making him flustered.

Since he found his internal turmoil appalling, he did not appreciate her provoking further suffering. He contemplated kissing the smirk off her face. Maybe kissing her until she forgot her name and apologized for causing him such gastrointestinal distress.

Instead, he closed his eyes, images of melancholy starlight and moonbeams drowning out what little coherency he possessed. "I'll go make your hot water."

Reaching for the only microwavable mug in the house, he winced, wishing they owned something that didn't resemble giant tits. With no alternative, he surrendered to his fate, pulling the heavily-titted ceramic mug clad in a yellow and magenta polka dot bikini from the shelf. *Practice your breaststroke* and *The Beachcomber, Florida,* graced the back.

Soft footsteps gathered as the microwave dinged. Jack turned toward the quiet patter, his eyes sweeping over pink-tipped toes and shapely legs hidden by his faded flannel. Something inside of him screamed he wanted more. More of this—her dry and comfy in his sweatshirt and pajamas while he brewed her subpar tea, preferably in non-heavily-titted ceramic-ware.

"Sorry," he managed through a cracking voice, handing it over to her. "We're not mug people, apparently."

Lydia studied the ridiculous mug while Jack grabbed a beer from the fridge.

"Well, this is—" She directed an amused gaze at Jack, taking a swig of his drink. "Do you think I should buy her dinner before I tea-bag her? Or…"

Beer fountained out of his useless mouth with impressive speed. He wiped the foam clean, a wide stretch of a smile following the swipe. Wrong time to take a sip.

Proud of herself, Lydia rummaged through her purse, mumbling, "I've got jokes now, too," and pulled out a sachet full of tea-bags.

There it was again—the easy familiarity. There was no way they could have met before. He wouldn't have forgotten about her, not when everything about her felt like it was imprinted on his soul years ago.

He leaned against the counter, trying to appear nonchalant while his insides whirred like a cartoon scribble. He probably would have pulled it off, too, if it wasn't for his sweaty palms on the counter, and heaven forbid they betray him, but his socks. Jack faltered, promptly landing flat on his ass.

Lydia jumped. "Oh my god, are you okay?"

"Yup. Just—fell." Heat rushed to his cheeks, and he bit back a string of expletives. Already covered in bruises from today's game, his ego didn't need one, too.

Sweet honey filled the air in soft titters as Lydia offered her hand. "Are you usually this much of a mess or is this a special occasion?"

No, his ego couldn't take much more of this. Ignoring her outstretched hand, he came back to a standing position with gritted teeth and muttered, "For god's sake, woman, I found you in a fountain."

"Hey! Low blow, Parker." She playfully swatted at him, and Jack caught her wrist.

Lydia's eyes widened at his hand wrapped around her own before relaxing into that infuriating smirk. "You caught me."

The desire to yank her to his chest and close the ever-shrinking space between them once and for all itched him to his core. He'd never felt a magnetism like this before.

Magic. It had to be. That was the only thing that could explain whatever spell he was under.

"Aulie?" Gus rasped behind him.

Lydia blinked. Once. Twice. And then glanced over Jack's shoulder. "Oh, darn it, Gus, you ruined my fun."

Wait. What did he call her? *Aulie?* Like Gus's *little sister—Aulie?* Jack quickly released Aulie's wrist as if he had been stung, trying to conceal his shock and horror.

Gus and Jack had grown up together in the small town of Chawton Falls. He wasn't just Jack's oldest friend, he was his closest, too.

Gus rubbed a hand over his buzzed haircut. "What are you doing here? And why are you bothering Jack? You know he hates when you do that."

"We were catching up. It's been a while since he's been home, and a lot has changed since then. I thought I'd fill him in on what he missed." She flashed Jack that *look* again. The one that made Jack feel like she could reach into his chest and rip out his heart, and he'd say *thank you*. It didn't matter now that he knew who she was. He still felt like somehow he was hers, like he always had been, even if he didn't know it. "He found my debriefing fairly interesting if I'm not mistaken."

Since they were little, Aulie Desfleurs had always been a terror, trying to tag along on fishing trips and dips in King's Pond, much to Jack's unsociable chagrin. She was chatty, annoying, with a flair for the dramatic, and a far too clingy disposition.

But *this*. This form of terror was entirely new, with a gentle slope to her nose and pink pouty lips that were being used for evil.

The day Jack turned eighteen and left his hometown of Chawton Falls for good, Aulie was fourteen and bawling her eyes out on the stoop of her childhood home because she had just dyed her hair an unfortunate shade of cotton candy pink. "It said spiced auburn. The box said spiced auburn," she had muttered, tears streaming down her face.

Jack, like any finely raised New England boy, was highly uncomfortable with fits of crying. In his discomfort, he had chuckled and said, "You've always been such a dramatic little thing," ruffling the offending hair with a passing hand on his way into the house.

"And you had to do this debriefing in his clothes on my campus because..." Gus narrowed his eyes at Aulie, crossing his arms. The veins on his corded forearms popped. Jack shivered, remembering the intimidating presence Gus brought to the ice for most of their high school years. It was at the core of his DNA to protect the people he loved—Aulie, especially.

"They looked cozy?" Aulie pulled at the tips of her fingers anxiously. She peeked at her brother with one eye. "And I missed you?"

Her brother's resolve strengthened. "Seriously, Alouette?" He used the family nickname for Aulie, unknowingly emphasizing the *little sister* aspect to Jack.

"I—um. Tyler picked me up and brought me down to spend the night. But things—ended poorly."

"I thought I told you to stay away from Tyler."

"So you did, and now I'm listening."

Gus's stare narrowed, resting on Aulie's face with an unrelenting sense of parental judgment.

"What?" Aulie tossed her hands up in exasperation, and Jack took a step back. He'd been on the sidelines of enough Desfleurs family conflicts to know not to interfere once they started. Gus loved Aulie more than anyone else in the world, but his protective side always clashed with Aulie's fiercely independent streak.

At least that hadn't changed.

"Nothing." Gus shook his head. A muscle in his jaw flexed. "You're growing up to be just like Mom. You know that, right?"

"I—um." Aulie bit her lip and lowered her gaze to her toes, rubbing tiny circles over an old nail head encased in a clear coating on the floor. Aulie and Gus hadn't seen their mother since Aulie was an infant, so whatever comparison Gus was making wasn't a good one. "I promise I learned my lesson this time. No more falling in love, okay?"

Jack's heart slowed, drumming against his chest in a melancholic rhythm he couldn't explain.

"That's not—" Gus scrubbed his hand over his face and suffocated a frustrated groan. "Forget it. You need a ride home?"

"If you don't mind."

"Yeah, I can do that. And you can tell me why you're wearing Jack's clothes on the way there."

With a swallow, Aulie's eyes flicked to Jack's face. Suddenly, she wasn't a little terror to be avoided at all costs. Her frivolity was a mask for that heavy weight that still clung around her shoulders. Chawton Falls was over an hour away, and judging by Gus's clipped tone, that would be a long, uncomfortable ride for Aulie.

"I can drive." The offer fell out of Jack's mouth before he had time to analyze the implications. He hadn't been home in four years. Yet here he was, risking creating an awkward situation for himself because of his recently jumpstarted heart.

Aulie's gaze shot up to meet his. "To Chawton Falls?"

He shrugged like this wasn't a momentous action for him. Like he hadn't avoided his hometown for so long for a reason. "I know the way. Do you guys actually trust that junker to get you back there?"

"No, not really. I don't even trust it to start in this cold," Gus sighed. He nodded to Jack's bottle. "Have you been drinking?"

Aulie smirked. "I wouldn't worry. Jack sprayed more of that than he drank."

Damn her.

Heat rose to the tips of Jack's ears, and he dipped his chin, ceding the fact.

"Yeah, if you don't mind, Parker, that would be helpful." Gus glanced at his room, his weary shoulders sagging with exhaustion. Having given up his hockey career his senior year of high school, Gus was on an academic scholarship, and the pressure to perform for the future welfare of his family hung like a heavy cloud over his head. "Let's go then, Alouette, come on." He beckoned Aulie to approach him, wrapping his arm around her as he walked to the door.

Out of the eyesight of both Desfleurses, Jack allowed his entire being to deflate for half a second. Clueless about the Bro Code, he understood enough to know that his best friend's little sister was a major penalty.

"Are you coming, Jack?" Aulie shot a glance over her shoulder with a single, dangerous dimple, and he swallowed down the tug, directing his thoughts to the neutral zone. God, he hated the neutral zone. But Gus was his teammate—metaphorically anyway, so that was where he'd have to stay.

"Right behind you," he said, grabbing his keys and heading out the door.

"Seriously though, why are you wearing Jack's sweatshirt? That one's his favorite," Gus asked, his breath escaping in wisps of vapor that spiraled through the night air.

"I may have lost a fight with a fountain, though the victor

remains unclear at present." A nervous titter escaped Aulie mixing with the shrieks wafting in from behind the house.

Jack raised his gaze to the moon, illuminated behind a sprouting branch. *This isn't the help I needed,* he thought, before hurrying his pace to join Gus and Aulie. His hand raised to his chest again, and his palm drew errant circles where a new percussive rhythm thrummed.

Like. At. All.

But the upward tilt of his lips and the joke dancing on the tip of his tongue suggested otherwise. "She probably doesn't want to gush about it, but she gave the fountain a run for its money."

Gus's steps halted. He narrowed his eyes at Jack. "Since when do you make dad jokes?"

"Thank you! That's what I said!" Aulie exclaimed. "He goes to college, and suddenly, the dude becomes Mr. Personality. You could have used some of that charm when you were pounding my Doritos, you know. I would have shared."

Jack shook his head with a smile. "Nah, stealing them was half of the fun."

Gus blinked. "Mr. Personality, huh? Must have missed that transformation."

"I think it suits him." Aulie's delicate voice became a melody for his beating chest. The music ignited a thousand little fires where darkness blanketed Jack's core.

Mr. Personality, huh?

Maybe he could be that kind of guy, after all.

Chapter One

Aulie Desfleurs

Five Years Later

Play: *Something's Got a Hold on Me by Etta James*

"He's *naked*, Emy! Naked! Why would you show this to me?" Glossy pages filled with pro-athletes *in the buff* rustle in the early morning wind as I fling the wretched magazine on my lap into the air. It falls with a plop on the patch of dirt in front of the garden bench my soon-to-be-ex-best-friend Emy and I are sharing. Like the cursed relic it is, it lands open to a page I'd do just about anything to forget.

What's the going rate for a lobotomy these days?

I blink at it. No, no, that won't do. Stop staring. Better yet, pray and repent for your sins or something.

My eyes flutter closed and despite the peaceful natural sensations surrounding me—slow waking waves, a subtle breeze, birds chirping in the trees—the image, equipped with hard lines of muscle and a devastating smolder still haunts me. Apparently, it took less than a second for my depraved mind to memorize the illicit content Emy shoved in my hand the minute I sat down beside her.

If it's going to haunt me, I might as well focus on the real thing. Because, well, I'm weak, and there's a decided thirst my pumpkin spice latte will not quench. No, I fear only looking, again, will satisfy this particular need, even if I know I absolutely, most positively, should *not*.

My eyes flicker open once more and greedily drink in the spread in front of them. Tattoos cover a forearm, flexed and corded, resting on a sheet of plexiglass. The ink dances up his bulging bicep, further defined in the high contrast of the black-and-white photo. I follow the line of his arm, meeting a set of powerful shoulders that hold the head of a man who exudes self-confidence.

A wild graphite gaze—a color I know to be sapphire in techni-color—bores heavily into mine, sinful and magnetic. Like it's reaching through the lens and page to steal my forsaken soul and claim it for himself. Which is a problem. A major, major problem.

If I were staring at a stranger, these descriptions would be fine. I'd feel zero guilt appreciating the craftsmanship of this photo. I could savor my pumpkin spice latte (that I only spilled a little of in my dramatics) with Emy, soak in the breathtaking view of King's Pond glittering in the golden hue of morning, and remark on the clever way the penalty box covers his unmentionables.

And we could sit here, unbothered, and it wouldn't matter that the words coming to mind are *devilishly handsome, compelling, commanding, devastating,* and *arresting,* because I'd be a nobody, admiring a somebody who willfully posed for a picture like this.

I'd be a nobody daydreaming about a rake that needs a bit of reforming. That spends more time in the penalty box than is good for him and needs someone to help him correct the dangerous game he's playing.

But here's the thing, while I, Aulie Desfleurs, am a cardigan-wearing nobody, the picture in front of me is of *somebody known.* Somebody important to me.

It's Jack Parker, one of my best friends.

Illicit feelings and thoughts, that are far too dangerous to entertain given my history, scramble my brain and fry my circuits.

With a groan, I bend down and pick up the *Iron Inspiration* Body Issue dusting it off and shoving it back into my traitorous roommate's hand. "I really didn't need to see him naked, you know."

"I think the correct term is nude since this is a rather artful representation of his body," Emy says, further digging her own grave. "I've never been more frustrated that someone is in a penalty box in my life."

"I've never been more thankful for the penalty box," I reply and try to keep my mind off the contraband still open in Emy's hands. My eyes draw back again to Jack's chest. Nondescript lines of cursive live on his left pectoral muscle, and they keep my attention for far longer than they should. He's had them since the first summer he came back to Chawton Falls after a few years away, but I've never been able to read them properly.

"Seriously, Emy, why did you have to torture me with this first thing in the morning?" I whine, stretching my legs on the wooden bench we're sharing.

"Because torturing you is fun, and I want you to have a fling with a hot hockey player who's head over heels in love with you."

I scoff at the notion that Jack Parker, the man who teases me to no end and sees me as his little sister, could be in love with me. No, there's a better chance that my brother Gus would join a commune and go on a digital detox, or Emy would stop trying to set me up with everyone with a pulse, oxygen intake optional.

"Fine. Ignore me," she says.

"I should have ignored you five minutes ago," I mumble.

"Fair. Unfortunately, I have some not so good news to share so I thought I'd soften it with something a little more...satisfying."

"I'm sorry, this is what you consider *satisfying*?"

Because I'm just all sorts of frustrated after looking at that.

She shrugs. "I found it delightful." She unlocks her phone,

hesitating and keeping it in her grasp. "Now, before I give this to you, promise me you'll keep a level head and don't freak out."

When has a person ever been told "don't freak out," and it actually prevented said freak out?

"I make no promises after the stunt you already pulled this morning."

With a sigh, she shoves her phone into my hand with the Instagram app open. At the top of her feed sits a photo of a couple kissing with a homemade wedding bouquet obscuring their faces.

Underneath, the caption reads "Surprise! We eloped! Next stop: moving to Cali with my hubby, peace out NH. It's been real, but it's time to become a star!"

"I don't get—" I squint, deciphering the handle. MrsEmmaJames. I don't know anyone with that—

Oh, no.

Oh, no. No. No. No. No. No.

"Lydia and Wickham eloped?" I panic. The devastating news floats out into the misty morning air. "Oh no, no, no, if this is real, I'm ruined."

Callen James and Emma Greene have been inseparable since they fell for each other at last year's Annual Chawton Falls in Love with Jane Austen Festival. It's a regency fair that I, as the events coordinator of the Wentworth Estate, host with the support of the local community college's English Department every October.

A fair that Callen and Emma had agreed to reprise their roles of Lydia and Wickham for again this year. Something they won't be able to do if they're in California.

This fair opens in three weeks and I'm months behind in my planning process, which is my fault, mostly. This summer, I stayed with Jack in his apartment in Boston and assisted him with a smattering of hockey injuries he suffered during his team's Stanley Cup run. It wasn't the smartest decision for the fair or my sanity, but the people in my inner circle will always come first.

"I should just cancel the fair." I groan. "Move to Canada and retire a disgraced, fair planning failure. Maybe start a goat farm.

Although the goats would probably mock me for my failures, too. Yes, solitude would be better."

"Yes, good. We're not panicking or overreacting to the news at all. Glad to see it." Emy wraps her Aurora-Berry-Alis lacquered nails around her steaming mug of homemade pumpkin spice goodness that I woke up way too early to brew.

While I adore waking up to the copper and rust-colored hills of Chawton Falls, there's unfortunately no Starbucks in sight. The closest one is two towns and twenty-five minutes over in a resort town on Lake Winnipesaukee.

Apparently, the moose and deer, which far outnumber the human population, don't appreciate the simple joys of life, like enjoying a hot cup of coffee on a chilly, relatively dreary, life-ruined morning.

Emy chuckles and inhales the wisps of steam from her mug with a soft smile. "You have to admit, it is kind of funny, though. Like what are the odds those two character-players would actually elope?"

I will admit nothing. Zero humor has been detected.

Dragging a collecting breath through my lungs, I resign myself to the situation, telling my frantically beating heart to relax.

I'm sure it'll be eager to comply after I drown it in copious amounts of caffeine?

Keeping my gaze trained forward, I revel in the quiet waves lapping to shore. My mind and my heart calm a fraction from the brown noise.

Which is all the peace I can hope to find when my sacred color-coded and tabbed-to-perfect planner is continuously taunting me with an overwhelming you-should-just-bury-yourself-alive-now to-do list.

The last thing I needed was to recast two consequential characters so close to opening day.

"Do you have your emergency back-ups at the ready?" Emy asks, smoothing down the flannel blanket spread across both our laps.

"No, my list has dwindled over the past few years, but I'll

reach out to the primary group when it's not so early in the day. Hopefully, somebody knows someone and can save me," I say. Inviting a newcomer into the fold sounds horrendous. But Lydia and Wickham are too important to leave uncasted, so I'll have to get out of my comfort zone.

Gross.

Taking a sip from my mug, I savor the warm coffee sliding down my tightened throat. Pumpkin, nutmeg, cinnamon, and a hint of maple syrup that was tapped and boiled from a maple in the front yard dance along my tastebuds.

My chest drums in an elevated rhythm.

Good morning, anxiety. So nice of you to join us so early in the day.

A playful twinkle passes through Emy's warm brown eyes as she picks up her chin and greets the rising sun. "You know, I might actually know someone who could help."

"You do?" I ask, shooting up from my resigned slump. Somewhere in my bedroom, my planner bursts into a spontaneous rendition of Handel's "Hallelujah Chorus". Maybe today won't be a total bust after all.

"Yeah, she used to be the lead in all the school plays in my high school."

Oddly suspicious, because Emy and I went to the same high school and that person was...

"But for whatever reason, she's resigned herself to playing Mary at the fair, where no one notices her goddess self."

Me. She's referring to me. I was always the lead in the school and town productions, and I play Mary now.

The jury is out on the whole goddess thing, though. Goddesses are usually powerful warriors, and I'm whatever the opposite of that is.

Maybe a flimsy chicken. Like those floppy rubber ones that you squeeze, and they make a dying squawk.

"No. No way am I playing Lydia." I shoot her some seriously dirty side-eye. Which, to be fair, given said flimsy chicken personality, is probably as dirty as a well-rinsed dish sitting futilely in the dishwasher for a second wash.

It's been five years since I buried the highly potent foolish gene I inherited from my mother. I can't risk it surfacing again, even if it's for the good of the fair.

Acting the part of the jester was never a good look on me.

"Oh, come on, Aulie. At least consider it."

"Absolutely not. You know my stance on Lydia. She's—"

"—Too foolish, impulsive, selfish, and naïve to the implications of falling heedlessly in love without suspect of character, much like Marianne—" Emy mimics me, in an insultingly docile tone. "Take out the selfish part, and that sounds like somebody who used to thrive under those conditions."

"I wouldn't exactly call my romantic history thriving, but sure," I say, because I hardly consider a handful of men who never made it past a second date and a cheating ex-fiancé who ruined acting for me, successful.

Emy's not wrong about how similar the youngest Bennet sister and I used to be, though. A huge part of my reluctance to take up the role is that there's a buried part of me that *is* like her. A part of me that is in love with love and happily-ever-afters and careless with my heart. A part that's in peril of falling head-over-heels with anything that pays me attention.

After far too many heartbreaks, I've learned to keep that piece hidden, and to approach any new relationships cautiously, because platonic or romantic, I'm doomed to love and hurt intensely. It's a part of my DNA I can't change, just as much as Gus can't change being protective, or Emy can't alter her tendency to meddle in other people's affairs.

I, Aulie Desfleurs, will always be a fool in love.

And so, I must be cautious in my approach to it. Avoid it at all costs.

Playing Lydia is too dangerous—what if the character unlocks that part of me again? What if I can't control her?

No, I've had enough heartbreak over the past few years

without bringing it on myself. It's best to stay safe and be the plain, boring Mary that both my safety and sanity require.

A spasm suddenly grips my lower half, and I discreetly press a hand to the right side of my abdomen. Hopefully, Emy won't notice the shift.

Almost immediately, her eyes narrow to my hand. Darn it all, I'm not even hiding my pain well today.

"Make sure you mention that pain in your appointment today," Emy says. "Those spasms are definitely happening more often than they used to."

I sigh. She's right. An unknown pain has been troubling me for half of my life, and recently, it's gotten worse. She shouldn't worry, though. I'm certainly not, since doctor's tell me all the time I'm just a total softie. Things like my period bother me way too much, usually curling me up in a ball and forcing me to crawl from room to room. Tough, strong people like Emy run marathons during theirs.

"It's probably nothing, like it always is." I suck in a breath. "It's fine. I'm fine."

"Mmhmm. Sure." Emy purses her lips. "I know it's not natural for you, but please try to be more assertive in there today. I'm sick of this for you."

Bringing my mug to my lips, I let the warm autumnal aromas steady my breath. *Hi brain, if you could not hyper-fixate on Emy's last sentence, that would be great. We have enough to panic about today. Okay?*

Emy is sick of my pain. Not *me*.

I repeat the reassurance again because, despite my pleas, my brain's already blurred the lines between my pain and me. We've been one for as long as I can remember.

"Yeah, I'll try to speak up. Promise." Which is a lie because I know myself well enough to be certain I'm going to melt the minute I'm in that office. In general, assertiveness is difficult for me, but at the doctor's office? With my feet hitched in the stirrups and all of me out on display? Too vulnerable. Too impossible. Not going to happen.

"Hey, maybe we try to go out this weekend? Take your mind off things and get out of the books for a second," Emy says, trying to be helpful. Unfortunately, her request only piles on top of my mountain of anxiety. Everything that's gone wrong already this morning tumbles down in an avalanche.

After years of keeping my feelings buried for Jack, one—far too alluring—picture is threatening to unearth everything.

I'm behind on planning for a fair that makes up over seventy percent of the museum's income for the year.

Lydia and Wickham eloped.

Which is only supposed to happen fictionally!

And I have a doctor's appointment in a few hours, and the odds of being dismissed for the twenty-millionth time are infinitely higher than coming away with answers.

"Uhm. Yeah, sure. We can go out." Or at least I'll try. Unfortunately, my obsession with reading isn't a choice. It's the result of my far too dramatic body gasping its dying breath whenever it comes time to socialize with others.

Again, another prick of anxiety bypasses the calming comfort of my warm mug of coffee and nettles its way into my chest.

The audacity of it all. Coffee should cure everything.

But seriously. What happens when Emy grows sick of my severe failings as a human?

Everyone has their limits. My parental figures certainly did. My father left my mother, brother, and me shortly after my birth. Then came my mother's turn. It was too hard for her to pursue new romantic relationships with children, so we were left in the care of our grandmother, Memere, and all of our great-tantes and oncles, when I was only four years old.

There's no way my "sick with nothing to show for it" disposition lately is fun to be around.

But Emy's a forever friend, right? That's what we promised each other in the third grade. The year we both learned during a family tree assignment that we had memeres who made the best baked beans and meat pies and spoke to us in a mix of French and English.

Panic seizes my lungs as I breathe through the escalating thoughts.

Directing my mind to the world around me, I try to calm the rapid-fire worries spiraling inside. In the crook of a shedding maple, a dew-spotted spiderweb glistens in the morning sun. The tips of the tree set ablaze in an autumnal flame of crimson red and blood orange leaves. The song of a black-capped chickadee greets the new day on the perch of a nearby birch. Queen's Anne Lace edges the banks of the pond.

Everything is fine.

"Hey." Emy clasps my hand. Her eyes land softly on my face and wrap me in a warm mocha embrace. "It's going to be okay. They're going to figure this out. I promise you. It's not in your head."

I nod and hope against all hopes that maybe this time, Emy is right. Even if ten years of experience with these appointments suggests otherwise.

Chapter Two

Aulie Desfleurs

Play: *Keep Breathing by Ingrid Michaelson*

It is a truth universally acknowledged that a doctor in possession of the wealth of knowledge provided from a single seminar class twelve years ago will consider themself an infallible expert regarding the hellish reproductive organs housed within their fragile, unstable, constipated patient.

Laying on the exam table, I recite the satirical line of Jane Austen Emy left on my car a few years ago to combat my anxiety. Reading the note before my appointment started as a calming ritual for me, until three years later and far too many doctor's appointments the note is tattered and tear stained. Luckily, I committed it to memory. Now, I mentally recite it when the appointment is going south and I need something else to focus on.

Today, I'm on recitation number nine.

Eleven is the record.

"Have you tried using a vibrator?" Two gray caterpillars in

serious need of grooming raise, meeting what brief eye contact I can muster in this position. Conversations are never a good idea while your feet are high in stirrups.

The flare of hope for a good appointment Emy sparked inside me flickers out with that question until only a smoldering ember of nope, no way, nuh-uh, not going to happen remains.

Thick bile churns in my stomach. For whatever reason, I feel queasy discussing my vibrator usage—or lack thereof—with a man that went to high school with my great-tantes and oncles.

Dr. Murdoch keeps his lips taut, elbow-deep in my cave of wonders, searching for a sign of the curse.

Spoiler alert: he won't find one there. They never have.

My vocal cords tighten, holding down a scream, and I clear my throat.

"No. But I feel like—" *Oh, punaise.* A band of cramps erupts across my abdomen. I suck in a breath, collecting myself. This pain, more than anything else, concerns me. Not the severe lack of orgasms in my life.

Which, truthfully, is my reclusive self's fault anyway.

Ugh, darn it all. This is going like all my other appointments in the past. The doctor hears one symptom in my list of complaints and tries to cure that specific ailment instead of assessing all my problems collectively.

Something more than my lack of orgasms and weak sphincter is plaguing me.

Why won't they trust me when I say that?

I could be wrong, and the professionals right. That's what the logical side of myself always tries to argue when I'm in the office being dismissed for the millionth time. I must be the problem if so many people with medical degrees are waving off my concerns. Maybe it's not the conclusion I feel deep in my bones, but it's the more believable one. Who knows, maybe the cave of wonders metaphor lands closer to the mark than I realize. Maybe the pain from all the poking and prodding is my neglected pelvic region's way of moaning and saying, *"Who disturbs my slumber?"*

"No vibrator," I say in an even tone, fixing my gaze on the

three-dimensional model of the vagina perched on the windowsill straight ahead. Huh, so that's where my clitoris is. "But if I'm honest, sir. I'm more concerned with the constant pain, bloating, and other symptoms I mentioned."

Like the deep, depressive thoughts near my period. Or bleeding through maxi pads in two hours and the inevitable anemia. Not to mention the nausea, vomiting, chronic fatigue, occasionally blacking out when trying to pass a bowel movement, insomnia, hot flashes, cold flashes, Violet-Beauregard-level-bloating, and the constant neck, back, and pelvic pain.

To name a few of my complaints.

He nods, caterpillar eyebrows furrowed, and then clamps down on a muscle in my cave-of-not-so-wonderful. My insides roar with pain. My teeth bare down on my lip, biting back a yelp, and I draw blood from the force.

"You're constipated," Dr. Murdoch says, pulling out his hand.

No. No. No. No. No. I've waited six months for this appointment. It can't be slipping away with another constipation diagnosis. I try to save face, contorting my expression into a more neutral one than the anguished look vying for real estate there. It's important I don't show too many emotions, or this appointment will be well and lost.

"I'm not—"

"I felt stool."

"I passed two bowel movements already today." My fingers twiddle, and my feet shake, still in the stirrups. A tremor of pain works its tendrils through my lower half and clenches my stomach, pelvic region, and the tops of my legs in a slow burst of intense, needling heat.

If this is what constipation feels like, I'd like my money back on the fiber supplements and probiotics I took religiously before this appointment.

Not to mention the stool softeners.

Water.

Yoga.

And daily runs.

I did everything right before this appointment, and somehow, I still ended up here.

Constipated.

What a load of crap.

Discussion over, Dr. Murdoch channels all his energy at the keyboard before him—his finger hovers over the keys, circling for its destination. A quick clack follows, and he repeats step one.

Hover. Click. Repeat.

With each agonizing episode of "Old Man Overcomes Inadequate Typing Skills," the weight of another failed appointment drags me below the surf.

I can't shake the feeling that I'm drowning in a bottomless ocean, but instead of throwing me a lifeline, everyone who comes along to rescue me keeps telling me that I'm actually safe on shore, and the hyperventilating and gasping are all in my head.

"I'm writing you a prescription for a probiotic. Focus on your diet, drink plenty of water, and exercise; you should be fine. I'm also resending a prescription for birth control. It's your choice if you want to fill it, but given your complaint regarding your periods, I think it's time to start."

I tilt my gaze heavenward. Birth control. The clicking tongues of ten devout Catholic tantes ring in my head. It's probably time for me to stop listening to ninety-year-old French-Canadian women who took their grudge over masses lead in English to the grave. But old habits die hard for me.

A frustrated tear rolls down my cheek. *No. No crying, Aulie. Not yet. Hold it in.*

Dr. Murdoch pauses his slow-moving struggle, glances at me, and emits a long, pronounced sigh.

Busted.

In my experience, medical professionals find people who emote in their office offensive.

Maybe it pricks their conscience, and they don't appreciate it. I don't know.

Maybe I should lean into it, and Dr. Murdoch, overcome with

an overwhelming sense of guilt, will see me in distress and reconsider dismissing me.

He clears his throat, taking a long sip of water. "I would also recommend seeing a therapist for whatever is bothering you. The chronic fatigue you mentioned is a depressive symptom, making you think you're in pain when you aren't."

Or maybe Dr. Murdoch doesn't have a conscience.

Can you have a conscience as a medical professional? Sometimes I wonder if there's some ritual they have to undergo to remove it before they can get the floppy hat at graduation.

Maybe it's the floppy hat that sucks it from their souls.

"I'll leave you to get dressed," Dr. Murdoch says, exiting the room.

With my feet still hitched, I lay on the exam table, stunned. The white sterile walls provide nothing but bitter silence. I waited six months for this? Let myself hope...for this?

What a fool.

Never hope.

I know that. I practice that. It's the one solid truth about life I've established in my almost twenty-four years on this planet.

Hope is an invitation to be disappointed. Nothing more.

I lace my legs into my tights and fumble with gravity. Oh, for Pete's sake. Why did I choose to wear hosiery to the doctor's office?

Wobbling, I hit a sliding tray. Metallic tools clang to the tile floor, and in their clatter, I admit defeat. My socks and boots will do. I ball my tights together and toss them into my purse.

With my peacoat and scarf wrapped around me, I take a breath and shuffle out to the lobby, pulling my crocheted hat over my ears.

Tears prick the edge of my eyelids, threatening to make another embarrassing appearance.

Hold it in. Five more minutes.

The fresh autumn air fills my lungs as I step out to the grey skies hanging overhead.

At least the weather has the good sense to reflect my mood.

Mrs. Bates, my Subaru, sits in the back of the parking lot. A distance I reveled in earlier as a chance to stretch my legs now mocks me as a burden I need to overcome. How many times will I have to go through this before someone listens to me and figures out what's wrong?

What if it's nothing?

Another tear trickles down my cheek, and I hurry my pace in the parking lot, fallen leaves crunching under my haste.

The local florist, Mrs. Beverly, offers me a broad smile stretching across her cheeks, kissed pink by the mid-September wind. "Good morning, Aulie."

"Hi, Mrs. Beverly." I force my lips into an unnatural upward curve and fight the tremble working through them.

"Almost time for the fair."

"Mmhmm." I slow my steps since my Memere taught me to be polite and kind above all else, even when I want to sob in solace in my Subaru.

"Looking forward to it."

"Me too. It should be a great year."

Liar.

According to my planner, I'm doomed and missing two key character pieces.

I'll be lucky if there *is* a fair this year at this rate.

Finally, I reach my car, and frustrated tears flood out of me like a flume. My head collapses on the steering wheel. A long overdramatic blare of the horn follows.

I jump at the blast. And then laugh.

And cry.

And laugh-cry.

After ten years of dismissals, my reserves to handle this are nonexistent.

Starting the car, a familiar post-appointment thought sinks like a stone in my gut. Without the hope of another appointment on the horizon, reality becomes clear. No one is throwing me a lifeline, so I'll have to gather the strength to just keep swimming.

Somehow.

Chapter Three

Aulie Desfleurs

Play: *Back to Autumn by Tall Heights*

Mrs. Bates didn't start on the first turn.

Of course, she didn't. Why would exiting the seventh level of diagnosis purgatory be easy?

"Come on, Mrs. Bates. We don't have time for this today," I plead with my spinster vehicle, turning the key again. After yelling for Mother, she settles into a softer purr.

Well, it's more like a clunky, clattering purr.

Nevertheless, she's alive, and that's all that matters today.

Note to self: get an oil change and tune-up at Pinard's Automotive, Greeting Cards, and Pie Shop next week.

I should get Emy's birthday card while I'm there too.

Connecting my phone to the car audio jack, I scroll to my post-appointment playlist and press "End of the World" by Herman's Hermits. It's a dramatic song that lifts my spirits on days like today because I can cry, wallow, and laugh at how ridiculous I am, all within three minutes.

I'm about to let the tears flow as my first crush, Peter Noone, soothes my soul when that eighties song, "Centerfold," suddenly blares through my speakers instead.

What the—

"Incoming Call: Jack," reads on my dashboard.

"When did that ridiculous woman even have time to change his ringtone?" I groan, ignoring how my traitorous heart leaped when it saw his name.

Add "change Jack's ringtone back to normal" to my never-ending to-do list.

Thanks for nothing, Emy.

Okay, when I answer this, I have to play it cool. I didn't just see a revealing picture of him or have a meltdown over the odd feelings spiraling inside because of said picture.

Nope. Totally unaffected by his merciless hard lines of muscle and piercing gaze. Everything is totally fi—

"Hello, you've reached Petunia's Pancake Parlor. Will this be for pickup or delivery?" I wince at my forced joke greeting the minute it leaves my mouth.

"Oh, god. Pancakes sound so good. Do you deliver?" Jack's morning voice, thick with gravel, rasps against my ear. Warmth blossoms in my chest.

"Are you still in bed?" I ask.

Shoot, no, I shouldn't be thinking about Jack in bed. That's a dangerous combo.

"Just enjoying my last day before the season's craziness starts tomorrow." He yawns. "How'd your appointment go?"

"Oh—um." I swipe at the tears dotting my cheeks, shifting into drive and leaving my disastrous visit in the rearview mirror. "How are you feeling about the game tomorrow?"

He chuckles, shifting in bed. I can practically hear him mussing his hair, still half asleep like he did so many times on the couch this summer under the influence of some serious narcotics. "Must have been a shitshow if you're avoiding telling me about it, huh?"

"Yeah, it was...less than ideal." The whites of my knuckles flash as I twist and tighten my grip on my steering wheel while

I pause at an intersection. Turning right, I wave at a few locals in passing cars headed to their jobs at the local resort. Soon, when the last leaves fall, and winter settles into the hills, the town will hibernate, but for now, Chawton Falls is alive and thriving.

"I'm sorry to hear that. I know you were looking forward to the appointment."

"I don't know if 'looking forward' is quite the terminology I'd use, but I was feeling something akin to hope, I guess. It's fine. I'll survive."

"You always do." The usual brashness of his teasing tone softens. "But I hate this for you. You know my offer from the summer still stands, right?"

I sigh. Jack offered to pay to send me to one of the doctors in Boston, hoping I'd have better luck in the metropolitan area. Still, I don't know if I could handle the guilt of another medical professional's dismissal, knowing I cost him thousands of dollars.

"And I appreciate it, but they're probably right, and I'm just a hypochondriac or something, and then you'd be out a buttload of money because of my neurosis, and I know I'm spiraling, and I swear I'm grateful for you—" Tears trickle again, and I pause to collect myself.

"Hey, hey, it's okay. Just know the offer is there if you want to take it. Not a big deal."

"Thank you again."

"Anytime. I've got you. So, anyway. How's the fair planning going this week?"

An ugly amount of snot runs down my nose, and I grab a nearby napkin and swipe at it, laughing at the mess I am this morning. "Oh god, that's an utter disaster too. You'll never guess what happened this morning."

"Did you lose the bonnet box?"

"Don't even joke about that!" I shriek. It took years to curate the bonnet collection thanks to my co-planner Bridget's stringent historical accuracy standards. I will guard it with my life until the end of times. "No, but two major characters eloped this morning, and they're headed to California now. So I have to find *two* replacements before next week. It's a nightmare."

"Damn. Any ideas of who could fill in?"

"Oh! Actually, I was hoping you'd bail me out," I joke, laughing at the thought of Jack running around in breeches and using a mangled British accent. The man would absolutely never.

"You know, I would love to, but I think I have a hockey game that day or something."

"You're so cute playing your little game with your little stick."

Where you get thrown into penalty boxes because—

Oh my word, no Aulie. Bad.

Momentarily losing all good sense and executive functions, I swerve, and Mrs. Robinson, out walking her labradoodle, gives me a nasty passing glance. I wave apologetically, heat blasting my cheeks with embarrassment.

"Oh, come now, Dessy. There's nothing little about my stick." Jack's cheeky tone has me doing a double-take. *Does he already know?* Am I being that obvious?

"Gross!"

"Kidding. Kidding. Well, I'm not, but—" A coughing fit rattles my speakers. "Ah shoot. I'm so heartbroken I won't be able to wear tights for you."

"Breeches," I correct. "And also, you're a dirty liar."

"No, really, I'm gutted I can't be there to help you, but darn it all, my job."

Speaking of.

"How'd Veronica take you breaking up with her?" I ask to change the topic. I don't have "get arrested for vehicular manslaughter" on the to-do list today, and Jack in breeches is too great a danger to entertain while driving.

"How do you know I have?"

"Because it's like you said, the season starts tomorrow. And you never date during the season."

Once hockey season starts, Jack has a one-track mind—hockey, hockey, hockey, cup, cup, cup. Gus, me, his family, Chawton Falls, relationships, and everything else fall to the wayside until July comes around again.

"Damn. I didn't think I was as predictable as you. But, yeah, let's say I made a good choice making sure it wasn't at a steakhouse."

"Very disappointed to hear you didn't get stabbed."

"See, this is why I call you first thing in the morning. You always make sure I feel so loved, Dessy," he teases. My heart does another stupid somersault at my nickname. It's a hockey nickname, the ultimate symbol I weaseled into Jack's inner circle after many years.

A feat that thirteen-year-old me, who harbored a massive crush on my brother's aloof, grumpy best friend, would be squealing over.

"Look, Parker. You have enough people inflating your ego. It's my job as the best friend to keep you humble."

"I don't remember hiring you for that."

"You didn't. The universe, however, considered it a vital role for a balanced axis—heavy heads tilting the weight of the world and all that. But let me tell you, the initiation process was brutal. I had to go into a fountain and pretend I was desperate for help. Charm your socks off until you were literally falling for me."

"I still contend my socks were extra slick that night."

"Mmhmm, sure." For whatever reason, if I want to rile Jack up, all I have to do is mention him slipping off the counter the night we were re-introduced, and he gets a little tongue-tied. Since Jack established pretty early on that we have a teasing relationship —and that's it—it's ammunition I refuse to let go of.

"Right, well. I'm sure you're getting close to the donut shop by now, so I'll let you go. Say hi to Memere for me."

I don't know if it's sweet or concerning that Jack knows my morning routine so well.

"Thanks. I will. Hey, do you think it's weird that I'm still doing this? Emy's giving me her patented total judgment look when I say I'm headed to the cemetery. But she doesn't know this side of things, you know?"

"Honestly, Dessy, I'm not sure I'm the right person to ask, but I don't think it's weird. I think you should take your time and do what you need to. There's no right way to get through any of this shit."

"You're right." I sigh.

"I'm sorry, you cut out. Can you say that again?"

"Didn't you have to go?"

"Ah, shit, yeah, I'm already running late for the morning skate."

"Surprise. Surprise," I say. "But hey, before you go—behave tomorrow. I know it'll be hard when you're playing against Alex, but I didn't give up my summer for you to do something silly in your first game back, okay? Get a good night's sleep and make good decisions tomorrow."

"Go out and drink a shit ton tonight and then pound the crap out of the fucker tomorrow. Got it."

"No! That's not what I—"

"See ya, Dessy!" Jack says, a broad smile clear in his tone. Jerk.

He hangs up, and my over-the-top dramatic music starts up again. With a sigh, I change the song. I'm well past my cry until I make myself laugh part of the drive.

Anne's Donuts, the local bakery housed in a whitewashed barn, appears on my right. I turn into the drive-thru lane equipped with a crackling, static two-way speaker installed in the 1970s when the shop opened. I stop in line behind another Subaru. A "This Car Climbed Mt. Washington" sticker clings to their rear bumper.

With a calming breath, I soak in the beauty of the surrounding area. Just down a gently sloping hill, Mr. Martin's cows graze peacefully in their pasture. Moulton's Apple Farm sits to the left. Tractors with wagons attached to the back are loaded with hay, ready for October. A pumpkin patch and corn maze stand as decorations on the farm, signaling fall has *arrived* in New Hampshire. The "Leaf Peepers" will head north this weekend for the autumn scenery, and we'll be ready.

The car in front of me pulls forward, and I follow suit.

"Welcome to Anne's Donuts. How can I help you?" The voice of Blake Bailey, the mastermind behind an over-the-top Mrs. Bennet and a pompous Mr. Elton, crackles through the frozen speaker.

"Hi, Blake! It's Aulie. Can I have my regular, please, and thank you?"

"You've got it! Drive up!"

Blake's sparkling green eyes greet me at the window. "Good morning!" they say, tucking a loose golden tendril falling out of the bun behind their ear. Powdered sugar is swept across their cheek, forehead, and nose, coating their pale skin in an early dusting of snow. The Chawton Falls landscape won't be too far behind if these frigid morning temperatures continue the way they have in the past week.

"Morning! How are you doing?"

"Oh, you know, same old! Hey—um—have you been on Instagram this morning?" Blake swallows, avoiding my eyes with the question.

"Unfortunately, yes." I groan. "Any chance you know anyone who could help us out? Because all Emy offered for a solution was for me to fill in. Wouldn't that be ridiculous?" I laugh off the suggestion, hoping Blake agrees with me.

It's a terrible idea. Probably. I don't know. I *am* desperate, and maybe I could play the naive, foolish woman in love and not let the role seep into my own life. Maybe I'm overthinking all of this and there isn't even a foolish side to unleash anymore.

"You totally should do it!" Blake brightens, a broad smile stretching wide across their face. "Getting into acting again could be good for you."

"It really wouldn't be," I grunt, feeling betrayed. I was looking for validation, not another person on Team Emy. "It's kind of the opposite of what I need."

"It's been a rough few years for you." Blake regards me sympathetically, hinting at what everyone always tiptoes around. Being raised by a group of people far older than me was a huge blessing when I was little. But now, after the past few years and far too many funerals, I only know the icy grip of mortality. "Maybe it's time you did something fun. Something for yourself. Besides, I miss my leading lady out there." They pass my tray of coffees through the window to me. "Wouldn't getting back out in the theater world be a great way to show you're over that shitty ex? Or maybe you could turn your attention to the hot hockey player who sends you moon eyes when you aren't looking."

The tray wobbles in my grasp, and I inhale sharply. I stabilize it and narrowly avoid spilling scalding hot coffee on my lap.

The whole "your best friend has the hots for you" theory my friends refuse to drop rattles my nerves more than it should. Probably because it's absurd, and I'm a practical, level-headed woman.

And entertaining the idea that the bad boy of the National Hockey League harbors feelings for me, a woman who holds the record for most cardigans owned, threatens my sensibility.

"I'm going to pass on the Jack idea," I say. "We're friends. That's it. That'd be like dating you or Emy."

"Or it could be more like Emy dating Gus, which is working out." Blake smirks, handing me a bag with three apple cider donuts—one for me and two for Emy and Gus.

While I was gone this summer, Blake played the part of matchmaker, encouraging a budding relationship between my brother and best friend. Alone in our house on King's Pond, the forced proximity and Blake's nudging allowed Emy and Gus to know the best parts of each other's hearts.

Parts that I adore in each of them.

Honestly, I love their relationship. I just sometimes wish I wasn't as privy to it since I'm now with them in the confines of that same house again.

"I wouldn't know. I have safety perimeters in place mentally where they're still in separate rooms at night, and the squeaking is Gus playing with a rubber duck."

"I worry about you sometimes."

"I always worry about me, so that's fair." I laugh.

A less-than-polite but understandable toot blares from the vehicle behind me.

"Thank you for the coffee, as always. I love you, bye!" Hastily, I take my foot off the brake and pull forward.

Turning the corner, I enter Main Street and blast some oldies. "I'll Follow the Sun" by the Beatles plays as I enter the center of town. "Centerfold" may be the newest music played in this car in some time. The music from the 50s and 60s is the only part of my childhood and family I have left, so I gladly wrap myself in a cocoon of British Invasion music and Bubblegum Retro Pop.

Nineteenth-century brick buildings line the widening road. The town square, housing a white gazebo, passes on my right. Two men, Gerald and John, lift bales of hay inside, setting the scene for the fall festivities.

Oh my gosh, I can't believe I almost forgot about the Scarecrow Contest. Emy and I should build Finchwilliam Darcy and Elizabeak Bennet this weekend.

I'm sure she'll fight my brilliantly punned creation, like she does every year, asking if we could try something else. She always does that, attempts to change things and get me out of my comfort zone.

But it's called a comfort zone for a reason, and who doesn't enjoy being cozy?

There's enough sadness and change in the world without actively seeking it out.

I pull at my sleeves, passing the old Neal's Mill. Just the thought of change makes me anxious.

The red structure towers over the square, visible from nearly every angle of Chawton Falls. The familiar rush of the rapids and falls of the Squam River below the cobblestoned bridge drowns out the chaotic whir of my mind.

My heart grows heavier as I pull the car down the winding driveway that leads to the serene cemetery sitting beside a wide, grassy meadow. Fog sits low over the horizon, and images of Mr. Darcy striding toward me in a billowy coat dance in my head.

Throwing the car in park, I undo the binding constraints wound around the sorrow in my heart.

Take a moment every day to remember them and let however

you feel out. I read that somewhere, and it works. Allowing myself ten minutes of raw reality means I can carry on for the rest of the day, locking all necessary feelings away in a tidy compartment until my allotted mourning time the next day.

I pop the trunk and fish out the trimmers and brush I store in the car to clean off the grave markers. A wood stove burns nearby, and the smoke delicately wafts over, steadying my breaths with the nostalgic comfort a good wood fire can bring. A few leaves from a nearby tree hug Uncle Eddie's gravestone.

In fall, all the leaves become flowers, Alouette, he used to whisper.

I pick up an orange frosted leaf, roll the dry stem on the pad of my thumb and stuff it in my pocket, humming to myself as I finish cleaning the rest of the family markers.

Breathing in the sun's warmth, I sigh. Aunt Camille, Uncle Edouard, my Memere, and their brothers and sisters are all laid out before me. Fourteen in all. Fourteen people who loved and cared for me. Old age released them one by one until it reduced their lives to granite in the ground and a legacy of the love they showered on those around them.

"I miss you all terribly."

A subtle breeze passes through the cemetery, rustling the leaves. I shiver against the wind and pull my peacoat tightly against me.

"I wore tights out. I swear," I say defensively, putting the trimmers back in the car and retrieving a blanket. I roll it out in front of my Memere, placing one coffee on her freshly laid marker, and sit cross-legged next to it with my cup, removing the *Jane Austen Seven Novels* book tucked underneath my armpit.

I close my eyes, channeling all my energy into my family and letting myself feel and reflect on whatever comes to me.

A soft fire flickers in the wood stove, a pot of ragout simmering on top.

My Memere's fingers fly freely with a joyful staccato rhythm on her dual-layer organ. Her high, beautiful voice fills the room.

"You sound like Snow White!" a little version of me giggles.

Uncle Edouard, sporting a flat tweed cap, enters the room with his ukelele, dancing around, strumming off-key and off-tempo.

"Edouard," Memere scolds, the big smile on her face at odds with her stern tone. "Will you quit that racket? It's not even in tune, heaven-to-Betsy."

Uncle Edouard shrugs and gathers me up.

"You'll wreck your hip!" Memere shrieks as I laugh and squirm in my uncle's arms.

"Oh hush, Ani. I'm not old yet."

Aunt Camile walks in with chunky black sunglasses shielding her eyes, even though we're inside. They're glasses half my aunts and uncles have started to wear. She sits on the couch with the hefty book I currently hold. "Come read to me, love," she beckons.

My eyes flicker open, and I clear my throat, thick with emotion. That's quite enough of that.

"Now, where were we? Oh, yes. The letter." I sip my coffee. The hot liquid warms everything down to my toes.

God bless hot coffee.

Opening the book to *Persuasion*, I flip to where Captain Wentworth's letter is penned across the page. I breathe through a sharp twinge in my pelvis and continue the story—one that promises the happy ending I'm beginning to fear my life will never have.

How could it without them?

Chapter Four

Jack Parker

Play: *Fat Lip by Sum 41*

Whoever said that there's nothing more beautiful than Boston in the fall has never actually been to Boston in the fall. They probably saw a postcard of the George Washington statue in Boston Common with a bright blue sky and yellow trees behind it and considered it idyllic. But that postcard is a damn lie because all it does in September and early October is fucking rain.

Headlights streak down the winding paved cow paths we call streets and spray the puddles on the poor bastards who are still out at this ungodly hour.

With a decided wobble, I stumble on the sidewalk, eliciting a groan from Captain Party-Killer, Grady O'Callaghan.

He levels a stare at me, and I snicker at the role reversal. Good. After all the times I hauled his humongous frame around campus, he owes me a few more nights of being the frustrated responsible one. Probably not too many more at this rate, but a few, anyway.

Drinking my feelings for Aulie Desfleurs away didn't work out as well I hoped tonight.

Fuck. They're still growing stronger, like she's a goddamn sorceress who stole my heart for her collection a long time ago.

Maybe she did. Maybe the sweet, innocent persona that I eat up every time I'm around her like a man starved for scraps is all a ruse. Maybe when I'm gone she whispers incantations over my long-lost organ and that's why nothing I ever try will release me from her grip.

There was a time when drinking her gone actually worked, and giving into other vices and impulses made it possible for me to stay away from my ultimate vice—*her*.

But now, after a month of her taking care of me and having the audacity to be lung-grippingly gorgeous the entire time—I'm officially done for.

Of course, I'll never act on it. My friendship with Gus, and honestly, with Aulie, is too important for me to risk on something I'm bound to screw up anyway.

"Come on, Parker. Stand up straight." Grady sighs, wrapping my arm over his shoulders and saving me from toppling to the ground.

Water beads down his face, flattening his curly mess of long-blond hair. Some strands stick to his forehead and cover the scar that's a relic of the first time we got drunk together. Apparently, Grady needs someone whispering "maybe you shouldn't" or he does things like smash a glass bottle to his forehead.

Between that and when he tried to cowboy a Swedish defenseman during the Olympics, barreled headfirst into the cot and dislocated his shoulder, he's had to learn to become responsible or stop playing hockey.

Giving up the sport isn't an option for either of us. It's in our blood. As much as being the serious fuddy-duddy goes against all of his DNA and impulses as well.

"Seriously," he grunts. "I only looked away for two seconds. How did you get like this?"

"I don't know. Some women wanted to take shots with the star forward of the Brawling Badgers and *Iron Inspiration's* centerfold. How could I say no?" I say, hopefully presenting evidence that will appeal to the sliver of Grady that's still fun.

"Uh-huh, and how many times did that happen?"

"Mmm. Six or seven...maybe ten times? I don't know. But have you seen the picture?"

"Yeah, totally fuckable. I get it," he says in a disinterested tone. So only boring Grady is going to exist tonight. Got it.

A group of women passes us, huddling under an umbrella and giggling.

I straighten slightly and wink at them.

"We loved the photo shoot, Parker. My friend needs a stripper for her bachelorette party if you want to join us!" one woman shouts.

"Oh my gosh, I can't believe you said that!" A blonde woman with a sash playfully swats at her emboldened friend as they walk further away. "You're so bad."

Huddled laughter continues as their heels splash along the cobblestoned sidewalk.

In the past, someone saying something like that to me may have made me blush. Now, it's all a part of the public persona I hide behind for protection.

Jack Parker, starting center for the Brawling Badgers, doesn't mind his body being celebrated in flatlays and soap commercials because it's not his. The trainers and nutritionists who changed me from an awkward college kid to someone with hard, immovable muscle own it. It's a tool I use for my job. That's it.

I pivot to join the ladies, but Grady's grip holds me firmly in place. I trip on the ledge of the sidewalk, and my ankle twists. My ass meets asphalt, and a large splash follows.

"Are you kidding me? We just got you walking again." Grady crosses his arms, casting a withering stare down at me. "Coach will kill me if you show up like this tomorrow."

"Dude, you gotta chill out." I laugh. "You know how often I've seen your ass on the ground?"

"This is different."

"How?"

"Because I was in college when I pulled this shit, and you're twenty-eight and have a team of guys relying on you to get them to the Cup this year."

The whole *you have a bunch of guys relying on you* bullshit always sobers me up. Well, kind of, anyway. As much as I can sober up after five shots of tequila.

It may have been seven. I don't know.

"Let's get back to my apartment," I say, standing and straightening my shirt.

"Thank you." Grady lifts his gaze heavenward, and drops of rain collect on his face. He blinks, wiping them away with agitation.

I should cool it before he blows a gasket.

My phone vibrates in my pocket. It's probably the same person who's called me the last four times, but just in case...I slide my hand into my soggy designer jeans and pull it out. Sure enough, *Veronica Burke, Mandy's friend*, sits at the top of the screen.

I hit the ignore button...again.

Grady glances over in time to see her name displayed and shakes his head. "She won't stop."

I slide my phone back into my pocket, and we continue to walk through the relatively empty streets of Boston. "I'll change my number tomorrow."

I don't understand why Veronica is bothering. Our arrangement was clear. Our dates were for the headlines, nothing else. "It's ridiculous that she's acting like me ending this caught her off guard. I was clear about my timetable from the beginning."

"No way someone like Veronica has experienced being dumped, real or fake." Grady shrugs. "She probably figured you'd fall in love if you spent some time with her. Like in that one Hallmark movie she starred in where she owned a failing bakery and had to fake date a movie star so people didn't catch on that he was dating some other starlet. What was it called? I can't remember, but I should watch that one this weekend. It was the right kind of cheesy for a rom-com, you know? Oh! *Fake It Till You Bake It,* that's the one."

"I'll—erm—I'll take your word for it." I shake my head, careful not to laugh at Grady. He's obsessed with cheesy movies about love, and I don't think it's cool to dump on something someone else is passionate about.

Although the humor of a tough hockey player watching Hallmark movies isn't lost on me.

"I made sure she knew about my No Dating During the Season Rule, though. That wasn't a flexible rule," I say. When the hockey season starts, only one thing matters to me—winning the cup and seeing my name next to my dad's on the trophy.

Sure, I still dabble in some extra-curricular stuff, like parties and drinking, but I'd argue it helps me stay loose and keep my screaming skull quiet between puck drops, so I don't tighten up on the ice.

Veronica was a publicity stunt, nothing more. My agent thought it would be a good idea to have a backup in Hollywood in case my injuries in the offseason didn't heal. Veronica needed her name in the gossip columns to pull away from her first failed attempt at film.

Going from playing cheesy Hallmark characters and a demon slayer to a British historical piece where her accent went from American to Cockney to Australian didn't go over well with the critics or the public.

A dizzying wave hits me, and I stumble along the sidewalk. The neon glow of the golden arches near my apartment blurs in my hazy line of vision. It beckons me in a whisper. *Poor dietary decisions don't count as long as they're done in the mid-of-night, Jack.*

"I need sustenance," I say.

"Really? The day before our opening game?" Grady groans. "Just cut me now, Coach. I realize I'm only on the team to keep the asshole under control, but really, he makes it impossible."

"It's just a burger. I'll be fine." I wave him off and enter the restaurant. A scrawny teenager stands behind the counter, leaning on the palm of his propped-up hand, half asleep. Our shadows fall over him, and he startles at the creeping darkness. Slowly, his eyes widen, and his mouth slackens as he recognizes us. Well, me specifically.

The open gawking doesn't faze me anymore. It's been happening ever since some TikTok went viral, crowning me the "Bad Boy of the National Hockey League." The video ushered thousands of follow-ups with montages of me in clubs in Boston, me fighting on the ice, and one even dream-cast me as the main character in some dark romance novel (whatever that means). I mistakenly asked Aulie about it, and she sent me the story summary, and I just have to ask: are people who read okay?

At least it gave me solace that some fictional version of myself got a happily ever after.

"I'll take two-quarter pounders with cheese, a large fry, and—" I glance again at the menu. My eyes draw to a limited-edition milkshake that Aulie ordered at alarming rates this summer. I snort to myself, a small smile tipping my lips up. Against my better judgment, images of her scream across my skull. I've never seen someone so content with something so small and frivolous. My heart thrums in a rhythm that only beats when I'm thinking of Aulie, recalling how her eyes lit up when she wrapped her pink pouty lips around the straw and hummed with satisfaction the minute the frozen concoction slid down the back of her throat.

Couch-bound after many injuries, the routine held me captive. The way her lashes fluttered to rest on her cheeks as she savored the first few sips and the content smile on her mouth for the hour after she'd finished.

God, that smile. Not even the most potent painkillers could dull the ache in my heart when she smiled like that.

Grady clears his throat, shaking me out of my Aulie spiral.

Sheepishly, I correct my posture and avoid his curious stare. "Sorry. Um, I'll take one of those s'mores milkshake things, and that will do it, thanks."

"Of course, he'd get a milkshake, too," Grady mutters. Hard worry lines cut across his forehead, highlighted under the harsh fluorescent light.

I shrug. "I mean, it sounds decent."

"So does sleep."

With a chuckle, I make my way over to a nearby booth.

A woman sporting a yellow cardigan with a ribbon tying her hair back stands outside the McDonald's. Discreetly, she snaps a picture of me, blushing when her eyes connect with mine, and realizes she's been caught. Her eyes rake over me, falling to the tattoos covering my arm. She motions for me to come out.

I shake my head. For all my want to forget, my milkshake spiral brought everything down. Aulie is the only one I want to see tonight. Even if she's hours away and off-limits.

The tray slides across the table and brings me back to reality. I nod in a silent thank you to the fast-food worker awkwardly moon-walking away.

Placing the s'mores shake under the halo of the lights hanging over the booth, I snap a picture and put it in my chat with Aulie. My fingers hesitate, hovering over the letters, but if I ruined my night already, I might as well poke the wound, too.

JACK

Want one?

DESSY

You have a game tomorrow. Why are you out this late?

JACK

Your up.

DESSY

You're* Darn it, Jack. Are you drunk?

JACK

No?

DESSY

Liar.

JACK

What are you reading?

DESSY

Actually, believe it or not, Emy dragged me out.

JACK

No way. Send proof.

A picture populates on her side of the conversation, and I swallow. In a dark, crowded room, Aulie stands dressed in a lace camisole, a cardigan that's her signature outfit topper falling slightly off her shoulder.

I tell my heart to behave, bracing myself to look at her eyes, the piece of her that holds me arrested more than any other. The part that's a window to her soul. But when my gaze falls upon hers, my ready heart sputters in an unfamiliar rhythm.

The starlight perpetually hung in Aulie's eyes no longer sparkles, and its absence feels like a direct punch in the gut.

For the first time since we were re-introduced, she looks exhausted. Defeated even. Like she's finally accepted the truth I stumbled upon years ago. Happy endings are a work of fiction, and there's no escape from the torture and heartache this world dumps on everyone.

For all the teasing I've given her over the years about her nauseatingly optimistic demeanor, I want to believe happily-ever-afters exist if only to provide a spark for her. One that would reignite the stars that had once burned in brilliant defiance.

JACK

Call me tomorrow?

DESSY

Sure. But please, Jack. I'm serious. Go home.

I pause, racking my brain for an appropriate response. But my head is thicketed with a blanket of tequila fog, and well—a thumbs up should be okay, right?

51

"Everything good?" Grady asks, sitting across from me at the table and sneaking fries out of my bag.

I swallow, dropping my phone on the table and sip my far too-sweet frozen confection.

"Yeah, fine. Just sobering up." I rub the heels of my hand into my eyes, trying to get the haunting image of Aulie's vacant stare out of my mind. "You were right. I probably overdid it."

Grady crosses his arms and snorts as if to say, *No shit.* "Aulie call you out?"

"Uh, yeah." I dip my head, ceding the fact. "Like she always does."

He laughs, growing bolder and stuffing a handful of fries into his mouth. "She's going to get sick of your shit one day. I'm surprised she hasn't already." He grabs one burger, unwraps it and inhales it.

"What are you—I didn't buy these to share." I press my lips into a thin line, biting down the panic Grady's unintentional earworm lays. It would probably be for the best if Aulie got sick of me one day and finally cut me loose, untethering me from the pull I can't quit that always leads me back to her.

Back to someone I can never have, even if she's everything I want.

"Figured. But I burned a shit ton of calories dragging your ass here the last block and a half, so it wouldn't have killed you to ask." A glob of ketchup falls to the outside of Grady's lips, and he tries to swipe it clean with his tongue.

"You're lucky I don't get sick of *your* shit," I say, shaking my head and passing him a napkin.

"Nah. We lifers, baby." Grady winks.

My chest warms. For most of my life I've lived in my dad's shadow, always unsure of who is friends with me, Jack the general grump and not Jack—son of John Parker. Grady, for all the shit I give him, is a loyal friend and I'm thankful for our friendship... most of the time.

Slaking his hand across the table, Grady grabs my milkshake. What is he—*no.* I cringe as he wraps his mouth around the straw.

"Dude. What the hell?"

His eyes close, savoring his sip, and a low hum vibrates his throat.

Yeah. It's definitely way cuter when Aulie does that.

Chapter Five

Jack Parker

Play: *Shipping Up to Boston by The Dropkick Murphys*

"Finally, the Prince has arrived." Assistant Captain Cooper Anderson's voice trumpets, heralding my haggard entrance. "Grady, you can stop shitting your pants now."

Grady's feet halt their frantic pacing across the outline of a hockey rink on our locker room floor. With a pivot, he takes me in and lowers his hands from his head on an exhale. "Oh, thank god. You're five minutes late for morning skate and look like shit, but at least you're here."

"You're going to get premature wrinkles if you keep wearing your face like that." I gesture to his furrowed brow and frown before taking a long sip of my iced Dunks. I'm five minutes late, but the caffeine pit stop was necessary for my headache this morning.

"Going to? He does not have wrinkles already?" Big Ed, our Captain, smirks, drawing out his dimple. The slight indent on his cheek does little to disarm him of his imposing stature. At six-foot-nine, Big Ed not only stands as one of the tallest players in the League but also one of the oldest. His battle-scarred face, from years of playing hockey in Slovakia, used to scare me when he was a young player on my father's team. Now I'm thankful I play with that face rather than against it.

"I definitely saw a few wrinkles in his player picture. Those high-definition cameras weren't forgiving this year." Coop shakes his head.

Wes Larsson lurks in a corner and shrugs on his practice sweater. "I thought he looked stately. Like an older Chris Hemsworth."

"I think Chris is older than him," Coop adds thoughtfully.

"No way. I'm googling it." Wes reaches for his phone in his locker, resting next to a picture of him with his mother.

Grady mutters something into his hands, scrubbing them over his face.

"No shit—a full eleven years older than you, Grady. Fuck, he looks good. I wonder if his skin routine is posted somewhere. I'll send it to you if I find it."

"He's eleven years older than me? Really?" Grady observes his anxiety-ridden face in the mirror. Normally, I'd feel bad the guys are tag-teaming on Grady—he's more sensitive than he lets others see. But with all their attention focused on him, I'm free to settle back into my locker and focus on centering my mind for gameday. "I bet he'd have wrinkles if he were left in charge of the asshole, too. So fuck all of you."

"I feel like the height difference between Big Ed and me would make it difficult, but okay," Coop says. "Just do me a favor and buy me dinner first. I haven't been out since Mandy had CJ, and I need to feel appreciated to reach my peak performance."

"Yeah, you know, Coop, I don't think I needed to know that about you." I laugh, tossing my pads on. "But I think I'd need more than dinner. No offense to any of you."

"Some offense taken," Big Ed says with a sigh. His calloused fingers nimbly work the laces on his skates. "I'm a very delicate lover."

A violent cough comes from Grady's corner. "Wrong fucking time to take a sip of water."

I slap his back a few times as he chokes and sputters.

"I'm sure that Katarina is a very lucky woman." I bite the inside of my cheek, holding back a laugh while Coop and Wes tactfully hide their faces in their cubbies.

A wistful gaze settles on Big Ed's face as he stands and turns his attention to a framed picture of his family. "And I'm a very lucky man."

"Hey, Parker. Did you see Veronica posted a break-up video about you guys?" Wes asks, his gaze locked on his phone.

Coop shakes his head. "I'm not surprised. Mandy said she's been a terror on set since you broke up with her." His wife, Mandy, plays a computer-hacking witch on Veronica's demon-slaying show that is shot locally in Salem, Mass. "What happened to you two? You seemed happy-ish."

"Didn't work out." I shrug. As much as I'd love to be honest and tell the guys it was a stunt, I signed a non-disclosure agreement.

Grady, of course, knows, but I didn't *tell* him. He figured it out because he's watched way too many rom-coms.

"My Katarina wasn't too surprised. She said you didn't have the look," Big Ed adds.

The pull of cloth tape slices through the air-conditioned locker room air. "Jack's never had the look," Wes says, winding the tape around the blade of his stick. "Except maybe at a beer or something."

"Oh, he has that look for someone, but he'll never make a move, so it doesn't matter." Grady chuckles, probably glad the conversation has shifted in my direction.

The jerk.

"That girl in his apartment this summer, right? What was her name?" Coop asks.

"Aulie—" Grady supplies before I can tell everyone to fuck off and mind their business.

"Aulie, right. What's up with her?" Coop picks his eyes up

from tying his skates and meets my narrowed stare. Suffering through a killer headache, I'm able to supply a little extra heat with my scowl. Coop greets it with the desired, eye-widening, shutting up-now reaction.

"Nothing is up with her," I growl. "We grew up together. I'm best friends with her brother, so we're close too. That's it."

"I didn't know you had a sister, Grady—" Wes mutters through clenched teeth, attempting to cut through the end of the tape. Unfortunately, he's missing a critical incisor, and it's my fault. During the playoffs last year, he was setting up for a pass in front of the net, and I blasted it from the blue line and accidentally lifted it right into his jaw.

I scoff. "I wasn't referring to Grady."

"Hey, ass. I don't see Gus dragging your ass across Boston." Fully dressed, Grady leans angrily against his locker. He *could* leave us and meet the rest of the team on the ice, but I know he won't. He's staying to make sure I get out there at a reasonable time because, fair or not, Grady will somehow get chewed out about it, too.

I slump down on the bench to latch on my shin pads and pull up my socks. The pressure in my temple softens a fraction from sitting and I sigh through the relief. "More like policing me."

"I used to be fun, you know." Grady shakes a finger in my face.

"I remember." A ghost of a smile on my lips. "No one is stopping you from sliding into walls in your underpants. I don't know why you're complaining."

Grady groans, stretching his shoulder. The rotator cuff he tore cowboying in the Olympics still haunts him. He doesn't have to say he regrets it out loud. I can see it on his face every time he spends the day after a game with an ice pack wrapped around his shoulder. His injury didn't heal correctly and has severely reduced the power behind his slapshot.

Unfortunately, this means Grady's a viable fourth-line option with a first-line salary, making him a target for Sports Radio fodder. The current rumor is that the only reason he's on the team is because I'm a diva and need him to function. The rumor is bullshit. I'm the furthest thing from a diva. Still, I don't know how Grady feels about it.

"It's probably better I didn't," Grady says. "Besides, someone has to keep you from hurting yourself. Hell if Aulie is going to want to take care of your prima donna ass again. I can't imagine how terrible that must have been for her."

"You know, that's the one thing I still can't puzzle out about this situation." Coop stands, wearing a tepid smirk, like he's aware it's dangerous to poke the bear, but he can't help himself. "I don't think the first person I'd ask to stay with me through all that would be my best friend's little sister, you know?"

I swallow. Coop is digging way too close to the truth for my comfort. I asked Aulie to stay with me this summer because when I was at the lowest point in my life, she was the only person I wanted near me. Even if it was complete and total torture in so many ways. The hit Alex Piotrowski put on me in the Finals stole my best chance at the cup. The one dream I've had since my dad passed when I was seventeen. For a moment, I feared he'd taken my chance at playing hockey ever again, too.

"She was just saving me from a summer of my mother and sisters smothering me."

"Can I have her number?" Wes asks, beating the butt end of his stick into the floor.

"What? No, you can't have her—"

"She was stunning." Big Ed nods. His eyes move around the room like he's sharing a secret with the other guys, and I'm not in on it. "And nice. A perfect match for Wes."

Again, I massacre the inside of my cheek. This time to stop myself from saying something too rude and grumpy for the Party-Parker-Persona. "I'm not—"

"Honestly, Wes would be better than half the duds she's dated," Grady adds.

Wes cocks his head to the side. "Thank you?"

"I'm not giving her number out to anyone. So can we move off

Aulie, please?" My headache surges to my frontal lobe, and I pinch the bridge of my nose.

I can't pretend to blame my hangover for the pain anymore. It's clearly from interacting with these pains in the asses.

"How's the leg doing?" Wes gestures to my knee with his newly taped stick.

The MCL tear in my knee and my dislocated shoulder from Piotrowski's cheap hit have healed, but hell. It required an enormous amount of dedication and rehab on my part to get there.

Piotrowski should have gotten a major penalty and ejection for that hit.

He didn't.

We should have won the game.

We didn't.

We were up three games to two in a best-of-seven series before that game.

We lost the next game without me, too.

"The leg is fine." I wave off his concerns.

"How do you feel about playing that rat today?" Big Ed tucks his gloves under his armpits and assesses me with an unnerving stare.

"Great," I lie.

Tonight, I plan on unleashing all my pent-up frustration over the situation on Alex; it will be glorious. It's his fault I had months of rehab and had to spend a summer holed up with a woman who lights every fiber of my being like a fall bonfire, licking my skin, blood, and bones alive.

Okay, so the last part was my fault. I'm a masochist. But still.

Alex Piotrowski will feel the extra five pounds of muscle I put on in the off-season.

Big Ed's stare rests heavily on me. Which is fair. He's been in the league long enough that when someone like me spills a bunch of bullshit, he's not going to buy it. "You're on thin ice with the league. It will not end well if you retaliate."

"I'll be fine. I have it all under control," I say, pulling my socks over my shin pads.

Big Ed's firm hand encompasses my shoulder. "We need you to be a team player tonight."

I shake his hand off my shoulder, standing to grab my practice sweater. "I'm always a team player."

A smattering of laughs and snickers undulates through the room from the rest of my teammates. They don't have the decency to hide their amusement as they did with our Captain. Apparently, I don't inspire the same level of fear as him.

I'll have to work on that.

"What?" I sigh, growing weary of interacting with people as much as I love these guys most of the time.

"You turn into a different player when we play Alex." Coop shrugs. "No offense, but would he have had the chance to lay into you like he did last year if you had passed the puck instead of trying to take him on your own?"

What the fuck? Does he think the hit was *my* fault?

"Do you all think this?" I ask, glancing around the room.

Wes doesn't meet my eye but bobs his head in slight affirmation.

Grady isn't as bashful and mouths, "No shit, fucker" to me while Big Ed wraps me up in a sympathetic smile.

"What happened between you two, anyway? I know he's a rat, but he's always worse when he plays you," Coop asks leaning against his locker.

The only advantage of getting to the practice stadium late is the usual peace and quiet in the locker room before Coach inevitably chews me out for my tardiness.

God, I could use some peace and quiet.

Instead, guilt bubbles in my gut. Images of my fists pummeling into Alex's face during our senior year of high school flash through my mind. Okay, so I at least have some blame regarding the beginning of our feud. But that fucker deserved it.

I had just read an online article about my dad having terminal cancer, a fact I didn't know personally, but it was plastered across a local sports site. Alex laughed and said my dad probably didn't tell me because he was disappointed with how emotional I could get.

And then. Well, I proved him right by driving my fists into his face.

It was the last time I remember emoting.

"Look." Big Ed's voice booms through the locker room and calls me back to the present, where I'm being annoyingly and aggressively tag-teamed by a bunch of assholes. "Whatever you need to play out of your mind tonight, I don't care. But we need you *on the ice.*"

A shiver wraps its icy grip around my spine. Again, I am thankful I play with Big Ed and not against him.

"I'll behave, Dad." I roll my eyes like the bitter seventeen-year-old being chastised that I've suddenly become.

"I'll take the job if it keeps you in check. Someone has to now, yeah?"

I swallow, unable to meet the Captain's gaze again. I don't talk about my history for a reason, and opening day isn't the day to start. So instead of getting emotional. Instead of hyper-focusing on the fact that I haven't processed a damn thing in the past ten years. Instead of fixing my mind on the fact that my family kept my dad's cancer a secret from me because, "It was your senior year, half-pint. He just wanted to protect you, and we had to respect that."

I shrug off a million things threatening to crack the ice around me and plunge me deep into frigid waters. "Only if you cut the crusts off my PB&J like you do for Lexi," I say, referencing his youngest daughter who has the right idea—the crust on the bread is the worst.

"Deal." A boisterous laugh rattles Big Ed's frame, and I sigh, knowing I've avoided the heavy, deep-in-your-feelings danger zone.

"Hey, Jack." Bill, the assistant coach, sticks his head in the locker room. "Coach wants to talk to you in his office before you go to skate."

"Got it."

"And then the training staff wants to see how your MCL is healing today."

Goddammit. When is all this extra shit going to stop?

It's freaking annoying that one stupid hit has made such a difference in my life.

"Tell Coach I'll be there in five, thanks." I finally shrug my practice sweater on, pulling the folds down over my pads.

"You got it."

Walking past Grady Sulking O'Callaghan, he extends a hand and clamps down on my shoulder pads, halting my steps. "If he asks, you went out alone last night after I begged you on my knees to stay inside and study tape or something else that will make me look good. And then I met up with you out of concern for our star player."

"And for the hot chick in the background of my snaps."

"She looked like Alicia Silverstone from *Blast from the Past,*" Grady sighs, turning his gaze heavenward, wrapped in a glow of Brendan Fraser reverie. "How could I not take a chance?"

"You're so weird." I shake my head. "But don't worry, I've got you. I doubt he'll even bring it up. How would he know what we did last night?"

"He has his ways." Grady's eyes widen, and he looks like that frightened/shocked emoji Aulie uses a lot when I tell her about my nights out.

Taking a deep breath, I collect myself after *all of that,* and walk to the coach's office. I'm sure he wants to check in on my injury and that everything is fine.

His door is cracked open ajar, and I rap twice before pushing it open.

Coach's stern gaze doesn't lift his focus from his iPad, and my stomach twists. "Come in, Parker."

Judging by that greeting, there's a decent chance this isn't about my injuries. I settle into the hard oak chair in front of his desk. The old wooden seating that's been here since the Big Bad Brawling Badgers of the 1960s groans under my weight.

At the sound of the creak, Coach takes his readers off and places his tablet on his desk. "How's the leg?" he asks.

"It's fine, but the training staff wants to see me. I should probably get going, so I'm not too late for skate." I stand.

"Make sure they check your ankle out, too. It looks like you took a nasty fall last night." Coach slides his iPad across the desk. A TMZ photo of Grady staring down at me, arms crossed, while I'm mid-fall, sits on the screen—center *of Attention: Boston Feelings Thawing for Hometown Hero.*

Well, that heading is entirely unnecessary.

I wince and sit back down.

"I just tripped on some loose cobblestone. The street was slick, not a big deal."

"The street was slick. As a professional hockey player, that's the story you're going with?"

"Just telling you the truth, Coach."

"Right, so the slip had nothing to do with this." He swipes his finger, and a video of me appears, downing two fistfuls of shots before grabbing another two.

Seven was probably the more accurate estimate, then.

"What are you going to do tomorrow?" a bubbly voice asks in the clip.

"Revenge." The bleary-eyed version of me laughs.

Yeah. I don't remember any of this.

"I don't know how much clearer I can be with you, Parker. But the team needs you. You were the top scorer last year by a runaway. And I get it. I do. You've been through a lot at a young age—" (*translation: sucks your dad died*) "—but you're nearing the backside of your prime in hockey years. So whatever hole you're trying to fill doing this, figure it out fast or bury it. I don't care. But if you keep doing shit like this, I will have to bench you for a few games."

"Got it. Anything else?" I ask, resting my hands on the arms of the chair and pushing up.

"Unfortunately, yes. The League has issued warnings to both teams before today's game. Because of Piotrowski and your history, and then this damn video, they're keeping a tight leash on the game to prevent an all-out brawl like last year. So, if either of you try anything that isn't an appropriate hockey move, they'll be quick with an ejection and suspension."

Shit. Well, I'm stuck with this pent-up frustration for longer. Neat.

I stand, pulling down my sweater. "So, don't hit the bastard. Got it. Anything else?"

Coach regards me with unwavering skepticism. "I'm serious, Jack. The team needs you. No retaliating. As much as I understand you wanting to. We need you to keep your emotions in check and be a team player today."

You would have been too emotional, half-pint. He couldn't handle that. My sisters' words to me after my father passed play in my mind.

I've had to dance around my dad too much today. I need to get out on the ice and clear my damn mind.

"Yeah. Team player. No emotions. Got it. I can do that."

Chapter Six

Jack Parker

Play: *Dirty Water by the Standells*

The artificial wintry air of the rink wraps a welcoming hand around me. We've played on our home ice plenty of times in the past few weeks getting ready for today, but opening night has a different feel. There's a certain excitement, that vibrates through the stadium, like everyone knows this is a day to shake off last season and focus on the new one, full of hope and possibilities. I inhale, letting the chill of the freshly laid Garden ice flood my airways and enter my veins. The deafening roar of the crowd quiets my mind. Logan Sloan, the opposing New York center, glides into the face-off position in the middle of the ice, and I do the same.

We nod to each other. Sloan's a well-respected player in the league, and I'd be okay that he finally got his name on the cup if it didn't mean that it came at my great expense. Still, he showed how classy he was after the series, sending me a gift basket full of recovery tools and a "see you next year" card.

That being said, the man is more than a few years off his prime—and I have the highest winning face-off percentage in the league, so there's no way I'm losing this drop.

"How's the leg, Jackass?" Alex's nauseating voice sounds over Sloan's shoulder.

Of course, he's on the ice now.

Since we're the home team, Coach could have paired our lines differently. Maybe put the fourth line out first to face Alex, and then it would have taken a while to get a match-up between us. But apparently, he's not interested in making this easy for me.

Maybe he's punishing me for coming to practice hungover.

I swallow the anger bubbling and channel my attention to the official raising the puck for the drop. Blinking lights slowly dance over the ice. The loud stadium music fades. The ref drops the puck, my stick finds it first, and last year falls away.

The first five minutes of the period pass with little excitement. The puck slides up and down the ice as bodies check each other, both teams shaking off the rest of the off-season rust. And the crowd quiets from their initial uproar, eager for a new season after our disappointing end last year.

On my third shift, I establish myself in front of the New York net. Alex attempts to push me out of position, but the extra mass I packed on in the off-season catches him off guard, and he loses his footing.

"Leg seems fine." I smirk.

Coop passes it my way, and I set my stick so it deflects the puck, changing its angle slightly as it heads toward the net. The goalie stretches out last minute and snags it. He grumbles at Alex, still sprawled on the ice, to get into position, and I glide back to the bench with a lightness in my skates.

Maybe I can get my revenge without laying into the bastard, after all.

Two shifts later, I chase a puck to the boards when I hear the furious slash of Alex's skates behind me. I halt my pursuit on a dime, and Alex, angling for a hit, careens into the boards. The puck inches by him, making him look like the pee-wee player he really is.

Excellent.

Thank you, agility training.

Which, for the record, was definitely not private dancing lessons with Big Ed as part of my rehab over the summer. It was something manly and gruff, like... log rolling?

Wes cuts through the zone, and I pass him the puck. He slams it into the net and scores our first goal. A foghorn sounds over the arena's sound system, and a choir of "ohs" follows along to our signature after-goal song.

God, I missed that sound.

Grady, Big Ed, Coop, and I huddle around Wes, slapping his helmet, whooping, and hollering as the crowd cheers.

Breaking our huddle and skating back to the bench, Big Ed tugs on my sweater. "You know he's going to play like a rat now." He nods over to Alex, getting chewed out by his coach on his bench.

As much as I'd love for things to keep going the way they are, I know Alex well enough to be certain he hasn't started poking and prodding yet.

Every team has a guy like him, and I'm usually on the raw end of their ire, but Alex is in a league of his own. He'll try to keep up at first, but when it's clear he can't compete with me skill-wise well, he goes to Plan B. Cheap hits and remarks to get under my skin are his calling card.

I'm used to it.

But I'm not immune.

The first period draws to a close with us up one to nothing.

In the locker room, Coach reinforces what Big Ed said on the ice and reminds me about the league's warning before the game. Over the past few years, they've suspended me enough that any suspension now will be lengthy.

Four minutes into the second period, I set myself up by the net. Alex hip-checks me. "Saw Veronica last night," he says.

Like I give a fuck.

"Ate her out. Poor thing was desperate for a man."

"That doesn't explain why she was with you," I mumble.

A stick cracks against my back. A cross-check. It's a move that should earn Alex two minutes in the penalty box with a minor. But, like always, the refs miss whatever he does, and he gets away with it.

I establish myself further out in the zone, distancing us. Grady passes me the puck.

I deke Alex out. It also draws the goalie off-balance to his left, and I use this, sending the puck into the high-right side of the net. It sneaks in under the cross-bar. Fuck, yes. The foghorn sounds. The crowd erupts with cheers.

Two-nothing.

Gliding by Alex, I give him a little wink. My line jumps on me.

"Hell of a pass, Grady." I smack his helmet. That goal is as much his point as it is mine.

Skating back to the bench, he puts his glove out for a fist bump. "I saw the cross-check. Let me take care of the prick, okay?"

I shake my head, sitting down. "Nah, I can handle him."

"Jack, this isn't up for discussion." Grady's voice drops several octaves, and his stare narrows on me behind his visor. "Do not fucking touch him. This isn't the time. We need you."

I'm tempted to roll my eyes, but ultimately, I relent, banging the head of my stick on the ground a few times and sliding down the bench during another line shift. "Okay. Fine. Fine. I'll let it go."

I'm confident I can manage Alex, but I also don't feel like arguing with everyone on opening day.

And for the rest of the second period, I let it go, finding satisfaction in dominating Alex enough that I ignore his nettling. Thankfully, he focuses his little prods and pricks around Veronica. A subject I find easy to turn to white noise.

I slam two more goals into the net before the second period ends. Hats fly to the ice at the sound of the third foghorn, and the game is paused to clean them up.

The rush of the game lifts me even higher. I've scored hat tricks before, but never before the third period's started.

On our last shift of the period, Grady lays Alex out on a play. It doesn't satisfy my thirst for revenge like I was hoping and I end up retreating to the locker room with my team up a somber four to nothing.

The team follows filling the locker room with a chorus of "fuck yeahs" as they take their sweaters and pads off for intermission. Coach tells us to keep it up. Big Ed encourages us to keep playing like a team. And they both level a warning glance in my direction when they remind the team that New York might go for heads rather than pucks in their desperation.

Let them come for me. I'm ready for the fight. Itching for it. But I know that's not what they want to hear, so I nod and say, "I've got it. I'll keep my head up and stay out of their way."

And I behave for most of the third period, even finding an opportunity to lay Alex out *the right way* on a play.

Five minutes are left in the game, and my last shift is coming. Coach will pull the first line soon since things are getting chippy, and our safety is his priority.

A stick finds my back, and I have one guess who the cross-check is from. I don't move.

"Veronica said you had some side piece in your apartment this summer," Alex says, bumping me with his hip and trying to move me out of position in front of his net.

"Fuck off," I grunt, battling for my position with a shoulder push back.

Coop passes the puck to Wes who passes it to Big Ed. It travels to Grady next. The four have established positions at the top of the zone and are killing time with a game of keep-away.

"Is the chick here?" Alex asks. "Maybe I could find her after the game. I figure if Veronica was so starved, she probably is, too. What do you think, Parker? Do you think I should eat her out? You know, I like licking pussy." A long wet tongue hits the side of my cheek, slowly dragging up near my temple before I register what's happening.

Did he... *lick me?*

What. The. Fuck.

Red washes over my line of vision. A puck rebounds off the boards. Quickly, I pivot to chase it. Alex follows. I have an opening. I poke my stick out way too far. Alex trips over it and flies, landing headfirst into the boards. He collapses on the ice, blood pouring out of his nose.

Shit, I didn't mean to draw blood.

One of his teammates slams me against the boards. An ugly, albeit toothless snarl is aimed in my direction. Fair.

Randy Collins, the owner of said snarl, pins my hands to the side.

"Just watch the face." I sigh, resigned to receive a flurry of punches from two other New York players. Grady, Wes, and Coop enter the hubbub, followed by Big Ed, who was on the other end of the ice, and a little out of breath after three periods of shifts. He grabs fists full of sweaters, pulling the entire New York first line off me.

Alex picks himself up off the ice and swipes at his blood. He skates back to his team's bench with a "gotcha" smirk on his face.

Fuck me. The sheer amount of blood from his nose doesn't bode well.

How does the douche even *bleed* overdramatically?

Over the mayhem, the officials break up the primary fight. Grady evades the refs, dragging one of the New York players out of the huddle. They both drop their gloves for round two. A linesman escorts me to the box before collecting Grady and his dueling partner for roughing. At the same time, another announces my fate to the crowd.

"Number Forty-Seven. Major Penalty: Tripping with the Intent to Injure."

That ruling has suspension written all over it.

Slumped over, I rub Alex's saliva off my cheek, ignoring Grady's death stare sitting next to me. The only positive of a major penalty is that I'm stuck in the box for the rest of the game and won't have to deal with Coach's chew-out until after. A whole three minutes later than a minor.

Maybe I should use this time to practice what I'll say to the Department of Player Safety.

I doubt *he asked to eat my friend out, licked me, and called me a pussy,* will cut it.

Chapter Seven

Aulie Desfleurs

Play: *Just One Look by Doris Troy*

"For the love of Peter Noone, Emy. Will you put that thing away?" I grunt as Emy leans on the desk in my bedroom, skimming through the body issue *again*. The heavy box in my arms slips, navigating around her, and I barely make it to the desk before it drops with a thud on the hard mahogany surface.

The ordeal is overly dramatic, so I play it off like I'm frustrated with her, contorting my face into a harsh scowl instead of acknowledging reality. I used to sort these boxes on my own, but recently, bending and picking things up has become torture. I'm almost twenty-four and in relatively good shape. This shouldn't be so hard.

In the past few days, Gus, Emy, and my co-planner Bridget have helped me unload everything from storage, placing them into my bedroom to inventory before they're moved to a white tent at the base of the fairground next week. As a result, my room looks less and less like a place to sleep—which is fine, I wasn't anyway—and more like the backstage for a Joanna Baillie production.

Still wrapped in plastic, costumes hang neatly on clothing racks in one corner. Opposite the explosion of muslin dresses, linen shirts, and buttoned waistcoats sits the pile of boxes I'm trying to organize. Usually, they'd be perfectly organized already, having packed them at the end of the last fair with the meticulous nature with which I do just about everything. Last year, in a moment of weakness, I let Emma and Callen help me. Neither of the two lovebirds wanted to leave the fairground, but they didn't want to acknowledge their feelings for each other... yet.

There has to be some joke about their love continuing to make more work for me, but I'm too tired to think of what it could be.

Opening a box labeled "Bonnets," I immediately find gloves, a fan, a roll of tickets, and a handful of our double-sided maps from last year that catalog the fairground on one side and Chawton Falls on the other, *so much for guarding this box with my life.*

The fair is a decent draw for foot traffic, and the local businesses have gotten involved to take advantage of it. The bookstore, Little Shop on the Square, will deck its window out with Jane Austen's books. Anne's Donuts has a Jamsfield Donut. Cup of Joe's, a small café on Main St. serves Elizabeth Beignets with a caramel cappuccino dipping sauce that I would happily bathe in a vat of. And Emy's toy store, Little Prints, gives a ten percent discount to anyone who presents a fair ticket stub at checkout.

"I just feel so inspired to get into shape when I look at this magazine," she says, staring at a picture of some football player catching a ball in the nude while mindlessly feeding herself bites of my tourtière, meat pie that is more butter than meat.

"Mmm, inspiration, sure. I heard everyone in the magazine has at least two helpings of meat pie daily." I swipe my hair out of my face. Today is hot for September, and my body isn't used to it after the chill of the last few days. "So, was your offer to help me sincere? Or are you going to be a bodily obstacle?"

I dance around her with another box. I packed this one since it's appropriately labeled, and its contents are organized. It's full of hats for our military characters and gentlemen who don caps during the festival. I pull out a stove pipe top hat that Mr. Bingley will wring his hands on in a few days as he apologizes for being an "unmitigated and comprehensive ass" and sigh happily.

Even though it's a lot of work, the fair is my favorite part of the year. For a few days, Chawton Falls, New Hampshire, becomes Chawton, Hampshire, where Jane wrote a good portion of her works. The first weekend, when the weather is typically better, we dedicate ourselves to *Pride and Prejudice,* her most famous novel. Players will run around the fair, some as background characters, and others will act out scenes from the book on a tight timeline.

Dances, balls, and social conversations happen in the main house. Mr. Darcy proposes disastrously on a stage to Elizabeth outside. Lydia and Wickham make a big production of their escape, and fair-goers can choose to aid or interfere with Mr. Darcy's frantic search. Usually, it becomes a giant search party that's a ton of wild fun.

I need to keep the big picture in mind. It will all be worth it when we're on the grounds. Even if it feels impossible.

"I'm sorry. I thought I *was* being helpful." Emy flashes me a teasing smile. "Maybe the problem is that you misunderstood what I offered to help with."

"How so?"

"I didn't mean I'd help you with manual labor. I meant I'd help you realize your feelings for a certain troubled hockey player."

She flips the page to the centerfold, and my cheeks heat. I've grown far too familiar with the contents of that page for my own sensibilities.

"I don't understand why I'm friends with you sometimes."

"My theory is that you Desfleurses are genetically programmed to love me, but your guess is as good as mine." She shrugs. "But, seriously, Aulie. Look me in the eye and tell me you've never thought about Jack like that, and I'll drop it."

I swallow. Emy knows me too well to get anything past her. But I steel my nerves and try anyway. "I've honestly never thought about it," I say, chewing on my bottom lip.

She snorts. "Yeah, okay, liar."

And I am. I've thought about Jack like that more than I'd care to admit over the years. First, when I was a pre-teen and he was the older, cooler guy who hung out with my brother.

And then, more recently, when at the lowest romantic point in my life, he rescued me from drowning in a fountain. Drenched, cold, and foolish, when the object of my childhood and teenage fantasies offered out his hand, everything inside of me screamed, *to the hell with Tyle this is Jack and my moment. The one we'll tell our grandkids about.*

The blows of a failed engagement fell away that night as the man who used to treat me like an amusing child seemed interested in me as a matured, alluring woman, however fleeting the moment was.

I'd endure it all again so you could finally see me. I'd say those words out loud someday to my hoodied knight. I was so sure.

I was a fool.

Because Jack Parker is not a knight, at least not one that dons shining armor. He is a pirate, a rogue, a Wickham, or a Willoughby. Somebody that the foolish ladies in the romantic novels I read fall for, only to be left with a broken heart.

So it's imperative for my safety that Jack stays where he belongs—the friend zone.

Not that it matters what I genuinely feel, anyway. I'm undoubtedly the antithesis of everything Jack seeks in his relationships, however temporary they usually are.

His last girlfriend, Veronica, all but confirms this with her raven-black hair, muscular physique, and chic wardrobe. My soft curves and cardigans would never stand a chance against someone like her.

Heck, the woman plays a demon slayer on television, and I'm still recovering from that one episode of *Are You Afraid of the Dark?* I watched at a sleepover when I was nine.

Public pools? No, thank you. I still can't think of them without shivering.

I'm a soft girl with a fragile heart and a penchant for falling wildly in love and fracturing into a thousand pieces when it's over.

A man like Jack would never find my wholesome personality and homebody tendencies appealing.

With a sigh, I swallow my pride. I'll admit to Emy that she may be on to something, but I'm also going to play the all-the-people-I-love-are-dead card, so she'll move on from this conversation post-haste.

I'm a soft girl, not a good one.

"Okay, so I've thought about him a few times. But I'd never act on it because he's not interested. I'm not ruining a perfectly good friendship when most of my best friends are dead. So, can you please leave me in peace about this situation and help me sort all this stuff?"

Emy lets out a long, frustrated breath. "I just want you to be happy."

"I love you, but this isn't the solution." I pick up the *Hats* box and grab the inventory checklist.

Since Emy and Gus's relationship took a more serious turn, my best friend's focus has shifted to finding me "the one." Which was tolerable until her "revelation" that Jack's my endgame—a notion I like to call hogwash.

"Did you ask Greta about being Lydia?" Emy thankfully takes the hint that I need a subject change.

"Yes, I did." I nod, pursing my lips. I'm one bonnet short. "And she can't do it either and doesn't know anyone interested."

"I know someone," Emy sings. "She's super talented—"

"And needs to run the fair," I snip back. I loathe derailed plans entirely, and yet here I am, derailed. Seriously, where is that bonnet?

I shuffle around the contents of another tossed-together box. Maybe it's in here. A crinkle of paper draws my attention. My heart drops. I know exactly what this is, and if Emy sees it, I'll never hear the end of it.

Discreetly, I reach into the box and slide the folded paper into my pocket. This thing should never be seen by another human. It proves I'm ridiculous and clueless about relationships.

It's a product of my boredom, an always dangerous state of mind for me. When I'm bored, I think too little and say too much.

During my free time as Mary or other small characters at the fair, when it's rainy and slow, I sometimes get bored and do silly things. Like, make "Aulie Desfleurs's List for a Suitable Suitor." Which is both a terrible name for a list and ammunition I don't want Emy to have.

I'm sure she'd laugh at my desire for loyalty and dependability more than anything else on the list, but Gus has both characteristics in spades, so she can bite me.

"Okay, but how much stuff has to be completed the day of, anyway?" Emy asks, placing the missing hat on her head and assessing herself in the dressing mirror I'll throw into the tent for character players during the fair.

It clashes with her indie band t-shirt, oversized cardigan, and leggings, but she still pulls it off. Emy could pull off just about anything with her confidence.

"A lot." I sift through the following box. A tiny pug-sized bonnet I made in a weird late-night crafting session surfaces. I giggle and happily place it on my pug Willoughby's head. His proud puss regards me unimpressed with his headwear as if to say, *Madam, I am a gentleman, and you've put a lady's bonnet on my head.*

He blinks once. Twice.

"Oh, hush. You look charming," I whisper. With a yawn, he moves to his bed in the corner. It's the only place safe from the regency bomb that's gone off in here.

"So, you need a helper." Emy turns her body, bringing her full attention to me.

"I can't hire one, and no one would want to volunteer for that this time of the year."

"Hi. My name is Emy LaBranche, and I'm interested in the position of assistant. I have a BA in Business and own and operate a toy store. I'd love to talk to you about taking some responsibility off your shoulders so you can have some fun, too." She extends her hand for a shake. As kind as her words sound, I'm not trusting them. Trusting them leads to me running around the fairground as a silly little thing. I accepted earlier today that in reality, I'll probably end up stuck with the role of Lydia, but I don't want to acknowledge it yet. Once I acknowledge it, panicking internally will be the next logical step and I'm too busy to be anxious. "Seriously, Lydia looks like she's so much fun to play."

"*You* want to do it, then?" I ask, trying to determine if the navy-colored Bicorne army hat in my hand should be Wickham's or Captain Wentworth's. I'm not as good with all the accuracy things as Bridget, but she'll let me hear it if I mess up.

Emy smiles. "If you think you can talk Gus into playing Mr. Wickham, sure."

There's no way my stuffy brother would be interested in that.

But...I *am* desperate. I heard my ex-fiancé Tyler was back in town and even briefly entertained the thought of asking him. Maybe I *should* try to ask Gus. He loves me and hates Tyler, so I have that going for me, anyway.

I creak the door open. "Gus?"

"No." His answer comes from the hollows of the living room.

"But I haven't even asked yet."

"Whatever fair thing you're trying to rope me into, absolutely not."

"But, please? I'd owe you."

"I'm not wearing those damn breeches. End of discussion."

"Why won't you wear breeches for me?" I whine.

"Sorry, Alouette. Even I have my limits." Gus's usage of my childhood nickname does little to soften the blow.

"Fine."

Emy picks up her piece of tourtière as Gus and I continue sparring. "You tried." She moans, slowly dragging the fork out of her mouth. "You seriously nailed the clove to all-spice combination with this one."

"It's still slightly off, but it's getting closer to her recipe." I doubt I'll ever be able to recreate Memere's recipe for her famous meat pie perfectly. Translating her recipes is an art. "A pinch of this, a dab of that," is really "pour half the salt-shaker in and dump in a carton of butter."

Adding that much butter to anything hurts, but it's a necessary pain.

Unlike the one currently spasming through my pelvic region. That one hardly seems necessary. I breathe through the cramp, keeping my face flat. No one needs to know I'm in pain.

"Please, at least consider playing Lydia, Aulie," Emy begs.

"Why are you so invested in this?"

"You were so happy on stage. I want you to have that again. Don't let the dickwad fiancé thing—or whatever he was—"

"A womanizing ass I warned her about multiple times," Gus contributes from the living room. A symphony of keyboard clacks follow his grumpy diatribe.

"What Gus said." Emy smiles softly. "Don't let him take more from you than he has." She gathers her sleeve and wipes some moisture off my cheek.

When did I start crying?

"I love you, Aulie. He was never worth it."

"I know." I nod, and I am over it.

It's just—that part of me that loves so intensely and gets emotionally attached to people has a hard time with the "letting go" part. I loved Tyler more than I'd ever let myself love before. We were engaged. And when I opened his dorm room and found a woman lying there waiting for him, something broke inside.

Worse yet was how Gus looked at me when he realized I'd lied and snuck around with Tyler for years even though he told me he was bad news. I thought I was being sensible, telling Tyler I wasn't comfortable going all the way until we were engaged. But all I did was foolishly put myself and my heart in a situation where Tyler never intended to keep his word.

He was seeing another woman behind my back and using his minimal power as the student director to make advances on the women at his new school.

Acting, which used to be our main point of bonding became tainted and joyless for me. There was no way around it.

"I am happy with you and planning things. Planning things makes me so happy. Do you realize how happy planning things makes me?"

"Yes, now plan yourself into a bigger role in the fair, since you don't have another option."

I toss a bonnet in Emy's direction. It falls slowly to the ground with an anti-climactic plop. Darn. Not exactly the cutting effect I was looking for. But Emy has a point. The first weekend of the fair is a week away, and Lydia is integral.

My shoulders droop. I have a few late nights ahead of me, which is fine. Since my Memere passed away, earlier this year, I've slept terribly. Nightmares plague me—ones where I frantically clear the dirt away from her grave. There's been a mistake. She's not gone. She can't be. I'm too young to navigate the rest of my life without her.

"I'll have to make a few things for Lydia's costume since I'm twice Emma's height."

"You're going to do it?" Emy shouts, flinging tourtière everywhere, before wrapping her arms around me.

Willoughby's placid countenance perks up, suddenly accessing stray meat pie filling.

"I kind of don't have a choice, do I?"

"No. You're screwed, and I love that for you," Emy says, releasing me from her embrace.

"We still have to find a Wickham, though."

"That shouldn't be a problem. Hey, random attractive man, want to flirt with my gorgeous self? Kiss me and get paid to do it?"

I roll my eyes. "You write the best sales pitches."

"It's like I have a degree in it or something." Emy brushes her dark silky hair over her shoulder for good sassy measure. Her eyes zero in on my chest. "Your bra doesn't fit."

I adjust my bra. My under-wire is poking into my side, making me fully aware of its ill-fitting nature. "I think it's the new birth control. The girls blew up overnight."

Cue choking from the living room. "Seriously? Close the door again, I'm right here."

"Your sister has boobs. Stop listening in on our conversations or get over it," I say back.

"I'm sorry, Alouette. Who technically owns this house?" Gus says with his signature parental tone. It was funny when we were younger, but now it's annoying. He's only four years older than me. That's it. Not the forty he pretends. I wish he would stop seeing me as the little girl he needs to protect and parent and start seeing me as an equal. He's dating Emy, for Pete's sake, and she's a few weeks younger than me.

"I'm sorry. Who does all the cooking and cleaning? Do you even know how to work the washing machine?"

"I have an IQ of 160. I could figure it out," Gus bellows.

"Did you have an IQ of 160 when you used the laundry detergent pads in the dishwasher?" I bite back a giggle. Last year, Gus boasted he figured out a way to load the dishwasher to its highest efficiency and banned anyone else from touching it. I didn't fight his ego. It meant less work for me. But then we all started feeling a little sick, Gus more so than anyone, so I took over his job for a week. The minute I went to load the dishwasher, I realized his mistake. He'd been using laundry pods instead of dishwasher ones.

"The packaging looked the same. That's a branding and marketing issue, not my fault."

I open my mouth to tell him that if he had taken the time to read, an activity he abhors, he'd have seen his error instantly, but Emy's warm hand covers my mouth.

"We love and appreciate you and your brain, Gus," she says.

"Love you too, Em." Gus's voice softens. It's sickening.

"I'd appreciate it if you could not work him up so much. I love you, but you need to remember he's lost his whole family and is dealing with depression, too," Emy whispers to me in the bedroom.

I sigh. Of course, he is. Gus gave everything up for our family. He left his one true love in hockey behind in high school to concentrate on his college-level studies because it promised greater financial security for the rest of the family. Then, away at college, he worked diligently at night on a code he sold to care for our Memere and the rest of our aging family.

He's my rock, and I hate to think I haven't been able to be that for him lately.

"I'll try to be better." I flatten a curled ribbon on one of the bonnets.

After a few guilt-laden moments, Gus's phone rings. "Hey, is your dumb ass almost here?" he answers with a slightly elevated voice. Here? What does he mean by "here?"

My eyes flicker to the magazine still sitting open on the table while a nervous flutter terrorizes my abdomen. There's only one man Gus speaks bro-ey to, and I hate that knowing who's on the other line is giving me belly swoops. Those should be reserved for fictional men who get decimated by a woman after lightly touching her ungloved hand or something.

"Huh, Jack usually calls you first." Emy smiles.

Which is a fair observation. When Jack needs either of us, he calls my phone since Gus notoriously never answers his, and I always do.

Well, I *did* always answer.

But three days ago, when they threw Jack into the penalty box, I, uhm, had a rash of thoughts that I will not pollute my mind with thinking about a second time.

Willoughby raises his head from his bed as if he can sense my spiraling indecency. A libidinous pug to his core—my sincerest apologies to my childhood stuffie, Quackers Von Quackenstine—I suspect he has a second sense for these things.

Jack leaning against that penalty box, needing saving, is a more pervasive image than I thought it would be. I don't trust my ability to remain calm around him and not give away how much I'm struggling with my feelings.

So I may have ignored his last three or five tries.

Guiltily, I shift the dresses on the rack. Veronica posted a nasty video about their break-up on Instagram a few days ago, coinciding with his bad temperament on the ice. I'm sure there is a relationship between the two, and he needs to talk to someone about it. The break-up meant more to him this time than he's letting on. It had to. From what I've gathered through her social media profiles, Veronica is as close to flawless as a human can get, with her charitable works, boss lady attitude, and dedication to nourishing her body, mind, and soul.

Gus peeks his head into my room. In a flash, I stand in front of the magazine, still open on the desk. With a hand behind my back, I slowly close it.

"That was Jack. He's running a little late, but thinks he'll be on time for dinner."

"Din-dinner?" I stammer. "Doesn't he have a game?"

Gus cocks his head to the side. "He's suspended for twenty games," he says slowly, like I should already know this. "And his agent thought it would be a good idea for him to get out of the city after that guy threw something at him yesterday. Didn't he tell you? Emy said you were—"

"Aulie's just been so busy with the fair planning, you know. She's been forgetting things," Emy says in an uneasy tone.

Wait, have I? I've been tired, sure, but I feel like I'm on top of some things.

Gus crosses his arms, furrowing his brow. "You do at least remember he's going to stay with us in three-ish weeks once Simone has the baby and needs the nursery, right? I'll need help getting the guest room set up."

Jack-They-Put-Me-In-The-Sin-Bin-For-a-Reason-Parker, here? Oh no. I would remember that, because instead of organizing bonnets I'd be barring all points of entry to the house while simultaneously researching local hypnotists.

I would never have agreed to it. Which means...I turn to Emy, whose lowered gaze is all the confirmation I need that she's guilty of meddling. "I told Aulie I'd take care of that," she says, not meeting my eye.

"Gus. Will you excuse us? I need to talk about my...period with Emy."

"Uhm. Yeah. Sure..." He tiptoes out. "We can talk about everything later."

"Looking forward to it," I say with a sing-songy voice and a fake, plastered smile.

The minute the door clicks shut, I turn and shoot daggers in Emy's direction.

"Remember, I love you, and you love me." She giggles, putting the bed between us.

"Yes, and I will plan the loveliest funeral for you after I kill you. Promise." I lunge, and she squeals, jumping from my clutches.

"Okay, but just no carnations. They're tacky."

"Like I would put carnations in your—stop distracting me! And don't you dare try to play the Emma part with us while he's here." I point an accusatory fan in her direction. "I'm serious. No matchmaking. Nothing good can come out of this. Jack will just get weirded out and leave if he knows I've caught feelings."

"Matchmake? Me? I'd never dream of doing such a thing," Emy says innocently. She crosses her heart, but the twinkle in her eyes suggests otherwise.

Chapter Eight

Jack Parker

Play: *Ever Fallen in Love by the Buzzcocks*

Friends can buy friends apology flowers, right? That's not something restricted to coupledom? Standing on Gus and Aulie's doorstep, I manage to overthinking everything—including if I should knock on the Desfleurs's door—because Aulie's ghosting me, and I need her like I need air to breathe. The last few days of silence have been suffocating.

The cellophane wrapped around the fresh-cut flowers I hesitantly picked up at a roadside stand on the way to Chawton Falls crinkles in my sweaty palms. I steady my breath. Usually, I wouldn't knock. Since I was little, the Desfleurses have had an open-door policy, but with a string of unanswered phone calls proving Aulie's mad at how I behaved on the ice, things feel different.

I balance a box of her favorite pizza from a small beach town in Seacoast, New Hampshire. Beach pizza is a weird phenomenon that doesn't exist this far north in the state, and Aulie's borderline obsessed. I'm hoping the gesture is enough to put an end to her silent treatment.

Since she showed up on my campus five years ago, we haven't gone a day without at least texting *something* to each other. Her radio silence has sucked, but I get it. I should have controlled my emotions better. I shouldn't have let Alex get to me like that, but... if I'm honest, I'd pummel just about any asshole who said anything about wanting to eat Aulie out, Alex most of all.

I regret not being on the ice and letting my team down. I regret disappointing Aulie after she gave up so much this summer and is busting her ass now. But I don't regret what I did to Alex. He *licked* me. Who the hell does that?

Goosebumps rise on my neck before I rap on the wooden door in front of me. Leaves rustle in a nearby bush like I'm being watched. By who? There's no way the paparazzi followed me up here. Although, I guess with Veronica's bullshit video, maybe. Numerous callers have asked if I care to comment on the video. I still haven't watched it, but from what I've gathered, Veronica is claiming I'm a jerk—a fact—and that I broke up with her because she wouldn't give up her charity work to spend more time with me —obviously false.

I have zero motivation to set the record straight. People will think what they want about me either way, and her fans are both hardcore and loyal. A "Veroniac" even threw an Iced Dunks at me on the street the other day, so it'd be wasted breath.

"Maa."

"What the fuck?" I jump at the foreign sound. The pizza wobbles in my grasp, and I almost fall ass-backward down the stairs.

With my head on a swivel, I search the overgrown foliage around me for whatever creature made the creepy sound. Golden leaves obscure a brown and white fur coat, and I raise my eye line slightly.

Two beady eyes cut into me as the creature chews on its cud.

Goat.

It's a goat.

That's not too bad. Goats are friendly, right? People do yoga with them and shit.

I can see my sister, Simone, rolling her eyes at my overreaction. *You've lived in the city for too long, half-pint. Goats are nothing to freak out about.*

Sure, goats don't usually just *happen*, but she's right. I'm Jack Parker. I play hockey and get paid to ram into people for a living. Simple farm creatures don't faze me.

My heart settles a fraction, and I finally bring myself to rap on the door, still very aware of what's transpiring over my shoulder. If that goat comes for me, I'm busting through this door with no fucks to give.

The giant oak barrier creaks open, and Gus greets me, his eyes trained on his laptop, and brows furrowed. "Why did you knock?"

So, knocking was the wrong move. Noted.

"I—uhm." *I panicked. Aulie hasn't talked to me in days, and I can't handle her being mad at me. And, oh yeah, that goat in the bushes fills me with a significant sense of dread, and I don't know why.*

Nope. Can't say that.

"I couldn't open the door with my hands full."

And yet, I knocked on the door...with my hand. Gus raises his gaze for half a fraction. He's a literal genius, so he'll see right through me.

"Whatever." He shrugs. "Just come in. The last time Gio got into the house, he shat everywhere."

"Gio?"

"Mr. Martin's goat. You know, the farm by you sister, Simone's house." He nods over to the bush. "The thing keeps getting loose and wandering the town."

"Ah." I step over the threshold, and Gus shuts the door behind me.

"Did you get the ring?"

"Oh, yeah. Hold on."

I fumble with my pocket, again proving I had a free hand, and pull out a box. The ring is a family heirloom that belonged to his

Memere. Gus gave it to me when he picked Aulie up from Boston this summer, leaving me responsible for finding a jeweler who could refinish it before Aulie's birthday. His Memere lost the stone in a grocery store years ago, and he couldn't replace it then. But now, we're both in better places financially, so we got it cleaned, resized, and added new diamonds and emeralds to it.

The jeweler at the store congratulated me on my upcoming engagement and complimented me on my taste. I didn't correct him because that would have required further conversation on my part—a horrifying notion.

I glance around for Aulie, not wanting to spoil her surprise. "She's in the family room playing the piano," Gus says, sensing my hesitation.

I pass the black velvet box over to him. He peeks inside and breathes a sigh of relief. "Memere was so upset when she lost the stone," he says. "I wish I could have gotten it fixed for her, but Aulie will love it. Thanks again for helping."

"Oh, yeah. No problem." I shift my weight. *I'd do just about anything to make your sister smile.*

"Aulie did a lot for me this summer, and you two have been through hell. Just happy to help."

"I should probably go hide it while she's distracted. Be right back." He turns briefly. "Beer's in the fridge. Aulie said dinner would be ready in an hour."

Inhaling, the smell of cloves and allspice fills my lungs. God bless the Desfleurs's family cooking. It is a genuine weakness of mine. When Aulie was over this summer, I basked in the scent of it blanketing my apartment with a warm coziness. Whenever I'd wake up from a heavy nap, onions cooking in butter or some other comforting smell would welcome me and I would escape into a momentary piece of paradise.

She gave me heaven, and I threw it away with one lift of the stick.

The thought sinks like a stone in my stomach. I need to make amends somehow. Even if the pizza isn't enough, I'm stuck in Chawton Falls for forty-some-odd days.

I have time.

I follow my nose toward the kitchen. Soft piano music fills the great room. Aulie always plays sweetly with a hint of a melancholy tone. Fire flickers in the stone hearth, framed by built-in bookshelves loaded with books from the floor to the ceiling. The curtains to the back windows are pulled open, revealing the pond and the rolling hills of red, orange, and yellow.

I rarely ever visit this time of the year, and as much as the reason why I'm here now sucks, there's a charm about Chawton Falls in autumn, that softens the blow a fraction.

Leaning against the doorframe to the family room, I listen, balancing the pizza and flowers in one hand and shoving my other hand in my pocket.

Her fingers fly over the black and ivory keys, playing a tune she hummed regularly while doing the dishes or helping me somewhere this summer. I sigh and let myself relax after three hours of driving. My head grows heavy and droops forward as the sound of her playing lulls me into a quiet doze.

Thud.

The music stops. Aulie's bench scratches against the hardwood. Blinking my eyes open, I find the bouquet on the floor.

"Sandra Bullock, Jack. Why the heck are you always so quiet?" Her tone isn't quite scolding, but she barely meets my gaze.

I need to lay the charm on thick if I'm going to get myself out of this. A broad smile stretches across my face. "Most people say I'm heavy-footed."

I'm never particularly verbally charming with this woman, but I can at least flash a devastating grin and hope for the best.

"Most people are liars, then." She smiles back. We're getting somewhere, good.

I lean down to pick up the flowers as she does the same.

"I've got it, Dessy." Sometimes, when Aulie bends, she has this face after, like she's clearly in pain, but she doesn't want anyone else to know, and I've messed up enough this week to add that face to my guilt-list. My fingers brush against hers, and I'm tempted to let the touch linger.

"You've got your hands full. Is that Tripoli's?"

"Of course, it is. I had to get my girl her favorite treat before I came up here." I wince the minute the words pass over my lips.

Wrong. Wrong. Wrong. Wrong. That's not something someone in the friend zone should say. Maybe I should have gone with something like, *I also drilled a man because he suggested he wanted to be intimate with you. Aren't I the best kind of friend?*

But never *"my girl," douche. What were you thinking?*

Her eyes snap to mine, and the sharp, curious stare catches me off guard. I snatch the flowers and stand straight, hitting my head on the wall behind me.

"Oh, my goodness. Are you okay?" Aulie's delicate fingers feel for a bump on the back of my skull. The touch incinerates any hope I have of handling this situation well. My eyes linger on her soft pillow lips, and she rakes her teeth over them.

Holy hell. This woman is going to be the death of me.

"Fine." I swallow, drowning in her intoxicating floral scent. The only time she smelled more dangerous was this summer, when she ran out of her soap and used mine. Something feral broke inside me when she bent to tend to my bandages, and I caught a whiff. If I closed my eyes, I could pretend she smelled like that because she was just as much mine as I've so desperately been hers for the past five years.

"Smashing. Really." I gently grab her hand and pull it down. Because she's not mine, and never will be.

She can't be.

"Wall, hello there." She smiles softly at me, but it doesn't reach her eyes like it normally does. A pang of longing sounds in the hollow of my chest cavity for the lines that usually rim the corner of her eyes when she's genuinely happy.

Her thumb runs errant circles on the top of my hand, and that hollow pang gives way to a dramatic thud. But she's touching and joking with me, which she doesn't do when she's angry, so maybe I read too much into her ignored calls and texts.

My gaze drops to our point of contact, and hers follows. Her eyes widen, almost like she didn't realize what she was doing, and she rips her hand from mine.

The sensations border dangerously close to morphing into feelings—and, can't have that.

In my avoid-all-emotions panic, I shove the box of pizza and flowers at her. "These are for you."

Luckily, Dessy is used to me operating at an eleven around her. I doubt she even knows that there's a side of me that is calm and collected, so she catches the box with relative ease. "Thank you?"

"I'm sorry, I uhm—broke my promise to be on my best behavior during the game. But I've missed you, so if you could find it in your heart to forgive me and stop this ghosting business, I'd appreciate it."

For a second, there's a flicker of her sparkle as she peeks into the box. Extra slices of provolone cheese sit on top of square pizza loaded with the sweet sauce that makes it signature "beach pizza." But then, as if she's conscious she's allowed herself a moment of happiness, she blinks, and it flames out as quickly as it appeared.

"Right. Yes. I haven't returned your phone calls because I'm angry. So angry," she says, stuffing a piece of pizza into her mouth and shifting the weight on her feet. I cock my head to the side at her awkward demeanor. I'm putting out too much nervous energy, and it's rubbing off on her. "Luckily for you, it's physically impossible for me to be both mad and holding this pizza, so I guess I can look into my heart and forgive you. Want one?" She offers me the box, sauce already covering her face.

"No. I need to save room for the meat pie. It smells great." I wipe a smidge of sauce off her cheek before I can even think about how weird that is. Aulie's face reddens, and her mouth parts. I swallow. My hand itches. It's had a taste of her touch and wants so much more. "But I'm glad we're okay. I missed you." I swipe at a fallen tendril along her cheek and tuck it behind her ear, smiling warmly at her as heat radiates from my thumb and tingles shoot down my arm.

Aulie opens her mouth and stammers.

God dammit, Jack. Stop being so fucking weird.

"*Quack. Quack. Quack. You're my best friend.*" The muffled sound of Aulie's childhood stuffed duck pulls us both out of whatever the hell that was.

Her eyes widen as her mouth deepens into a frown. "Excuse me. I need to save Quackers from that darn dog." She stuffs her slice back into the box and slides it into my grasp. "Thank you again." She flashes me a hesitant smile before trudging down the hall and disappearing into her bedroom. "No. Bad dog. Off. Out."

The quacking continues.

"I'm serious."

I love you.

I bite the inside of my cheek, stifling my laugh. Aulie's dog loves humping that doll, and whenever he pokes the stomach, it cycles between quacking and other various phrases. Since I became emotionally stunted at seventeen, I'm still not mature enough to handle the situation.

"Hey, Willoughby. Do you want a treat?" The quacks fall silent and sharp claws clatter on the hardwood floor toward the kitchen.

Willoughby haughtily marches into the room. "Yeah. That'll teach him."

"Hush. We're good enough friends know that you know this dog walks all over me—all creatures do." She stares pointedly at me, and I put a hand on my chest.

"Creature? Me?" I feign offense. "Since when do I walk all over you?"

"Oh please, we both know the only reason you asked me over this summer is because I'd give you anything you wanted when your mother and sisters would give you a hard time."

My cheeks heat. I didn't beg Aulie for help because she was a pushover, I asked her there because she was the only thing I needed. "That's not entirely accurate," I croak.

"The truth is somewhere around there though." She shrugs, opening a cabinet door and missing my blush. Pulling out a canister of homemade biscuits she dips her long, elegant fingers into the container and gives him one.

Willoughby scoffs it up and tilts his head to the side, waiting for another.

No way he doesn't get at least three more from her.

"You'll ruin your dinner," she says.

The fawn pug with a plump, happy figure, sits patiently. His stubby pink tongue pants in expectation.

"One. You get one more."

At a distance, I take her in. Heavy lines and circles darken her eyes, and her mouth tilts in an unfamiliar downward turn.

She's wearing the last few years like a heavy, tattered cloak, and someone needs to wrap her up in something more befitting the queen she is.

I don't know if I can do anything for her, but I have to do something.

She reaches in and grabs another biscuit, which is again swallowed greedily by the recipient. Hesitating, her hand remains in the canister.

Walking over, I gently take it from her, careful not to let our fingers graze again. "All done," I say firmly to Willoughby. He growls but waddles bitterly back to his bed near the crackling fire.

"I think I found my mission while I'm here," I say, stretching over her to put the biscuits away.

Aulie's back hits the counter, a gust of air escaping her. "What would that be?"

"I'm going to teach you to stick up for yourself."

"Yes, because your stick did you so much good," she says with a quiver in her voice.

My foot stumbles over something as I extend my reach..

Not something. *Someone.*

Shit. I stepped on Aulie's foot.

"Sorry!"

She wraps a hand around my back to keep me from wobbling. "It's fine. Just a six-three hockey player clamping down on my pinky toe. No big deal." She glances up at me, and tears rim her eyes.

Fuck. I hurt her.

"First lesson, Dessy." I put my hands on either side of her on the counter, leaning in with a mischievous grin. Seeing her cry is like a deep slash to my heart. I need to make her laugh or smile before I bleed out. "Milk that pain for all it's worth. If you played your cards right, I would have waited on you hand and foot today."

"Is that so?" She quirks a brow at me, a small smile tugging on the tips of her lips. *Bingo*. "I think it was one of those delayed pains, but my foot might be bruised after all. There may even be some residual pain radiating up my legs and arms. I don't know how I'll finish sorting the mound of boxes in my room on my own."

"I guess I could help you with that." This close, my gaze betrays me. It flickers over her soft, light brown hair tied high in a messy bun and lingers on her hazelnut chocolate eyes searching mine.

Sparkle or not, she's still Aulie.

And she's still Gus's little sister.

I repeat the mantra that's drilled into my mind for whenever I find myself in this situation.

Gus and I are like brothers.

So, logically... Aulie is...

She runs her teeth over her lower lip.

Yeah, maybe I could find a hypnotist that could convince me she's a bad idea once and for all.

I step back, clear my throat, and glance out the kitchen window. Aulie sidesteps me and heads to the stove, grabbing an onion to chop up.

Outside, Gus is standing by the pond, draping his arm around someone affectionately. It looks like it's their third roommate and Aulie's best friend, Emy, with her long brown hair and tiny frame, but...

She faces him with a massive smile.

That's definitely Emy. I've seen her enough to—

Gus grabs her face with both hands and lowers his head, pressing his lips against hers.

"What the fuck?" The words fly out of my mouth louder than necessary. That's not—they shouldn't be...

Metal clatters in the corner of the kitchen. "Ow. Fudge nuggets!" I glance at Aulie. Blood is flowing out from her finger.

I rush over, grabbing a towel and wrapping it tightly around her finger. "Shit, shit, shit."

"It's fine." She breathes out.

Like hell it is. My gashed out heart hemorrhages in my panic.

"Seriously? It's not fine. It was pretty deep." I frown. She might need stitches. "You need to be more careful."

"Okay, Gus." She snorts. "But I'm not the one shouting next to someone with a knife. What was that about?"

I don't know what to say. Does Aulie know Gus is going around kissing her best friend? Shouldn't that be off-limits? Or maybe girl code is different? But that doesn't seem right—twenty-first century and all that.

"I just saw something that caught me off-guard, sorry." I blush, keeping the pressure on her finger.

Aulie glances out the window. "Ah. Yeah, that's new-ish." She smiles. "But they're cute together. Huh?"

"Isn't that...weird...for you? Your brother and your best friend, I mean."

She shrugs. "It was at first. But I love them both so much that it's a bonus that they love each other too. You know?"

I nod. I'd never thought about it like that. Would Gus feel the same way? Probably not. He's protective, and I'm a no-good ass, so there's that. Not that it matters what either Gus or I think. Aulie's showed no interest in me. After suffering through the last few days without communication, there's no way I'd risk ruining our friendship and losing her for good.

She deserves better than someone who can't handle their emotions and hides behind a bad boy image.

"Where are your band-aids?" I ask, shaking myself back to reality. I shouldn't be entertaining any of this, anyway.

"They're in the medicine cabinet in the bathroom, but I can get them—"

"Let me take care of *you* for once, Dessy," I say as softly as possible, but inside I want to yell, *Woman, chill the fuck out before you bleed to death.* Bit dramatic? Sure, but I can't handle the sight of her blood without panicking.

"Oh. Uhm. Okay." She barely meets my eyes as she smiles.

Grabbing some Neosporin and the band-aids, I return to Aulie hanging near the couch in the great room and gently unwrap the towel. Thankfully, the bleeding's slowed.

Cleaned and washed, I put another band-aid on top of the smaller one, just in case, and smile sheepishly at her. "Good to go."

Aulie bats her eyelashes. "My hero," she says in a faux Southern accent.

I snort, mind flailing, because that woman's long, dark eyelashes do terrible things to me, and I ruffle her hair.

With a blush, her gaze flickers to mine, and then she brushes past me. "I should get that meat pie out before it gets too dry."

"Good call." I cough.

Note to self: never ruffle that woman's hair again.

Chapter Nine

Jack Parker

Play: *Can't Fight This Feeling Anymore by REO Speedwagon*

I might be ninety percent meat pie now, but I can't stop eating it.

The nutmeg, cloves, and cinnamon meld with the melted slice of American Cheese perfectly, and every "last" bite becomes a "well, maybe I'll have just one more."

It doesn't help that I'm incredibly anxious, which is a foreign feeling in this house. Ever since I was little, this place has been my comfort place. Aulie's Memere and aunts and uncles were always around, talking over each other with their Franglish. And I could sit in a corner, eating Aulie's Doritos or whatever was on the menu for the day, and people watch in the shadows.

Unlike my house, where my older sisters treated me like a dress-up doll, and I was the center of my mother's attention well into my teen years.

But today, my knee is shaking under the table, and there's a decided itch under my skin.

Gus is dating *Emy*. The girl we used to catch peeking behind trees, watching us when we'd go swimming in King's Pond.

And the world hasn't exploded.

Her friendship with Aulie seems fine.

Aulie and Gus are fine.

So what the hell have I been doing?

"Jack? Are you all right?" Aulie tilts her head a fraction. Her eyes scan over me, and the crawling feeling inside intensifies.

"Yeah, fine. Why?"

"You're clutching your knife pretty hard." She gestures to my left hand holding my butter knife's slim handle like I might need to stab someone at this table.

"Oh. Yeah. Erm. Fine." I smile slightly, releasing the knife and tugging at the collar of my shirt. "So, when did this happen?" I nod to Emy and Gus, holding hands across the table.

Gus looks sheepishly at Emy, and it's cute and stupid and nauseating.

Lucky bastard.

"I think we'd been flirting for a while, but stuff fell into place when Aulie took care of you in Boston. You know it's funny—we don't have a specific date we can point to. It just happened. Easy, you know?"

"Friends to lovers is the superior trope in my experience." Emy smiles broadly at Gus and winks.

Aulie clears her throat.

Easy.

It just happened.

Nope. I can't say I understand any of that.

"Cool. Cool." I stab at my meat pie and stuff a heaping bite into my mouth to keep myself from saying something stupid.

The bite is too big, and it lodges itself in the back of my throat, clogging my airways.

Play it cool.

I go for a sip of water, but I'm obviously choking and probably dying, and oh my god, I'm a giant weenie. That's it. Because I could fucking say something to Aulie now, and I'm literally choking on the idea.

"Jack?" Aulie stands, a worried look plastered on her face, and comes over to whack my back. Once. Twice. "Oh, punaise, how does that hemlock thing work?"

"It's the Heimlich," Gus provides.

"Okay, great, Einstein, but do you know how to do it?"

"No." He frowns. "But I'm sure there's a YouTube video." He pulls his phone out.

"I think you have to wrap your arms around his waist somehow. Like a hug," Emy adds while I continue to cough and sputter.

"A hug, really, that's helpful. I'm sorry, Jack, I'm trying. Shoot, I should take a class for the fair. This would be an important skill to have on hand."

"Mrs. King's apple crisp was too dry last year; I almost died myself." Emy leans over to watch the video on Gus's phone.

Aulie whacks my back a second time. "I told her she needed to add more butter, but she's been on a health kick since Mr. King had his heart attack."

"See, that's definitely a hug," Emy says, leaning over and watching the video.

"Okay, but what do I do with my hands while I hug him?"

Something passes between Emy and Aulie that I can't decipher, mainly because I'm actively trying not to die, but it ends with Aulie scowling and pointing a stern finger in Emy's direction. "Don't."

She whacks my back several times, and I clear whatever is stuck in my windpipe.

"I'm good. I'm fine." I catch my breath. "Thank you all for your contributions."

I take another sip of water, but I've downed the contents of my glass. So, with shaky hands, I reach for the wineglass and knock it over in my flustered state.

Aulie jumps back, avoiding a waterfall of red wine that rushes down to the carpet below. "What the heck is wrong with you today? You didn't get a concussion when you hit your head on the wall, did you?" She puts her hands on my face, cupping my cheeks and staring straight into my soul. A slight dusting of freckles dances over the bridge of her nose, bleeding into the rosy blush of her cheeks. God, she's perfect.

And I clearly can't handle my shit.

"Excuse me." I stand and promptly bolt to the bathroom to collect myself.

What the hell was that?

She's not off-limits. The thought echoes as I splash my face with water and get a hold of myself.

She's not interested. I don't date during the season. I know all this.

Do you, though? Or are you being the wimp you've always been?

What I'm not—

And I'm conversing with myself in the mirror. This situation has finally broken me.

Maybe admitting my feelings to Aulie wouldn't be so bad—if only to save whatever sanity I have left. I weigh the decision to talk to Aulie, turning the knob. A rush of cold air slaps my damp cheeks as I step into the hallway. It's probably better if I wait until the end of the season to tell her. When my mind can focus and prioritize her.

Willoughby cuts across my path, emerging from Aulie's bedroom with a small piece of paper in his mouth. "What have you got here, bud?" I ask, bending down and rescuing whatever it is from his teeth.

The text "Aulie's List for a Suitable Suitor" sits among a pool of slobber.

I shouldn't read it. It's none of my business... then again, I'm a known asshole, so...

I hazard a glance at my surroundings, but Emy, Gus, and Aulie are all talking in the dining room a good two rooms away. The only person to judge me for my assholery is the picture of

John F. Kennedy hanging in the hallway, a remnant from when Gus and Aulie's Memere owned the house.

"Ideas live on, am I right?" I joke, before shaking my head—having a conversation with a picture of a dead president probably isn't much better than having one with myself.

Must be kind, dependable, and loyal.

"Not off to a great start there," I chuckle.
JFK says nothing.

I would prefer he worships the ground I walk on since I'm bound to become overly attached and want a balanced emotional relationship.

"Well, at least I've got that one covered."

He is comfortable showing affection and expressing his feelings to me.

"There goes any shot in hell I ever had. Should I even read on?"
Again, JFK ponders but remains silent.

Shares the same values about family and children and having them sooner rather than later. I want someone I can grow old with surrounded by a gaggle of loved ones.

"Well, shit," I say with a swallow. I've never really thought about what a relationship with Aulie would look like because I've been so focused on the "off-limits" part.

I'm not interested in starting a family for at least the next ten years. I have too much hockey to focus on. Plus, I'm too much of a mess myself. Me responsible for another human should be illegal. And Aulie? I know she has a massive hole in her heart for her family, and she deserves to start her own as soon as she wants to.

If she was interested, and that's a big, no-way in hell *if*, it wouldn't be fair to her if I asked her to give that up. So maybe biting my tongue and saying nothing is the best way to go. There's a greater chance I'll ruin a romantic relationship than a platonic one.

Below four, item five sits half-heartedly crossed out.

> ~~I want someone I can have wild chemistry with (if that's not foolish to ask for). I want that soul-crushing, tingling, toe-curling feeling. I want his kisses to destroy me. I want to be utterly wrecked.~~

The thought of Aulie finding that with someone else boils my blood. But it doesn't matter. I can be angry. I can use that fuel and be miserable on the ice as long as Aulie gets the happy ending she deserves.

Below line five an arrow points to it with a little text bubble that reads *that one is too foolish. I'll be content with a safe, stout love, after all. Was Charlotte Lucas's ending really that tragic?*

Oh no. *Well, that won't do, Dessy. You deserve fireworks and whatever happy shit is in those Jane Austen novels of yours.*

With a sigh, I leave the paper on a side table littered with family photos of Gus and Aulie's Memere, aunts and uncles, and finally return to the crew in the dining room. That list was a friendly reminder that there are other reasons I shouldn't act on my feelings for Aulie besides her being Gus's little sister. Mainly, she deserves the world and someone who's nearly as good as she is, and I'm—well, me. She shouldn't settle for someone like me instead of waiting for the great romantic hero she deserves.

"You should ask Jack."

The sound of my name causes my steps to slow.

"No way he's going to want to do it," Aulie's sweet-honey voice answers.

"You never know. Didn't he say he'd love to help?"

"Yeah, as a joke, there's no way he planned on actually being able to come through."

Dependable.

The word from her list screams past my skull. But it doesn't matter; I'm not trying to show that I can be anything for Aulie. We want different things, and above all, I want her to have the world, not take it from her.

But maybe, this list isn't a terrible idea to keep in mind. So, I can't be a suitor, but she deserves good people in her life, and that's what that list was, right? Maybe it can be a bit of a moral compass for me while I'm up here, and I can show her she has someone on her side who can help her through all this.

Yup, that's a logical explanation for why I want to incorporate those characteristics into my life.

"You never know, though. Now that he's here, there's not much to do, so maybe he'll be down to help."

"I don't know, Emy." Gus's chair creaks. "I don't think it's his thing either."

"But what's the harm in asking?" Emy continues.

"No, you're right," Gus says, a phrase I seldom hear him use. "You should ask him, at least. Maybe he'll be bored or something."

"Ask me what?" I ask, finally entering the dining room. I search for Aulie in her seat, but she's not there. My head swivels to the floor. She's on her hands and knees cleaning up my puddle of spilled wine. Shit.

At this point, I'm not even sure I deserve this woman's friendship.

"Nothing, it's fine." She waves me off.

"Aulie needs help with the fair because she's behind on planning after caring for you," Emy says.

Grabbing a napkin off the table, I bend to finish cleaning up the mess. "Whatever it is, count me in, Dessy."

"No, Jack. I couldn't possibly ask you to—" She raises her head. We're a lot closer than we were when I started my crouch. My breath catches and echoes off the walls like it's coming from somewhere else rather than internally. I shift my weight, leaning further back. "This isn't your type of thing, trust me."

"You're so sure you know what my thing is?"

"I mean, after five years? Yeah. I have a pretty good idea. And trust me. This isn't it. It's fine. Emy's just upset because I'm beyond desperate and I'm considering asking Tyler since he's in town."

Fucking hate that idea.

"Nah. Why torture yourself with that ass? Whatever you need, Dessy, I've got you."

"Thank you," Emy breathes out.

"I hate the prick too, but they should explain what you're getting into before you agree, man. It's not manual labor or something. It's—"

"Unnecessary. I owe Dessy for taking care of me this summer and saving my life." My gaze lands on her. Lilacs, violets, and rosewater hit my nostrils, and my heart hammers against my chest. I'd put up with just about anything if it meant keeping her away from that asshole. "And my PR team suggested I do some charity work after whatever Veronica posted, so it's a win-win."

"This isn't something you can flake on, Jack. If you commit, I need you there."

"You don't think I'd keep my word?"

"Your track record suggests otherwise."

My mouth presses into a grim, hard line as I study her.

"What?" she whispers.

"You don't think I'm dependable?"

A rush of color dusts her cheeks. Shit, I shouldn't have used that word, it's a dead giveaway that I read her list.

"I mean, no offense, but yeah. Look where you are, Jack. You should be with your team, but you're here, in Chawton Falls, because you're suspended. That doesn't exactly exude dependability."

A muscle tics in my jaw. She has a point there.

"That settles it, then. Whatever it is, count me in, and I promise you," I lift my eyes so they land on her and keep them there, far more steady and sure than my frantically beating heart. "Aurelie Lunette Desfleurs, I'm going to be there."

"You'll have to work the fair, just like everyone else. I can't give you special treatment, or there will be anarchy."

"Wouldn't expect you to."

"That means coming to set up days on time."

"Fine. Got it."

"I'm serious. You can't be late."

"I'm a professional athlete. I can get to places on time just fine."

Her gaze narrows skeptically.

"Okay, so like five minutes late. But I'll be good, I promise. Just trust me."

"Okay." She nods. "Yeah, I mean, it *would* be really helpful, actually—"

"Deal. Great." Emy jumps in, casually sipping her glass of wine. "Aulie, you officially have your Wickham. How do you feel?"

"Great." Aulie's gaze hastily meets mine before darting away in a nervous flutter.

Wait. Wickham?

Who?

What?

Huh?

Chapter Ten

Jack Parker

Play: *Teenage Dirtbag by Wheatus*

My body was not made for hard twin mattresses. I'm not sure anyone's is. I groan, pushing off the poor excuse of a bed resting on an antique iron frame in my sister's nursery, ready for my new nephew. After a minute of waking from my groggy sleep, I crack my back and let out a long-suffering sigh. My recently recovered shoulder is frozen. I rotate it a few times until it loosens from immovable to stiff.

My toes press against the hardwood floor, and they're greeted with a significant chill. A shiver works up my spine.

The tangy scent of freshly baked cranberry scones wafts under the door and a second wind of full-bodied coffee follows.

When it comes to my sister, fresh-baked pastries are never a good sign.

It's her tell that she wants to have a talk and is planning on softening me up with something sweet and warm.

When I was twelve, and she wanted my basement game room

for her bedroom because being twenty-two and living at home was stifling, she baked apple crisp.

At fourteen, she wanted to talk to me about how she was moving out of the house to live with Tom, her now husband, but wanted to make sure I knew she wasn't leaving me. I got brownies and a brother-in-law out of that one.

And when she wanted to talk to me about Dad's cancer, she baked a whole ass cheesecake.

God, I hate cheesecake.

But cranberry scones? If she wants a kidney, she can have it. No questions asked.

I pull a crew-neck sweatshirt over my white t-shirt, still in my boxers. Goosebumps rise on my arm. I'm sure it's a lot warmer in the central part of the house, but I need a few minutes to wake up before whatever Simone wants to talk about.

Stretching, I open the blinds in my room, hoping the streaming sun will warm the room up during the day.

The blinds shoot up after a firm tug, and the sun instantly floods the ten-by-ten light blue room, transforming it with a cheerful, warming effect that exudes my sister's personality.

I blink a few times. Two soulless eyes laser their way through the window.

I jump. My heart hammers against my chest. "What the fuck?"

A goat.

With its brown and white spotted coat and deadened gaze, I get the sense that it's the same goat from Gus and Aulie's. His gaze levels...at my crotch?

I breathe. I'm inside. The goat—what did Gus call him? Gio? Is outside. This is fine.

After a minute of mindless staring, Gio opens his mouth and lets out a long boisterous bleat. His head flails, and his eyes widen to an alarming size, as if to say *I'm a goat, and I'm going to mess you up.*

I step back on my heels.

And just as quick as the bleating began, Gio closes his mouth.

His long floppy tongue hangs out the side. Like a hiccup, he follows with a tiny "maa."

I don't break our stare as I retreat into the center of the room because I'm seriously concerned he can somehow Houdini his ass through the window. Pulling my sweatpants on, I back out into the hallway and close the door behind me.

Silverware clatters in the kitchen, and I follow the alluring mixture of coffee beans and warm pastries through the maze of rooms tacked on to the back of the house. Warmth grows as I near the hearth and a crackling fire.

"Simone?" I ask.

"Ah, there's the bad boy of the National Hockey League," my sister teases as I bow under the doorframe to the small galley kitchen. I doubt bad boys are worried about goats hexing them, but sure. "I made your favorite scones."

I want to prompt her to get the inevitable conversation over with, but if she's not jumping right in, I'll take a second to eat my scones in peace.

She smoothes down her chocolate brown hair, slightly lighter than mine, and rubs her pregnant belly—her midlife crisis, as she likes to refer to it. "You okay?"

"Yeah, fine." I try to shake off the memory of Gio's blank stare. I'm unsure how good goats are at witchcraft, but I feel cursed "You guys didn't get a goat, did you?"

"Oh, is Gio out again? I'll call Mr. Martin." Simone wipes her hands on her apron. "He's been getting out and wandering the field ever since Tom fixed him a few weeks ago—actually—Tom!" Simone calls her husband down the long corridor leading to their dining room. "Gio's out again. Are you going up to Mr. Martin's farm today?"

"Yeah, I'll bring him back."

"Make sure he doesn't get into the flowers before then."

"He'll be fine. The fence I built should keep him out."

"Just like the one you built that was supposed to keep him in?"

"You make solid points."

A flurry of papers rustles, and a chair scrapes against the well-worn floor a few rooms away. Tom shuffles his way into the kitchen. He's the local farm veterinarian, and since he's handy and incapable of saying no to people, he is also the resident odd-job man.

"Hey, Jack," he greets me with a wide, toothy smile. "Welcome. Welcome. How was the drive up?" He stuffs his feet into a pair of mud-caked boots.

"Long but fine."

Simone's eyes sparkle. "That happens when you detour to the Seacoast for pizza."

I blush. "You may have already guessed, but the box in the fridge is for you guys. I put a few cannolis in there too."

"Yes!" Tom triumphantly shoots his fist in the air before hanging it out for me to bump. He plops a hat over his head and ears. "If you'll excuse me, I have an overly adventurous goat to attend to, a bee to milk, and a cow hive I should extract honey from, anyway."

Simone walks over and kisses Tom on the cheek. "Please don't milk the bees, dear."

"You know what I meant…" Tom pinches his pointer and thumb together, pretending like he's milking some tiny-ass nipple. "Can you imagine?"

"Go save my flowers from Gio, love."

"Right! The wether!"

My brow furrows. "What the hell is a wether?" Maybe it's the name for a goat who's joined the occult.

"It's the proper terminology for a castrated goat."

"Ah."

"We should catch up later, though, half-pint." Tom winks, using Simone's nickname for me. Even though I'm almost a foot taller than her now, our ten-year age difference meant I was half her size well into her twenties.

"Sure. Looking forward to sharing a beer or something."

"Yes. That is something we will do." Tom shoots weird finger guns at me, slowly backing out of the kitchen.

Simone's laughter follows his departure. "He's surrounded by so many women, and all the farmers he works with are sixty-plus. I don't think he knows how to interact with a guy your age."

"I can take him out with Gus while I'm up here—show him a stripper or something." I flash a big teasing grin, running a hand through my bedhead. Getting Simone riled up is still my favorite pastime, no matter how old we get. She hates whatever I'm doing with my "tattoos, fist fights on the ice, drunken nights, and rotating list of women," and she never lets me hear the end of it.

My sister scoffs, pulling a tray of scones out of the oven. Oh, are those blueberries?

Damn, maybe she needs two kidneys.

"Drop the act while you're home. I've seen you pee yourself because I tickled you too hard. We all know you're a softie."

"It's not an act." It's totally an act. "But to be fair, you were the cruelest fucking tickler."

"There are little ears here!" Simone slaps my hand away with her dishrag as I reach for a scone. "Little ears that look up to their uncle and could use a better example than someone who trips guys into the boards and breaks their nose."

"It was an accident."

"Oh, that's complete horse poop," she says, dipping into the fridge and grabbing a milk pitcher. She pours a glass and hands me a plate piled high with scones.

When is she going to get to whatever she wants to ask?

Heat from the oven clouds the space between the narrow walls, and I push up my sleeves, suddenly wishing I had a t-shirt on under here.

Simone sighs, focusing on the new tattoos I've recently had inked below my elbow. "Dad would hate those."

"They're mostly about him."

"That's why he'd hate them. They're like a perpetual reminder that you stopped living at seventeen."

I clear my throat and wash down my scone with milk. Well, this visit is off to a good start. "I've lived to twenty-eight just fine."

"'The man who gets the most out of life is not the one who has lived it longest, but the one who has felt life most deeply.' That's—"

"Rousseau. I know." I roll my eyes. Dad's favorite. "He also said God made me and broke the mold. Which I prefer to live by."

Simone swats at me with her towel, and I avoid the assault with a tiny giggle, reverting back to the ten-year-old who swore her oldest sister hung the moon.

"Okay, Smart Ass. But seriously, Jack, I'm worried about you. It's like you've repressed all the goodness that was stuffed inside you—and just stopped feeling. That's not a life. That's a…a vessel."

"A vessel?" I quirk a brow. I don't remember that quote.

"Yes, and that's a Simone Finnigan original, buddy." Her shoulders deflate as she lowers herself onto a kitchen chair nestled nearby. Her hand rakes through her floured hair, leaving a few more white streaks in its wake. "I just don't know what you're trying to prove with this image you have. You could do so much more with your position and your money than you're doing now. He'd want so much more for you."

Is *this* what she wanted to talk to me about? I mean, the scones are good and all, but… "He'd want me to win the Cup."

"That's complete bull. Dad was so much more than just hockey. You know that. You lived that. Mom and Dad had already had two children at your age. I had Luce. And you're pulling punk-ass, tripping-guys-into-sideboards stuff, falling on your drunken ass in public, and running around with a different woman every night."

I could throw it in Simone's face that I've volunteered to work at Aulie's fair for a few days. The fair benefits the local museum and the town, and that's benevolent and shit. But telling her would require extending this conversation, and it's too early in the morning to deal with any of this.

"Thanks for the scone." I push off the counter.

A firm hand wraps around my wrist before I can exit the kitchen. "I didn't mean to mom you the minute you got here. I'm just worried about you, half-pint."

The harsh lines on my face soften. "I appreciate your concern and that you cushioned this conversation with scones, but I'm fine. I promise."

"Yeah...that's not why I baked the scones." Simone flashes me a weak smile. "Do you know what tomorrow is?"

Since my suspension came down three days ago, the only thing keeping me somewhat aware of the concept of time is the text message I get from Grady every morning with a countdown to when I can play again.

GRADY

Forty-three days until your suspension is over.

"I thought that'd be your answer." Simone presses her lips into a thin line. "It's Dad's birthday."

My stomach drops. That means it's also Stand Up to Cancer night for the Badgers. A game where I'm usually made the honorary captain. A game where a camera stays on me while the stadium watches a video montage of my dad kicking ass on the ice and hoisting a miniature version of myself in the air after he won his first cup. A game where I spend more time in the penalty box than on the ice, and none of my teammates question it.

And a day where my family spends time together, going to his grave and having family dinner. I've been all too happy to have an excuse for why I couldn't join them over the past ten years.

Until now.

"And I think—" Simone hedges her words, handing me another plate piled high with scones and homemade jam. "No, *I know* it would mean the world to Mom if you joined us for everything. Including going to the cemetery to see him."

"I—ugh—" My hand holding the plate shakes. I've never been to his gravesite. Without seeing that marker, I can pretend like he's on a broadcast trip or just not great with phones. But that marker —it's a final reminder of where he is now.

That's not him.

"Uncle Jack!" My niece, Lucy, miraculously saves me as she

enters the kitchen and lunges at me. I catch her, but the scones fall to the floor.

"Hey, there's my favorite girl." I clear my throat and paste a grin on my face. Lucy has been running into my arms like this forever, but now that she's nine, her launch comes with a little more force behind it.

"Mom says you'll be in town for the entire month." Her finger traces a small shiner on my face from the scrum after I tripped Alex.

"If you'll let me." I press a kiss to her cheek.

"That's just enough time to meet little Jack!"

I glance at Simone, quirking a brow.

"It was going to be a surprise." She shrugs. "We wanted to honor Dad, and well, you didn't ruin the name, even if you sometimes do questionable things."

"Are you going to get traded to Alberta, Uncle Jack?"

I cock my head to the side. "Not that I know of, but maybe your sources are better than mine."

I know anything is possible in the league, but I've always felt like my spot, as the Hometown Boy and the Son of John Parker gave me a little more security than some other players.

"Some boys at school told me that their dads think you act like a diva rat, and they want to trade you to a Canadian team. And if you were in Canada, we'd see you even less."

"Well—luckily, as far as I know, those dads don't handle the trades for the Badgers, so don't worry. I'm not going anywhere, okay?" I squeeze her extra tight before lowering her to the ground.

I swallow down all the times I worried my dad would be traded too.

I'm not going anywhere, Jack. Don't worry.

Right, I never gave much thought to the fact that some people who love me would be impacted by something like that. It's so much easier to think of myself as a lone wolf.

"Hey, Luce—" Simone says softly, like she knows I need a second to process. "Grant and Coby will be here to see Uncle Jack soon, so why don't you prepare your room and hide anything you don't want broken."

Little Luce sighs, lowering her shoulders and gazing at the ceiling.

"They'll grow out of it, dear. I promise."

"They're six. They should have grown out of it already!" Lucy continues her sulk as she marches to her bedroom.

"Amy's still a bit of an enabler," Simone says, grabbing a broom to sweep up the crumbs from the fallen scones.

"Our Amy? Really?" I stick my hand out and commandeer the broom. No way will I stand here and let the thirty-six-week pregnant woman sweep up my shit. "Didn't see that one coming."

Growing up, Amy was my favorite sister because she always let me have my way. Simone called me on my shit way too much—she still does.

"I'm sorry for springing tomorrow on you, half-pint, but I think you should come. It'd be good for you."

I shake my head, trying to sweep under the cabinet's lips. "I can manage the dinner, but I'm still not ready for the cemetery."

Simone reaches out and grabs my hand. "Will you ever be ready? It's been ten years—and we already lost you for four when you were in college. What's really going on, Jack?"

I chew on the inside of my cheek. I've never told my family why I vanished or that I still feel bitter that everyone had time to process and say goodbye to him when I only had a week. One fucking week before he was gone. News outlets knew before I did.

All because, what? They thought I wouldn't be able to handle it? I'd be too emotional. Well—I'm doing what they wanted, right? I'm handling it by not handling it. I'm not emoting. And every time I want to feel pain over the situation, I get a tattoo. Healthy.

"Probably just a man processes death differently thing. I'm over it. I've moved on. That's it." I shrug, bending down, collecting the crumbs in the dustbin and walking them over to the trash can. "We good? Was that it?"

"Yeah. We're good." Simone frowns. "I'll let you eat your scones in peace before—"

Bang.

Simone's front door slams open.

A thunder of footsteps that sound like they belong to a herd of galloping horses follows.

Lucy screams.

Something crashes.

"Coby, don't jump on the table, dear." My mother's voice follows in the hallway. "And where's my baby boy?"

Simone eyes the back door, handing me a plate of scones. "Save yourself," she whispers, straightening her apron and heading into the chaos. "Grant. No, please don't lick the floor."

Yeah. Getting out of here for a few minutes sounds like the right move.

I open the back door, only to die of a heart attack right there on the spot. Nothing matters now. Those damn two lifeless eyes stare, unblinking, at me on the porch.

So maybe inside is better —

"Amy—Grant's wiggled his way to the top of the bookshelf, and he's too heavy for me now," Simone says, exhaustion clear in her voice. "Coby, love, you can't sit on the cat. Amy?"

"Boys, listen to your Auntie Simone and be good, okay?" Amy says in the sweetest, most non-threatening way.

Or outside, outside works too.

"Maa."

"The fuck!" I recoil, turning and facing Gio again. Staring. Hexing.

"Language, half-pint!" Simone calls from the other room.

Only forty-three more days until this suspension ends, and this hellscape of domesticity is over.

Chapter Eleven

Aulie Desfleurs

Play: *Needles and Pins by the Searchers*

"So, what do you think?"

I blink through the layer of film coating my eyes and refocus on my co-planner, Bridget Funk.

Did she—did she finish her lecture?

I've perfected falling asleep with my eyes open during Bridget's diatribes. Today, she honored me with a long-winded dissertation on the umbrella scene in *Persuasion*. People seem to have forgotten the cultural significance of Captain Wentworth offering Anne Elliot an umbrella. I'm not entirely clear why, since before traveling to dreamland, my mind took a detour to the Land of Panic and Chaos.

There, a festival of *Oh no, Jack is Playing Wickham, and I'm Going to Have to Deal with the Forced Proximity Situation* is in full swing.

You're Going to Have to Flirt and Touch Him While Being a Silly Little Thing is the main attraction, with flashing neon lights, and a small version of Whack-A-Mole featuring Emy's adorable-but-meddling face.

I blink again.

Bridget peers at me beneath her thick black bifocals, which make her look a good forty years older than me, rather than the four, and brings her cup of tea to her lips, patiently waiting for me to respond. "It's a lot to take in, I know. It blew my mind too."

Yeah, that's not the problem here. I wipe at my mouth, collecting the drool that formed at one corner of my lips as I dozed. Luckily, no one in Cup of Joe's is paying attention to us.

"About the umbrella?" I finally manage, dusting cobwebs off my vocal cords.

At this point, I'm not sure what I'm supposed to be responding to. She went on for fifteen minutes, and I caught about five of it. Bless Charlotte Lucas' plain heart and all of Bridget's students if her classes are that dry.

"Mmhmm."

Tapping my pen on my notepad in front of me, the mountain of materials we still need to address taunts me.

Twenty.

Twenty items we need to discuss immediately for *Pride and Prejudice* weekend. And we somehow just wasted fifteen minutes on an umbrella from *Persuasion* five weeks before its weekend at the fair.

"Do you think you'd be able to find a period-appropriate one? I mean, I'm not expecting elephant bones. That's abhorrent. But at least, visually close to period?" Bridget asks.

"Oh, uh. No." I purse my lips and tap my pad again. My foot shakes under the hard oak table, sending residual ripples through my tea. "That's why I haven't attempted to give him one."

"But the implications—" Bridget groans, picking at her gluten-free scone. "Captain Wentworth bought an umbrella just to talk to Anne. We'd be doing him and our dear Jane a serious disservice if we didn't include it this year."

Do you *want to find a nineteenth-century British umbrella, then?*

I chew on my lip, glancing at my ever-growing to-do list, and sigh. "I'll see what I can do, but no promises."

The cynical part of my brain laughs. *Yeah, right. No promises. That's a good joke.*

The minute I agree to something, it's only a matter of time before I bend myself backward to ensure I come through. I pencil in, *find a period-appropriate umbrella* at the bottom of my two-page to-do list and shift in my seat as pain surges through my abdomen.

Yesterday, I'd nearly finished my run when it felt like my uterus and other organs went on a stabbing rampage inside. I only had a mile left, so I was determined to push through and keep going.

Jack, coming for a visit from his sister's house, found me on my death stroll.

After I almost blacked out, he wrapped his hand around my waist to catch me, and I conceded defeat. We rode the rest of the road in his Escalade in silence.

I'm fairly certain our continued silence was due to the fact that he's figuring a way out of the fair now that he knows what he volunteered for. He probably would have done it yesterday if my hasty exit didn't cut our visit short. I rushed into the house and vomited before curling up on the bathroom floor.

I was too embarrassed to face Jack after my dramatics, so Emy met me in my bedroom with my heating pad and a cup of tea. God bless that woman.

This morning, I thought my pain had faded, but now it's intensifying again.

I squirm on my stool as another stabbing sensation seizes my midsection—*son of a dandy.*

Bridget's brows furrow as I fail to hide my distress. "Are you okay?"

"Fine. Just typical woman's stuff." I force a tight-lipped smile and let the air escape through a pinprick, attempting to steady my breaths.

"Ah." Bridget nods. "I have Advil if you want some."

"Actually," I say on an exhale. "That would be great. Thank you."

"Yeah, of course." Bridget bends down and retrieves her purse. Pill bottles rustle inside as she searches. "Did you find someone to fill the Lydia and Wickham roles?"

"Yeah. I did." I clear my throat. Part of the reason I let her umbrella diatribe go on for so long is because I was avoiding this subject. I'm not sure how Bridget's going to react to the news. If I take the role of Lydia, that means there's still an empty spot— Mary. True, Mary's part is less significant, and we could get on without her—sorry, Mary, I love you—but Bridget is a stickler for accuracy, and the only solution I've come up with is that *she* plays Mary.

She's maybe a little too much like the character for me to have total confidence that she'll take up the role.

"So, I was wondering—how would you feel about playing a small role this year?"

Bridget quirks a brow, glancing up from her Mary Poppins-style purse. "How small?"

"Mary?" I wince.

Breathing a sigh of relief, Bridget a family-size bottle of Advil on the table. "Mary, I can do. I was worried you were going to ask *me* to be Lydia for a second. Can you imagine?"

A little giggle escapes me. Now, *that* would be something I'd pay to see. "No. I wouldn't torture you like that. I volunteered as tribute."

"A noble sacrifice." Bridget nods, grasping her cup with both hands and inhaling the curls of steam. "And who, pray-tell, is the unsuspecting Wickham?"

The term "unsuspecting" is a little too on the nose.

"Uhm, Jack Parker—the hockey player? He's my brother's best friend and is up for that weekend." I gulp down the pills along with the ball of anxiety that's lodged itself firmly in my throat.

"The one you stayed with this summer?"

"Yup, that's the one."

"No offense, but do you think he'll show up the day of?" she asks with a pointed look. "He doesn't seem like the type of guy who would want to take part in a regency fair, and according to Veronica Burke, he's a major ass."

I didn't take Bridget for someone who followed Veronica Burke's social media, but okay. I file that fact in my tiny mental folder of "things Bridget Funk does that surprise me." It's a small folder, but occasionally, she says something so against her Grandma Chic personality that I have to note it.

She's also not wrong about Jack. He's not the most trustworthy human and typically doesn't do things that make him uncomfortable.

"He's not the ass that Veronica said he was—I can promise that anyway. But, we don't have another option. We have to trust he'll be there or accept that we won't have that part of the novel conveyed properly the day of."

Bridget taps her chin, deep in thought, and shrugs. "If he bails, I'll have to manage the part."

I snort and fan myself. "I don't think I could handle you in such close quarters."

"Well, let's hope this Jack Parker comes through. I wouldn't want to ruin my friendship with you with some sexual tension." Bridget wiggles her brows. A smile I seldom see stretches wide across her cheeks, reminding me how gorgeous Bridget, with her auburn hair and rosy complexion, really is. "Because I don't like many people, and I don't feel like having to make a new friend."

Trying to squash my surprise at Bridget's declaration of friendship, I bring my tea to my lips. I didn't know she considered us friends, but after five years of planning this fair together, maybe we have settled into something akin to friendship.

"From the sounds of it, he's a modern-day Wickham anyway, so maybe he'll settle into the role easier, and it won't bother him as much."

I laugh. "Yeah, maybe."

No matter how much I adore Jack as a friend, I can't deny his dating history is rather Wickham-like. He doesn't put himself out there in relationships, typically settling for ones that are convenient or advantageous and ending them long before they reach any commitment stage.

He's a cruel flirt—with just about everyone but me.

Not that I've secretly wished he would flirt with me because that would be silly.

It's probably better that he never has—I couldn't handle it. For Pete's sake, I almost had a heart attack, because he reached up to put the biscuits away, and my mind, thoroughly plagued by that magazine spread and stare, betrayed me.

I swallow, recalling the way my belly swooped when his chest pressed against mine. My eyes zeroed in on the pulse above his collarbone, itching to trace the dips and curves with my fingers. He just had to lean his head down and—

A shallow breath escapes me. I clear my throat and join reality once more.

"You okay, there?" Bridget asks, slowly arching her eyebrow. It's a pointed skill she humbly brags about with its frequent employment.

But I can't blame her. Her eyebrows are fire.

"Yeah. Fine." Slowly, I take another sip of tea, hoping the cup partially obscures the growing heat on my cheeks.

"Don't get into character on me yet, Desfleurs. We're still a week out."

"All good. Promise. Only Aulie here." I laugh nervously.

"You wouldn't have a thing for attractive hockey players, would you?"

I choke on my sip of tea. "What? No." I narrow my gaze on the hot liquid before me, avoiding Bridget and her fire eyebrows.

"So, this whole thing with Jack is—"

"Completely professional and entirely out of necessity. Neither one of us wants to do it."

"Sounds good to me." Bridget nonchalantly sips her tea. Suddenly, I'm overcome with jealousy that she has nothing in her life causing her panic, and she can do things like calmly sip tea. "So, we won't have to worry about you two running off before you're supposed to, like we did with Emma and James last year?"

"Nope. Everything will be completely proper. Scout's honor."

"Don't keep it too proper. Nobody wants a boring Lydia. You'd kill her sparkle."

"Wouldn't want that," I say, shifting in my seat and trying to ignore the little voice whispering that's precisely what I've done in my own life.

Chapter Twelve

Aulie Desfleurs

Play: *The Way I Feel Inside by the Zombies*

The pain in my side hasn't receded. Since I met with Bridget this morning, I've been bound to my couch, wrapped under my heating pad.

It is, thankfully, a comfy couch. It's not so soft that I sink into an inescapable I-live-here-now abyss, but somewhere I can live my best cozy life. But I've seen too much of the darn thing the past year and am *sofa-king over it*.

Hopefully, Emy hasn't developed a mind-reading skill because she would judge me for that pun.

Having clacked out the final edits to the schedule and expectations sheets for the volunteers at the fair, I close my laptop, taking a moment to soak in the warmth of the fireplace crackling in the hearth. The flickering fire illuminates an otherwise dark living room.

The fall sun is setting earlier every day. It's the one thing I dislike about this season. It's a reminder that the long, dark winter is slowly approaching.

Ah, well. I'll savor my favorite time of year while I can and worry about our depressing winters later.

The floorboards creak overhead. Gus and Emy journeyed upstairs while I was working, so I'm on my own tonight, alone with Willoughby, of course. Who's currently curled up in his bed by the fire.

What to do.

What to do.

Sit here and overthink everything that's transpired over the last few days?

That's a hard pass.

Go outside and watch TV by the fire?

Maybe, but I don't know if there's a show I want to watch right now.

2005 *Pride and Prejudice* in here with some takeout?

Oh. Productivity and TLC all in one? Yes, please!

FRIED RICE IS ALWAYS A GOOD IDEA. HAVING ALREADY PUT the *Pride and Prejudice* DVD into the player—we're old school in this house regarding the classics—I happily settle back into my tweed sofa with a carton of fried rice in hand.

Cooking is one of my favorite hobbies, and it's where I feel closest to my Memere since the kitchen was her palace. But every now and then it's nice to have someone else bring me food, knowing I can enjoy it without worrying about cleaning anything up afterward.

Pressing play, the weight of the world, or at least a very important fair, slowly lifts as the melodious *dos* feed my soul.

In two hours, Mr. Darcy will traipse through a meadow illuminated by the early morning glow of the sunrise. His coat will billow in the wind, and he'll proclaim his undying love to me again.

Sorry, Elizabeth.

In reality, I'm more of a Jane Bennet than an Elizabeth, but the idea of somebody leaving someone they loved at the behest of another's opinion is an unconscionable offense. Flippant behavior that injures others is unforgivable. Jane Bennet deserved better.

Our front door busts open, and the large, blustery bang straightens my spine.

Willoughby lets out a tiny bark in his bed by the fire before sleepily lowering his head once more.

"Good watchdog." I roll my eyes, clutching the remote, the only hard item near me. I'm not sure I'll be able to bludgeon someone with this, but I'll try. Fried rice is a tasty treat, but I can't see it being used as a defense weapon.

This is why we shouldn't have an open-door policy because murderers, salespeople, and nosy neighbors exist.

"That damn goat," a breathless, agitated voice says from around the corner.

My shoulders relax. *Jack*.

My heart doesn't get the "we don't have to worry anymore" memo and continues to beat wildly in my chest.

Footsteps gather closer. I glance down at my tank top, hoodie, and faded, apathetic leggings—another reason our open-door policy is the worst.

I stare over my shoulder as Jack enters the room, running his hand through his hair and catching his breath.

My carton of fried rice burns in the palm of my hand. My Memere wouldn't just encourage me to offer him some—she would demand it. "Grab a spoon and dish from the kitchen if you want some rice."

Darn it—why do I have to be such a wonderful hostess? With my hyper-focusing, I forgot to have lunch, and now I'm super hungry. Memere would have gotten up to get him the cutlery herself, so I guess I'll never be as hospitable as her, but she was setting an impossible standard to begin with.

Jack waves me off. "My mom force-fed me more than enough. I needed to get out. Where's Gus?"

Right. Of course, he's here to see Gus. Why would he be here to see me? I settle back into the couch now that I know I won't be murdered, and resume eating my unhelpful fried rice without bothering to pause the movie.

"Aulie?"

I peek back up at Jack. His hands are on his hips, pulling his already snug athletic shirt even tighter, and highlighting his hard, firm chest. Slowly, one of his thick dark brows arches. At this juncture, responding to him would be wise if I don't want to give myself away.

"I'm sorry. Did you need something?" I ask, trying my best to hide the pang of hurt that he's here to see my brother and not me.

"I asked you where Gus is?"

"Oh. Right. He's upstairs with Emy." I bring my attention back to the screen in an act of self-preservation. "Is Gio out again?" I clear my throat as the question comes out squeakier than I hoped.

"Yup. Unless there's another creepy ass goat that gets loose."

"No, Chawton Falls has just the one. I bet you'd find a few if you went to a bigger town like Wolfeboro."

"Good thing I avoid Wolfeboro like the plague then."

"It's lovely when you get past the crowds this time of the year." I glance up at Jack, and my lips twitch. Regarding his disdain for crowded spaces, he might as well be Mr. Darcy. "Did you run here?" I fight the temptation to focus on the sweat beading down his corded forearms.

He scratches his head, his figure still looming over the couch. He's likely planning a dignified escape now that he knows Gus is busy. "Yeah. Made good time thanks to that goat, too. Unlike some people."

Okay, rude. I was making excellent time yesterday until I almost died. And I contend that my death crawl was relatively speedy for an adult. I might even consider entering a crawling competition.

"Show off."

"Are you feeling any better?" he asks, coming over to an empty space on the couch and sitting down near my outstretched feet.

Is he staying, then? I hope he doesn't expect me to deviate

from my plan of watching *P&P*. I've already missed Mr. and Mrs. Bennet's conversation about Bingley with our small talk.

"Aulie?"

"Huh?" I finally pause the movie.

"I asked if you were feeling okay." Soft eyes search mine, and I squirm under the attention.

"Oh, yeah. Fine," I lie through another stab in my pelvic region and shift on the couch. "How are you doing?"

"Great," he says in an unconvincing tone. His fingers drum against the arm of the couch for a few seconds before he pops back up and meanders into the kitchen. He returns with a beer. "What is this crap?" He gestures to the TV.

"Crap? Seriously? The cinematography of this movie alone is magical. Just look at the use of light in this scene."

He rolls his eyes, popping the bottle cap off with his keychain opener and taking a swig of his beer. "My apologies. I should have asked—what is this masterpiece of cinematography gracing your television set?"

"Yes, much better. It's *Pride and Prejudice*. You know—the book we're covering next weekend? I suggested you watch this."

His mouth flattens into a grimace. "Right."

"And..."

"And now I'm here, watching it." He settles back into the couch. Heat radiates off him, filling the empty space between us. Not that I notice. Not that my side yearns to press against to his...

Not a chance.

Because I am sen-si-ble.

Who needs Jack's broad shoulders for support when I have a perfectly good fried rice in my hand?

Not me.

Admittedly, there's a large portion of me that's anxious if Jack watches this and sees how intimate he and I are going to have to be—walking around the fair married for the latter half of the day— then he's going to want to back out of his role. But I can't control that, and I'd rather be left in the lurch now when there's a hope of scrambling and finding someone else than be let down on Opening Day.

Before I press play, I angle my shoulders in his direction. "Can you just promise me, if this is too awkward or seems like too much, you'll let me know you're not going to do it now instead of deserting me at the last minute?"

"I told you I'm doing it. Why would you think I'd back out now?"

"It's just..."

"You still don't trust that I can be dependable." He narrows his eyes, and I squirm under a stare growing increasingly cold and unwelcoming with every word out of my mouth.

"No, well—kind of—not really, it's more...you didn't know what you were getting into when you said you would do it. And sure, Wickham is pretty close to—" I gesture at him, like *well, you know*. "So, you don't have to do too much character acting—but you're going to have to wear breeches and a funny hat. I don't want you to feel compelled to do something you agreed to without knowing what it was."

"I don't feel compelled to do anything. I want to help you." Jack's usually teasing mouth presses into a harsh slash. He takes another swig of his beer, diverting his attention to the screen in front of us. There, paused on the TV, Mr. Bennet readies to tell Mrs. Bennet that her nerves have been his constant companion for the last twenty years. "You good, Coach?"

"Uhm, yeah. All good." I shift, giving us the distance on the couch Jack's sudden frigid demeanor requires.

"All right, let's watch the game tape, then."

The nervous energy balled up in my chest dissolves. He's going through with this. I half-smile, snuggling into my corner of the couch, and press play.

Forty-five minutes later, fatigue wraps its heavy hand around me, and I yawn. I'm still not sleeping well at night, and I haven't been able to nap either.

Jack grabs a throw pillow and places it on his lap. "C'mere, Dessy. Get some rest."

I hesitate. Over the summer, high on painkillers, Jack reclined his head on a pillow on my lap several times. But my buried feelings were still successfully repressed then and I was never the one lying down.

Lowering my head to his lap, my racing pulse thuds wildly in my ears.

Do not focus on how close we are to his thighs and hockey butt.

Jack pulls a blanket down from the back of the couch and drapes it over my shoulder as I hug my heating pad tight to my abdomen.

I sigh happily. This, for all the terror, is a moment of heaven.

I learned a long time ago to soak in the quiet wonder and joys of a moment before they're lost forever.

In the room, the fire continues to crackle in the hearth, providing more than enough heat and ambiance on this chilly fall night. Smoke wafts off the fire, mixing with Jack's signature pine and cedar and his post-workout sweat. Willoughby quietly dozes in the corner. Half-way through the movie, Darcy and Elizabeth dance on-screen with a heated intensity. Everyone else fades to the background, and a gorgeous accompaniment heightens the tension between them.

Yeah, I could live off this moment for a while.

My eyes flutter closed, heavy with sleep.

Jack's hand falls to the small of my back.

I tense, surprised by his touch, and my eyes shoot open.

"Sorry." His hand recoils, and I instantly feel the void of his warmth. "My shoulder was bothering me resting on the top of the couch—"

"It's fine. You were fine," I squeak. *Sure, your touch lit a blaze in the pit of my stomach that could rival the one blaring in the fireplace, but it was fine. Sensations, that's all they are.*

"You sure?" His voice cracks.

"Mmhmm. Rest your hand wherever is best. No big deal."

"Right." His fingers fall lightly against me again, and I don't flinch this time.

Externally, anyway.

Internally, everything is one massive fire drill.

Don't make this weird. Don't make this weird.

"I wouldn't say no to a back rub while you're there," I blurt. Jack's fingers stiffen.

Darn it. I made it weird.

"I was just kid—" My words die as Jack's hand falls under my blanket. His thumb presses firmly to the right of my spine and makes a tiny circle.

And then another.

I hum as his strong fingers undo a fair number of knots.

"Is this helping at all?" he asks, his voice husky and low, like it's coated with a thick layer of smoke from the fire.

"Yeah, it is, actually." I try to draw more oxygen into my lungs, afraid my breathy delivery will give me away.

Calm down. Jack's done way more than this with plenty of women. You don't need to show how desperate you are.

"I may have to coerce you into doing this more often."

I peek up, and Jack's lips are curled into a small smile. "No coercion needed. I've got you, Dessy. Whatever you need." He takes another swig of his beer, and my insides warm. "But you're going to have to explain to me what the big deal is about Wickham because I don't get it."

"It's coming."

The scene where Wickham and Lydia run off together eventually begins. My entire being buzzes, and restless energy surges through my legs. I sit up, discreetly stealing glances at Jack.

His brow raises slightly. His mouth flattens into a frown, and he brings his beer bottle to his mouth, and I follow the work of his throat.

Is he agitated?

Oh, god. Is it because he doesn't want to have to run away with me? Did I put him in an impossibly awkward sitatuation when I asked him to help at the fair?

Wait, did I ask him?

No. Emy did. This isn't my fault. I need to chill.

The credits roll. Jack's spine straightens. And I ready myself for the awkward conversation about to occur.

You know I'd do anything for you, Aulie, but asking me to marry you? Even for pretend? That's a bit much.

He stands and stretches his neck from side to side.

Rubbing the stubble on his cheek, his bright blue eyes bore into me.

Here it comes, the letdown. I brace myself.

He opens his mouth and sighs before shaking his head and walking to the recycling bin to dispose of his beer bottle.

Huh.

Crawling up on my knees, I peer over the edge of the couch. Jack's shoulders sit high and tight around his ears with a frustrated tension. "Are you okay?"

"Yup." He pops his "p," staring at the ceiling. Slowly, his shoulders drop, and he turns to me with a soft smile on his lips.

I don't buy it.

"Something's wrong."

"Nah. Everything's fine." His keys jingle in his pocket as he rustles around for them. "Hey, want to go out with me?"

That is the million-dollar question. Yeah, I want to go out with Jack. He's kind and handsome, and I like the way I can be myself around him and—

Jack's brow furrows, looking at me like I have two heads.

"Huh?" I blink.

"I asked if you want to go to the bar with me. The game is about to start, and I thought I'd catch it out."

"Oh!" Right. Going out to a bar. The bar where there's a game. The bar where there's a game that Jack wants to watch. That bar. That kind of going out. I glance down to where my heating pad rests on the couch. It's been separated from my midsection for maybe a minute, and I'm already feeling the effects of its absence. "What if we do a fire out back? We have enough beer here, and I can put the game on the big screen."

Jack shakes his head and bounces on his toes. "Don't you want to get out of the house? You never leave."

I bite my lip. "I left earlier in the week."

Jack scrubs his hand over his face. Cast in the fire's light, his dark circles and longer stubble come into focus. Something's off, but he's not telling me what it is.

For all his silence, one thing is clear.

He needs me.

I can overcome my pain to be there for him. I have to.

I don't pay my midsection another second and drag myself up off the couch. "Just give me a second to change." I walk past Jack. "Do you have clothes to change into? You'll catch a cold in your wet shirt and shorts."

"I'll go back and grab the Escalade while you change into one of your sweater dress things and meet you here."

"Sounds good." I smile, entering my bedroom and ignoring the pull on my side. Pain radiates down my leg with every step.

Alone, I let a few tears escape.

A cramp works itself deep into my abdomen. I hunch over the bed, biting down a yelp, and blink through the black dots spotting my vision.

I wouldn't say I enjoy going to bars or clubs. They're chaotic, smelly, and running into the drunk versions of everyone I know doesn't appeal to me. But I'd rather avoid them because I want to, not because my body sabotages me. I want it to be my choice.

In the past year, my body has become a prison—one that my mind can't seem to escape.

No amount of rest, no amount of distraction has been enough to overcome it.

Because part of me is in a constant state of torture.

I'm tired and frustrated. And I am tired of being frustrated. If this pain isn't a big deal, why can't I overcome it?

What's wrong with me that everyone around me seems unfazed by the day-to-day while I'm demolished by normalcy?

Another round of frustrated tears down my cheeks, and then the dam bursts. My chest heaves through the uncontrollable sobs, and I let myself feel everything I've ignored. I very well can't stop now.

Thankfully, no one is here to witness any of this.

But Jack will be back soon, so I must suck it up and get over it.

The tears slow. I shuffle through my closet, trying to find something comfortable to wear. My hands stop on a sweater I usually pass without a second thought. It's a short dress rather than a top that shows off my legs and a fair amount of my shoulders.

I've never had the nerve to wear it out.

Put on one of your sweater dress things.

I chuckle to myself. Jack probably meant for me to throw on a dress and a cardigan because that's my signature look. But I feel less than spectacular, and I want to change that.

Sometimes masks are easier to wear when you have a costume to accompany them—my countless years in theater taught me that.

With a deep breath, I collect myself. Wipe my eyes dry. Put the mask back on and prepare to return to a world that could never know the strength I have to gather simply to live.

Chapter Thirteen

Jack Parker

Play: *All These Things That I've Done by the Killers*

After ten years, I should be more prepared to handle my dad's birthday.

But it still stings just as much as it did the first year.

Not that I let on how damaged I am by the whole thing. I can hear everyone now. *It's been ten years. Are you still not over that? Let go, man.*

For whatever reason, my masochist tendencies are determined to keep their sharp talons embedded in a world of grief. No matter how much I hoped I'd move past this eventually.

I hoped that this year, without game theatrics hanging over me, I could muscle through the day differently.

But I was wrong. This day still sucks ass.

And when Big Ed texted me this morning, *This one's for him,* that was it. That's all it took to send me spiraling.

I stayed in bed most of the morning, ignoring the eerie scratches on the window and a muffled "maa."

Simone came and asked if I was ready to go to the cemetery. I declined but agreed to be at dinner.

Dinner was miserable. My family was overly cheery considering the circumstances, regaling my dad's life stories. Tales that I've repressed because I've overanalyzed my actions in every single one.

Why did my dad keep his cancer a secret from me?

From what I've gathered from my sisters over the years, Alex Piotrowski wasn't too far off, he thought I'd be too emotional. But what had I done that made him think I'd react that way?

After dinner, the threat of watching home movies had my skin crawling, so I bolted, claiming I was behind on my fitness training.

And then I ran.

And ran.

And when a particular goat who's formed an odd obsession with me joined in the chaos, I didn't think. I just kept running on instinct. My feet followed an unfamiliar dirt path dusted with oranges, reds, and yellows.

And, like a sick twist of fate, it landed me *there*.

The last person I wanted to see in my fucked-up state was once again the only person I needed.

I tried to play it off like I was there to see Gus, but I knew I was lying to myself the minute I saw Aulie bathed in the fire's flickering light.

When her head fell to my lap and I pulled the blanket down over her shoulders, the thoughts spiraling like a cartoon scribble inside my head quieted.

Until they didn't.

Until an entirely new panic set in.

I wanted more of this, and this alone. Of Aulie. Of the quiet. Of a soft flicker of a flame that burned for her instead of the wild, hungry blaze that constantly held me prisoner.

My *she's off-limits* mantra didn't provide its usual dousing effect, and once again, I faced the reality of the situation.

I can act on my feelings and finally have a conversation with

Aulie. One where I see only two logical outcomes, one much more likely than the other.

Either Aulie will return my affections and release me from five years of pent-up frustration and turmoil—or—and this is much more likely, she'll tell me she's sorry, but she doesn't see me romantically and that I've made our friendship weird. She'll need a break, and I'll live the rest of my life in deeper agony without her.

Waiting for her in the car in the Desfleurs' driveway, I square myself in my rearview mirror and admit the truth. "I am a giant weenie."

"Are you now?" A sweet honey voice giggles over my right shoulder.

"Holy shit, Dessy." My hand shoots to my hammering heart. "When did you get in here?"

"Did I finally get you? It's all fun and games until you're the one having the heart attack, right?" She drums her fingers together, all evil-like, with a mischievous smirk.

The woman doesn't need to sneak up on me to give me a heart attack. Her bare legs crossed over each other do that just fine. I try to keep my eyes trained on her face, but they're pulled in way too many fucking directions. In the little time I left her, Aulie changed into a sweater that drapes off one of her shoulders, and her hem, fuck, it's landing mid-thigh. Her hair is now loose, cascading down her exposed back.

With a white-knuckle grip on the steering wheel, I put the car into reverse.

"You okay?" Dessy asks.

I wear a hard, very necessary expression because I can't let her see how much I want her. How much she's decimating me. And I'm too tired, too fucked-up to control my emotions around her today.

"You forgot to wear pants." A muscle clenches in my jaw, and I don't know what I'm angry about. Me? Because of the weenie thing? Or because the only thing holding me back is that I don't want to start a family for a while? Probably. Fuck it. I could start a family—with her.

Or is it that Aulie told me she thought I could play Wickham because I was like him, and the man is an asshole.

How shitty does she think I am?

"Oh." She shifts uncomfortably in the seat, trying to pull her hem down, and now I feel like an even bigger ass. "Yeah. You probably don't want to see that, huh? Sorry. I thought I'd try something new, but—"

"You look great, Dessy." I put my hand on hers. "Really. Ignore me. I'm just in my head about some things—but you look —" I swallow down my pride. "You look beautiful, honest."

Aulie turns her head, her mocha stare boring into me, but I keep my attention trained on the road. "Is it—is it the weenie thing?" she whispers.

"Hmm?"

"What you're in your head about."

"Yeah, that and a few other things."

You think I'm a man whore. It's my dad's birthday, and I'm not at the game, and holy hell, you have nice legs, and I'm tempted to turn this car around so nobody else at the bar will see them.

Caveman. I am a caveman.

"Any thoughts on the whole Wickham thing?" she asks after a few beats of silence. "Like how you want to play it now that you've seen the movie?"

Images of Aulie's fingers slipped into the crook of my arm as my wife come to mind.

As uncomfortable as the pants the men in the movie were wearing look, pretending she's mine even for a small sliver of the day sounds glorious.

"Not really. Whatever you usually do with the characters is fine."

"Well, last year, the characters ran off before they were supposed to, and we found them—" She shifts in her seat. "Anyway, I don't know if we can go off that. Unless you want to get that into the characters. I could follow your lead, whatever you're comfortable with. This is going to be weird, isn't it? I'm sorry, it's weird."

We stop at a red light, and I turn to face her. There's no way she knows the invitation she just gave me. All I can think about is how I'd love nothing more than an excuse to kiss her senseless and have her carrying this torch for fucking once.

But again, the whole "don't make this friendship weird" neon light blinks on over her head.

I grip the steering wheel and slow the indecent thoughts I have of slamming her back against a wall in the museum where the fair is taking place. "Do you want to feel it out tonight? See what we're comfortable with? When one of us goes too far, we can let the other know that's our limit."

"Honestly, after a few shots, that might be a nice way to ease into it. I haven't acted in a while, and I'm worried I'll be rusty."

"Same. Same." I nod.

And she laughs in return. "I need to warn you I used to get really into character when I did these kinds of things."

"Do whatever you think is best. I'm sure I can handle it."

"Okay. I'm kind of excited." She wiggles in her seat. "Give me the rest of the ride to get into character. I need to meditate on it. Yes. I am silly. I fall easily in love. I—" She peeks at me with one eye. "When is go-time? Are you sure this isn't going to be too weird?"

"We'll be fine. Let's say we're Jack and Aulie until we cross the threshold of the bar."

"Deal. Okay. Getting back into character. You're lucky yours isn't too far from the real Jack."

What the hell? Does she really think that?

"Indeed," I say, biting the inside of my cheek just to elicit a different pain.

We ride in a terse silence for the rest of the ten-minute drive.

"Park here." Aulie points to an open space a block down from the bar. "The lot gets tight, and your definitely-overcompensating for something car would probably get stuck there until closing."

"Ouch, hey! What do you have against my car?"

"It's just a bit much, don't you think? Your sports car would have been fine up here."

"My sports car wouldn't fit my family in it if we all wanted to go somewhere together."

"Oh." Aulie blinks. A slow smile creeps across her face, and my eyes linger on upturned lips. She leans in. "I'm on to you, you know."

I fight to catch my breath. Of course she is, ever since I saw Emy and Gus together I haven't been able to get my shit under control.

"On—on to what?" I stammer. Entranced by the curve of her neck, and slope of her bare shoulder. God, my lips can't be this close and not brush against hers. What the hell is this torture?

"You, Jack Parker, are secretly a bigger softie than I am." With her devious grin, she boops my nose and I shake out of her spell.

I fashion a hard slash to my mouth to hide my current decimated state. "I thought I was an ass like Wickham."

"With women, sure." She shrugs. "But with your family you're a big ol' squish. And I love that about you. If you have a hat and don't want to be recognized, grab it." She opens her and gets out while I'm left processing the fact that there's something about me she loves. The level of my gaze naturally follows her in her dress that hits barely below...

Yup. If I look there much longer I'll be the furthest thing from soft. Reaching into the back seat, I grab the flannel and hat I bring on every outing in case I want to go under the radar.

Since my suspension roughly a week ago, I haven't shaved, and the hair on my face covers a good portion of my cheeks and jawline. Hopefully, it's enough to obscure me somewhat. I wanted to get out and drink and forget, but there's still the part of me that hates crowds and people and regrets this decision.

Walking to the bar, Aulie huddles against the wind. What was she thinking coming out without a jacket? At some point tonight, this flannel will find its way onto her shoulders.

I stop at the door, grabbing the handle and holding it open for her.

"Last chance to back out," she whispers.

"We'll be fine."

Aulie's lips quirk, traveling down my hat and flannel.

"What?" I ask.

"Nothing, you just look like a lumber*jack*," she says. "Get it?"

I shake my head. "In with you."

"You're never any fun. Come on. You've got to give me some props for that one." She crosses the threshold and turns around to face me, unleashing a broad, soul-crushing smile. The brilliance of it explodes in the dim light of Collin's Pub, the local bar whose menu boasts the greatest collection of potato dishes in the State.

"Nope. Not dignifying it." I cross my arms and flash a faux stern look her way. "You should know better by now that I'm too mature for name-calling."

"Yeah, okay." She giggles. "You're supposed to be Wickham, not Darcy, by the way."

Stepping inside the pub, a familiarity overwhelms me. I've never actually visited this Chawton Falls establishment, but an Irish bar in New England is an Irish bar in New England—wooden paneled walls, cracked wooden support beams, and a less-than-pretentious bar in the middle. Forty-year-old men with sad, weathered faces stare emptily into their pint glasses, occasionally glancing at the big-screen TVs covering every corner of the bar. An old, well-used pool table sits up on a platform, and two dartboards hang nearby.

The door shuts behind us, and a few faces gaze at us. Recognition briefly flashes over their faces, but no one makes a move to say anything or approach.

Relief washes over me. The bar isn't full, and they're going to let me exist.

Eighties rock blares over the speakers, and I bring my mouth to Aulie's ear. "I thought you said this place would be crowded."

"Oh, just wait." Her fingers wrap gently around mine, and she tugs me past the bar. Sparks shoot up my arm from the contact. "Hi, Frank!" she says to the bartender.

"Hey, there's my girl! I haven't seen you in a while." He narrows in on our hands and directs a less-than-warm stare toward me. "You two be good. I'll be in here if you need anything, Aurelie."

"Always!" she says, dragging me out the back door. It takes a few blinks for my eyes to adjust to the fenced-in area that greets us. Twinkling lights weave through the branches lining the edge of the seating area. A fire blazes in a large, square fire pit with a bar top raised along its circumference. Twenty-somethings huddle around it, warming their hands and drinking beers.

TVs hang in wooden boxes. All tuned to the pre-game show. Boston has some nice rooftop bars, but this is something only a small town like Chawton Falls can have.

Again, a few eyes fall on us, but no one moves to ask for an autograph or a selfie.

Instead, Aulie falls prey to the attention of the people around us, stopping and saying hello to excited faces every few feet.

Eventually, we make it to a tiny booth in the back. Aulie slides in, and the diplomatic smile she's had plastered on her face falls a fraction. "Give me a second, and I'll get our beers and shots."

"I've got them. Take a second to catch your breath, Ms. Popular." I grin, and she rolls her eyes. "Oh, now that's not very Lydia Bennet of you."

"I'm choosing to interpret her character as unsociable and taciturn at the moment."

"I wonder what the head of the fair would think of that."

"Get me a shot of tequila, and I'll flirt you into a stupor, Parker. I just need a second."

"I'll be right back. Try not to get in too much trouble while I'm gone."

"No promises." She giggles.

I dip my head and press a kiss to her temple. Her lips part with a gasp, and I swallow down the misstep. That was probably laying it on too thick. "Anything—erm—any particular beer you want?"

"Oh, something pumpkiny please."

"You've got it, Dessy." I turn and head to the bar, the feel of her skin and a slight saltiness dance on my lips.

Everything is still. Everything is quiet and good in the world. But then I see the TV, the headline—Jack Parker, Absent for Night Dedicated to Late-Father Due to Suspension, sits below a desk full of talking heads.

And my thoughts spiral out of control once again.

Chapter Fourteen

Aulie Desfleurs

Play: *Something is Happening by Hermans Hermits*

While I haven't conferred personally with Jane Austen, I'm fairly certain that George Wickham was not a forehead-kisser. Jack Parker, though, apparently is. A surge of electricity courses through my body as soon as his soft lips touch my skin, like a carnival circuit coming to life. The residual flips in my stomach feel like a never-ending rollercoaster ride, and with each twist and turn an anxiety-filled nausea increases.

I've never liked rollercoasters, and after five minutes stuck on this one, I'd kindly like to exit the ride.

Shivers work down my spine in the chill autumn air.

Yes, the air. That's definitely why there is gooseflesh puckering my skin. The finely raised bumps have nothing to do with the five-second montage of Jack leaning over me, his lips quirked softly and his hand finding my shoulder, playing in a loop in my mind. As I breathed in, the scent of pine and cedar filled my nostrils, wrapping me up in a warm, flannel-clad blanket.

The whole thing has thoroughly ruined me, and that's a problem because we'll need to do more than kiss each other's foreheads during the fair. In the past, Lydia and Wickham were found huddled together in compromising situations. Initially, it was supposed to be just enough to offend regency sensibilities, but we lost the drama in a generational translation.

When Emma and Callen took on the characters, keeping them to regency standards was nearly impossible, so we embraced a more intimate approach, and it ended up adding to the fair-goer enjoyment.

Well, until last year, when things started going a little too far.

But kissing and forced proximity have become a part of the characters' roles. And me? I can't even handle a simple forehead kiss.

"...Say what you want about Jack Parker's skill level. But today's game is a perfect argument for trading him," a tin, hearty voice echoes from the multiple televisions, bouncing off the star-chipped trees that twinkle in the night sky. *"He couldn't control his emotions in the first game, and now he's missing Stand Up to Cancer Night and the celebration of his dad's birthday. If playing tonight didn't motivate him to be a team player, nothing will. The man's pathetic, Scott. I'm sorry."*

The rollercoaster car in my stomach careens off an unfinished track, hurtling into a freefall and crashing into the Ferris Wheel of Guilt. A long ride with no ending in sight. How could I have forgotten about his dad's birthday? I never forget that.

Glancing up, I seek Jack standing by the bar. He's been gone for longer than necessary if all he's doing is buying our drinks. His shoulders slump over the bar top as Andrew, one of my high school classmates, pours a shot into a glass and slides it over to him, muting the televisions with his free hand. Jack throws his head back. His throat works as he swallows the shot, and I watch transfixed, following the lines of his bearded jaw.

He looks too darn good in a baseball hat, and it's rude.

And distracting.

I blame his taut, tan skin and smoldering looks for frying my brain and making me forget something important, like his dad's birthday.

Don't forget how self-involved you've become with your own grief.

There's also that. First Gus, now Jack—I'm letting a lot of important stuff slip because my grief's suffocating me.

"Aurelie Desfleurs, you are a sight for sore eyes." A slimy purr from an even slimier figure draws my attention from Jack's broad shoulders. Standing in front of me in a white button-up and an infuriating smirk, is my ex-Fiancé, Tyler Higgins.

Sure, the train car in my stomach has already crashed, but now it's tunneling past my stomach, firmly lodged in my lower calf. My deepest apologies to all the passengers on board. Refunds will be available upon exiting.

Sweat coats my palms, and I fold them onto my lap, discreetly wiping them on the rough wool of my sweater.

Why did I come out with Jack when I knew Tyler was in town?

His blue-green eyes flicker with amusement as his infuriating smirk widens into his devastating grin—a grin that got him just about anything when we were dating.

As pathetic as it sounds, Tyler's the only person I've let myself love romantically—it was a shallow love built on the flimsiest foundation—and yet, I let it go too far.

Just like my mother used to do.

After Gus went away to college, I dated Tyler for three years. At night, I'd sneak out, meeting him on the banks of King's Pond for late-night kisses under the stars and hot and heavy clothes-on make-out sessions.

It wasn't until he proposed that we went further, and I gave him my heart and body, safeguarded by a promise. My first lesson in humanity, some people don't keep their word. Tyler was one of them.

Five years later, I know now it was for the best, even if it devastated me then.

After him, I shut my heart off to love. I'm too foolish to trust myself with matters of the heart.

Clearing the thick bile in my throat, I go to speak and find I'm far too parched for speech. "Tyler, hi," I croak. "How are you?"

"Much better now that you're here," he says, passing a hand through his blond hair. He's wearing it differently. It used to be down to his ears. Now, the sides are short, and he's kept the top long and slicked sideways. "Listen, Beautiful. I'm hoping maybe we can catch up while I'm in town. Can I get you something to drink? A Shirley Temple, maybe, or..."

"I already told you I'm taking care of Dessy tonight." Jack looms over Tyler. Looking down the slope of his nose, he gestures for my ex to move out of his way, brushing past his shoulder and laying two shots, two beers, and a piling heap of glorious poutine on the table.

"Right, you did," Tyler barks out a laugh. "But if any of those drinks are for Aulie, I'm sorry to tell you, man, you've wasted your money. She doesn't touch that kind of stuff."

Oh, for the love of Peter Noone, why is this guy standing here after five years and pretending he still knows me?

Yeah, before I was twenty-one and it was illegal to drink, I was too timid to try anything more than the sips of beer I'd have with my cousins when they visited from Canada. But now, it's not illegal, and occasionally, I let myself drink—even if I regret it with a flare of pain the next day.

Jack drapes an arm over my shoulders. He turns the brim of his hat around to the back before he leans in close, and I feel the warmth of his breath on my neck, sending shivers down my spine once more. "Who is this asshole, and why is he on the receiving end of your awkward face?"

"This is Tyler, and I don't have an awkward face. What the heck is that?"

"You do, but we can revisit that point later. Permission to act like an even bigger asshole than usual to get him to leave?"

"Okay, but don't be too mean."

Tyler clears his throat. Even after five years he probably still hates not being the center of attention.

Jack's arm tightens around me. He nuzzles into the crook of my neck. "Kitten, you haven't introduced me to your little friend," he says softly enough that it sounds like it should be between us but loud enough that Tyler, a man very proud of his six-foot status, hears.

"Oh, right! Where are my manners?" I press a kiss to his cheek. His extra-long stubble falls like rough sandpaper against my skin. A rogue thought wonders what other pieces of him would feel like on my lips and I shut it down immediately. "Jack, this is one of my high school classmates, Tyler."

"Oh, come on, babe. Classmates? We were more than that." Tyler winks.

I ignore Tyler being, well, Tyler. "And Tyler, this is Jack Parker, we—he—" My tongue stumbles over how to introduce Jack. I doubt he'd appreciate me labeling us more than friends since word about whom he's dating travels fast, even this far north in New Hampshire.

Sure, we're playing tonight. But Jack getting cozy with a girl isn't exactly newsworthy. It's only when he labels it that the press explodes.

"Jack is a good friend of mine," I say, finally settling on the truth.

"Friend—that makes more sense." Tyler chuckles. "For a second, the crew almost thought you were dating." He hitches his thumb over at a group of old classmates watching us curiously. "But I told them there's no way our class princess is involved with *the* Jack Parker."

In my senior year, my classmates decided I was too sweet to bear the title of queen, so they voted me the court *princess* at prom. They even made me a special sash as a joke. Though Tyler was still voted prom king.

While I was thankful that so many people seemed to like me well enough to vote for me, the joke stung. Princesses need saving,

Queens rule. It was a reminder of my tendency to be the damsel and victim in my life rather than the heroine.

If I'm being honest, I'm not entirely sure I've overcome that bad habit.

"Believe me, Trevor—" Jack drawls.

"Tyler."

"Right, whatever." He dismisses this correction with a wave, like he's bored to death of this guy already. "I hate when she uses the friend label. If it were up to me, I'd lock this shit down and never let her go. I'd be a fool not to." Jack's sapphire gaze turns to me, resting heavily on my face and regarding me like I'm something worth revering. The arm wrapped around me, pulls me in tighter, and his thumb strokes my cheek. "You know, I'd do anything for you, right, kitten?" His eyes move to my mouth, as if I hold some kind of spell over him. "And I mean—" his nose traces the line of my jaw. "Any" —a soft kiss punctuates the break in the word— "thing."

My lips part involuntarily. "That is a very tempting offer," I say breathlessly. My chin tilts a fraction, resting too close to his own to be sensible for much longer. The need to kiss him consumes me as the ache in my chest grows almost unbearable. I'm momentarily distracted by the tremor I swear I feel in his fingers, still caressing my cheek. His eyes come back to mine, searching and slightly unfocused for a beat, before he blinks and takes a breath.

"It was nice to meet you, Taylor," Jack says in a final dismissal, not bothering to look in Tyler's direction. A devious, crooked grin quirks his lips, and I can't believe I ever doubted he could slide into character. The man's a natural. Between that and the darn baseball cap, he looks like sin incarnate, and I'm currently too weak not to give into temptation.

"Tyler." The vague image of a man over my shoulder corrects.

"Sure," Jack murmurs, his hand tenderly cradling my face. "Fuck, you're beautiful. C'mere."

My body reacts without hesitation, pressing into him and resting my hand on his chest—I

Bang. The glittering crack of a tray full of glasses crashing to the cement tiles below reluctantly separates me from whatever trance Jack had me under.

Tyler stands in a halted retreat with beer cascading down the front of his shirt. A tray rests in Andrew's hand. Beer funnels down the sides and a glass lays shattered on the pavement. "Shit, man. I'm so sorry, I uh—" He runs his hands through his hair, glancing at the wreckage. "I—fuck." He slumps away, rejoining his friends.

Guilt churns my stomach, incinerating the butterflies fluttering in a flurry this close to Jack.

Next to me, Jack chuckles. "Serves that jerk right," he says under his breath.

"Darn it, I think we were too mean. I should go help clean him up before that stains." I wiggle out of Jack's arms.

A warm hand wraps around my wrist. "Don't you dare, kitten. Let him go."

"Okay, what's up with this whole kitten thing?" I laugh.

"I panicked, but I figured it was a play on Kitty Bennet, maybe?" He regards me almost bashfully.

His reasoning is cute, and I'm torn. Something about the innocent, helpless vibe of the name doesn't sit well with me, but also…Jack Parker is calling me "kitten," even if it is for a bit, how can I be mad at that? "I don't think Lydia would like being called something close to her sister's name, but we can keep it for tonight."

Jack's grip stays locked on my wrist, but if I wiggle a bit, I may be able to shimmy free. My heart protests, like it's comfortable in our little flannel cocoon with Jack and it fears the cold. But I should leave and help Tyler—it's the right thing to do. I think.

Could snuggling with a man you have intense growing feelings for, but who doesn't feel the same way about you, also be the right thing to do?

Because I want it to be.

Desperately.

"You make a very valid point. I'll come up with something

else." He nods. "Now, do me a favor before you try to escape my grasp and look at Tyler."

I glance up, seeing a gorgeous chestnut brunette drawing near a downtrodden Tyler with a bunch of napkins. In the next moment, she pats his chest down.

The action does little to assuage my guilt.

Until the twinkling lights overhead catch a sparkle on her finger.

"Is he...engaged?"

"Seems it. He was at the bar when I went to get us drinks and tried to start a conversation about you and me. I didn't give him much, but he kept running his mouth and saying stupid shit, like how I should stay single. He said he recently got engaged but hates it because 'it's hard to keep people like us tied down to one person,' implying I was the same kind of asshole he was." Gently, Jack grips my chin and turns my attention to him. His eyes meet mine, hard and intentional, like what he's about to say holds a significant amount of weight. I try my best to keep my stare connected with his, but the temptation to dip lower, to his lips, grows stronger with every second his sapphire gaze bares into me. "I wouldn't do that to you, Dessy. If you were mine, I'd worship you like the fucking queen you are."

My heart somersaults at Jack's words. I'm not entirely sure what to make of them. *If* I was his? It's a hypothetical situation Jack has no intention of making a reality, I'm sure of it. Still, the thought that the notion has passed through his mind, even for a microsecond, has rainbows all but exploding out of my chest.

Couple that with him calling me a queen, and well, I'm toast.

Scrambled eggs and bacon. Here comes me.

With a sigh, I lean back, finding Jack's arm still open and waiting for me. I burrow into the crook again. "Thank you for rescuing me."

"Anytime." He reaches forward, grabs a shot, and hands it to me before grabbing one himself. We clink before I throw my head back and swallow. The liquid slides down the back of my throat, incinerating anything it touches. Blech. "Now eat your poutine before it gets cold," he says, handing me the cheesy curd goodness I didn't ask for but desperately need.

"I love you for knowing to get me this. Serious best friend benefit right here." I happily squirm, taking a bite. Savory brown gravy dances on my tastebuds, and I greedily shove a few more fries in my mouth.

Jack tsks in a disapproving manner.

"What?"

"I'm not your friend tonight, Aulie, remember?" Gently, Jack's thumb swipes across my cheek. His touch leaves a passing, shimmering tingle along my skin. The playful light in his eyes flickers out, replaced by a deep, smoldering intensity.

With his eyes still locked on mine, he takes his thumb in his mouth and sucks the remnants of brown gravy off.

I—uhm suddenly forget my name. It's Lydia or something like that, right?

"Definitely not friends tonight," I stammer.

A wide, devastating grin breaks across his face. "That shit's pretty good," he says, leaning back and rubbing lazy circles on my exposed shoulder. He reaches over to my plate of poutine and grabs himself another fry, acting like we didn't just have a moment.

Because we didn't.

He's playing George flawlessly.

And just like that, the truth I've been trying to ignore all night rears its ugly head. I'm still that silly girl falling head-over-heels for her brother's best friend, the one guy that could well and truly ruin me.

It's too late to go back. The fair is too important, so I'm going to have to accept reality. Lydia Bennet, my sensible self, whoever I am, we're well and truly doomed.

Chapter Fifteen

Aulie Desfleurs

Play: *A Kiss to Build a Dream On by Louis Armstrong*

One hour, two pumpkin beers, and three shots later—I'm certain Jack has had more—the dizzying feeling in my gut rivals the twinkling lights overhead.

For the entire first period of the game, Jack draped his arm over my shoulders. Not that I minded. The chill of the night is creeping in, so the extra warmth from his side is soothing.

Sort of.

There's a loud portion of my brain sounding the alarm that I like all of this—quietly watching a game in the crook of his arm—way too much.

With a content sigh, I let my head tip back during a commercial and admire the string of lights mirroring the stars above. Jack follows suit. "They did a good job with this back patio. I could see myself coming here a lot if I lived here," he says.

"I love it. I've wanted to do the same thing in our backyard. But the lights are sitting in the garage collecting dust because Gus won't let me climb a ladder alone, and he never has the free time to help."

"Did you want them near the fire pit?"

"Yeah."

"That would be nice."

With our eyes locked on the sky above, a gentle hum vibrates through me. This, right here, stargazing with Jack, is another moment of perfection that I refuse to take for granted.

Jack hasn't mentioned what today is, and I don't know how to bring the subject up organically. Since the game started, we haven't talked about anything. Jack muttered a few things, sure, but they've mostly been about Peter, the usual second-liner who's filling his spot. He's frustrated that Peter can't anticipate the pass and is too meek establishing himself in front of the opponent's net (personally, I think Peter's doing a fantastic job).

After the first two periods end, the score remains zero-all, despite the Badgers putting a fair number of shots on goal.

Their opponent, Seattle, isn't supposed to be good this season. So, this game should be a gimme. But even I can see the issue. The team hasn't found their chemistry without Jack. If they don't find it soon, the Badgers might have to fight for a playoff spot later in the season—even though they have the talent to clinch a first-place finish.

For intermission, the local sports station cuts to a panel of suit-clad men who dissect the highs and lows of the game. Earlier, when they were bashing Jack, Andrew turned the sound off the TVs, but once the game started, he turned the volume back up. Some sports are fine to watch without sound, but hockey should never be one of them. The sound of the skates cutting across the ice and the clash of the sticks in battle is some serious ASMR.

Scott, I think it's obvious what the problem is with the Badgers. They've relied too heavily on Jack Parker, a guy who isn't dependable, and now their chickens are coming home to roost.

Jack tenses next to me at the sound of his name.

"Oh, screw you," I yell at the TV. A few faces turn in our direction. At the bar, Andrew frowns and immediately grabs the remote to mute the sound again. "Thank you, Andrew. You're a gem."

"Anytime, Aulie." He waves.

"But seriously, Jack, don't listen to guys like him. Like he's ever played hockey or knows anything about you."

"That's Richard Brousseau."

That name doesn't resonate with me; I just see a crabby old man who's been too hard on him. Why should he care?

"He played with my dad, and he's my godfather," Jack says, scrubbing a hand down his face. "I'm going to get another beer. Want one?"

Jack's arm slips from its perch on my shoulders, the ghost of his warmth lingers along my bare skin. I shiver through the sensation and furrow my brow while Jack rises from the booth. I can't imagine how he's feeling. If someone that close to me said something like that on national TV on an already rough day, I wouldn't be able to cope. I'd be an absolute puddle. I shift in the booth, not knowing what to say or how to make any of this better.

"Oh. Well, he's still a meanie pants, and I don't like him."

"Noted. Beer, Dessy. Want one?"

If my random outburst at the TV is a sign, I shouldn't have another drink. "I'm good, but thank you."

He nods, slipping his hands into his pockets and making his way to the bar once again. His shoulders sag, burdened by something he's keeping to himself.

I squirm in my seat, trying to make myself comfortable without Jack's warmth. A fair number of people I went to high school with are here tonight, and it's a reminder of how this town entraps its inhabitants.

Some people left to attend the state university in the southern part of New Hampshire, but with another state college only a town over, a substantial population here has never lived beyond the county line, including myself.

I used to think that made Chawton Falls special, and maybe it is. I love it here, especially in fall when red, orange, and yellow dust the hills beyond King's Pond and pumpkins sit on every doorstep.

But since most of my family has passed, there's a decided chill to the usual warm glow downtown. The sunsets over Squam River are a little less vibrant and the colonial architecture stands a little less proudly.

In other words, the charm of this town has faded ever so slightly.

Jack wanders back to me with two beers in hand. I shiver against the wind, huddling into myself. I was foolish not to bring a jacket, but I didn't have one that went with this dress.

"You want my flannel?" he asks, pointing his chin at my crossed arms.

"I'm sure you need it more than I do, but thank you. I'm regretting not choosing a seat closer to the fire, though."

"But then we would have had to talk to people." He grimaces, placing his drinks on the table. Still standing, he pulls one arm out of his flannel and then the other. With each movement, the fabric of his grey Henley molds to his muscular biceps and chest.

Don't ogle your best friend. That's rude.

"Here, seriously. I run hot when I drink, anyway."

Wrapping the warm fabric around my shoulders, Jack's woodsy smell swirls around me. With my boundary issues in full swing, I bury my face into the collar of his shirt, relishing the enticing scent.

This summer, I had to use his soap when I ran out, and it took a good month before I stopped smelling like the man. I didn't think it was a problem then, but that was before the *Iron Inspiration* spread and the man ate gravy off my face.

Now, well, everything's changed.

Jack settles into the booth with a sigh. He nods to the TV. "They talk about anything worth repeating?"

I shake my head. "I wasn't paying attention. Are you sure *you* don't want to talk about anything?"

"Nah, I'm good." He brings the bottle to his mouth and takes a swig, letting his arm lazily drape against the back of the booth again.

Cool. Calm. Nonchalant.

Meanwhile, my insides are on fire, and I'm too many drinks in to handle any of this sensibly.

"C'mere, kitten. Keep me warm," he beckons, nodding to the crook of his arm where I've spent most of the night.

Without a second thought, I lean back into him, telling myself this is *something* we naturally do. Yes, a random man is giving me attention, and I'm just—

That random man is Jack. Your best friend. The guy that you had feelings for from the age of five to eighteen. Strong ones. Ones that won't be stamped down easily.

Proceed with caution unless you want to die from broken heart syndrome.

"When you want to talk, you know I'm here for you, right?" I ask, keeping my attention on the TV where yet another commercial for Dunks is playing. "I'm sorry I've been busy and haven't been there for you, but if you ever want to talk about your dad—"

"I won't want to talk about it, Dessy," he sighs.

"Well, is there something you want to do? Whatever it is, I'm here for it—for you."

"Let practicing be my distraction, like it always is."

I peek over my shoulder to glance at him and his almost-beard grazes my skin. Our lips all but brush against each other as we stay nose to nose. "I can do that. What do you want to practice?"

"This." He tucks a finger under my chin and raises his brow as if asking permission.

That single eyebrow raise sends a million questions spiraling through me. What if this wasn't an act? How would he kiss me, for real? Would he be gentle or demanding? Would he cup my face and trace the seam of my lips like I've read in so many of my romance novels? Would I feel the sparks and fireworks I've long since given up on?

And then, maybe the most important question of all crashes through all the rest: Can I kiss him now and not get too attached?

Doubtful.

What would happen to us when my heart inevitably becomes irrevocably his?

But there's an undeniable ache torturing my chest, and the yearning to know what his lips feel like pressed against mine wins out over everything else.

My teeth rake over my lower lip, and I nod. Jack leans in slowly and brushes his lips against mine in a gentle embrace. A warm feeling skitters down my bare legs and curls my toes. The intensity of the touch startles me, and I jolt away.

"I need to go pee," I declare far too loudly. "You know, all that liquor—whoosh."

Whoosh? Whoosh! You're killing me, woman.

With incredible haste, I stand and bolt for the bathroom.

"Shit. Dessy—I didn't mean—"

I don't hear the rest of whatever Jack has to say, my feet carrying me faster than his words.

In the bathroom, I let the cool water from the sink fall along my wrists and calm my nerves. What the heck am I doing?

We're supposed to be playing, *practicing*. *This* should all be fine.

But there's a pit in my stomach screaming that I'm not acting, and as far as Jack is concerned, I don't need a mask or a character to be that foolish girl again.

I *want* to kiss Jack Parker.

And that's a problem.

I've never wanted to kiss a romantic opposite in a play. It's just been something we've had to do. Feelings were never involved.

So why can't I turn my feelings off now?

Oh, heck, I'm such a terrible friend.

Jack is saving my butt and the fair, and I'm royally mucking it all up. Why am I letting my feelings get in the way when they should be tucked neatly in the bonnet box they belong in?

No, I can't ruin the fair because of a silly crush. I can kiss Jack and have it mean nothing.

Our lips can touch, and my heart will remain unaffected. I'm sure of it.

But Jack needs to stop muddling my heart with all the sweet things he's doing. Yes, that's the problem. It has to be. George Wickham would not do sweet things like kiss my forehead and give me his flannel. How am I supposed to behave like Lydia Bennet when Jack's suddenly more of a Bingley?

Swinging the bathroom door open, I'm greeted by the six-foot-four center shrouded in the hallway's darkness. I can barely make out the bashful expression plastered on his face.

It's endearing.

And endearing simply won't do.

We need to correct this posthaste.

"Dessy...I didn't mean to—well, I did, but—shit." He scrubs a hand over his face with a groan. "I'm sorry."

"Hey, hey. No, it's fine." A soft smile curls my lips. So we both don't know what the heck we're doing. For some reason, that makes me feel a little better. I grab the hand covering his face and rub small circles into his calloused palm. "I think we need to set some ground rules because the action took me off guard."

"Ground rules, right. That sounds good." His shoulders relax as he finally brings his attention to my face.

"I need you to stop being sweet and be more of a rake."

"Like... the gardening tool?"

"No." I laugh. "A rake. It's a term they used in the nineteenth century to describe a man who had lower moral standards and was a playboy. When we're practicing, I need you to pretend like all that matters to you is having me wrapped around your finger to get what you want. I don't have feelings that concern you."

This request sounds dangerous, but I'm relatively confident I'll be able to play off of Playboy Jack better than Slightly Flirty Jack. That version is too easy to pretend is real and it's confusing my heart.

If Jack acts like he does at a club, a part of his life I don't belong in, I can separate the two. Jack Parker, the best friend, will be safe.

I think.

I hope.

I can do this.

"You—want—I'm sorry? What do you want me to do?" Jack scratches the back of his neck, staring at me like I have multiple heads. "No offense, but I tried to kiss you—uh, for practice, you know...and you bolted. This doesn't sound like a great next step."

"I promise you I was slightly rattled after the Tyler thing, but I'm good. I'm ready to take this seriously. And I don't think it'll be that hard for you, either. We, uhm, we've been flirting all night, right? And now we're in this dark, secluded hallway. What would you do if I wasn't your Dessy, and instead I was someone you—I don't know, just met at the bar tonight?"

"Dessy, I don't do—"

"Uh, uh, Parker. Dessy's not here. It's like you said, we aren't friends tonight." My fingers reach up and play with the three fastened buttons on his shirt. With each exposed inch of skin revealed, the binding of hesitation around my heart falls away. I graze the small patch of hair dusting his chest, sparks searing my fingertips with every passing touch.

Like everything else tonight, touching Jack feels like a natural fit, as if I was born to do it.

My head was made to rest in the crook of his arm. Our lips were made to join together, and his skin was meant for my fingers and touch alone.

Jack's eyes shutter closed. His chest rises and falls in a pronounced rhythm. With every exaggerated breath he takes, I grow increasingly hopeful that he feels the inevitability of us too.

"I'm just a girl who pretended to be cold, so you would give me your flannel," I say, pressing up on my toes and bringing my lips a few inches from his. His breath falls hot against my cheek as his eyes flutter open. "And then I pulled you into a hallway to tease you some more. So, Parker, as a rake, as someone who wants to get me wrapped around your finger because I have something you want—what do you do?"

"Dessy—" he whispers, impossibly soft. His forehead falls to mine like he's in agony.

He's not going to play the game and I can't force him to do this when it looks like it's torture for him.

"You know what? Let's forget it. This was clearly a mistake. Maybe I could ask Tyler. He's obviously got the rake thing down —" I turn. I'd rather leave the role vacant than actually ask Tyler, but Jack doesn't need to know that's the road I'm going to take. All he needs to know is he's off the hook.

Jack's hand firmly envelops my wrist and tugs me toward him. The warmth of his chest slams into my back before he pivots us and gently presses me into the wall. The black ink on his wrist swirls into the cuff of his shirt above my head. My breath hitches in my throat as my lungs struggle to adjust to the sudden shift in our positions.

"Put your hands on the wall," he says low and gruff.

Like the doomed shmuck I am, I follow his orders. The electric current humming inside sparks alive, buzzing through my veins and licking my nerve endings to life. While touching Jack may have felt natural, this is anything but.

This is something unearthly. A sensation I can only compare to one other paradoxical sensation in my life—thunder snow on the shores of King's Pond. That's what it feels like when Jack looms this close—not a bland blanket of goodness, but a collective. confusing beauty in all its forms and powers.

Jack lowers his mouth to my ear. "Promise me if I do this, you won't act weird around me after."

"Why—why would I act weird?" I ask. Delicate snow falls along my spine and goosebumps pucker my arms.

"I'm serious, Dessy. I need you—this can't ruin that, so I need to hear you promise."

I manage a nod, forcing my lungs to produce enough oxygen to respond. "I understand we're just practicing. I promise I won't get the two confused."

Liar.

"Good." Suddenly, the flannel draped along my shoulders drops to the ground with a thud.

With a feather-light touch, Jack brushes my hair over my

shoulder. His rough cheek scratches against my skin, before he places a warm kiss on the nape of my neck. In a tortuous and meticulous manner, his mouth moves down my neck, claiming every millimeter of skin with care. "Do you know how fucking wild this dress has driven me tonight?" he asks. His left hand grazes my bare legs and the pressure between them grows as he plays dangerously close to the hem of my mid-thigh dress. "Between this bare shoulder and your damn legs, I swear you wore it just to torture me."

With every light trail of his finger and brush of his mouth over my skin, lightning licks my nerves alive.

If I cared an ounce for myself, I wouldn't let this continue, but the fair is too important. It's possible I'm using Lydia as an excuse, but I don't care. Lydia Bennet would relish this kind of attention.

So instead of calling a timeout like I probably should, I let the fool out to play.

"I mean—" I giggle, putting on the sweetest, flirty airs I can muster. "You told me to put my sweater dress on. I was just following orders."

"Next time, I'll tell you to wear a potato sack out," he snarls.

"I look that good in it, huh? Maybe I'll wear it to the club with Emy, then."

His hand grips my hip, and he turns me around. I lose a breath as his chest presses against mine, his body caging me in.

His eyes have turned wild and dark, and his lips are swollen from the kisses he pressed into my skin. "Maybe I'll tear it off tonight, so no one else will ever see you in it."

Images of Jack ripping my sweater off in one swift, hungry motion, flash through my mind and desire pools between my thighs.

"I'd like to see you try."

His gaze devours me as he leans in closer, pressing a tender kiss to the corner of my mouth.

I whimper, completely unsatisfied. It's been so long since I've felt the softness of someone else's lips or the heat of another's skin against mine, and the desire, now, is overwhelming. "Something tells me you'd willingly take part in the destruction." He grins, wide and dangerous. "I've been racking my brain trying to figure out what motive I would have here, and I think I've finally got it. Do you want to know or should I keep it a secret?"

"Tell me, please." I slide my hand to his lower back and under his shirt. His skin scorches my fingertips and I pull his hips in tight against mine.

"This, Aulie. I want you—you out of your mind for me. I want you begging for me, like I'm the key to your relief."

I nervously bite down on my bottom lip, hoping the pressure of the action will ease the growing tension everywhere else.

It doesn't help. I'm seconds from becoming exactly what Jack wants, desperate and begging.

Gently, he cups my face with his hand, his rough palm sliding against my cheek, and I nuzzle into it. If he searches my gaze, I'm sure he'll see how much of my heart he's stolen tonight.

"Then kiss me already." It comes out more breathy than I'd like.

He tsks. The pad of his thumb runs over my mouth which grows slack under his gentle touch. "Now Aurelie. I know those aren't the manners your Memere taught you."

The sensible part of me jerks against this, wanting to roll my eyes and tell him to quit his teasing and kiss me already, but she's no longer in control. Foolish, foolish, Aulie, the girl who'd wear her heart on the sleeve for the taking if it wasn't his already is captain of this ship now.

"Please," I beg.

"There you go. Good girl."

Finally, Jack tilts his head. Anticipation courses through my body, making my limbs heavy as lead. I exhale as his lips press against mine, as if a world of unrealized tension is escaping my body with his touch. I deepen the kiss, savoring the taste of his lips, malt, cinnamon, and nutmeg dancing along my tongue.

"Dessy—" he says, the words low and hush. Almost a moan, as if he's making sure I understand this kiss isn't being shared between Lydia and Wickham, but it's a real one just for us.

That's all I need to adjust the angle of the kiss, ride the thrashing waves, and let go.

"Dessy—I'm shit—" This time when he speaks, it isn't as soft but much more desperate. The dark hunger in his eyes fades to one of alarm. Suddenly, two hands fall on my shoulders, and he gently pushes himself off of me.

I blink back to reality just in time to see Jack bolt for the men's bathroom.

An ungodly retching sound follows.

Oh. Heck. He wasn't making sure I knew the kiss was something passing between us and not Lydia and Wickham. He was trying to tell me he was about to vomit.

My fingers trace my lips, swollen and sore from the shocking storm they just endured.

And Jack threw up.

Even worse, I thought his request for release was some great declaration of love or something.

Definitely misread that one.

I brush my hair out of my face with a sigh. This is why I keep the hopeless romantic under lock and key.

Another round of Jack retching sounds beyond the bathroom door. I straighten my dress and collect myself. Now isn't the time for misplaced pity. I need to overcome my bruised ego and help my friend.

Holding my nose, I enter the bathroom. Jack is in the first stall with the door open, hugging the toilet bowl.

He looks at me and groans, before leaning his head against the wall.

"You okay?" I ask, tepidly approaching.

"I should be there, Dessy," he says, closing his eyes. "I fucked up so bad."

I slide down to the ground next to him, trying not to wince as my bare legs meet the cold tile. Jack's head falls to my shoulder. "I don't deserve you," he says, sounding far more drunk than he did a few minutes ago. How did I miss that? Well, to be fair, whatever he was doing made me miss a lot of things, so maybe I shouldn't dwell on that. "You're too good and pure, and I'm going to ruin" — he hiccups— "someday."

I don't know precisely what he means to ruin, but I'm doing a pretty good job ruining our friendship, so he doesn't have to worry about that.

Jack's head lays on my shoulder for a few minutes longer, and I count his breaths, trying to settle my own. "We should get you home," I whisper, pulling out my phone and texting Emy for a ride.

"I can't let Simone see me like this."

"Don't worry. I'll take care of it," I say, pushing him off my shoulder and trying to get him to stand.

At that moment, the door swings open. I breathe a sigh of relief when I see it's Andrew. He's always been a solid guy. I can trust him to be discreet. Without asking, he puts his shoulder around the other side of Jack to keep both of us from falling over.

Thank you, I mouth.

"I should have cut him off sooner, but I couldn't with what day it is, you know?"

I nod. "I enabled him, too." My mind goes to all the out-of-character stuff Jack did tonight, and his words before he leaned in to kiss me. He literally told me I was a distraction and I still let myself get caught up in that.

Good to know I'm still terrible with the whole not giving my heart over to someone the minute they pay me a compliment thing. I'm going to have to do better in the future.

In tandem, we walk Jack to the front, where Emy said she'd meet us.

Her car pulls up, and we stuff Jack into the back seat. The car ride home is silent, save for Emy's eclectic playlist, which does little to quiet my mind as it spirals over the fact that I kissed Jack.

And it was everything I've ever wanted in a kiss. My toes curled, my heart raced, and electricity spiraled inside.

And he...vomited.

That's going to do wonders for our friendship.

Chapter Sixteen

Jack Parker

Play: *Northern Attitude by Noah Kahan*

I'm suffocating in a heavy blanket of rosewater and lilacs. With each shallow breath, my stomach churns, and my head pounds with growing pressure. I'm engulfed, sinking deeper and deeper into an endless abyss. Aulie's going to be the death of me.

Just like I always knew she would.

Another knot twists my stomach.

With a groan, I turn on my side. The mattress, softer than I'm used to, gives easily.

Flickers of last night string together in a hazy, incoherent mess. Couple that with my throbbing headache and a queasy stomach, and I think it's safe to say I overdid it at the bar.

Simone is going to kill me.

Another dose of lightning surges through my frontal lobe.

Well, she will if I don't have an aneurysm first.

Nearby, pages ruffle. My stomach drops. I don't know how last night ended, but I know who I started it with, and after a few shots, the usual ache in my chest for her was getting insufferable.

Cracking one eye open, I hesitantly take stock of the room. The floral wallpaper, wooden panels, and floor-to-ceiling built-in bookcases confirm my fears. I'm in Aulie's bed. Last night's shrouded in a dense fog, and I can't recall anything after the first period of the game.

The gentle morning light filters through the wooden blinds and illuminates Aulie's curved figure as she reads in her cozy window seat. She's settled in with a pillow propped up behind her and a blanket wrapped around her legs.

Again, my stomach turns.

That window seat is about four feet long, and Aulie is five-eight or five-nine. If she slept there last night, that couldn't have been comfortable.

Her gaze doesn't meet mine and I let my stare linger on her bee-stung lips glowing in the morning sun before following the curve of her neck and resting on the patch of exposed skin between the strap of her lace camisole and a tattered cardigan.

While my memory is fuzzy, I remember that shoulder torturing me all night long. A yearning swells to trace her delicate shoulder with my mouth and hear a soft exhale pass over her lips in response.

"Morning," she says.

"Morning." Sandpaper coats my throat forcing a strangled greeting.

"There's water on the side table." She runs a finger over her lips, focusing on the book before her.

My hand twitches at my side, eager to follow hers. Waking up to Aulie in the same room—to have her be the first thing I see in the morning—it's a dangerous experience I can't afford to repeat.

"Thank you," I say, sitting up. My blanket falls away, exposing my bare chest to the chilly air, and I shiver.

I try to catch a glance at Aulie to see her reaction. Pink cheeks, a nervous work of the throat, something, anything to tell me I might have a chance someday, but her attention stays glued to her book.

Forget it. I've made too many messes that she's cleaned up. There's no way she sees me as anything more than a problem to solve. And I don't know that I'd want to subject her to my non-existent dating skills, even if she cared for me in that way. I'm not the hero she deserves, and I never will be.

"Dessy, about last night—" I don't know what I should apologize for, but waking up in her bed suggests last night didn't end well.

"Already forgotten. You were hurting and drunk. I promise I understand." She snaps her book shut. "Your shirt should be clean. Hold on, I'll go get it for you."

"What happened to it?"

She stands and cocks her head to the side. "You vomited on it?"

"Of course, I did."

I'm lucky Aulie's still showing me kindness if she cleaned that up.

A corner of her mouth tilts up into something mischievous. "How much of last night do you remember, Jack?"

I scoff, leaning against her headboard and muss the back of my hair with my hand. "I'm not that much of a lightweight, Dessy."

"Right. Right. So obviously you remember agreeing to let me sell your organs for profit."

"I'd give you a kidney if you asked." I shrug. "But I feel like giving you the money instead would be less messy."

"Less messy, sure, but far less fun. Though I don't know how much your liver would get me on the Black Market these days."

I train my gaze on the water cup in front of me, not able to meet her stare again. I shouldn't have let my emotions get the better of me last night, but when Richard went after me on the pre-game show, I lost it and the temptation to stop feeling anything for a while grew too strong to overcome. "I'm sorry I drank too much last night. How can I make it up to you?"

"I was thinking some waffles at the diner, and the use of your giant car for fair errands would do the trick."

"Wow." I chuckle, taking another sip of water. "You had that one ready, huh?"

"Didn't sleep much last night." She raises one of her shoulders in a shrug. The strap from the lace camisole falls, and I'm too tired not to stare.

Pink dusts her cheeks. "Right! Your shirt. If Gus asks, you slept in the guest room. I tried to get you to lie down in there, but you kept saying you couldn't be alone—so, here you are."

"Here I am." I nod into the empty remnants of my glass. Her soft feet patter across the hardwood as she exits the room.

And I'm left sitting here, staring at her pillow and blanket lying in a huddled mess in the window.

Between Aulie's sleeping position, my hangover, and the black hole in my memory, I should feel like total shit—and I do mostly—but there's a warmth slowly growing in my chest. Waking up to Aulie—fuck, I could do that every damn day.

~

"How can you listen to this garbage? I'm not even hungover, and this music is giving me a headache," Aulie groans, reaching for the volume knob and turning my driving playlist down as we barrel south on Route 16 to Portsmouth.

"What do you have against Blink-182?"

"It's chaos. It sounds like he's being castrated, and they asked him to sing through the procedure."

A sudden burst of laughter escapes me in surprise. I've never heard Aulie be that negative about...well, anything. "Put on whatever you want, your highness," I say, tossing her my phone.

"Oh, thank heavens." Aulie purses her lips and browses my Spotify. I don't know why she's bothering. There's zero percent chance she's choosing something other than oldies music.

Without fail, a harmony of voices I recognize as the Beach Boys kick in behind a snare drum.

"Much better," Aulie says. Her head falls back on the rest, and she closes her eyes, a serene smile plastered on her face.

"What's your obsession with oldies, anyway?" I ask.

Her shoulders rise in a shrug as the sun softly flickers over her features with every passing, shedding maple. "There's something cozy about the music. Oldies were always on in the house, and they make up so many of my favorite rom-com soundtracks. When I hear them now, I smile and think, this is it, a happily ever after is about to happen. Like hearing Stevie Wonder sing "Signed, Sealed, Delivered I'm Yours" and knowing Joe Fox is about to take care of Kathleen Kelly—which is the single greatest scene in rom-com history if you ask me. Love a good caretaking scene."

"I'll take your word for it. I've never seen it."

"Considering you're like the least romantic human ever, I'm not surprised."

"Ouch." I play off the insult, rubbing my palm over my chest.

"It's okay. You're pretty and good at other things, I'm sure." She hums.

"Thanks?" I try to tell myself to focus on the part when Aulie said I was pretty and not on the fact that burying my feelings for her the past few years has ensured there will never be a future with us. How could there be when she thinks I'm incapable of being romantic and compares me to the likes of George Wickham?

She yawns beside me, and another pang of guilt pricks my chest. There's no way she got any sleep in the window seat last night.

"Why don't you try to nap? It should be another half hour before we're at the antique store."

She cracks an eye open. "We just left Chawton Falls. It should be a good hour."

"Sweetheart, we both know I drive like I skate."

Aulie shifts uncomfortably in her seat. "Recklessly, with no regard for other people's safety?"

Note to self: never use the term sweetheart again.

"Shit! Dessy, did I do something last night, or are you just this grumpy in the morning?"

She pulls on her seatbelt, loosening its hold on her neck and chest. "Nothing happened. Just grumpy, I guess." The lack of conviction in her voice tells me everything her answer didn't.

Something happened.

"Care to fill me in on what I missed, anyway?" I ask softly. Something I did last night put us off-balance, and until I know what I can't set us right.

"What's the last thing you remember?" she asks.

I scrub a hand over my cheek, scratching at my facial hair and thinking. Images of nuzzling into Aulie's neck and calling her "kitten" come to mind. I try not to grimace—I wasn't on a good trajectory if those are my last memories.

"I remember eating an excellent batch of poutine, and that's where it ends." That's a lie, I remember wiping some gravy off of Aulie's cheek with a weird sexually charged energy. I was so fucking gone for her, I just wanted to taste something that was so close to the skin and lips I was truly hungry for.

"Gotcha. Well, let's see—" She taps her chin with her finger. "You missed the alien abduction. It turns out Tyler isn't from Planet Earth, and his family came to bring him home."

"You know, I vaguely remember the spaceship. Looked like a giant penis, right?"

"Exactly. And then, the first period happened. Peter didn't anticipate a pass, and you were upset."

"Yup, that tracks."

"And then the first intermission."

"Usually follows the first period. So, good."

"And the second period..."

"Dessy, I know the flow of a hockey game—that's not what I'm asking you."

"What are you asking me, then?"

I run my hand through my hair. "I want to know if there's a reason you're suddenly the embodiment of a grumpy, awkward turtle around me."

"What? That's not a thing." She forces a laugh.

"Hear that laugh? That's not the laugh you usually give me,

Aulie. I need to know whatever I did because I don't like this—whatever this is between us."

She tugs at the tips of her fingers. "I suppose there may be some residual awkward tension leftover from the kiss," she says, glancing out the window.

It takes every ounce of my energy not to swerve off the road. Pulling over and collecting myself might not be a terrible idea because my brain is sputtering, and I don't know if operating heavy machinery in this condition is advisable.

"Between us?" I ask.

"No, between you and Andrew, the bartender. It came as quite a shock—"

"Aulie—" I grit my teeth. I don't care if I'm, as Elizabeth Bennet called Mr. Darcy last night, a "humorless poppycock"—I can't just cross into teasing mode. If we kissed, there's no way I withheld how I felt about her. And now she's uncomfortable.

"Yes, between us. But it was just for practice for the fair. I didn't notice you were drunk until you threw up immediately after. Jack, honest, I'm so sorry. I wouldn't have done that with you if I'd known. I get that you—that we—" She sighs. "I get where you stand on the matter. I promise not to let it ruin our friendship."

I wince. Vomiting immediately after our first kiss isn't exactly the storybook ending I've envisioned over the past few years. In a perfect world, I would have been sober and given Aulie the kiss she deserves. One that shattered her senses and left her wanting more. Instead, I'm lucky this woman is talking to me this morning. But because I'm a masochist, I can't help but ask, "Was the kiss good, at least? I mean, for the fair?"

"Well—" she starts, staring straight ahead, "I mean, if I'm being honest, it felt a bit like kissing a family member, you know? Since we're so close. But it'll have to do."

"Right." I grip the steering wheel. "Well, I'm glad it'll do. I wouldn't want to ruin the fair over something so insignificant as a kiss."

She doesn't respond, and we ride in silence for the next twenty minutes. Meanwhile, my head is alive and loud.

You kissed her, you fucker? Well, there goes your shot. Friend zone it is.

"Antique shop should be right around the corner if you want to start looking for parking," Aulie says as we arrive in downtown Portsmouth.

"What did you need to get this far from Chawton Falls?" I ask, pulling into a rare-on-street parking spot in front of a small Parisian café, with colorful meringues and pastries sitting in a floral covered window.

"An early nineteenth-century umbrella." She sighs. "And I bet there will still be something wrong with it."

"Let me guess. Bridget?" I ask. I've never met the woman, but from the stories Aulie's told me, she tends to make more work for Aulie than she takes off her plate.

"Yup," Aulie says, popping the "p" at the end of the word.

Something in her tone itches at me that something more than a poor kiss transpired between us last night. I need to figure it out before this trip is over or else she'll let it fester. I can't risk losing our friendship on top of everything else today.

"Hey, Dessy?" I cut the engine and smile at her. "You wouldn't have room after all those waffles this morning for some beach pizza, would you? It'd be a shame to be so close to the ocean and not go the extra twenty minutes to get some, don't you think?"

"Only if it's not a bother," she says, back turned to me, her hand on the car door handle. Since this morning, she's kept eye contact with me at a minimum, and it has me on high alert. I don't know what I did, but I'm going to fix this.

"Never for you," I say softly to an empty car since she's already out the door and headed for her umbrella.

~

THE WAVES CRASH ALONG THE SEAWALL WE SETTLED ON after we grabbed a box of Tripoli's extra cheese. The wind whips around us, and Aulie pulls her cardigan tighter. With her gaze on the waves, a flash of uncertainty flickers over her features. She takes a bite of her square pizza, and her eyes shutter closed as a small smile curls her lips.

Exhaling, I take a bite of my own and savor the sweet sauce dancing along my tastebuds. At least whatever is bothering her, pizza still seems to be the remedy.

A smattering of sauce covers her cheeks, and I fight down the unrelenting tug in my abdomen to swipe my thumb across her velvety skin.

"You're wearing your pizza again," I say, gesturing to her left cheek and offering her a napkin.

She blushes, grabbing the napkin to clean herself up. "Thank you," she says with a sigh. Apparently, there's only so much this pizza is going to fix.

"Hey." I nudge her with my foot. "What's going on in that head of yours?"

"Nothing." Aulie shifts, tucking her legs underneath her. A seagull flies overhead, battling against the growing headwind.

Same, bro. Same.

"It's something," I say as gently as possible. "I have a feeling something else besides a kiss happened last night."

Aulie shakes her head.

"Tell me. Please. I can't fix it if I don't know what asshole thing I did."

"You didn't do anything. It's stupid."

"I doubt that."

She faces me and takes a deep breath before dropping her gaze, tracing the eroded ridges of the gritty rock beneath us. "I'm upset with myself. I've been so busy with the fair and wallowing in my own stuff that I didn't even know what yesterday was until we went to the bar. I should have known your father's birthday would have been extra hard for you up here and had a game plan ready, but I didn't—and I'm just—I'm sorry I let you down."

"Hey." I gently lift her chin and guide her gaze to mine. "That's not your job, Dessy."

"Isn't it, though?" She shakes herself, refusing to look at me again, like she somehow thinks my behavior is her fault and not my inability to navigate the emotions that surfaced yesterday. "I'm the emotional support best friend, right? That's why you keep me around."

"If anyone is keeping anyone, it's *you* tolerating *me*. Not the other way around. You're stuck with me until you kick me to the curb, got it? I need you."

She picks up a discarded mussel shell and studies the black and blue coloring on the outside. "You said that last night. The needing me thing." She chews on her lip as if she's weighing if she should say whatever it is she's thinking.

"We're always honest with each other, Aulie. Don't change that now."

And by that I mean she's always honest with me. I'm harboring a million secrets and lie to her and myself daily, but who's keeping score here?

"Last night, I got the impression that you were using me as a distraction, so you didn't have to be vulnerable with your feelings. If that's the kind of friend you need, I don't know that I love being that person for you." A tear falls down her cheek. "I'm sorry. I'm tired and overly sensitive, but sometimes it feels like I'm your friend and not the other way around. Like, of course, you'll keep me around—I bail you out of situations and care for you, but what happens when I can't or don't want to do that anymore?"

I don't know how to answer her. Guilt tears my nerves to shreds. Apparently, I've hidden how I feel about Aulie so well that she somehow thinks she's expendable when I need her in my life as much as I need oxygen to breathe or water to survive.

I lean forward and wipe a tear from her cheek. "I'm so sorry I've made you feel this way."

Hiding my feelings is doing more damage than I realized. Aulie can't think like this for another minute, even if it means I have to show her more of me than I'd like to.

I can—I will—do better *for her*.

With the fresh air clearing my lungs and Aulie's words tight to my chest, my perspective shifts for the first time. I've been too in my head to think about anyone else, and it's hurt one of the most important people in my life.

"I promise. I'm going to make this up to you." The hollow spring in my chest bursts forth, and suddenly I'm overwhelmed with feelings I'd usually rather not deal with.

There's a spot, not too far from here, that means more to me than any other place in the state, and suddenly, I have the courage to go there. As long as Aulie's with me.

"Come on." I stand, offering her my hand. "There's one last place I want to stop before we go home."

Warily, Aulie regards my outstretched hand and narrows her eyes at me. "Where do you want to go?"

"Nowhere that'd make sense until we're there—but trust me."

Her palm slips into mine. Sparks fly up my arm on contact, and I let them, not bothering to hide how much such an insignificant touch decimates me. If she glanced up she'd see one of those ridiculous looks of longing plastered on my face that the rom-coms Grady watches love to slow pan in on. "That's not as easy a command to comply with as you'd think," she says, flashing a teasing smile my way.

"Oh good, she's coming back to me." I chuckle, packing our pizza and turning the car down Route 27.

Thirty minutes and one Italian sub shop later, I park my car in front of an ice rink in Exeter, a small seacoast town in New Hampshire.

Rummaging through the plastic bag, I place two ginger ales in the console, a large bag of salt and vinegar chips between us, and hand Aulie one-half of the sub. Onions, pickles, and vinegar fill the car with nostalgia, and I swallow the ball in my throat, begging me to run away from the sensation.

With curiosity, Aulie watches as I undo the tape and paper on my sub half. I ignore the attention, trying to let myself ride the waves of emotions as they crash into me. The sharp bite of the onion does little to quiet the tide, and after a second bite and a hit of the spicy oil, the danger I'll start crying in this parking lot becomes a genuine possibility.

Shit. This is hard. Okay. We can do this.

Aulie still keeps her gaze on me, blinking a few times and then looking at the rink like she can't understand why we're here. That's fair.

"My dad used to bring me here," I say after my third bite.

Aulie's sandwich stops, resting against her lips.

"We had a lot of tournaments at this rink, and my dad would usually bring me. If there was a big break between games, or sometimes before them, we'd grab these sandwiches, sit here in the parking lot, and talk. Sometimes about a girl. Sometimes he'd get philosophical and share quotes he had just read, but we never talked about hockey. It was the one time where it was just me, my dad and this sandwich—no one else fighting for John Parker the hockey legend's attention."

A warm hand encompasses mine, and I glance down to see that I'd started trembling at some point.

An unyielding pressure challenges the confines of my chest, pushing and threatening to explode.

"Anyway, that's the story." I shrug, hoping to bury the swell of emotions. That's enough growth for today.

"Jack?" Aulie says, her thumb rubs tiny circles on the top of my hand. "Thank you for bringing me here. This means a lot, you sharing this with me."

"Thank you for being the friend I could do this with." I smile back. "I'm sorry I've been taking you for granted. I've been so up my ass. Seriously, I'm happy we're friends."

Aulie regards me, a well of tears rimming her eyes, but her smile rests more naturally than it did a few hours ago, telling me I'm successfully rebuilding whatever broke between us last night. "I guess we've both been up each other's asses."

I raise my brow, and her eyes widen. "I didn't mean—it came out wrong!" She playfully swats at me. "You're literally the worst, Parker. I don't know why I'm friends with you."

"Yeah, but you're stuck with me, Dessy." I wrap my arm

around her, holding my sub in the other hand, and press a kiss into her hair.

"I guess it could be worse," she grumbles, the hint of a smile suggesting that being stuck with me might not be such a terrible thing after all.

Chapter Seventeen

Aulie Desfleurs

Play: *Be My Baby by The Ronettes*

"Everyone's here that should be. Roger," Emy's voice rings in my ear.

Last year, I invested in two-way radio headsets to make communication more accessible across the fairgrounds. The Wentworth Estates' acreage is vast and hilly, and cell service is spotty on a good day, so after four years of torturing my poor legs, the purchase felt necessary.

"Perfect. I'm just unloading a few more boxes, and I'll be over in a second," I say, pulling the bonnet box from my car and walking it to the white crew tent in the back corner of the fair. It's tucked away behind an enormous willow tree and obscured as best as possible, so we don't ruin the illusion.

Although Food Truck Row may do that just fine. But I doubt anyone would complain about easy access to fried dough and poutine.

A long pause, not characteristic of my best friend's loquacious demeanor, sounds on the other side.

Oh. Darn it. "Rabbit," I say, ending my side of the transmission. This morning, when I gave Emy the earpiece, it was with extreme hesitation. I love my friend, but having her in my ear is a dangerous prospect.

She promptly confirmed my fears when she held her device in the sky and declared, "Unlimited power!" like Darth Sidious from Star Wars.

She's spending too much time with Gus.

When I tried to establish some ground rules like keep the channel open in case I need you and don't litter it with every thought that crosses your gorgeous mind, she agreed.

But she had a few rules of her own.

One was our call and response—Emy thought it a wasted opportunity for walkie-talkie users everywhere who didn't use "Roger" and "Rabbit" as their sign-offs.

With the fair opening in five days, I'm thankful that Emy gave her employees at the toy store extra shifts and came to help. I don't think I'd be able to navigate managing the players, setting up inside of the estate, and the grounds crew and players' tent without her and Bridget stepping up. Even Jack pitched in; taking me to Portsmouth a few days ago was a big help. We stopped at Costco on our way home for water and snacks for everyone, and I took advantage of his powerful muscles to load up the car.

I don't know how I've done most of this on my own the past four years.

But I've always been a bit of an overachiever. It helps me manage my pain if I can hyper-focus on something else.

Or at least, it *used* to. I'm unsure if I can overcompensate for the pain torturing my pelvic region this year.

"I can start the introductions where you know everyone already—Roger," Emy says.

"I'd say yes, but we should hold off on that until Jack gets here. He's the only newbie, and the rest of the cast knows each other. Oh, but maybe it will be a good idea to prep them. Tell them we'll have a quasi-celebrity joining us this year and that they should treat him like he's Wickham at the fair and not Jack...rabbit."

"Heh. Jackrabbit. I bet he wants to do you like a—"

"Oh my god, I regret giving you a headpiece."

Silence.

I roll my eyes. "Rabbit."

"You knew what you were getting into. But yes, I can give them a heads up. See you soon! Roger Rabbit over and out."

I don't think that's how ending a call works, but I'm more than happy to let Emy be her best self when she's helping me. Pulling a box of props from my trunk, the chorus to "Centerfold" blares in the slim pocket of my leggings. My heart skips a beat.

I need to remember to change that before Jack accidentally hears it.

"Hey, what's up? You almost here?"

"Already here. I was calling to see where I should meet you, but I see you," his voice echoes.

I turn around and—sweet love of Peter Noone! Jack looms only a few steps away. Water droplets fall from his hair like he's freshly showered. A curious look and a crooked grin sit on his face as he regards me with the phone still up to his ear.

"I'm hanging up now," I say, trying to draw oxygen to my lungs and settle my wildly beating heart. "Hi."

"Hello." He slides his phone into his pocket, stuffing both hands in his jeans immediately after. His grey t-shirt billows in the wind, highlighting his chest and revealing a bit of his chiseled abdominal muscles. "That's not the type of oldies I'm used to you listening to."

My eyes fixate on the swirling ink on his arm. He's been in long sleeves most of his visit, so I missed a few new tattoos. A vine full of thorns twists from his forearm, around his elbow, and up to the image hiding under his sleeves of him skating with his dad on a cranberry bog.

I've studied the ink on his arms and chest more than I'd like to admit. I love every piece. His hockey number nestled among the thorns on his forearm. The Jean-Jacques Rousseau quote that was his dad's favorite sits below it, "Teach him to live rather than to avoid death; life is not breath, but action." And of course there's the mysterious black scroll of script on his chest that I'll someday work up the courage to about.

"Dessy? You awake?" Jack snaps his fingers, and I blink alive, settling on his crooked grin again.

Oh, that thing is almost as dangerous as his tattoos.

"Yeah, yeah. I'm here." I laugh awkwardly. "What did you ask me again?"

"I didn't know you liked that song... whatever it was, it's not very rom-comy."

"Oh! 'Centerfold!' Yes." I wince. Admitting the title was not the best way to start this. Actually, it may have been the absolute worst. "It's a prank. Emy set it as my ringtone, for, um, no particular reason. Hi! How are you?" A cheesy, forced grin spreads across my face.

"Great." His brow furrows as he searches my face for something, but he shakes his head. "Do you need help with those?" He nods to the boxes in the trunk.

"If you don't mind, that would be great."

There are only a few boxes left. We pull them in relative silence. I haven't seen Jack since we ate subs at the ice rink on Thursday. We invited him to Sunday dinner yesterday, but he told Gus he was going on an uncle adventure with his niece and nephews, which only slightly increased the recent pulse between my thighs when I thought of him.

"How was your weekend?" I finally ask.

He snorts, pulling the last box out of the trunk and following me back into the white tent one last time. "Mine was fine, but I doubt the people playing Peter Pan and Tinkerbell at StoryLand would say the same."

My heart skips. StoryLand is an adorable amusement park in New Hampshire that my Memere used to take us to once a year. There are princesses, princes, pirates, and everything else you could want in a magic fairy tale world, and it's one reason this fair exists today.

That first summer Jack returned home to Chawton Falls we took Lucy to StoryLand to celebrate his signing. As a literary nerd, it reinvigorated me to see the park through adult eyes. Cinderella's pumpkin coach, Captain Hook's pirate ship, and the swan boats helped create a magical storybook feel. And then I thought, *Why does this feeling have to stop as a child? Why can't we feel like we've stepped inside a book as adults?*

I'd always had a personal connection to Jane Austen, and being from Chawton Falls, New Hampshire, New England, the leap to the regency fair seemed natural since dear Jane wrote most of her works in Chawton, Hampshire, England.

"What did Coby and Grant do?" I ask, wincing internally. He doesn't need to say they were the problem. I've never met greater terrors than those two. They're twin tornados.

"Well, Amy signed them up for the pirate classes. That was our first mistake." He runs his hand through his hair and shudders. "And then—uhm—they somehow found rope. I don't even know where it came from because the class was just Peter and Tink teaching the kids to talk like pirates. I swear I only looked away for two seconds—"

"They tied Peter and Tinkerbell up, didn't they?"

He nods. "And commandeered the ship. Which was, fun fact, actually fully functioning and improperly docked."

"Dear god. You may want to set some of your salary aside for bond money as they age."

"Not a bad idea." He stretches from side to side. "Coby kicked me when I picked him up to end their coup, and I swear his feet are made of lead or something. I don't remember having that much power in my legs at that age."

His hand goes to the folds of his shirt, pulling up on the left side and slowly revealing his black-and-blue ribcage.

I gasp. "Oh my god, did you make sure he didn't break something?"

He shakes his head. "Nah, I've had a busted rib before, and it doesn't feel like that. But still, I don't know if I should be impressed or terrified that he marked my body better than some pro hockey players do. Kid's going to be an enforcer for sure."

Closing my trunk, I wipe my hands on my leggings. "Well, I'm glad you're okay. Finding another Wickham at this hour would have been terribly inconvenient." *Especially because I liked last Wednesday at the bar a little too much.*

"Wouldn't want anyone filling my space, either." He smiles, nudging me playfully with his shoulder.

Warmth and hope bloom where they have no business growing. Relax, he's just being friendly, because we're *friends*.

"All right, let's meet the rest of the crew, shall we?"

I gesture for Jack to step out in front of me as we traverse up the hill, but instead of walking, he offers his elbow. "After you, Ms. Bennet," he says.

The hint of a smile dances on my lips as I wrap my hand around his bicep. "What a gentleman."

"We try," he says softly, almost like I wasn't supposed to hear it.

~

THIS MAY HAVE BEEN A MISTAKE. TWELVE PAIRS OF EYES stare unblinkingly at Jack. I don't know what Emy told them or if they thought she was joking, but the minute Jack and I appear over the rolling hill and meet the group in the Wentworth Mansion's foyer, the group falls into an odd silence.

"I'm sorry. *He's* going to be one of the actors... for the fair?" Henry, a cherub-faced twenty-something who plays Mr. Bingley, rubs the back of his head. "No offense, but do you think that's a good idea?"

"I mean, we don't have a choice." I shrug. "Emma and Callen left us pretty high and dry when they eloped. But I'm confident that Jack can fill the role perfectly." I put my hand on his shoulder for extra *I support you* emphasis.

"What about his accent? Does he do a British accent?" Lucas asks, arms crossed. He's our Mr. Darcy and usually the most charming individual you will ever meet, but he's also a method actor who's getting his undergrad at the college a few towns over and takes his job at the fair very seriously.

"*He's* right here," Jack says, staring at Lucas down the slope of his nose. "And, uhm, no, I didn't know that was part of the deal." He frowns. "But I'll work on it."

I smile at him. Jack's stepping out of his comfort zone for us, and I'm so incredibly grateful and frankly surprised by it. "There you go! And if Emy hasn't gotten to the other news yet, I'll be filling in as Lydia—"

"Wonder why," snorts Sabrina, our resident mightier-than-thou Caroline Bingley who is definitely not type-cast because that would be awfully rude of me.

"So," I continue, ignoring her jab. "If Jack gets in a pickle, I'm confident either I or Chloe, as Elizabeth, can help him."

Lucas nods, not fully satisfied with the answer, but again, we don't have much of a choice, so everyone has to accept the situation.

Jack Parker, infamous hockey player and hometown hero, will be a member of our troupe for the next few days. Nothing weird about that at all.

"So, that's all the casting news I have," I say, grabbing a stack of papers containing a rundown of the fair, expectations, schedule, and a map. After giving the players their directives, they disperse and I ready to trudge down the hill again to set up the snack station in the tent.

After a few years of participating, the crew doesn't need a checklist to know what to do. While the Estate hires professionals to set up the stages and the booths, a lot still needs to be done. The piano must be tuned so that Alyssa, as Georgiana, can play a multitude of reels and other classical songs. In an hour, the fairgrounds open for vendors, and they need to be checked in and assigned their areas. Not all of them will start setting up today, but I like to give them a few days in advance in case they want it.

Tables and chairs need to be moved inside to make room for the ball and dancing lessons which start tomorrow.

Hopefully Lucas and Chloe take that on, since they do it the way I like.

But it's okay if they don't. It doesn't have to be perfect.

Right?

I don't buy my own reassurances. I'd rather everything be just so, and take on most of the jobs myself, but...I can't. Not this year, and I don't know if that's bothering me more than letting go.

I wish I was good at delegation instead of being forced to delegate because I'm exhausted and keep having these random flares of pain.

There's a tiny carnival portion of the fair—with only a few rides and a petting zoo, but Bridget will be there so I can set up the tent.

I usually handle the tent the week before, but I let it slip and didn't order the darn thing until last week, when the guy called me to see if I'd need one this year because it surprised him he hadn't heard from me.

As the rest of the crew disperses, Jack stands with his head on a swivel, eyes large taking in the chaos around him.

Sabrina's direction? Jack.

Big surprise.

She takes two steps forward, extending her hand. "I'm Sabrina, by the way. I think it's so nice that you're here helping our little Aulie out. Don't hesitate to ask if you need someone to show you around. It can be overwhelming, and Aulie is a busy beaver." She glances over her shoulder, flashing a less-than-genuine smile in my direction, and I bite down the nauseating feelings bubbling in my chest.

Sabrina's a knockout; she'd probably make a great Jane if I weren't the type of person who held a grudge. But I doubt Sabrina can even pretend to be the most essential thing about Jane's character.

Nice.

"Thanks." Jack flashes her a smile and his dimples pop.

From what I've observed, Jack doesn't seem to have "nice" high on his must-have list for his dalliances with women.

A strange, guttural noise vibrates in the back my throat. Am I jealous?

No, if the angry inferno currently blazing in my stomach is

any indication, I'm *incredibly* jealous, and I hate it, thanks. I have to get this crush under control before the hockey season is over and Jack starts dating around again, or I'm doomed to be a grump.

Jack's eyes shoot over Sabrina's shoulder and meet mine. "Where do you want me?" he asks.

"Unfortunately, you're stuck with *my* beaver. Sabrina, I think Bridget could use some help with the carnival stuff," I grumble, grabbing Jack's hand and leading him out of the house.

Right on cue, Jack's gut-busting laugh follows me down the slope and into the crew tent. "I guess there are worse beavers to be stuck with."

It shouldn't, but his joke warms my chest, just a little.

Chapter Eighteen

Jack Parker

Play: *Howlin' for You by the Black Keys*

French doors leading to the Wentworth Garden swing open, bringing a rush of fresh autumn air into the solarium. The tranquil sound of water trickling greets us as we step out into the rows of flowers, twisted trees, and water fountains.

"And this is the garden," Aulie says on an inhale.

"So I've gathered."

She tips her chin up and soaks in the rays of sun blinking through the red and orange trees that center each garden bed. The serene look on her face allows my anxiety to calm just a fraction.

I *wanted* her to take an actual break after lunch because she couldn't mask the intensity of her pain while we were bending and carrying things into the crew tent. Given that I caught on, it must be significantly worse than usual. Despite knowing about Aulie's busy schedule this week, I asked if we could pause for a break, but when she denied that request, I thought up a different angle.

I need to get a sense of the fairgrounds before Saturday. So, my new plan is to explore the area at a leisurely pace while strategically finding places for her to rest.

Unfortunately, none of the damn chairs inside the house are for actual sitting, so all I've done so far is make her walk uphill, upstairs, downstairs, and all over the rest of the damn estate.

Scanning my surroundings, I take in the explosion of colors from the garden beds where tall flowers in hues of yellow, red, and orange sway in the breeze. They're beautiful if you like flowers and shit, but not what I'm looking for.

Hopefully, this garden has benches, and I can pretend my knee is hurting or something and ask her to sit with me for a moment.

Bees buzz around us as I search and make no progress in finding a suitable place to pause.

Rounding the winding path, a fountain with a flat brick ledge appears. The water in the basin seems to come alive as the sun's light reflects off its surface, illuminating everything around it.

That'll do. I hasten my steps.

"The fall layout is my favorite," Aulie says, slowly walking beside me. "Marigolds and daisies are two of my favorite flowers, and they do a good job showcasing them, don't you think?"

I'm not thinking about showcasing marigolds. Aulie's left hand is pressed into her abdomen, and pain rims the edge of her eyes, causing them to tighten a fraction in a wince.

I ball my hands into fists at my sides. Aulie's told me she's been having problems. But this is the first time I've seen the problem firsthand. It's taking all my strength and self-control not to throw her over my shoulder, march her to my car, take her home, and make her stay in bed for the rest of the day.

"*Shit.*" A quiet, rare swear passes over Aulie's lips. She bends a fraction with a sharp intake, and that's enough to send me over the edge. I can handle being in pain, but her? No fucking way.

"Sit." I point to the fountain, a scowl slashing hard across my face.

Aulie quirks a brow slowly, her eyes narrowing in suspicion.

"I'm sorry. Are you under the impression that you can command me to do things suddenly?"

No, I'm just about to have a goddamn aneurysm because you're clearly in pain.

I let out a deep sigh and run my fingers through my hair as Aulie stands with her arms crossed. I don't want total control of her like some old-school dude, but if she could just listen to me this one freaking time…

Something tells me that Lydia was too headstrong to listen to Wickham as well, but her pangs of pain and discomfort probably didn't bother him like the shot in the heart that wounds me every time she winces.

"You know, on the fairgrounds, I think I do have that right." The corner of my lip tugs into a smirk. I mirror her stance with my arms crossed and stare at her with a new challenge.

If Aulie wants authenticity, consider this my dedication to the craft.

"Come again?" She cocks her head to the side. A bee buzzes lazily around her head as if drawn to her sweetness.

Aren't we all?

"You're my wife at the fairgrounds, right? And this is a regency fair."

"For some of the day," she warns, drawing attention to the knife's edge I'm balancing on.

"Well, we should practice that too, right? Not just the seduction part."

"You want to practice being married to me?"

Sweetheart, if it'll get you to sit your ass down, I'd wear tights and recite Shakespeare's sonnets to you.

"That depends." I nod my head toward the fountain. "Married couples sit in gardens and admire the flowers, don't they?"

"I supposed they do."

"Come sit, Dessy. Please." I offer my hand, and she slips her palm over mine, letting me lead her to the ledge.

Settling onto the brick platform, she exhales, and the tension in her shoulders dissipates. Good.

"You're going to have to come up with a different nickname for when we're married. 'Dessy's' a weird thing to call Lydia Bennet."

"I figured I'd just go with something simple like 'my wife.'" I shrug. "Is that okay?"

"Oh, yeah. Fine," Aulie says in a rushed manner. There's a decided shift in her posture at the question, as if she's suddenly being pulled taut like a rubber band. She doesn't meet my stare, as her knee bounces wildly up and down. I put my hand on top of it to hopefully calm her down.

"If that's too much for you or stupid or something, we can think of something else."

"My wife is fine—if that's what you wanted," she says, her voice an octave higher than usual. She clears her throat. "Totally chill with it."

"Right, so you're not looking at me because..."

"This garden is beautiful this time of the year, you know? I just love how they showcase—"

"The marigolds and daisies. We've visited that topic already. Aulie, what's going on?"

The breeze blows her caramel hair in tiny wisps around her face while she shakes her head. Her hand slides over mine, still resting on her knee. "Nothing is wrong. I just—it's funny, thinking of being married to you."

I resist the urge to frown. "Thanks."

"Could you imagine how sick of me you'd get? I'd probably drive you away in two seconds."

"You'd be running from me in one," I mutter, trying to hide my frustration. Although I'm not ready for anything serious, the thought of waking up to Aulie every day and sharing quiet nights with her by the fire is tempting.

It's everything I could ever dream of.

And nothing I deserve.

"Oh, I don't know. It'd take at least five seconds to look at you and another ten for the mental victory lap that I'd tricked you into marrying me."

Wait. What?

My eyes snap to focus on her face, and Aulie recoils in horror, her hand covering her mouth with a gasp.

I'm comfortable enough in my skin to say that most people consider me conventionally attractive. There's a reason a soap company put me in an ad about playing dirty and getting clean with my naked torso covered in suds. But I've never dared include Aulie in that grouping.

"I didn't—that—that came out wrong," Aulie finally manages through her hand.

"Did it?" I cock my head, shifting my leg closer so it bumps against hers.

"Obviously. Because why would I think that?" She scoffs. "You're like my brother—ew. Honestly, we should forget the whole marriage thing. Maybe we won't touch at all. People will be so into their fried dough they won't even care." Aulie's cheeks bloom with a shade of pink so gorgeous none of the flowers in this garden can compare.

Interesting.

Shamelessly, I graze my fingers over my bottom lip pretending I'm lost in thought. It's a move Grady taught me when we started going out to bars together. He said it draws attention to the mouth, and I can usually gauge someone's interest from their reaction.

Aulie's eyes flick down to my lips. Desire colors her expression with a sultry hue I've desperately waited five years to see her wear.

Brother, my ass, you little liar.

"Nah, neither of us does anything half-assed. Let's not start now." I turn toward her, a new dare in my stare. "Unless you're worried you'll fall in love with me."

"What? Get out of here." She laughs. It's tinged with discomfort as if I've stumbled upon something that she doesn't want me to discover.

And like hell am I going to let this go.

"I don't know. Running away with me could be tricky if you're already doing mental victory laps over marrying me."

"I know this is hard for you to believe, considering your massive ego, but I can consider you attractive and you still not be my type." She gently pats my face, and I catch her wrist.

The hope swelling in my heart shrivels away to nothing. A dark heaviness hangs where the delicious feeling of possibility rose just a few moments ago, and I stamp the sensation down, burying it in my feelings graveyard.

Not wanting to dwell, I say a quick eulogy and turn my attention to flustering Aulie instead.

"I guess you're just going to have to prove it, or I'll have no other option but to think you're already madly in love with me and afraid I'll find out," I say. A teasing grin spreads across my lips, eliciting an eye roll from her. "It'll make our friendship weird, sure, but I'll overcome your massive feelings for me, eventually."

"Maybe I'm just worried you'll vomit on me again. Ever think of that?"

Touché.

"Pretty sober if you want to test it out."

"Fine." She huffs, turning to me. "If you want a silly little wife so bad, then I'm yours. Now do what you will with me, Mr. Wickham, for you've already well and truly ruined me." She says the last sentence with a dramatic flair, resting her hand on my chest. Right on the spot that's hers.

My throat bobs as the heat of her palm seeps through and becomes one with the ink resting beneath my shirt.

With a small smirk and a raised eyebrow, she silently dares me to follow through, as if she knows I'm all talk and no game.

My competitive side kicks in. There's no way I can let that look slide.

"Mine, huh?" My arm wraps around her waist. With a growl, I pull her into me. Her breath hitches, and her eyes widen as her body molds to mine. Delicately, my fingers trace the shape of her jaw. A hushed reverie overcomes me. "*My* wife." The words slip out, but I don't have the wherewithal to regret them. It's intoxicating to hold her like this and imagine it's real. I'll be chasing this high forever.

We're suspended in time, our lips mere centimeters apart, and the following second stretches into eternity. The temptation to taste her overwhelms any other want or need I could have, but I've gotten the impression that we're playing a game of chess, and it's not my move.

"Mr. Wickham, are you—" Her mouth pulls toward mine, and her breath grows ragged. But she remains restrained, never letting our lips brush. "Are you going to kiss me anytime soon?"

"Do you want that, my dearest?" I press a kiss to the corner of her mouth, enjoying her struggle to stay composed. Maybe her attraction will be enough to satisfy me for now. At least, it's something.

"It seems rather improper to leave my lips so out in the cold like this. I fear they shall be plagued with consumption shortly and wither away."

"Well, we wouldn't want that." Lightly, I brush my mouth against hers. It's a gentle caress when I want so much more. "They're far too lovely for an untimely death."

With a tender touch, I glide my palm across her cheek and weave my fingers through her hair. With a slight slant of my mouth, I capture her ragged breath.

The eagerness in Aulie's kiss is so unexpected and intense that it leaves me momentarily stunned. Hungrily, her tongue slides across the seam of my lips, taking me with a fiery possession. Heat courses through my veins as she slowly melts the steel cage around my heart with every pass of her mouth against mine.

My brain jumbles into an incoherent mess, trying to catch up. I've wanted Aulie for so long, wanted to tangle my hand in her hair and pull her close, but now that she's here, in my arms, I can't shake the feeling that "want" isn't the right word anymore.

I *wanted* Aulie when I saw her caramel hair barreled in curls, tumbling along her back. I *wanted* Aulie when she was warm and dry in my pajamas the day I pulled her from the fountain. I've *wanted* Aulie and her starry-stare, gently freckled nose, and soft-pouty lips every second of every day for the past five years.

But lying in the weeds of wanting, something else slowly crept in.

Maybe it was her sweetness or her kindness. Maybe it was all the teasing and banter. Maybe it's that she has the most gorgeous heart I've ever known. Maybe it's that I feel more comfortable with her than any other human on this earth. Or a combination of all these things, that have led to her soul being a treasure I'd travel to the ends of the earth to uncover.

Whatever the reason.

I haven't just wanted Aulie for a while now.

I've loved her.

Desperately.

And knowing that, realizing that now, as I drink in the sweetness of her lips and develop a severe sweet tooth, I don't know if I'm emotionally prepared to handle that revelation.

A small moan escapes her as her hands travel under my shirt. The want on her end, mixed with my revelation, surprises me, and I lose my balance.

At some point in the last minute of kissing, I shifted my sitting position, and now I'm on the fountain's ledge. I wobble, trying not to pull away and ruin the moment. Who knows if I'll ever get the chance to kiss Aulie again?

Aulie nips at my bottom lip in a slow drag that's far less innocent than I expected from her. My heart leaps in my chest, and the force propels my entire body backward. My wobble on the ledge becomes an all-out tumble, and I fall over, splashing into the pool of the fountain. Frigid waters soak my chest, before a delicate body collapses on top of me and a secondary wave threatens to drown us both in the shallow pool.

Aulie' chest heaves against mine. Her mouth falls into a shocked "o" as droplets fall from her thick, hooded eyelashes. Hell, she is gorgeous. My lungs seize. Whether my lack of oxygen is a result of our kiss or the shock of the icy water spilling all over us, I can't tell.

"I uhm—" She quivers, and I tighten my hold on the small of her back. Her eyes flash to my lips again, and for a second a hope burns deep in my chest that she's about to lean in for round two. "I—think that's enough practice for today. Good job." She pats my chest with chattering teeth. "I have a change of clothes—I'm going to—yup." She pushes herself up out of the fountain. "You're good for today. You can go home now if you want to. Bye," she says frantically, hurrying away.

"Bye?" I manage as she lightnings out of the garden, dripping wet, and I'm left wanting everything we almost had. Even if it selfish. Even if I'm nothing like the dream guy on her list.

Shit. This is going to be a problem.

～

I LOVE HER.

Splashing my face in the bathroom mirror, the thought that's looped in my mind for the last twenty-four hours continues to scream past my skull.

The tattoo spiraled across my chest, the one about *her,* laughs at me like "no shit, fucker."

I pull my shirt over my body, trying to silence the ink that was a late-night, too-drunk-to-function decision.

My muscles scream with the stretch. I overdid it at morning skate, trying to get that kiss out of my head.

I should have figured out that I was in love with Aulie before this—but saying she ripped out and possessed my heart years ago is different than saying I'd willingly rip it out for her if she asked, and I've never wanted to dwell on how completely gone I am for her.

Because if I'm gone for her, I'm still capable of feeling—both the good and bad, and I have zero interest in feeling the miserable stuff again. Numb has always been my preferred sensation.

Numb is just about the opposite of what I felt yesterday when Aulie filled my hollow chest with every pass of her lips.

Shoving my phone in my pocket, I walk into the living room, ready to head out the door for dance lessons. Not an activity I'm particularly looking forward to, but I'm willing to give it a chance if gives me another excuse to be near Dessy.

Unfortunately, she needs to run rehearsals so Sabrina will be my partner today, but Aulie will dance with me on fair days.

I should be grateful I get to give my heart a break from all the cardio, but something about losing another chance to have her body pressed against mine is disappointing.

In the living room, Simone is sitting in a chair, soaking in the early morning sun and folding laundry. "So, are you going to explain why you came home soggy yesterday?"

"I uhm." I flex my hand at my side to keep it from rising to my lips and tracing the phantom tingling sensation that's lived there ever since Aulie's mouth left mine. "I lost a game of chicken."

Simone clucks her tongue. "I heard the chicken got pretty wet, too."

"How?"

"Aulie picked up Lucy after school like she usually does on Tuesdays, and Luce said that Aulie was soaked. Said she fell at work and left her change of clothes at home. I put two and two together."

"Why was Aulie picking Lucy up? She's too busy. I could have done that."

"And deny Lucy her big sister time? Oh, no. You don't want to be on the end of that ire."

I tilt my head to the side. "She's still doing that?"

"No way I could separate Luce from her." Simone shakes her head.

Since I started returning to Chawton Falls regularly, Aulie's bond with my family has only grown. Luce, in particular, became overly attached. When she was seven, she threw a massive tantrum when it was time for me to head back to Boston for the start of the season because it meant she wouldn't see Aulie for another few months. Aulie promised she'd take Lucy out for ice cream alone, and Lucy screamed, "Like big sister time?" It was a sweet gesture, but that was four years ago. I didn't know that was something she was still doing.

I rake a hand through my hair. Yeah, this new information will not help me squash my feelings for her. "I'll have to thank her."

"You know, Aulie's just about as pretty as she is nice." Simone flashes a smile, folding a tiny onesie.

"Really? Hadn't noticed." I shrug with a nonchalance that would earn me an Oscar if the Academy was watching.

"So you're helping with this fair for no reason besides the goodness of your heart."

"You told me to use my position to help others. Well, here I am, helping."

"Uh-huh, okay." Simone smirks, folding a small pair of pants with Baby Yoda printed on them. "So, the puppy dog eyes you set on her all summer?"

"I was high on painkillers. I would have looked at Grady like that, too," I grump, putting on shoes that wouldn't be as heavy as yesterday's work boots.

Boots probably weren't great for ballroom dancing.

Now there's a thought that the bad boy of the NHL probably shouldn't have. Lord, what kind of hold does this woman have on me that I'm over-analyzing my footwear and getting ready for dance rehearsals?

I swear, this woman owns every ounce of me. She's unearthed the ugliest parts—the ones that haven't seen the light of day in years—and now, whether she wants them or not, they're hers.

Chapter Nineteen

Aulie Desfleurs

Play: *Sway by Rosemary Clooney*

My wife. Jack's fingers delicately glide over my jaw in a phantom memory. It's been four days since his lips brushed against mine, and I returned his gentle caress with a hungry possession. Four days, and still, his touch, coupled with his gaze of adoration as he grazed my skin, is all I can think about.

This distraction isn't appreciated considering it's opening day for the fair. There are a million and one things that require my attention—the fairground maps, character jobs, sign-in sheets, and ticket sales—and currently, they're all drowned out by the syrupy rasp of Jack's voice as he held me tightly.

A sharp pain catches my left side. Oh heck. Good to know that still cuts through everything else.

Dr. Murdoch suggested that since the pain is mental, I'd be fine if I found something to distract me. Now, I can't help but think he's wrong if Jack Parker's lips aren't enough to overcome my hypochondriac tendencies.

"Why don't you get changed and put your feet up for a second?" Emy nods in my direction. "I can go to the barn and update Mr. Martin on our change of plans."

We just finished a walk-through and made sure that the third-floor ballroom in Wentworth Mansion is ready to hold all the ticketed spectators for the dance lesson and exposition at two o'clock.

We're inspecting the horse-drawn carriages next, but today is unseasonably warm for the first week of October. I'm uncomfortable asking the horses to walk around the fairgrounds, so we'll have them in their stables, with plenty of treats for guests to feed them. The carriages will sit outside the barn for kids to play and take pictures in. I'm sure Emy can handle telling Mr. Martin herself, but there's still a part of me that can't let go.

"Nah, I'm fine. I can handle a little more walking," I say. Another cramp shoots down my left leg, and I stumble, hastily regaining composure before Emy notices.

Emy sighs. "Pumpkin, I can handle Mr. Martin. I'm serious. You have a big day ahead of you flirting with a gorgeous man so in love with you it's disgusting. Please take a second. All your hard work has paid off. We're good. We're ready."

My cheeks heat, and *my wife* loops again in my brain. I didn't think Jack would be this good of an actor, but the only other explanation is that he harbors *some* feelings for me. I can't figure out which of the two is more plausible. At the very least, Emy's wrong about the magnitude. There's no way he's in love with me.

Jack's never been in love with anyone. And if there were ever going to be someone who could earn that kind of affection, it would be someone like Veronica Burke. Not me.

Another spasm grips my stomach, and I double over with a shriek, the intensity catching me off-guard.

Emy opens her mouth to order me back to the tent, and I wave her off. "I'm going. I'm going. You're the best. I love you. Thank you. Oh—also—" I pause my retreat down the hill. "Speaking of pumpkins, can you—"

"I already checked with Mr. Martin yesterday about the pumpkin patch. He's having his son Robert bring them by and set them up in the next hour, and his wife will put all the tools for carving on the tables like she did last year. She even figured out how to do silhouettes, so don't worry. We've got this, all of us."

I nod. I should be thankful that the fair is self-sufficient this many years in that other people can lend a hand, and that it runs just as smoothly. But there's a weird feeling creeping in my chest, whispering that I'm replaceable.

Who wants someone who always thinks they're in pain working for them when they could have someone without those complications? What else do I bring to the table? Nothing.

With heavy thoughts about my expendability, I stroll down the hill at the back of the mansion leading to the cast tent and admire the fair unfolding to the left in the rising morning light. Sitting on seventy acres of land, the Wentworth Mansion is the perfect spot to hold an event of this scale.

A Ferris Wheel stands proudly among the rides. The multi-colored seats sway in the breeze, the sun catching off the acrylic chipped paint. Hopefully, I'll have time to ride it later and see the fair from the bird's eye. I've been too busy the last few years, but maybe with Emy assisting me, I can let go for once—at least, there's a silver lining in learning I'm superfluous.

Besides the Ferris Wheel, the glint of the gilded carousel sparkles in all its turn-of-the-century glory, and a few other rides that are new this year. Bridget coordinated most of that side of the fair, so I'm not entirely sure what shrieks and thrills rest over there, but I'm excited to wander later.

Next to the rides and games are the booths and stalls. Pastel-colored bunting blows in the breeze from above a handful of shops, selling everything from hats, fans, books, jewelry, Jane Austen-themed t-shirts and sweatshirts, and art.

The breeze picks up, blowing wisps out of my updo and wrapping them around my face. The heavy scent of fried everything follows along the wings of the wind, and I stop and inhale the melding aromas. Apples, cinnamon, fried dough, everything good and fall, kiss my nostrils, and I happily sigh.

As great as the fear was that this wouldn't come together, we did it.

~

WITH A WICKER PICNIC BASKET HANGING ON MY ARM AND A rumbling stomach, I trudge up the hill, following my fellow sisters, Jane, Elizabeth, Mary, and Kitty, to a bare patch of grass. It's the designated picnic area, abutting the "gothic ruins" that we take full advantage of during *Northanger Abbey* weekend on Halloween.

We're due for a "luncheon with the characters" in its shadows, where fairgoers are invited to bring their fried food findings to the grassy knoll and interact with us. We sit in the middle, chatting about everything and nothing, while Wickham flirts with Elizabeth, and Mr. Bingley and Mr. Darcy stumble across us about halfway through. Mr. Bingley will have his heart and soul laser-focused on Jane. At the same time, Mr. Darcy and Wickham have a tense interaction.

As the two gentlemen depart, they will loudly invite us to a ball, giving the gathered crowd one last opportunity to purchase tickets for the dance lessons and ball that will shortly follow.

After spending the morning walking around the fairgrounds, including a long stroll through the stalls and booths with my sisters pretending to want absolutely everything, I'm looking forward to sitting down and resting my legs. Who knew playing Lydia would be so exhausting? She's on twenty-four-seven.

As we make our way to our picnic destination, Cassie-as-Kitty huddles into my arm with a bright smile on her face. It's easier to act like her silly little sister with her sparkling personality to play off of. "Have you seen your officer yet?" she whispers with a giggle.

"I have no clue who you're talking about." I stick my nose up in the air. I've tried my best not to think about Jack in the first few hours of the fair because thinking would lead to me looking for his presence, and Lydia wouldn't have her head on a swivel for him, not yet.

"I caught a peek while he was getting ready. His shoulders fill that jacket out better than Callen's. I didn't even know that was possible. And oh my god, his butt in those pants."

Ahead of us, Bridget's auburn hair sparkles in the sun. She's far too striking and fierce to play the role of the sister who, by all accounts, is supposed to be rather plain, so we tried to dull her down in a grey cotton dress.

We failed. She's still spectacular.

"What are you two talking about?" she calls over her shoulder, gathering her skirt as we march up an incline.

"The officers," Cassie-as-Kitty says.

"Oh yes, I heard a rumor they were gathered not too far from here. You two best behave."

"Never." Cassie continues to giggle. "I am determined to be the most incorrigible flirt. What about you, sister?" She leans in with a conspiring gleam in her eye.

I hesitate. Shaking off the rust and matching my castmates isn't going as naturally as I hoped. Given my enthusiasm for acting in my youth, I thought it would be something I could slip back into, like a second skin or riding a bike. But I'm finding something heavy holding me back from fully leaning into the character.

I've spent so long actively killing the part of me that resembled Lydia, and now, trying to resurrect it in its complete form feels impossible.

Sure, I've seen winks of it the past few days, but pulling it out is like trying to complete a puzzle that's missing half of its pieces.

A tall figure blocks our path, obscuring the rays of the sun. "Yours, I believe." A voice with a subtle British lilt sounds from the shadowy figure extending a handkerchief to Chloe-as-Elizabeth. My heart skips an irrational beat.

It's Jack.

But it's not. When my feet halt and my eyes adjust, the man standing before me is someone entirely new.

With a smooth, shaven face I haven't seen in years, Jack looks younger and more like a wolf in sheep's clothing than the wolf himself.

His red wool jacket sits tight, pulling across his broad shoulders. The brass buckles that adorn his chest wink in the shining light, and I drag my eyes down and away over white wool breeches that, uhm—

Oh, look at those black gaiters. Those are some nice gaiters.

My traitorous gaze refuses to be content with feasting on his boots and pulls north to his pants again, which hug his thick thighs in a way that's somehow more deadly than the peek the penalty box picture supplied.

Bridget steps back, brushing against my shoulder and whispering into my ear, "His appearance was greatly in his favor; he had all the best part of beauty, a fine countenance, a good figure, and a very pleasing address."

"Huh?" I blink back to reality.

"It's a line from *P&P*."

"Do you have the whole book memorized?" I whisper, arching a brow and telling my mouth to close.

It doesn't.

I fear it will be stuck in the openly gawking position until the end of days now.

She shrugs. "I might have a photographic memory."

"Oh well, that's impressive."

"My sister, Lydia." Chloe-as-Elizabeth's voice cuts through my stupor.

"Pleasure." The red-coated gentleman I vaguely register as Jack, my best friend, reaches out for my hand. I extend it, and mischief sparkles in his gaze as his lips press against my skin.

Suddenly, all the pieces I've been missing to complete the Lydia Bennet puzzle make themselves known. The sound of my own ridiculous giggle echoes through me as a swarm of butterflies flutters in my gut.

If every officer looked this stunning, then at least half of Lydia's foolishness makes sense now.

Jack's stare rests on my face like he's trying to parse something out.

"Hi," I whisper, my brain utterly devoid of any other word in the English language this close to him.

"Hello, pet." He winks.

"Mr. Wickham, are you coming?" Chloe asks, exasperation in her tone. And I find myself at war with how I feel about her reaction because I completely understand. I promised her a luncheon where a professional hockey player wearing *this outfit* flirts with her for the entire event. If I were in her shoes, I'd be impatient, too. Nothing like this ever happens in Chawton Falls.

But there's an ugly part of me I didn't know existed that wants to growl "mine" at her, take Jack's arm, and run away for real.

I'm supposed to be silly. I get it. But that's probably taking this whole thing too far.

Ultimately, I know I need to be a team player and do what's best for the fair and well—boo because that's the far more torturous option.

With a sigh, I pull my hand away from Jack's grasp. "You need to be giving Chloe all the attention right now. The thicker, the better," I whisper.

"Are you sure we can't deviate from the story?" he asks with a teasing grin, and everything inside of me wants to shout, *Oh, god, yes, we could do that this one time.*

"Patience, Mr. Wickham, I promise you'll be married to me soon enough." I flutter my eyelashes. "And then you'll be stuck with me for the rest of the day and regret our nuptials entirely."

Fingering a loose curl resting on my cheek, he gazes softly and almost longingly at me. "If I was lucky enough to marry you, the only thing I'd ever regret is that you deserve better than someone like me." A smile tugs at the corner of his lips. He pivots on his gaiters, his hands tucked behind his back, and approaches Chloe with a charming smile.

And I'm left wondering who was talking, the playboy best friend or the selfish-manipulative rake he's playing.

Either way, it was incredibly out of character.

~

MY AUNT CAMILLE BROUGHT ME TO THE WENTWORTH Ballroom for the first time when I was five. It stole my heart and breath away, and I haven't been the same since. My Memere was anxious that I was too young to handle staying still in a place full of many breakable, irreplaceable things. Still, after begging day after day on our drive home from mass to see the inside of the imposing mansion on the hill, my Memere finally relented.

She wouldn't be the one to take me, though. Her nerves couldn't handle it.

So Aunt Camille, a marvelous woman who had once paraded down our staircase in a long red dress for dinner (before promptly tumbling down the final three, getting up, and gliding to the table), took me.

We put on our finest clothes for the visit. Looking back, I think she knew me well enough to realize that if she dressed me like a lady, I'd feel inclined to act like one. And I walked the halls of the Wentworth Mansion, home to the last British governor of New Hampshire, totally enraptured by the Georgian architecture, French landscape wallpapers, and ornate woodwork.

I stood under the crystal chandeliers that still hang in the ballroom, twirling in my pink sparkly dress and admiring how the light hit my skirt as it flared out. Aunt Camille gathered me up, leading me around the polished hardwood floor and teaching me the first few steps of a simple waltz.

"Someday, Alouette, you'll find someone who will sweep you off your feet. Some people in this family think it's a curse how easily we give our hearts away, but promise me you won't let that part fade. There's no kind of life to live without love, and you've been blessed to love to extremes that other people never will. Revel in it, my love, but make sure you only give your heart to someone willing to match you, piece for piece, in sharing their heart right back. There's no greater pain than an unrequited love, and you're worth a good worship. You always will be." She winked, twirling me as my gaze admired the ceiling decked with teals and yellow.

"How will I know if he'll love me back?" I asked.

"He'll tell you, more than just with cheap words, but with his glances and actions."

"What kind of things will he do?" At five years old, I was already a hopeless romantic, waiting for my Prince Eric or Phillip to come and waltz me away. Princes who vanquished dragons and... well, I'm not entirely sure what Eric did, but he was handsome and had a dog named Max and a fancy boat. Which was cool.

Aunt Camille smiled softly at me, "He'll do the things that don't come naturally to him just to make you happy."

"Is that what Uncle Guy did for you? Is that how you knew?"

"Every day, love. He reminded me every day."

"Lydia, the dance—" A tug on my arm brings me standing fully in the ballroom and glancing at Bridget's perfect eyebrows. I wipe my cheek. I didn't have crying on my bingo card today, but that's the thing about grief. Something that should be safe—like a room I've entered at least a thousand times since I was five—will suddenly unlock a memory, like ballroom dancing with an aunt you love and miss more than life itself. That's all it takes for the hole to open up in your chest and grief to flood your body, settling more heavily on your limbs than you're used to carrying around daily.

"Go find one of the closed-off rooms and take a beat. I can fill in," Bridget whispers. Mary dancing would be *Pride and Prejudice* heresy, yet the same woman who just sent me halfway across the state for a time period-appropriate umbrella—okay, I did that to myself—is offering to commit blasphemy *for me*.

A huge part of me knows I should disregard Bridget's offer. I should push through and join the dancing group—be a team player at all costs. Lydia's supposed to dance the entire night with multiple partners and look like an absolute fool. It's one reason that Mr. Darcy finds the Bennet family so inferior in their behaviors.

And no one will care. You're torturing yourself for nothing.

The thought crystalizes, and I remember how I felt when we ran into Tyler. I desperately wanted to do the kind, dependable thing and help wipe down his shirt, even though it felt oddly wrong. Like sometimes, the right thing is actually being a little selfish, and maybe what I think is selfish isn't that selfish at all.

I swipe at another tear, glancing briefly at Jack who is hovering in a corner out of character. Wickham doesn't come to this ball; it's part of why Darcy and Elizabeth fight. But since our aim is to involve every cast member, he's wearing formal attire, including knee breeches, a white shirt, and a navy tailcoat.

He's been marvelous today. Although his British accent needs work, he's still trying, and I couldn't be more grateful for him.

A cloud outside breaks, and the sun falls on his dark curls, catching the lighter streaks. My heart drums in my chest, and sweat coats my palms.

Again, the words *my wife* become a dangerous earworm in my mind. I'm supposed to dance with Jack after the first song, and after the reaction to his lips against my hand, I don't know how I will handle that.

He smiles lightly, but then his brow furrows, and he mouths, "Are you okay?"

My eyes grab his lower lip, and I drag my teeth across mine.

You love him. The thought pierces my heart like the ill-timed arrow it truly is.

I shake my head. No, I can't do this. Not now. Aunt Camille told me to give my heart to someone who could match me, and I gave it to the one man incapable of ever sharing his back, the one man I have no shot in hell with. What's worse, I gave it to a man that freaks out and leaves when women get too serious. I've lost too many people in my life to navigate that.

I won't be strong enough to handle another heartbreak.

So, I do the only logical thing in this situation. I thank Bridget for her offer, and then I turn around and run.

My feet patter down the long hallway, through a pair of grand doors into the parlor decked with green pastured wallpaper.

I pace with my hands on my hips, tears threatening to break through again. Everything is a mess. How could I have fallen for Jack Parker? What the hell was I thinking?

The swinging doors bust open, and I jump. Jack stands, gasping. "Jesus, Dessy, you're fast."

Alyssa's fingers flying over the ivory keys waft in through the oak barrier.

"What are you doing here?" I all but shriek. "You should be dancing."

"No one is going to miss my two left feet, trust me." He rolls his eyes. "What's going on with you?"

I just realized that I'm in love with you. "Nothing."

"So you just sprinted from the ballroom for fun?" He shifts toward me, and I step back on my heel.

"Thought I'd spice up the storyline." I laugh nervously.

"You know we could speed it up. I think people finding us here would be pretty risque, right?"

"Sure, but then we'd ruin the game, and who would really—" Jack puts a hand around my waist and pulls me against him. "What are you doing?" I ask in a breathless daze.

"What my dad used to do when my mom was upset. Sway with me, Dessy. It'll relax you." Gently, he grabs my hand and guides it to his chest. For whatever reason, all the chaos and panic spiraling inside calms. As long as we're touching, as long as we're close, I will be okay, even if it's the last thing we should be doing.

"Better?" he asks, adjusting his grip on my waist and tugging me tighter against him. Slowly, he moves his hips. This isn't close to a proper Regency dance, but it's exactly what I need.

"Yeah." I breathe in, resting my head on his shoulder. "Thank you for everything. I appreciate how seriously you've taken today. It means a lot to me."

"Whatever makes you happy, Dessy. You know I'd do anything for you," he whispers as the soft piano music from the other room accompanies us. It's a classical piano version of "Yellow" by Coldplay. Alyssa's been into playing modern songs like that since *Bridgerton,* and people seem to like it better than going full-on classical.

I let myself collapse into Jack's hold, swaying on the antique rug in the parlor. Everything is quiet for a second; my heart settles close to its owner, and I bask in the glow of the perfect moment.

"Thank you for being my friend," I say, to remind myself that this right here is more than enough. I should be happy with the now. "I don't know what I'd do without you."

Jack clears his throat. "Anytime, pal."

Chapter Twenty

Aulie Desfleurs

Play: *Then He Kissed Me by the Crystals*

"You're such a silly little thing." Sabrina-as-Caroline Bingley flashes me a condescending grin, towering over me on the hill in her yellow silk gown. The terrible part of me hates how well she can pull off the high-waistline and puffed sleeve look, but Sabrina is the picture of regency elegance. Even I have to admit that. Apparently, she's still going with her belittle me as much as possible strategy today, too, the second day of the fair.

It's fitting, given that Caroline is supposed to be a snooty woman with aristocratic airs, but I can't shake the feeling that there's more behind her characters' interactions.

It shouldn't bother me, not as much as it is, anyway. Lydia is a silly character, so mission accomplished. Still, something about that name makes me feel like a failure.

Letting Lydia out to play near Jack was a bad idea. He's the only one who could have me fumbling around a fountain basin, desperate to keep kissing him instead of dashing away like I knew I should.

Falling in love.

My fingers rub over the printed cotton of my white-country dress. Evening my breaths, I let a giggle pass my lips. It's the actor filler I've gone with when I have no clue what to do or say. Yesterday, it was an effective fallback—so I'm hoping today it'll do similarly.

"Yes, very silly." Sophie-as-Lousia Hurst nods. The ribbon tied atop her high-brimmed bonnet blows in the wind. The breeze is welcome after another warm day. I *should* shed my pelisse, but I'm worried it's obscuring some severe sweat stains, so I'll have to suffer for a few more hours.

Sophie, unlike Sabrina, is just about the most likable human you will ever meet, so her words lack the venom that Sabrina supplied.

My lips twist into a small smile. True, I was rustier than I imagined yesterday with my improv, but today, slipping into the dress and putting on Lydia's persona like a mask feels far more natural. "You may think what you'd like, but I'd prefer to be silly while soaking in the joys of life than constantly turning my nose up at people. Your time at the ball looked miserable while I danced with officers!" I say, skipping around the two and letting the handful of ribbons in my clutches dance in the breeze.

A few fairgoers stop and snap photos of our interaction. The crowd is a welcome sight since Sabrina and Sophie are scheduled to give a tour of the house soon.

Sabrina rolls her eyes and links her arms with Sophie. "Sister, I think it's time to retire inside the house. The company out here feels far too close to producing a piglet and making us chase it."

Women clad in t-shirts that say things like "Half agony, half hope" and "What would Jane do?" laugh at Sabrina's snark. She pivots on her heel with her nose turned up. "If anyone of status would like a tour of our fabulous home, we'll be inside where our perfect complexions can remain undamaged by the sun." Her eyes fall on me once more. "I fear it's too late to hide for some people, though."

Scrunching my nose, I stick my tongue out to emphasize my maturity. I like my freckles.

After encouraging the crowd to join the tour, I bounce down the hill to the tent. Sabrina and Sophie have everything at the mansion under control, and Lizzie is visiting Charlotte at Rosings on the stage, so now is an excellent time for me to take a break.

And some ibuprofen.

Unlacing my bonnet, I sigh, entering the tent. Blake-as-Mrs. Bennet is lounging on the couch, their hair wrapped in a white linen mobcap. I'm surprised to see them here since most of the day they run around the fairgrounds attacking random attendees with news about Jane's impending advantageous marriage to Mr. Bingley, saying things like "Five thousand pounds a year! Can you believe it? Oh, they will make a most handsome couple. And rich, to be sure!"

They grin. "There's my favorite daughter."

"Oh, hi, Mama," I reply, opening the cooler full of water. The ice has melted, and I wipe off the condensation.

"Is it almost time to be ruined?"

"I fear it so." Heat pricks my cheeks, recalling Jack's body pressed against mine in the barn yesterday during our game of hide-and-seek. His eyes were dark and dangerous, tracing the edge of my lips. He just had to dip his head and— "Have you seen the first aid kit?" I clear my throat.

"It's over by the muffins. Gio escaped the petting zoo, and our poor Mr. Wickham scraped his knee in a mad dash to get away. It was quite the sight watching a large man in military regalia scramble. Apparently, he's not a goat person."

"He's not a Gio person, that's for sure. Was it anything serious?" I shake my head, trying to bite down the smile threatening to erupt on my face at the image Blake painted. I feel terrible that Jack got injured, but as long as it wasn't anything serious—I mean, how many grown men have laid Jack out as part of his job, but it's the goat that gets him?

"Nothing more than a minor scrape. I think most of the damage was mental. If you're looking for the kit—how are you feeling?"

"I'm fine, just sore. All that walking," I say, locating the white plastic caddy with all the medical supplies players should require. I'm unsure if the pain in my abdomen radiating down my leg is really just because I'm sore, especially because other characters have to walk up and down the hill way more than me, and they seem fine. Still, I'm lacking any further explanation for the cramps plaguing me.

Emptying two white pills into my hand, I tip my head back and swallow them. Blake motions for me and points to the ground, and I nod, unbuttoning my pelisse and finally shedding the unnecessary layer.

Sitting in front of them, Blake's thumbs dig into my shoulders, and I sigh as tension floats away.

"How's the Jack Parker situation?" Blake asks. My posture straightens, and they laugh. "That good, huh?"

"I may have caught some unfortunate intense feelings." I swallow. I haven't admitted that fact to anyone, but there's no use trying to hide it from Blake. We've known each other too long and shared too many intimate moments in the theater to sneak anything past one another. "But it doesn't matter. He's only here for a few more weeks and doesn't date during the season. Plus, he's that—" I gesture vaguely toward the tent's entrance. "And I'm not compliment-seeking here, but I'm very aware that I'm not in the same league as him, and that's okay. I'm not supposed to be."

"Oh, come on, you could give Veronica Burke a run for her money."

Now that's a good joke. I throw my head back and let out a hearty laugh. "I don't need any false affirmations, Blake. I'm at peace with being the country-bumpkin best friend to the superstar athlete. It's where I belong."

"You're not giving yourself enough credit." Blake shakes their head, digging their thumbs under my shoulder blades. "Veronica has a team of people making sure she always looks flawless. You do that naturally."

"Oh yeah, sure." I snort.

"Plus, you're smart, kind, and real. Can Veronica say that?"

"She does a lot of charity work."

"I'm sure she does." I can hear the sarcasm in Blake's tone.

"What do you have against Veronica Burke?" I ask.

"Nothing. She's just making a dear friend think less of themselves, and I don't like it." Blake pats my back. "Remind me to get your back again after the fair. You're too tight. But I've got to get ready to start screaming wildly around the fairground that we're all ruined."

Standing, I crack my neck a few times, feeling far more relaxed than I did entering the tent. "I'll take you up on that. Sorry for the panic I'm about to cause, Mama, but I'm sure you'd have done similarly if you were in my position."

"I definitely would have let Wickham whisper sweet nothings in my ear, my dear. You're right. Oh, shit, Aulie?" Blake furrows a brow, glancing at me. "You've ugh—" They clear their throat.

"What? I've what?"

They rub the back of their neck. "You have something on your...butt."

"Is it dirt?" I ask, inspecting the fabric at the back of my skirt. A crimson stain catches my attention, and my heart drops to my stomach. That's not dirt.

I'm not supposed to have my period for another week. What the heck!

"The birth control," I groan. "Emy warned me the first few months would make me wonky. Thank you for letting me know, though. You're a lifesaver." I press a kiss to their cheek. "Now go bring the house down with your panic-ridden screams, Mama."

I rush over to the rack of dresses I keep in the tent for all the characters just in case something like this happens.

"Do you need help changing?" Blake asks.

I do, but they're running late for their moment to shine. "Jack should be here soon. I'll have him help."

"What am I helping with?" a deep, rich voice asks.

"Well, that's my cue." Blake chuckles, patting Jack's shoulder on the way out. "I'm sure you'll take care of our girl just fine."

I turn to face Jack as Blake breaks through the tent flaps and meanders to the fairgrounds. A familiar shriek follows shortly after.

"I need you to undress me," I say as matter-of-fact as possible, considering the request.

Jack's eyes widen, and a surprised cough rattles his chest. "I'm sorry, you—what?"

"Please, we don't have time for questions. I've got something on my dress, so I need to change into something else, and we need to be as far away from the tent for the search soon."

Jack blinks at me like I'm asking him to do the most unpleasant thing I could ask.

"Oh, for heaven's sake, it's just me, and I'm more clothed under here than you were in that damn photo shoot." I turn my back, giving him access to the zipper.

"You've—seen that?" he asks. His fingers lightly graze my neck, and a shiver works down my spine.

I panic. "Yes. No. Maybe." Slowly, Jack brushes my sleeves off my bare shoulders, and all words in my brain go up in smoke.

The dress falls to the grass with a thud. And I'm left in my underwear, in the tent, with Jack, not having thought this through. Growing up in the theater, I've been in my underwear for quick changes backstage more times than I can count. At first, they were awkward, but I learned to grow comfortable with them and my body eventually. We were like a family in the theater group; our bodies were instruments we used to tell stories together. To make art.

Standing here exposed, it feels like I've finally shed the last of my defenses, and now I'm holding out the heart that's been Jack's for a while, waiting for him to finally claim it.

With a deep breath, I turn to face him. The first aid kit is sitting on the table directly behind him, and I need to grab a pad and put it on in the cast port-a-potty.

His gaze sticks to my face like he's determined not to let it roam any lower, and a pang of misplaced disappointment drops in my stomach.

"I—uhm—I need to—" I motion to the table behind him. "I have to get something from the kit if you'll—" I reach around him. My chest brushes against his arm, and I hear a frustrated exhale over my head.

"Seriously, Dessy. You're killing me here," he says in a clipped tone. "Get whatever you need and get dressed. We're running late."

"Right. Right. Sorry." I don't glance at Jack again, knowing whatever agitated facial expression he's wearing will only make me feel worse. That's not fair to him. I'm the one who put so much pressure on his reaction to me. It's fine that he's not attracted to me, isn't it? I already knew that, more or less, given his actions. The man tried to escape kissing me twice now; once, he vomited, and the second, he plunged into the depths of an icy fountain.

Message received. This crush isn't mutual.

Padded and dressed, I exit the tent, finding Jack leaning against a nearby tree.

The agitation I heard in his voice wears heavily on his face. His lips are twisted into a harsh scowl, and his eyes, hidden by furrowed brows, narrow in anger.

"I'm sorry. Can you zip me up?" I sigh, turning around and exposing my back to him.

Jack's fingers brusquely fall on my lower back, and the zipper meets the top of my shoulder blades in a flash. I'm lucky he didn't catch my skin or my hair in his haste.

"Consider it noted I should make Blake wait and be late next time something like this happens." I ruefully smile at him. "Sorry. That seemed like that was torture for you. I know you're used to seeing—uhm—more attractive women in their underwear than me."

Jack's expression softens a fraction. His hand reaches out and cups my face. "Dessy, if you think that was the fucking problem, then we need to talk later," he says, his eyes moving over my shoulder. "But right now, the search party is way too close to finding us, and Lucas said there was a reporter from the *Chawton Falls Chronicle* looking forward to this game, so we need to run and hide."

"Diana is here?" I ask, snapping my attention to the hill where Lucas-as-Mr. Darcy is leading a group of people. A mop of red hair sparkles in the sun piled high on the woman's head. Diana is one of those people you can pick out of a crowd miles away, and today is no different. I've also been trying to get her to do an article about the fair for years, and she's never actually come. "I wonder why she's come this year—" I turn my attention to Jack. Oh. Right. Mr. Big-League Hockey Player was probably the draw. "This is a wicked big deal! Her event articles gather so much traffic, and maybe if she enjoys herself, it'll help keep attendance up the next few weeks."

My hands quake with excitement, and Jack reaches out to grab one, tugging me out of view. "Then we should probably get a move on, Lydia. I can't ruin you behind the crew tent."

"You could really..." I say as I let him pull me along at a hurried pace. We bob and weave through vendor carts. Fried everything fills the air and makes my mouth water. Oh, a fried Oreo sounds oddly enticing.

"Do you think we could put on a good show for her? Are you feeling up to it?" I ask as he continues dragging me past the food booths. "Your apple crisp smells heavenly this year, Mrs. King," I holler.

Jack swings me around, and my back hits the stone wall of the old ruins on the property. His hands fall next to my head, and he cages me with his body. "How good of a show are you talking because I saw children in that group."

I gulp.

"I don't know. I don't want you to do anything you're uncomfortable with. After I scarred you in the tent, I think it's safe to say I shouldn't be the one taking charge here."

"So you want me to take charge?" he asks a decided gleam that looks dangerously closer to desire than disgust passes through his sapphire gaze.

No, they're not sapphire. They're navy. When have they ever appeared this intense? This foreboding?

"That might be best. I'm sorry, I didn't mean to put you in that position back there. I'm just used to—"

"Shh. You didn't scar me, Aulie. I'm fine. Okay? Now take a second because I hear voices coming, and I'm going to get back into character."

"Right. Character. Back into character." I shake my hands at my side, trying to let my embarrassment slip away. "Okay, we're good. Go."

Suddenly, Jack grips my neck, raising my chin so my eyes connect with his. With one look, he incinerates every nerve ending in my body, and I feel more likely to collapse than the structure behind me.

"Hello, pet," he says, running the pad of his thumb over the lower part of my cheek. Slowly, his grip softens, and he trails a finger over the bare skin of my neck and traces the hollow space north of my collarbone. "Hell, you are beautiful, you know that?" He plays with the edge of my sleeve.

Want pools in between my thighs. His left leg falls just so, placing pressure there as if he senses it. He lowers his mouth to my ear. "Beautiful and *mine*." His teeth find my earlobe. My breath hitches, and he smirks. "Are you regretting leaving a scoundrel like me in charge?" He meets my eyes again, that dangerous gleam growing more potent in his gaze.

The practical side of me that's grown smaller by the day knows I shouldn't be pleased with this situation. I'm nobody's plaything, and Jack isn't serious. He's playing his part—remarkably well.

But after five years of feeling nothing but pain and misery, left for dead with the rest of my family—the fire currently licking me back alive is too good, too addicting to let go of. Maybe what I said to Sabrina earlier holds some truth. Maybe it's time to say to the hell with my good sense and chase some joy for once.

And for Peter Noone's sake, when a wildly attractive hockey player puts on a regency costume that hugs him in all the right places slams me up a dilapidated castle, maybe I'd be a fool *not* to take advantage of the situation.

"You're going to have to do far more than that to shock me, Mr. Wickham."

"What would it take, pet? I owe you after the tent." His nose brushes against my cheek.

"I don't think that reaction is what we're going for."

His lips curve into a dangerous, playful smirk. "I'd argue you misjudged my reaction."

"You were frustrated."

"Yes, would you like me to return the favor?"

"I don't see—"

Jack presses a kiss on the corner of my mouth and mine part with the request for more. "I don't know if I can do a full workup without getting us arrested," he whispers, grazing the edge of my jaw. "But hopefully, you'll understand where my frustrations lay after this."

His finger glides down my arm, leaving a trail of goosebumps in its wake.

He brings his mouth to my cheek, impossibly close, but his lips don't meet my skin like I want them to. Instead, he blows hot air down the nape of my neck.

The pulse between my thighs grows stronger with every *almost*.

I don't just *want* Jack in this moment. I've tipped over the edge into need.

My hand twists into Jack's coat with a slight whine, and he chuckles.

His hand comes up, gripping my ribs, and he runs the pad of his thumb right under my breast. The feel of him, faint over the fabric, isn't enough. I need more of him. More of his mouth on my skin, more of his touch.

"Please—" I whisper without caring how desperate it makes me seem.

Jack's hands move over my body relentlessly as he blows a steady stream of air against my skin and ignores my pleas to put me out of my misery.

"Jack, I need—"

A throat clears nearby, and suddenly, my senses flood back. The man tormenting me isn't Jack. It's George Wickham, putting on a show for the people that have gathered for my ruining.

It's a ruining that went way too far. We just needed to kiss. Chastely. That was all.

Instead, I've shocked a small family of five, the mother with her hair concealed behind a Badgers baseball cap, pauses mid-stuff of popcorn, kernels now falling out of her mouth.

A camera flashes. I blink, and Diana and her red hair stand with a pleased smirk on her face. She will probably write a scathing article about my impropriety after this. It'll work well for her, but it won't be the best marketing for the fair.

Jack pulls away, wearing a wicked, crooked grin. He fingers a curl falling on my cheek, bringing his mouth to my ear. "Do you understand my frustration now?"

I nod, slack-jawed. "I think so," I whisper back.

I *should* understand anyway. If Jack was sending a message, it was one of sexual frustration, but him feeling that way about me doesn't compute.

How could I be frustrating *him*? The man who could have just about any woman he wanted.

Including me.

If he just asked.

"Good. Now hurry along so I can marry you."

Lucas drops his Darcy mask for half a second before regaining composure.

"That will be enough, Wickham," he says. "Come, we have business to discuss."

Jack glances at me one last time. His eyes sparkle with satisfaction as he takes in my heaving chest, trying to gain composure.

And I have the regrettable feeling that Lydia wasn't the one who was just completely and utterly ruined.

Chapter Twenty-One

Jack Parker

Play: *Baby I'm Yours by the Artic Monkeys*

Mindlessly, I run a finger over my bottom lip, relishing the lingering feeling of Aulie's velvety skin resting there. A few minutes ago, she bowed out from under my arm and left me in a stupor.

I've never dared be that brave with Aulie or come that close to showing her how I truly feel. Terror should be coursing through my veins, but it's not. I'm oddly...good. Calm? Like I'm finally giving in to things my body knew we should be doing all along and now I'm...free.

Something strangely akin to hope sparks in my chest after our time in the garden earlier in the week, our dance yesterday where I swear something passed between us, and...*that*... five minutes where she almost seemed desperate for *me*. Maybe my affections aren't as one-sided as I believed.

A firm hand falls on my shoulder. I glance at it and find myself on the wrong end of a scowl. Lucas-as-Mr. Darcy glares at me, and I blink back to reality. Right. I'm supposed to be in character.

He leans in, like he's about to give me a piece of his mind, and as Darcy, he should. "You have a boner, bud," he whispers.

I panic. A camera flashes. And I turn away from a still-gathered crowd that hasn't dispersed like it did yesterday.

Shit. Shit. Shit. These damn pants hide nothing. How did men of this time manage? Were inner boners a thing?

"Come, Wickham. We have much to discuss," Lucas declares loudly. "Privately."

He leads me back to the tent, and I sigh as we bow under the flaps and enter seclusion.

My wedding to Lydia isn't for another half-hour, so I have a second to take a break.

We both do.

Lucas gets himself a cup of water and hands me one as well.

"Thank you," I sigh, slumping into a folding chair.

"No problem, man." Lucas laughs. "I'm used to this. Last year, Callen and Emma got pretty heated, and his breeches weren't subtle either. They're married now, you know."

"So I heard."

A pang of jealousy at Callen's situation roils in my stomach. If I'm honest with myself, I'd love nothing more than a story that ends like the previous Lydia and Wickham.

But it never will. I won't let my shit impact her.

Lucas's brow wiggles. "Do you think we might need to find a new Lydia and Wickham next year, too?"

"Wickham will be new, anyway, since I'll be well into my season, and I have zero intention of getting suspended for this long again."

"I don't think she'd look at anyone else like that." Lucas shakes his head. He sits across from me, leisurely resting his arm on the chair beside him. "It's not my place, but you know almost every guy up here has tried to make a move on her at least once, and she's always turned them down. She doesn't seem as keen to do that with you."

I've never asked Aulie why she doesn't date, but I doubt it has anything to do with me.

"She has a bad track record. I'm sure she's just protecting herself."

Lucas shrugs. "Or she's waiting for someone in particular."

"She's not interested." I shake my head, although that statement is growing less convincing by the day. "And we're just friends."

Another statement I'm suddenly more reluctant to buy.

Lucas laughs, glancing at his watch and rising. "Yeah, whatever, bud. You keep telling yourself that so you don't have to act on it."

No, that's not why I'm denying her feelings for me...there's a grander, more virtuous reason beyond my hesitation to open myself up and take a risk. I just can't access said reasoning.

Oh, right! The list! Aulie wants a family and nope—still out on that. Definitely can't do a damn thing about it either. Darn.

Aulie squeals and bursts through the tent with a huge smile she's fashioned often as Lydia. She takes us in and freezes.

"Oh, hi!" She tries to suppress her smile as she clears her throat and adopts a more serious expression. When her eyes meet mine, her cheeks turn a bright pink and her neck flushes.

A pesky ember of hope sparks in my chest. *Friends don't make friends blush from simple eye contact.*

Family, Jack. Family.

Sounds like heaven with her. Fuck.

"We're needed on the stage in a few, Mr. Wickham. Darcy, you, too."

My eyes rest on her, studying the nervous bob of her throat and how a flash of uncertainty passes through her gaze. The list and all the other reasons why I shouldn't go up in flames as hope and yearning burn in my chest in a blazing wildfire.

I should talk to Aulie after the fair today before I have time to talk myself out of it.

"Earth to Jack." Aulie's honey voice draws me back to reality.

Standing up, I offer her my arm. "Shall we, my love?" I move the tent flaps aside, soaking in the admiring gaze Aulie is directing to my face. A look that says she's mine.

It's for the fair.

I'm not naïve enough to think she's that far gone in real life. But I choose to hug the expression tight to my chest for now and hope she'll glance at me like that for real someday.

"Thirty more minutes, and you're officially a free man, Mr. Wickham. How do you feel?" she asks.

Half agony I won't have an excuse to touch you tomorrow, and half hope you might let me anyways.

~

"Are you coming?" Aulie pulls her dress over her head, and I blink back the shock at seeing her in a bra and panties for the second time today.

Yesterday, I left after my scheduled time, so I missed how comfortable everyone in this group is changing in front of each other—almost like a locker room, except it's co-ed and has Aulie in it. Today, reluctant to release her grip on my arm and this role where I could flirt with her, I remained in character and wandered around the fairgrounds with Aulie, even though our characters were no longer required for the rest of the story.

A handful of excited fairgoers asked if we would pose with them for selfies, and we obliged them. The smile I tepidly wore yesterday grew stronger, proud to share my "wife" with others and basking in the sparkle that had all but returned to her gaze.

"Jack?"

I blink and rub a hand over the stubble on my cheeks after two days of letting it grow. "Huh?"

"I asked if you're coming." Aulie's eyes connect with mine, and she blushes, understanding my stupor. She's right there, within arm's reach, and my hand tingles with the urge to wrap an arm around her waist and pull her tight against me and see if she'd mold into me the way she did in the garden. What sound would pass over her lips this time if I dragged my teeth across her earlobe?

"Coming where?" I ask, powering up my phone. Hopefully, I

have a text message or something that will pull my attention away from this damn woman who changes impossibly slowly.

"To the afterparty. We host one in the backyard after the first Sunday of the fair for the crew."

"Oh. Right." I scratch my head. If this conversation goes poorly, I doubt I'll want to spend time at a party with my rejection hovering around me, but then again, if it goes well, I won't want to share Aulie with a bunch of people for the night, either. "I—uhm, I wanted to talk to you first, if that's okay."

"Oh? Yeah, what's up?"

"So about today."

"Oh, yes, right." The blush on Aulie's face grows, and she grabs her shirt and throws it on with an embarrassed gusto.

My phone vibrates wildly in my hand.

Mom: Simone is going into labor.

Tom: Hey, half-pint, can you meet us at the hospital and grab Lucy? Amy was supposed to take her, but Coby and Grant have a stomach bug.

Simone: Need you. Now.

Shit. Shit. Shit. In haste, I shrug off my breeches, pull my pants on, and button them. I was going to change after the conversation, but never mind then. "I have to go."

"Now?"

"Unfortunately, yes." I tug my shirt off and shrug on my green Henley. Aulie's mouth drops into an "o." My lips quirk at the flash of desire that cuts across her face. She's tortured me enough for years with her existence. It's about time I return the favor. "Simone's having the baby—or had. I don't know. I didn't check the timestamps on the texts."

"Oh! That's fantastic! Are you going to the hospital? Do you want me to come?"

Aulie's request seems ordinary enough, but with my anxiety surrounding hospitals, I know there's something grander behind her offer.

If I weren't already falling head-over-feet, stuff like this would push me off the edge of whatever cliff of delusion I've desperately clung to.

Leaning down, I press a kiss on her cheek. "I appreciate you, Dessy. But I need you to rest. I'll see you soon, okay?"

Her eyelashes flutter as her fingers lightly graze where my lips brushed against her skin.

There's a decided lightness in my step while I rush to the car. Starting the engine, I speed away and head to the hospital, an intoxicating swell of hope and butterflies mixing with anxiety and dread for my current destination.

Gripping the steering wheel, I call Tom and tell him on my way. Simone delivered an hour ago so I don't feel as bad asking him to meet me outside so I don't have to spend a second in the waiting room since I loathe that place entirely. While it's not the same hospital, I elected to stay in the waiting room when my dad passed, and I haven't been in one since.

The news was still so new to me then, and I was filled with a fit of overwhelming anger that everyone had kept it from me. So I wasn't at his bedside when he passed. I didn't hold his hand or say goodbye like my sisters. I didn't give myself or him any sense of closure. Instead, I sat in the waiting room and watched a shitty Hallmark movie about finding love at Christmas, where a city-slicker businessman came home and fell in love with his childhood best friend, all grown up.

Okay, maybe the premise wasn't that bad.

Throwing the car in park, I rush to the entrance Tom told me was closest to the maternity/delivery wing and find him standing outside.

Rushing through the sliding doors, my heart speeds up a fraction passing the rows of chair and white sterile walls in the lobby. Thankfully, Tom's glow is infectious and helps settle my nerves. Simone is resting in one room while Little Jack is being monitored in another.

Tom leads me down a long, winding hallway, finally pausing at Suite Forty-Seven, and I bite down a laugh at their room matching my sweater number.

Tom motions for the door but doesn't enter. "I'm going to get a coffee and something to eat, but you go in. Want anything?"

I shake my head. The last thing I need is something in my stomach when I'm anxious; I'll hurl any moment. "I'm good, but thank you."

With a collecting breath, I step into Simone's room. A strong antiseptic smell greets me suggesting the room was recently scrubbed with a gallon of bleach.

"Hey, half-pint," Simone says, still sedated. She reaches for me, and I swallow down the ball of anxiety lodged in my throat. I can't show my family how uncomfortable this makes me.

Simone looks...okay, though. And I guess, given that she just pushed an entire human out, okay is better than expected.

But her skin is paler than usual. Her hair is in a high, frizzy bun. Her eyes are sunken, and her lips are pallid.

Couple that with the clamoring of machines around her, and it's hard to tell myself that she *is* fine. That all of this is normal. That I'm not about to lose my big sister to something no one is telling me about.

What if she's had a complication this entire time, and no one wanted to worry me?

What if they think I'm still the little kid who needs protecting after I've spent the last ten years showing them I'm no longer that soft teenager I once was?

I clear my throat. "Hey."

Chill. If you have a panic attack and pass out in the hospital, no one will ever tell you anything again.

Simone squints at my chest. "Your shirt is on inside out."

I glance down and find my buttons facing inward. "So it is."

"Half-pint," Simone says with a sympathetic sigh. "It's okay, I'm okay. Come here." She beckons for me to move closer, and I slowly oblige her, kissing her forehead.

"You look like shit."

"Well, I just pushed a child and a bunch of that out, too, so that tracks." She smiles and my chest lightens a smidge.

"But you're okay? Tom said there weren't any complications, and that's the truth, right? Because I can handle it, I promise."

"Ah. So that's what's going on." She grabs my hand. Hers has an IV taped to it. Would she have an IV if she was okay? "I'm fine, and I'm sorry. If I could do everything with Dad over again, I wouldn't listen to him. I'd tell you the minute we knew. That wasn't fair to you. But he didn't ask us not to tell you because he didn't think you could handle it. I'm sorry if you've been carrying that around with you, Jack. He was the one that couldn't handle facing *you*. He was so determined to be that strong hero for you to the end." A tear rolls down Simone's cheek. "I'm sorry, I'm just—I'm so hormonal, and I love you and—"

"Hey, hey." I pluck a tissue from a box on a bedside tray and hand it to her. "No crying. Today is a good day."

"It is, it really is. And now you're going to have a little Jack to be a hero to, and he's going to love you so much because we love you—" At this, Simone breaks. Her chest heaves and large sobs follow. I've never seen my sister cry, and something about it cracks the dam I've carefully constructed inside to keep my emotions at bay.

I don't know how much stock I should put in the words of a woman who's probably high on painkillers and just endured what she did, but at the very least, Simone is presenting a new perspective I've never imagined.

What if my dad really kept everything hidden, not because of me, but because of how he'd change in my eyes? *Would* it have changed anything if I knew he had cancer? Not to me. He would have been the best dad and hockey player; none of that would have altered my mind.

Still, the man's pride created a situation that's nearly destroyed me. I've walked around like an emotionless zombie without him because I thought he was embarrassed by me—so maybe he was fallible after all. That fallibility doesn't mean he didn't deserve love though, or that he wasn't capable of being who everyone needed and wanted most of the time.

So why am I letting my faults dictate what I do and do not deserve?

Maybe it's time to let go, too.

"Where's Luce?" I ask. As life-altering as this moment is, I have enough revelations to ponder for today.

"Tom gave her some money to spend at the gift shop. She was getting a little restless. I'm sure she'll be happy to see you and finally go home."

"Yeah, sorry about that. I had my phone off for the fair."

"No, that makes total sense. How did it go?"

The heat in Aulie's eyes, fixed on me and begging, sends a slight curl of fire through me. "It went well. Really well." A stupid grin breaks across my face, and I don't stamp it down.

"Did it now?" Simone quirks an eyebrow before glancing over my shoulder. A nurse enters, wheeling in Little Jack and handing him to her.

"You want to hold him?" Simone asks.

I hesitate. Because of my hockey seasons, I didn't meet my niece and nephews until they were a few months older. Little Jack looks too delicate and tiny for me to hold safely.

"You won't hurt him, half-pint. The dude just squeezed out of my vagina," she says matter-of-factly. I cough at her frankness, which is in direct contrast to the maternal, admiring gaze on her new son cradled in her arms. "Wash your hands and sit in that chair; the nurse will hand him over to you."

Following orders, I scrub clean before lowering myself on a bound leather chair.

The grey-haired nurse smiles softly, taking him back from Simone. "Make sure you brace his head."

My calloused hand cradles the back of his head as fine baby hairs tickle my palm. I hold the bundled little guy in front of me. Small crusties dust the eyelids of his scrunched-up face with its perfect button nose.

Little Jack's tongue darts out and wets his lip. His eyes open for a second, showcasing a blue-grey iris, just like his mom.

The waters behind the dam that's held my emotions for so

long, the one that Simone's tears slowly crumbled, burst through, and a swell of everything good and evil, but primarily good, washes over me.

"Hey, little guy," I croak, marveling at the peace that follows the initial surge of feelings.

I'm holding Simone's baby. A piece of her. A bit of Tom. I missed this with Lucy, Coby, and Grant. I missed this miracle of the first few moments, missed being a part of the welcoming party.

What would it be like to hold something that was a piece of me?

A piece of her.

"Quite the legacy, huh?" Simone asks.

"Yeah. He's—he's something."

In the back of my mind, a quiet voice I've left silent for far too long shouts, *This is what you've been missing. This is what you want. This peace. This miracle.*

And there's only one person who I want it with.

The faint memory of our kiss on the fountain and small passing smiles on the fairground sends tingles spiraling throughout my body.

A Hallmark movie montage of holiday kisses, engagements, weddings, and babies flashes in front of my eyes, and my wide, peaceful smile somehow stretches further across my face than I knew it could. Apparently, to this point, I've only been using half of my cheek muscles.

"I'm going to tell her." The sentence passes my lips before I have time to realize the implications of saying it out loud.

"That's great, half-pint! Now, how are we going to do it?"

Chapter Twenty-Two

Jack Parker

Play: *Mr. November by the National*

Announcing I was going to declare my feelings for Aulie in a hospital room in front of my sister was a terrible idea.

Given that my sisters and mother had a new family member to dote on, you'd think that I could have escaped the entire situation unscathed, but apparently, old habits die hard in this family. This habit, the one where they smother me and I become their plaything, is getting old. In the three days after my hospital room proclamation, Simone and Amy have been throwing out grand gesture ideas. Considering the most realistic option was me riding in on a horse dressed as Mr. Darcy, I dismissed each one.

I've tried telling them I'm not planning on proposing to the woman. I'm just going to be honest and casually mention that I have feelings for her that run deeper than the platonic ones.

For whatever reason, this answer hasn't placated them the way I hoped it would.

Yesterday, after Lucy had a tiny stuck-in-the-house meltdown, I decided today would be perfect to take her, Coby, and Grant apple-picking. Amy could take care of Simone and Tom's house while they rested.

All three women encouraged me to ask Aulie to come and help, claiming Coby and Grant alone would be too much for me to handle on my own at the orchard.

With a sigh, I agreed. I'd procrastinated the terrifying conversation long enough, and an orchard was as good a place as any for the planned discussion.

Splashing water on my face in Simone's guest bathroom sink, I tell my hammering heart to chill. The conversation isn't happening for a few more hours. There's no use going through cardiac distress this early in the day.

With my glasses on and my contacts resting in their solution, I do a once over at the outfit I have planned for today—ripped jeans, that according to my stylist hugs my butt in all the right places, and a tight grey Henley. I've overthought every aspect of this conversation except the actual words I'll say. Those keep getting stuck somewhere I don't have access to in my mind.

Two shrill shrieks carry into the house as a stampede of wild, hungry animals clamber through the living room.

So, the terrors have arrived, then.

Coby and Grant aren't as bad as everyone makes them out to be. They're high energy, sure, but so was Grady in college, and I handled him fine.

With a final once over, I nod at my reflection, and walk out to greet my overly invested family.

"Coby—" Amy's far too soft voice floats away in the wood-fire air. "Is this a good choice? Or a bad one?"

"It's a fun one." The springs of the old rickety sofa creak in a consistent rhythm. "So it has to be good."

I round the corner, tucking Coby smoothly under my arm. He wiggles and giggles as I spin him around a few times and gently place him on the ground. I ruffle my hand through his hair. "Be good today so we can get a treat on the way home."

"What kind of treat?" Coby asks, already sizing up his next misdeed.

"I was thinking ice cream?"

"With sprinkles?"

I scoff. "As if I'd get you ice cream without sprinkles. Who do you think I am?"

He reaches for my back. "Up. Up."

Kneeling, Coby climbs onto my back and I curl my hands under his legs just as my mother walks into the living room. She's wearing her typical blonde pixie cut longer these days and looks better rested than I've seen in years. Right now, she's grinning, wide and suspiciously.

Which, in my experience, doesn't bode well for me.

"I have something for you," she says.

"For me?" I ask skeptically, bending down and kissing her cheek while Coby wiggles behind me.

"Yes. For your date with Aulie today," she says, her eyes sparkling.

I chew the inside of my cheek, trying to fight back a sigh. "I don't have a date with Aulie. I have a date with this squirt." I pretend I'm about to flip Coby over my back, and he squeals, tightening his grip around my shoulders, almost choking me. "And Aulie just happens to be coming."

"Oh, hush. Your sisters told me what you plan to do today—Grant, don't sit on the cat, dear—so I'll tag along."

"What? Why?" My chest tightens. Coby's hands wrap around my neck, obstructing my airways, and I sputter, lowering to the ground and unloading my passenger.

"You're going to want some alone time with her, and the orchard is the perfect place for a nice walk."

A crash and the shatter of glass follow from the dining room. I cringe. Simone and Lucy rush to the crime scene from different areas of the house, but Amy remains on the couch, staring into space, drinking a coffee she bought on the way here. "How are your flowers doing, Simone?" she asks.

I blink.

Is my sister seriously this checked out? What the hell happened to her?

My mom rummages through her oversized purse, pulling out a plastic bag. "Anyway, if you think I'm going to let you talk to Aulie in one of those holey denim pants and that leather jacket, you have another thing coming." She thrusts the bag into my hand. "These are just something I picked up while getting baby clothes yesterday. I think they'll suit you better."

I swallow, opening the bag. A pair of dark-washed jeans and a cream cable-knit sweater sit inside.

I laugh. No freakin' way am I wearing this.

An avalanche of books crashes to the floor and I flinch at the clamor.

Tom runs through the living room, almost slipping on the hardwood floor with his socks. "Not the medical journals! I just organized those."

The picture of calm, Amy continues to sip her coffee. "Were you able to get Gio back up to Mr. Martin's today? I imagine living so close to that goat must be such a pain."

Again, I blink, taking in my absent-minded sister who I've always looked up to.

Do none of the adults in my life have their shit together?

Why the hell have I kept thinking *I'm* the fuck up?

"Thanks for the clothes." I smile softly at my mother. "But I think I'm going to have to pass for today. I'm already dressed, and it sounds like we should be going soon."

"I think it would be nice if you stopped covering up your sweet side, half-pint," Amy says.

"Please don't rip that page, Coby. Grant, seriously, where did you get that pen? That's from my locked drawer. For the love of god, where did you find my scapula?" Tom's horrified declarations continue, and I glance at Amy like, *Maybe you should be doing something?*

She merely takes another sip of her coffee and sighs happily, leaning deeper into the couch. "The fire feels nice in here, Simone. Is this your first one of the season?"

"Just humor your mother and try them on, please." My mom presses a gentle hand to my arm, and I can't deny a request like that.

"I'll try them on for you, but I'm not promising to wear them today." I march back to the bathroom, raise my shirt over my head, pull my sweater on, and change into the jeans.

With one glance in the mirror, I tip my head back and laugh. This is worse than I imagined. I look like the before in any rom-com Grady's made me watch where the guy gets a makeover to win the girl over.

I need *more* confidence to be honest with Aulie, not less.

No, this won't do.

But I'll humor my mother and show her—I'm sure she'll be happy enough just to see me in the outfit, and then I can change.

Walking back out to the living room, my sisters and mom all stand with their hands pressed to their hearts.

"Oh, there's my handsome baby boy." My mom sighs. "I've missed you."

I grunt, tugging on the collar of the sweater. "It's kind of itchy, but I'll wear it for Thanksgiving. Thank you."

"You sure you don't want to wear it today?"

Positive. There's no way Aulie's seeing me dressed like this today. Like hell if I'm going to risk her friend zoning me after all my hard-earned movement into the offensive zone these past few weeks.

A peculiar silence fills the living room. My stomach drops. "Where are the boys?"

A splash of water and a distinctive plop follow my foreboding question.

Plop. Plop.

Coby's giggles grow far more mischievous.

Shit. Shit. Shit.

I rush to the bathroom. Why did I leave the door open? Why were they left anywhere unattended?

Plop.

Pausing in the doorframe, a display of horror show proportions unveils around me.

Coby's huddled over the toilet, tossing my various possessions in.

Like my shirt.

And my watch.

And my pants.

And then, with a certain confidence I've failed to achieve in my twenty-eight years on this planet, the devil looks me square in the eye and pees all over my shit.

"What are these, Uncle Jack?" Grant asks, holding my contacts in his grubby palm.

"No. No." I reach for them in a panic, but I'm too late. He tosses them into the toilet.

Delicate titters sound over my shoulder, and I grab the two terrors and stuff them under my arms.

Turning, I'm greeted by Amy and Simone standing in the doorway with enormous grins.

"The rest of your stuff is in the wash." Simone bites back a laugh.

"I know." I was trying to be responsible and do a load of laundry before I moved over to Gus and Aulie's next week since Little Jack is about to move into the nursery. Damn adulting to hell.

"You have to wear the sweater."

"I'm aware," I say, scowling at Amy. "Your children are actual demons."

She shrugs. "But they're cute demons, aren't they?" She brushes some hair from Coby's face, still tucked securely under my arm.

Simone follows suit, raising on her toes and smoothing my hair down.

I'm glad I'm on the same level of respect with these women as these two devil spawns.

I place the boys down, ushering them out of the bathroom. "Go."

Slamming the door in everyone's face, I groan and glance at the mirror.

I might as well get cozy with the friend zone again, because, like hell am I breaking free looking like this.

Chapter Twenty-Three

Aulie Desfleurs

Play: *Cupid by Sam Cooke*

Moulton's Apple Farm is a pillar in the Chawton Falls community. Established in the early 1700s, the original white barn and orchard is one of the oldest buildings left in our small town. The colonial structure expanded over time, with additional buildings added across its sprawling acreage to become what it is today.

A temple to all things fall.

Locals and tourists stuff their baskets with homemade bread, apple cider donuts, gourmet spreads, and fresh-cut flowers inside the year-round Farmer's Market. While also collecting a fair amount of tea—and not just the herbal, green, or black kind.

Hushed whispers and side-eye stares angle in my direction as I slowly browse the produce aisles, waiting for Jack and his family to arrive. Apparently, I'm one of today's hot topics.

Since my Memere passed, I've grown used to receiving sympathetic smiles and passing the few hushed, "Don't you feel sorry for her? Those two were attached at the hip," whispers. But these glances aren't sympathetic. They're conspiratorial, almost—they're gleaming.

My cheeks heat from the continued attention. Whatever these people think they have on me, they're keeping their whispers low enough that I haven't been able to overhear anything.

Which is a first.

And annoying.

Amidst the chaos, my gaze settles on a crate overflowing with gourds, each one unique in shape, size, and texture. I have a particular weakness for the smallest of pumpkins, and I'm not ashamed to admit it. I palm one in my hand, studying the orange skin from multiple angles.

"Yes, you would look cute with a tiny hat, I agree," I muse. "Oh. How would you feel about wearing a bonnet and becoming Catherine Gourdland for Halloween?"

"Are you talking to a pumpkin...about bonnets?" An all too familiar, deep voice says with a teasing lilt.

I keep my gaze on my little pumpkin. Despite the hammering of my heart, I refuse to let Jack know that his sneak attack was successful.

"Don't you have something better to do than sneak up on unsuspecting women in—" I look up, and my words fall short as I come face to face with a cream-colored, wool covered chest. With his cable-knit sweater, black-framed eyeglasses, and unsure look, if I hadn't heard Jack's voice first, I may not have recognized him.

His finger tugs on his sleeve as his attention roams in a nervous flutter over my face.

A smile slowly rakes across my face before a quick snort escapes me.

Jack's lips press into a harsh line. "Don't."

"I'm sorry." I lean in conspiratorially. "Did we—did I miss hitting my head on something, and now we're in an alternate reality?" With a gasp, I place a hand on my heart. It should bother me I'm being silly, but flirting with him almost seems natural when he's dressed like this. It's like for the first time, Jack and I belong in the same world. "Wait, let me guess. I'm the city slicker girl who needs to learn a lesson about slowing down, and you're the small-town guy who's going to teach me about falling in love at an apple orchard?"

He crosses his arm and arches his eyebrow. A confident, challenging gleam settles in his eyes, eradicating all the nervous flitters. "Would you like me to teach you about love, Aurelie? You seem to create an awful lot of hypotheticals where we find ourselves in romantic situations. There wouldn't be a reason for that, would there?" With his hands on either side of the crate, he leans in, his eyes fixated on my lips.

"Oh, just put the girl out of her misery and kiss her, for heaven's sake," a loud, shrill voice cries, reverberating off the wooden walls.

I turn my head and see thirty townspeople staring at us, their eyes curious.

Fire burns my cheeks, and I swallow down a ball of embarrassment in my throat. Jack, to his credit, seems unfazed with the heckling and attention. Although, I suppose, given his profession, he's used to being heckled. "I'm uhm—I'm going to buy this pumpkin and grab the bags for apple picking. They're kind of expensive, so do you want to just do one, or do you want to grab one for each kid?"

Jack's eyes dip to my lips again, but he shakes his head. "Three sounds good, I'll go with you to pay."

"Where are the kids?"

"They're over at the petting zoo. My mom is watching them."

"Oh, your mom came?" I ask, standing in line and trying to hide my disappointment. A small part of me felt excited when Jack asked me to help with his niece and nephews, especially after the weekend we'd had. I thought it was a good sign that after all the tension on my end, he wasn't freaked out and wanted to spend more time with me. But like most of my time with Jack, I'm just making something out of nothing. Coby and Grant are terrors, and Jack needs all hands on deck to get through the day. "That's nice."

Mr. Gardiner, an older man with a penchant for making a

game of Bingo way more intense than it has any right to be, turns, smirking when he sees Jack and me standing behind him.

"That was quite the show you two put on the other day," he says, winking. My brow dips, furrowing as I try to puzzle out what he's talking about. As far as I know, Mr. Gardiner wasn't at the fair. "Good man. Of course, if I were fortunate enough to have a woman like this one look at me that way, I'd quickly lock her down. Marry her soon, son. You won't find anyone better—take it from a man who's lived eighty years. I know what I'm talking about."

"I'll uhm—I'll be sure to heed your advice. Thank you." Jack dips his head. The tips of his ears turn red. He catches my eyes roaming his face and flashes me a tiny, bashful smile as if to say, *Don't read into that. I hate conversations, and this is the best way to shut him down.*

I tell myself to hold on to the nonverbal message he's conveying instead of his words. Still, the daydreamer in me swoons a little, imagining Jack seriously considering Mr. Gardiner's advice.

Just then, a twinge passes through my lower half. I breathe through it, careful not to show too much discomfort. Since he's been here, Jack's been more attuned to my pain than I'd like, and I've caught him trying to make me rest a couple of times. The last thing either of us needs is for him to be worrying about me today on top of watching the kiddos. I'm here to help, not add more stress.

I'm here to help.

I repeat the mantra one last time for good measure. Telling my nerves to shake themselves out, no matter what revelations I may have had at the fair. They don't matter now. I've stamped down my feelings for him before. I can bury them again. We're friends. That's it. That's the only way we fit.

It's like we're two puzzle pieces where the shapes are right, but the pictures don't match because they come from different boxes.

Buzzing with too much nervous energy, I let myself get lost in the what-ifs. What if this was real life? What if Jack wasn't a big-time hockey player? What if five years ago, he came home with Gus for the holidays, and that was it? We fell in love. Game over. Or maybe he'd have recognized his feelings before Tyler and I dated. Perhaps we would have fallen in love with softer versions of ourselves, ones that didn't know all the heartbreak I've lived through or had a list of conquests as long as Jack's had become.

I'd joke about Veronica Burke, and Jack would blush because she was an actress he thought was pretty and nothing more. We'd snuggle and watch hockey games, maybe roast s'mores by the fire, and neither of us would know that there was a world where the pieces fit but the pictures didn't match.

Mr. Gardiner moves ahead. We slide up, occupying his space, and that's when I see it.

The reason everyone is staring and whispering. The reason we were vehemently heckled over a crate of pumpkins and why Mr. Gardiner thinks he's seen anything.

A lone newspaper sits on the *Chawton Falls Chronicle* news-stand. The headline in big, bold letters reads, "The Badboy of the NHL Plays the OG at the Annual Chawton Falls in Love with Jane Austen Festival." A picture of Jack caging me with his body, his leg wedged between mine, and an absolute look of decimation on my face, covers the front page. If he sees this, there's no way he won't know how bad I have it for him.

I grab the newspaper in a flash and clutch it behind my back.

Jack cocks his head to the side. "What do you have there?"

"Nothing," I say way too fast and suspiciously.

"Come on, kitten, give it over." He motions, and the name does little to help calm my nerves.

"Give what over? I said it was nothing."

"Uh-huh." His stare stays heavy and unnerving. But he shrugs it off and faces forward again.

I breathe a sigh of relief, relaxing my shoulders.

In a sudden movement, Jack puts his arm around me, pressing me against his chest and reaching behind me. I should have known better than to let my guard down. Who did I think I was dealing with? An adult?

That cable-knit sweater is doing things to my head.

"Really it—"

"Doesn't feel like nothing. Feels like a newspaper to me. What the hell are you trying to hide, Dessy?"

Slowly, he peels my fingers off and plucks the paper out of my hands. "Gotcha."

"No. Jack, I—please, don't. It's embarrassing for me."

"I can help whoever is next down here," Gabbie, one of my former classmates, calls down at her counter station. It's our turn, and I resign myself to humiliation, walking to the register. Jack puts the newspaper back on the stand face down, without ever glancing at the front page.

As I tilt my head in confusion, he meets my gaze and offers a nonchalant shrug in response. "I don't want you to feel embarrassed. If you don't want me looking at whatever it is, I won't. I just wanted an excuse to touch you, anyway." He nudges me with his shoulder and hands Gabbie his credit card. A playful smile dances on his lips and sends tingles down my spine.

Wait. Is Jack flirting with *me*? Maybe this *is* an alternate reality.

~

"Has anyone seen Coby?" Jack's panicked voice carries over the mish-mash of afternoon fall sounds: multiple pairs of boots crunching over the leaves and bees buzzing in the trees. Tractors with wagons hitched to their back, bump along the dirt gravel paths, escorting people to the various varieties of apple trees ready for picking. Jack's mom prefers McIntosh apples for her pies, so she and Luce continued further into the orchard, while we stayed on the outskirts for the Cortlands.

I pivot on my heel, scanning the surroundings. Sunlight filters below the bowing branches, leaning heavily with clusters of apples and creating multiple shadows. Shadows that Coby could easily hide in.

Suddenly, the sound of rustling leaves and snapping twigs fill the air as a barrage of apples descend from the tree above. An apple plunks me on the top of the head, and I yelp, covering my noggin with my hands. Jack tugs on my arm, pulling me toward the dirt path, narrowly avoiding Part Two of Newton's Revenge. My back presses against his chest, warm and firm, and I'm tempted to lean into him. But I don't have the chance to be weak because his hands fall on my hip, and he whips me around to face him.

"Are you okay? Do you think you need to be checked for a concussion?" His hand works over my head as he feels for a bump, and all the while, my eyes narrow in on his lips, contorted into an adorable, concerned frown.

"I'm fine—but—" I gesture to the tree, shaking violently.

Jack nods. "I should, yeah." He breathes out, going over to the tree. His hands reach up, obscured by the branches, and then he pulls down a wiggling menace.

"I made it snow apples, Uncle Jack. Wasn't that funny?" Coby puts his arms out like an airplane, flying on Jack's palm.

"You could have seriously hurt somebody, bud. You need to apologize to Ms. Desfleurs, one of those apples fell on her head." He brings him in for a landing near my face.

Coby's blue eyes meet mine, a hint of guilt hanging there. "Sorry, Aulie. I didn't mean to hurt anybody. I couldn't reach the apples, and it was getting wicked frustrating, you know? But now we've got a bunch on the ground to pick from!"

Grant walks over to the collection of fallen apples, picks one up, and promptly pitches it. Luckily, he misses beaming Mrs. Cardew, innocently picking apples from a nearby tree. Startled, she sighs when she catches the perpetrator. Coby and Grant's reputation precedes them almost anywhere in town.

"Sorry, Mrs. Cardew," I holler with an apologetic wave.

"Not a problem, dear. Traffic was great this weekend at the antique store, by the way."

"Happy to hear it! Hopefully, that keeps up."

"Keep things up with that handsome fellow of yours, and I'm sure it will. I loved that picture of you two, by the way! That bloom of young love—you just can't beat it!"

My eyes drop to my brown boots and a collection of maple leaves and apples on the surrounding ground. A wave of heat envelops me, spreading from the tips of my ears to the base of my neck as sweat gathers on my palms.

Jack looms above me, narrowing a curious stare on my face. I don't look back. It was nice of him not to peek at the newspaper, but there have been enough people here making implications about its contents that I'm sure he's figured out the gist.

I wasn't acting.

I'm in love with him.

~

THERE IS PRECIOUS LITTLE THAT A HOT CUP OF CIDER AND A homemade apple cider donut cannot cure. Resting at a picnic table Jack may not have subtly commanded me to sit at, I happily savor the cinnamon and sugar dancing on my taste buds. Currently, Jack is sprinting across the pumpkin patch, trying to catch Coby and Grant who have learned there's power in splitting up when trying to beat a professional athlete. Coby jumps on a pumpkin, and it explodes under him.

"I'm going to pay for that; I'm so sorry," Jack hollers to the teenager managing the area. He pushes his sweater sleeves up over his elbows, and the black ink that's a reminder that we come from different worlds is revealed.

The ember of hope that sparked alive when I thought Jack was flirting with me wilts in my chest. So he's flirted with me today? Big deal. That doesn't mean he's feeling things the same way I am.

On the other side of the patch, Grant picks up a pumpkin and spikes it down atop another. "You know what, better yet, I'll just buy the whole patch today, let anyone who wants one come in and grab one, and I'll just—yup." He finally gets a grip on Grant and tucks him under his arm. With a scowl, he marches to the bench and slumps down with his nephews firmly in his grasp.

"Definitely didn't need my help, huh?" I laugh as bits of donut crumbs fall from my mouth.

"I handled it."

"You bought an entire pumpkin patch."

"Quiet, you." He shakes his head as Coby and Grant wiggle and bite his arms. "If I let go, will you two sit here and eat your donuts?"

"I want to see the goats again." Coby whines.

"Later. Donuts. You two. Eat them or don't. I don't care, but don't you dare move from this bench, or I'm canceling our ice skating date on Thursday."

I wince internally at the chaos they'll find on the ice rink, but maybe having them in a contained space on skates will be better.

I grab two donuts from the box we purchased, place them on napkins, and hand them over to Coby and Grant. They slowly shake their evil façade as the sun breaks behind a cloud, and suddenly, they appear almost angelic.

Happily, they munch on their donuts, and Jack sighs, relieving the tension in his shoulders and gazes over the rolling hills that lead back down to the orchard below.

I pass a donut over to him and pour him a cup of cider. He takes both with a harrowed expression.

"Do you think they have something stronger than cider?" he asks.

"I think you need your wits about you with these two."

"Remind me never to have twins. I think only evil ones run in my family." He passes his hands through his hair, and I get lost in the winks of auburn and gold that settle in his curls in the dancing sunlight.

"I didn't think you wanted kids at all. Have you changed your mind?" I ask, licking the cinnamon and sugar off my fingers.

"If it was with the right person, I don't think it'd be that bad."

He smiles softly at me, and the earnestness of his gaze makes my heart thump to the sound of *me, he means me.*

"Uncle Jack! Aulie! Did you see you're on the front page of the newspaper?" Lucy comes barreling over to the picnic table, clutching a copy of *The Chronicle.* My eyes widen as they connect with Jack's, but it's too late. Before I can react, Lucy slams the newspaper down on the picnic table. The picture of Jack destroying me is sitting there for all to see.

For Jack to see.

Jack blinks. His brow furrows at the picture before raising his gaze to me and then back to the picture. I shift in my seat.

"It's a lovely photo of both of you, and the article was positively glowing," Jack's mom says, grabbing a donut and patting the boys on the head. "I thought you might like a copy as a keepsake, Aulie, and they only had one copy left!"

"Imagine that." I chuckle nervously. "Thank you. That was very kind of you to think of me."

"Did you boys have fun? Were you good for Uncle Jack?" Mrs. Parker lays kisses on the boy's heads.

Coby nods. "We were the best. We helped get apples down for Uncle Jack and everything."

"And I threw the rotting ones away," Grant says.

I glance at Jack, expecting a grunt or something from him, but his eyes are still glued to the picture, a slight wrinkle appearing between his brow.

"Oh, shoot, you know—I wanted to buy Simone a bouquet while we were here, but I forgot," Mrs. Parker says, an odd glimmer in her eye. "Jack, why don't you take Aulie to help you pick a nice one? My feet don't want to walk those cement floors again."

In a trance, Jack nods, rubbing the back of his head with his hand, his eyes fixed on something in the Deke photo.

"Jack?" his mother repeats herself.

"Huh? Oh yeah, flowers. Yes. I can go grab some." He bows out of the table and stands, offering me his hand.

I slide my palm in, searching his expression for some tell. He had to have seen something in that photo the way he was staring at it, but if he's not freaked out, maybe it's not as bad as I thought it would be.

We walk to the flower stand in silence, and he keeps his gaze fixed on the ground.

Perusing through the aisles of flowers, he remains silent. My words tumble out in a nervous stream as I ramble on about my affinity for Marguerite daisies and the bold shades of pink and orange flowers around us.

With a decided panic in his eyes, I have to accept the truth. I've freaked him out so much he can't even speak.

After we check out, I put on my brakes outside of the market. "Jack, should we...talk?" I ask. "You know, before we go back to your mom?"

"Talk, yes. I want to talk." He slides his hands into his pants, his eyes roaming over the flowers, pumpkins, and other wooden crates outside. In other words, anything that isn't me. "Good. Thank you. I uhm—right, so about this weekend...well, I guess the last week. Things between us have been...different."

Different doesn't mean bad. Don't read too much into this.

"And I just—well, I don't want to ruin our friendship..."

"Me either," I cut in. "Promise. Your friendship is important to me."

"Right, so it's hard for me to say...what I want to say...because of that friendship...and not wanting to ruin it, because you know Dessy, I don't want to lose you, but I think..." Jack's brows furrow, glancing over my shoulder. Before his eyes widen in horror. "Alpaca!" he shouts, wrapping an arm around my waist and pulling me to the side. A gust of wind slaps my cheeks as a charging alpaca speeds by on my right.

"What the—"

"Oh shit. Oh my god. No." Jack releases his grip on me and busts out into a full sprint toward the petting zoo.

I spin around, watching him careen past a picket fence and a door flapping in the wind.

In the pen, where sheep, alpacas, goats, and pigs usually stay, two little boys are on all fours "baaing." Farm animals scatter in every direction. Lucy and Mrs. Parker scramble like herd dogs, trying to shoo the animals back into the pen.

Sprinting down the hill toward the swath of animals that have escaped the farthest, Jack's words before he bolted play in my mind. He doesn't want to ruin our friendship, but that could mean two things. I don't know if the two terrors just saved me from an unfortunate letdown where Jack wanted to tell me we're friends and nothing more, or possibly from hearing everything I've ever wanted.

Chances are, the former.

But for some reason, I can't convince my heart the latter is impossible.

Chapter Twenty-Four

Aulie Desfleurs

Play: *Remember (Walkin' in the Sand)—The Oh No Song by the Shangri-Las*

"Happy Birthday!" Emy's cheery voice greets me as I blink the heavy sleep from my eyes.

Is she in the kitchen? Cooking? Am I still dreaming?

"Thank you," I croak, clearing my throat and shuffling into the kitchen. A giant yawn passes through me, and I stretch my limbs, still fatigued.

Even though I haven't slept well in six months, a special weariness falls on my shoulders after the second weekend of the fair—our *Emma* weekend, which had a smaller cast and ran smoothly, thankfully. But it still feels like running a marathon, and I'm in the middle of the race where the excitement of the beginning has worn off, but the end, *Persuasion* in November, isn't in sight.

We still have *Sense and Sensibility*, *Mansfield Park*, and *Northanger Abbey* to go through first.

Food trucks rotate through every week, and as an over month-long weekend event, some of the carnival elements change too, so there's always some kind of coordination needed, always something to stay on top of.

The smell of blueberries and flour hit my nostrils. "What are you doing?" I ask, peeking over Emy's shoulder. An uneven glob of lumpy batter slowly bubbles in an overly-greased frying pan. I hide my wince. "Are those *pancakes?*"

"An attempt at pancakes, anyway." She frowns.

"I accept attempts." I smile. "Thank you. You're the best."

Since I was little, blueberry pancakes for my birthday have been a Desfleurs household staple. I didn't know how I'd do waking up today with them, without *her*. It's my first birthday, without my Memere. But with Emy, Gus, and begrudgingly Jack, I still have so many people to be thankful for.

Even when they're massacring a perfectly good pancake.

With incredible stealth, I try to slip the spatula out of Emy's hand, but she bats me away.

"Get out of here!"

"But I can fix this."

"No, absolutely not. You will eat my subpar food, and you will like it," she says, pointing an accusatory spatula in my face. "Now go sit on the stool and open your present."

In my slippers, I shuffle over to one of our rickety counter stools that are just about as old as this house.

"Pancakes *and* a present, my goodness. You're spoiling me." I pick up the pink unicorn gift bag that Emy and I have been using for each other for the past few years. What's the point of buying another one when this one has sparkles?

My heart warms a smidge.

The only expectation I had for today was to stay in my pajamas, a pair of plaid flannel pants and the Sublime sweatshirt that Jack gave me the night we first met. It's the comfiest thing I own, and I refuse to leave its confines today.

I'd be worried about Jack seeing me in it, but I doubt he'll come over, considering he hasn't been here since he tried to let me down gently last week. He keeps saying he's busying helping Simone when we invite him over for things. Which is probably true and fine.

It's easier for me to get this crush under control if he isn't hovering twenty-four-seven, anyway.

Tissue paper sits crumpled on the top, and I pluck it from the bag, ready to uncover whatever is inside.

"Before you go further, this one is from me—and only me. Your brother wasn't involved. I feel you'll get that in a second, but still—probably best to preface that your brother's gift will come later."

"Okay?" My greedy fingers twitch. Emy and I have many inside jokes. There's no telling what's meant for my eyes only, not Gus's.

Reaching inside, I feel the glossy pages of a manual or book and slip it out of the bag.

It's not a manual—it's a magazine—binder clipped to a specific page.

Jack's smolder threatens to burn off the page and set my heart on fire. I glance away, looking at his forearm resting on the penalty box. Images of him pinning me against a wall and resting that same arm above my head flash at lightning speed. No. Well, that won't do.

"Really, Emy, you think this joke has gone on long enough?" I croak. She's drawn little hearts around the picture and, in her infinite ability to make me uncomfortable, has scribbled, "I love Jack." And "Mrs. Jack Parker" just about everywhere. I flash her a scowl that suggests she may want to consider running and hiding if she desires self-preservation.

"I'm going to wait to run away from you after you completely open your gift."

"I can't see anything else in here making up for this," I grumble.

"I don't think it'll make it better, to be honest. I just want to buy myself time to hide the knives."

Oh, well, that's encouraging.

With extreme hesitation, I reach into the bag, scared whatever else lurks within the glittery paper walls might bite me.

A box sits inside, and I pull it out, furrowing my eyebrows as I try to decipher what it is. It looks like a rose, but I narrow in on the pink printed words on the box until my brain registers what they read, and my eyes widen to saucers rivaling Rapunzel's in *Tangled*.

"You got me a vibrator!" I say in a harsh whisper. "What the actual fudge, Emy. This is officially too far."

"Read the sticky note," she says with a quirk of her lips. She flips her poor excuse of a pancake and frowns at the mess of batter all over the stove that follows.

"What sticky note?"

"It was on the box? Maybe it's still in the bag."

"I think I'll pass." I roll my eyes.

Pausing her pancake massacre, Emy comes over, gently grasping my hands which are holding the box and shaking.

Being raised by several Catholic women in New England didn't exactly set me up to feel comfortable around these devices, let alone receive one from a friend as a birthday gift.

Heat singes my cheeks.

"Okay, so listen," Emy starts. "That magazine, I'll admit, was a total joke. But I know you'd never buy something like this for yourself." She taps the vibrator box. "And I truly believe that you deserve to give yourself this outlet. It's good—healthy even, and I think it might help you with some things you're dealing with."

I swallow. After all the weird sensations that have built up inside me the past month, Emy's probably not wrong. It'd be healthier to have a safe channel to get all of that out of my system instead of letting it grow. "You're right. I wouldn't even know where to shop for one of these, so this was actually—in a strange and very you way—a thoughtful gift. Thank you."

Burnt batter tickles my nostrils. "Are you still cooking the pancakes?" I ask.

Emy groans and drops her head to the counter. "How does going out for pancakes sound?"

"Fine by me. Out has breakfast poutine, too."

The shower in the bathroom stops, drawing my attention to the fact that it was running when I woke up. Gus had a meeting today—I thought early in the morning—since he told me he would do something with me tomorrow to make up for missing my birthday, but maybe I misunderstood him since he hasn't left yet.

"I should go put this in my room before he gets out of the shower," I say, swirling off the stool. I grab the gift bag, fold it, and put it back in its special spot in the closet hallway, where I'll pull it in a few short weeks for Emy's birthday gift.

I open the closet and balance the vibrator box and magazine on the shelf.

The bathroom opens behind me causing the closet door to bump into my back from behind. Heavy feet shuffle beyond.

"Hey, I'm in here," I grump. Seriously, Gus couldn't wait for two more seconds in the bathroom instead of almost crushing me here?

"Oh. Sorry," A low, raspy voice that does not belong to my older brother says on the other side.

And I suffer from an acute form of cardiac arrest.

Death and I are now one.

Jack peeks back at me on the other side of the hallway. A towel hangs low on his waist. The sculpted Adonis V I've seen far too much in the past few weeks is more alluring in person.

He's...hypnotic.

The ominous feeling in the air intensifies as I take in the water droplets trailing down his hair and the intricate tattoos etched into his skin.

Couple that with the just-showered sandalwood scent overwhelming me, and all my good sense has suddenly gone up in flames.

Quickly, I avert my eyes. But it's too late. The smirk on his face and the slight raise of his eyebrow tell me I've been caught ogling.

"Why—what—when—who—" I shake myself out of the various forms of the interrogative rattling around in my brain and clear my throat. I'm currently barely obscuring a magazine clipped to an indecent picture of him with—if he thinks they're coming from me—obsessive hearts that should give him the creeps...and a vibrator. "Why are you here?"

"Simone moved little Jack into the nursery. Gus should have told you."

And yet, he didn't.

Seriously? This would have been helpful to know—I don't know—before I put on his sweatshirt and looked like I had a total Jack Parker problem.

What was I doing again?

Right—the bag.

I fumble, trying to reach the gift bag box, but it's a shelf too high. Gus must have been the last one to grab something from it.

I press up on my tiptoes, but still, it's out of reach.

"You want me to get it?" Jack asks over my shoulder.

"No, that's completely unnecessary. Thank you, though."

"It seems kind of necessary." He steps toward me.

Panic sets in. I can't risk him getting any closer and seeing— any of my "Obsessive Lover Who Can't Take a Hint" collection. If he notices any of this, there's no way he'll want to be friends with me anymore, and I'd lose a fair amount of respect for him if he did.

"Pants," I shriek. "Why don't you have pants?"

"Is that what got you flustered? Relax, Birthday Girl, you've seen more of me before, remember?" He winks. The corner of his mouth twitches in a quick smile before he narrows his eyes and takes another step forward. "Is that my sweatshirt?"

"What? This?" I turn a little hiding the Sublime logo plastered across the front with the giant sun. "No."

"Didn't take you for a Sublime fan. Not very rom-comy." Again, he steps forward, and my heart leaps out of my chest. Between his little smirk, that towel, and everything that's going to come crashing down on me if he comes over and sees what I'm trying to hide—I'm going to have to move to a different country, and I've never even left New England.

"Huge fan," I lie through my teeth. Maybe I can at least get out of this one fiasco. Save a tiny portion of my face—like the lower left quadrant, where I have that one freckle that's pretty cute.

"Sure." He snorts. "Not that I'm doubting you, but for shits and giggles, could you name any song by them?"

With every smooth step toward me Jack takes, I get the sense that he knows how much of an upper hand he has and is enjoying my flustered state.

Well, that's very rude because it's one thing to almost ask me to reign in my crush, but it's another thing entirely to tease me along.

I stand with my chin pointed up. If I'm about to go down with this ship, I should do it with dignity. "Santeria. Love that song, total banger."

He rolls his eyes. "Fair. Can I just—" He motions for me to move to the side, leaning over my shoulder and bringing our chests together. I try to hide my gasp when his bare chest hugs the small patch of exposed skin near my collarbone. I'm only wearing a camisole under the zip-up, and my breasts are a little more exposed than I would typically feel comfortable around Jack... and now they're pressed against him.

His lips hover inches from mine, and I close my eyes, feeling his finger trail across the back of my neck.

"What are you doing?" I ask.

"My mom labeled all my clothes before I went to college. It annoyed me when she did it, but—gotcha. Well, I'll be. It's faded, but that sure looks like a J.P. to me. A peculiar thing to label your own sweatshirt, Aulie Desfleurs." His breath falls hot against my cheek. If I just turn my head I could capture his mouth with mine. The yearning to do so, pulls my gut tight, like I've suddenly been poisoned, and his lips are the antidote.

I swallow. Hopefully, that's the only thing decorated with Emy's penmanship he uncovers today.

Cracking my eyes open, a teasing smile and a dangerous

dimple greet me. Jack's gaze bores into me, slowly searching my face for something—I don't know what.

His hand falls to the small of my back, resting there.

The mask I've muscled to keep on my face the past few weeks slips. And I freaking swoon. How could I not?

Jack's standing here all infuriatingly smug, with tattoos, a towel, and a face—looking like every dark fairy prince or rake I've read about in my varied romances that could destroy a woman with one look. Is this the new us? Him just lording my affections over me? Teasing me and stringing me along in a completely different way?

Ugh, I don't think I could take too much of that—that may be worse than him being weirded out. But *he is* a cruel flirt, so I don't know why I didn't see this as a possibility.

I hesitate. "I may have kept the sweatshirt."

"Did you now?"

"But it doesn't have anything to do with you. It's just comfy."

Slowly, his eyebrow arches, and his gaze lands on my lips and turns hooded. "I'm kind of starting to doubt that."

Gently, he lifts my chin. My back hits the door, and his body leans into mine. My footing stumbles, and I grab the ledge of the closet to stabilize myself.

A little paper wafts to the floor between us and shakes Jack out of his trancelike state.

The post-it note Emy was talking about.

I stare down at it, laying face up. *For jacking off* is written in big black Sharpie. My eyes widen. Oh fuck.

"I'll get it," Jack says.

"Oh, no, I'm good. I've got it." Quickly, I go to bend, and my hand flails, knocking the magazine and the box with the vibrator down with it. Oh. No. No. No. "No, seriously, Jack—"

Before I can stop him, Jack's bending down to retrieve every-thing. He picks up the contraband. He quirks that darn brow again, and a whir of emotions fight for real estate on his face.

I clear my throat as a wildfire blazes across my cheeks. "I can explain. It, um, was a joke. A birthday gift from Emy—a terrible, in poor taste present—" I say the last part a little louder because there's no way my best friend isn't around the corner listening to this entire interaction.

Jack's eyes widen, glancing at the spread littered with hearts. His jaw tightens. "She got you the body issue and a vibrator...as a joke?"

"I'm so sorry." Oh, dear Lord Jesus, please just strike me down now. Tears prick my eyes, and I cover my face. "I promise, I heard you loud and clear at the orchard. I will get this crush under control—please don't let this ruin our friendship. I know how it must look, but I'll—I'll work harder at making sure whatever feelings I've been harboring the past few weeks stay stamped down—I did it once before, you know, and you didn't know then, so I'm sure—"

"Wait, wait, wait... Dessy, what do you think I was about to say at the orchard?" Slowly, he peels my fingers down and regards me with—what is that look...pity? That's better than cruelly flirting with me or being creeped out...I guess.

"I need to get my feelings in check because they're starting to make you uncomfortable because you clearly don't feel that way about me and never will. And I promise, this—this wasn't me. Emy drew the hearts and the Mrs. Jack Parker stuff."

Jack's lips part, waffling between open and closed, and I wait for the gentle letdown. He shakes his head, his lips tugging into a smirk on one side. "I—uhm, I need to go get dressed and run some errands, but we can talk about this later, yeah?"

That's...it?

"Yeah...okay," I stammer, swiping some hair out of my face and aiming my gaze at the floorboards in front of me.

"Happy Birthday, Dessy," he says, a smile laced in his tone.

When the guest room door clicks shut, I finally allow myself to breathe.

"That went well," Emy yells from the kitchen.

I grunt and stick my middle finger in the air. Of course, when I finally break my no-swearing rule, no one can see it. "I'm sticking a certain appendage high in the air that implies I hate you."

"Aww. Proud of you, boo."

~

"I really don't think it's the big deal you're making it out to be." Emy grabs a fry slathered in gravy. Chatter swirls around us in a mix of French-Canadian twang and a word now and then of English. Chez LaBranche, the local diner that caters to the second and third-generation Franco-Americans in Chawton Falls, is my comfort food place. After this morning, I needed the fix that only fries, cheese curds, and brown gravy could supply.

God bless Poutine.

"He bolted." I glare, twiddling my fork between my fingers. Emy's too nonchalant about this situation, considering it was her fault.

I'm not sure when Jack left the house, but he wasn't there when I finally gathered enough courage to knock on his door.

A simple "Had to grab a few things. Happy Birthday again" text from him sat on my phone, and that was it.

No acknowledgment of the debacle that transpired that morning.

Our waitress, Delia, a former classmate—like everyone in the service industry here—refills my water for the fifth time.

"Thirsty today, are we?" she asks.

"Something like that." I nervously laugh, taking a sip.

Delia smirks and leans in conspiratorially. "I would be too if I spent that much time with Jack Parker. Good for you."

I choke, and Emy giggles, hanging out her first for Delia to bump.

"I always liked her," Emy says as she sashays to another table.

"No, you didn't. You threatened to fight her on the dirt road multiple times."

Emy frowns, stealing another fry. "When?"

"Let's see. There was the time she spread the rumor I was stuffing because I kept changing in the stalls in the locker room. Or the time she spread the rumor I was pregnant because I was having issues with bloating." I'm still having issues, and the "congratulations," and "when are your due," conversations still sting, but when Delia spread that rumor—well, high school bodies are hard enough to love.

"Sounds like you should have been the one challenging her on the dirt road." Emy shakes her head. She's right. I'm terrible at sticking up for myself and always have been.

I'd never admit it to Emy because the stink-eye would be unbearable, but I tutored Delia on the side in French while she was bullying me at school, too.

I don't know why I have such a problem. Maybe it's because I hate being lonely, and I find myself with that hollow feeling far too often.

Or maybe it's because my Memere firmly believed and drilled into me that a woman should approach every situation with kindness above anything else. That was true classiness. Even when the people on the receiving end of your kindness don't deserve it.

Whatever the reason, I can't shake the feeling that I got something wrong. Maybe kindness, much like people, needs a balancing partner to it.

"There's probably a statute of limitations on the whole challenging someone to a fight thing, huh?" I ask, picking up my fork and sinking it into the fluffy buttermilk pancakes before me.

"Might appear a big unhinged if you did it now. But I'd totally support you." A twinkle of mischief flashes in Emy's deep brown eyes. And I believe her. She's always been my biggest cheerleader.

Which is why something has been itching at me since this morning.

"Okay, but back to Jack. Emylou," I start, using her memere's nickname for her. "If you were so determined to give me that present—which I still question, did you really have to give it to me when you knew Jack was just down the hall? If I had known, I never would have opened it then."

"Honestly? I thought you knew." Emy sips her coffee, inhaling the curls of steam wafting off. "Who did you think was in the shower?"

"Gus seemed like the more logical answer."

"But Gus's on a trip. You knew that. That's why he's taking you out for breakfast tomorrow."

I sigh. My logic is seriously beginning to fail with this lack of sleep situation.

With a loud, over-dramatic groan, I let my head fall into my arms, braced on the table. Emy's phone vibrates, reverberating across the wooden tabletop and into my skull.

"Hey, pumpkin. Look at me."

I pick my head up and reluctantly meet her gaze.

"No more worrying about this, okay? Now, why don't we have a girl's day out? Hair, nails, and maybe a new outfit.

I shake my head. "I have work to do."

"On your birthday? Absolutely not. I forbid it."

Consider my suspicions officially raised. I always work on my birthday. It's a nasty side effect of my birthday being smack dab in the middle of the fair.

Maybe Gus isn't actually out of town, and Emy just needs to get me out of the house.

"What do you have planned?" I ask. I'm too tired for a surprise party and would rather know the situation so I can be prepared to people.

"Oh me? Nothing." An indescribable twinkle passes through Emy's eyes again. "I just think a spa day and shopping sounds like heaven, that's all." She shrugs, smugly sipping her coffee..

Chapter Twenty-Five

Aulie Desfleurs

Play: *Don't Worry, Baby by the Beach Boys*

A blanket of stars in the cloudless sky hangs over me as I stand in my backyard. Water laps to shore along the banks of King's Pond in the wake of a boat on a late-night ride. It's too quiet, save for the crickets and a loon cooing in the distance. Either I'm early or something went wrong with Emy's plans.

A light breeze rustles the leaves above my head. Gooseflesh prickles a swath of exposed midriff. I fight against the urge to pull down the hem of my white, long-sleeve crop top Emy convinced me to purchase with a pink tulle skirt. I love it, but I don't know, maybe I should have gone with the cable knit sweater. That would have been more me.

Not that it seems to matter. No one besides Emy will see tonight, judging by the current solitude in which I've found myself.

Emy shooed me back here when we got home to start a fire... but now that it's been a few minutes, I'm wondering why.

Suddenly, a flash of light has me blinking and adjusting to the shift in luminescence. I direct my stare overhead. Thousands of white lights twinkle in the maple branches overhead, glittering against the black sky. I chew on my lip—if this is a surprise party, they're certainly playing the long game.

And they're also really good at being stealthy—which doesn't sound like my friends.

A drum beats over the speakers Gus set up a few summers ago in the backyard.

Followed by a harmony of male voices.

My heart stops.

"The Beach Boys," I whisper as "Don't Worry, Baby" floods the crisp night air.

Leaves rustle as if someone is gathering closer, and I swirl, trying to figure out the direction they're coming from.

In the light of the crackling bonfire, Jack stands illuminated. His hair is neatly styled into a gelled coif, the style he wears for special galas or fancy dates. A neatly pressed blue button-up stretches across his broad shoulders. He's rolled his sleeves, and ink dances on his overly thick and corded forearms.

With a swallow, I raise my eyes, and they connect with his. My breath grows more erratic by the moment, and I bite back the urge to cover my stomach.

"Jack?" I finally manage.

"You look beautiful," he says with a labored breath.

Jack has commented on my appearance before, sure, but this one feels more profound than a surface compliment, like he gave me a part of his soul he keeps hidden.

"Thank you," I say, dipping into a curtsy and immediately wincing. "Where is everyone else?"

He clears his throat, glancing hesitantly at the screened porch where an outdoor dining table rests, shrouded in darkness. "Uhm, I was hoping it would just be the two of us."

Understanding and a dangerous dose of hope dawn on me. "Us?"

He slides his hands into his pockets and peeks at me almost

bashfully. "If that's okay, that was the plan—but I can go get Emy if you—"

"No. No, I like the plan." My gaze moves over the lights in the trees I've begged Gus to string up for years and the music that kickstarts the perfect scene from *Never Been Kissed*. Is Jack Parker big gesturing me?

With things he picked up from *listening*?

I'm so done for.

Neither of us moves. Jack stands, blinking, for what seems like an eternity, and I don't know what to do. Should I proceed to the table? Should I approach him?

"Jack?" I whisper.

"Right!" He shakes his head, offering me his hand. I take it, fighting the tremor working through mine, and let him lead me to the porch. The speakers serenading us shift to the next song, "Then He Kissed Me." Swearing under his breath, Jack fumbles with his free hand, trying to get his phone out of his pants. "Shit. This is what I get for thinking I'd be smoother."

"Jack?" I repeat his name, this time with a smile.

"One second," he mumbles.

I turn into him. For whatever reason, I cannot possibly fathom this man who skates around burly men with a cool demeanor is flustered because of me—Aulie "Too Sweet To Be Prom Queen" Desfleurs.

Gently, I grab his shaking hand, scrolling furtively on his screen.

He exhales, meeting my eyes and flashing me a sheepish smile. "I'll just hit shuffle."

"Did you make me a playlist?" I quirk a brow, leaning in closer.

I don't understand how what happened this morning has led to this moment, with him bumbling around, playing romantic songs over a speaker—but I'll gladly accept it.

"Maybe. Yes. I—" He winces as "A Kiss to Build a Dream On" starts, and I have to bite back a giggle.

I intertwine my fingers with his. "I think the songs are conspiring against you."

"So it would seem."

"Maybe you should do something about it." I drop my gaze to his lips, catching my bottom lip with my teeth.

Jack doesn't budge, and I hesitate.

The quirk of my lips falters after a few seconds of silence. "Shall we?" I smile half-heartedly, gesturing back to the table. Disappointment roils in the pit of my very exposed and chilly stomach.

A frustrated sigh registers behind me.

"Oh, what the hell? I already fucked this up enough," Jack says. Suddenly, a strong hand grabs my wrist and I'm forcefully spun around to face him. Colliding with Jack's chest, I feel the warmth of his body and the frantic rise and fall of his breath. His fingers brush against my skin as he cups my cheek, and I look up at him. In an instant, his lips crash into mine with a desperate urgency I never imagined this man could possess. Like I'm not the only one with unresolved feelings.

With an insatiable hunger, he coaxes my lips apart, and I let out a soft moan.

Ominous music plays in the faint part of my brain that's still registering reality, and then a woman's voice comes over the speaker. *He swore to protect her heart, but he stabbed it thirty-seven times. This is Kill Death Do Us Part, the murder podcast about those times when it would have been better to have never loved at all.*

I pull away, quirking an eyebrow. "Are you about to murder me? Because if you are, this is a very elaborate murder plot."

"Oh, my god." Emy shoots her head out of an upstairs window. "I'm so sorry. Please carry on as you were."

Jack waves up to the window. "Not the type of murder I had in mind tonight. *La petite mort* later, maybe." He winks.

"One kiss, and suddenly you're so cheeky."

"To be fair, it was one hell of a kiss." He exhales before pressing his forehead against mine. "Hi."

"Oh, had we not said that yet?" A euphoric giggle bubbles out of my chest.

He lays another soft, far more chaste kiss on my lips and then tugs on my hand to walk me to our dining arrangement.

He holds the door open, and I slip onto our screened porch as he flicks something on his phone. For the fifty-thousandth time today, the center for the Brawling Badgers, my Wickham, leaves me speechless. More string lights than I purchased cover every inch of the porch, including the ceiling, making it feel like we're under a canopy of fallen stars. The table is set with antique dinner plates and glasses and a lace tablecloth that doesn't look new, but none of it is ours. An eclectic collection of opalescent hobnail vases are filled with fresh-cut farm flowers, full of blooms in pink, orange, and purple. Between each vase rests a white candlestick and crystal holder.

On a cake platter, meat pie from Chez Labranche is adorned with a swig of rosemary, two bowls of poutine sandwiching each side, and what looks like the Elizabeth Beignets from Cup of Joe's with all the caramel sauce on a serving dish below.

"You did all this? For me?"

"Lucy helped," he says, walking over to the table and lighting the candles. "She told me very seriously that she's wicked into cottagecore."

"Well, it's beautiful."

"I'm glad you think so." Jack pulls out my seat, gesturing for me to sit down, and I accept it with a smile. My legs wobble, having turned to Jello. Hopefully my ridiculously poofy skirt obscures the shake enough that Jack doesn't notice.

"Hi," I manage.

"Hello," he says, sitting next to me. "Happy Birthday."

My practical side wants to hug those two words tight to my chest. I remind myself that Jack is a good friend and doing something special for me because he knows this would be a tough birthday. I shouldn't let myself get lost in the fantasy of a big gesture, but—maybe the practical side of me is the one being foolish.

If the only information I had was how Jack kisses me—like a

man starved—then I would say he has feelings for me—strong ones. It's getting harder to deny myself the hope that something more is passing between us.

"Before we eat, I was hoping we might continue our conversation from this morning." Jack folds his hands on the table, and I find it difficult to meet his eyes. The conversation where I looked like a total stalker?

No, thank you. Pass the poutine, please.

"Do we have to?"

He nods, and a smile tugs on his lips. "I think we should clarify a few things between us."

"Right. Sure. Well, clarify away." I fidget in my seat, unable to meet his eyes. Despite the lights twinkling overhead, and his lips crashing down on mine with obvious hunger, I can't shake the feeling of anticipation for a beautiful letdown.

"I wasn't bringing up our friendship because I thought you had feelings for me at the orchard and wanted you to stop."

"You weren't?"

"No. Not even close." Jack grabs my right hand. His thumb gently caresses a small freckle on the top. "Dessy, I want our friendship to grow into something more—and I was hoping maybe you want the same thing."

"To be *more* than friends?" I blink. Am I hearing this correctly? There's no way I could misinterpret what he's saying, right?

"Yes."

"What if it ruins what we have already?"

"I've been worried about that, too. That's why I've kept my feelings suppressed for so long, but I can't hold them in any longer. I've tried—and I was doing okay as long as I thought I didn't have a shot in hell with you. But Aulie, if you feel even an ounce of what I do, I think risking our friendship is worth exploring what's between us. It's up to you. If you don't see it that way, one word from you will silence me on the issue."

I cycle through all the information he just laid on me. How long exactly has had feelings for me? And how could the man sitting in front of me think he didn't have a shot with me? I've been pretty obvious about my affections for him.

I sit there and think.

And think.

And think.

While his thumb continues to stroke the top of my hand.

The passion behind Jack's kisses and the recent looks of longing gives more weight to his declaration, rather than my practical side's argument that he couldn't possibly feel a thing for me.

"What do you think, Dessy? You're kind of hanging me out to dry here." He laughs nervously.

"It doesn't make sense."

"What doesn't?"

I toss my hands in the air. "Any of it. Jack, I don't fit."

He purses his lips. "What do you mean, you don't 'fit'"

"Into your life. I'm not your type. I'm not a supermodel capable of orgasming five times in one session. I don't use the GOOP egg." At this, Jack raises his brow. "I read it on Veronica's Instagram. But seriously. I don't even know if I'm good at sex. I've only done it with Tyler a few times—and oh my god—why am I sharing that with you? I can't go out often. And even if I could, I wouldn't want to. You'd get bored with me in two seconds. No, I think risking our friendship would be a bad idea. There's no way you're thinking this through; you've just never thought about me like this, and you're suspended and confused—"

"Hey, hey, hey, come here."

I lean forward, and Jack pushes a strand of hair away from my face before gesturing me to scoot closer. I shift, and he gathers me up onto his lap.

Laying a hand on his chest, I feel his heartbeat pound under my pulse, and again I can't deny my way out of this reality.

For whatever reason, Jack likes me—as more than a friend.

"First off. I didn't do anything with Veronica, so I can't speak to her abilities."

My wandering gaze searches his face. How? I've seen all the pictures on the gossip sites of them holding hands, renting out restaurants, and her security moving her bags into his apartment. Did he have the markings of a man in love? Not exactly, but Jack's typically a stoic guy, so I didn't read anything into that—all I knew was he'd stumbled into a relationship with a woman that was as close to perfection on this earth as I'd ever known. The kind of person he deserved. "You didn't?"

"No. We weren't really dating. But even if I had, that wouldn't change my feelings about us. This isn't some sudden development for me, Aulie. I've never had a type that wasn't you. I don't know how I can be clearer about that. And I don't need to go out—those are things I do to quiet my brain. But just sitting with you on the couch or having you here makes everything quiet, too. So if all you want to do is cuddle on the couch or out here—I don't care. I want to be with you."

"What about when you go back?"

He blinks for half a second. "I don't know."

"You hadn't thought that far."

"I'm still figuring this out—hell, Dessy, until the last few days, I didn't even realize you had feelings for me."

"Really?" I laugh. "I thought I had been very obvious."

His eyes narrow. "I'm clueless about this stuff. You're going to have to be gentle with me."

"I can be gentle." I slowly work on undoing one button on his shirt.

"I wish I could promise you the fairy tale ending with the Prince Charming you deserve instead of a bumpy ride with the court jester. But if you're okay with all the bumps along the way, I promise I'm going to do my best to become somebody you deserve."

"I don't want somebody else. I want you," I whisper, letting my lips brush against Jack's in what I hope is a reassuring kiss. *You're so much more to me than you seem to know.*

It's reckless, really, to risk our friendship. One that's so important to me, especially since I've had far too many people leave. Jack has a no-dating during the season rule for a reason, and who's saying he won't re-enact it when he re-joins his team? The thought terrifies me.

But the prospect of not trying at all—we're beyond that. For once, safe isn't an option.

And with that, I deepen our embrace, and we stay there, kissing under a blanket of twinkling lights, until our lips are raw and our poutine grows cold.

Chapter Twenty-Six

Jack Parker

Play: *Slide by the Goo Goo Dolls*

"**M**aybe she went for a run?" The muffled panic of Emy's voice forces me awake. I blink against the unfamiliar filtering of light from an east-facing window. The guest room shouldn't be getting this much sun yet.

A heavy arm drapes across my bare chest, tightening as its owner presses further into the side of my body.

Aulie.

This isn't a dream. She's right here, flush against me in her cute-ass PJs.. Warmth radiates from every point of contact, and for once, I don't suffocate the fire that flickers in the core of my chest from our touch. I let it burn, relishing the soft heat that licks my nerve endings awake.

I hadn't meant to fall asleep. We only came in here to talk some more, but that led to cuddling, and somehow, Aulie fell asleep on me almost immediately. She's had such a hard time sleeping lately that I didn't dare try to wake her up. I wanted to sneak away to the guest room, but she didn't stir while I was conscious.

Gus's heavy footsteps sound on the other side of the door, coming closer. Shit. I really shouldn't have stayed so long last night.

"Her running shoes are still by the door."

"Maybe an errand, then."

"No, her car's here, too. Right next to Jack's. Didn't he say he had an early morning skate he had to get to?"

I wince. Yup. And I'm definitely missing that, too.

"That's weird." Emy laughs; it's high and tense—and way too close to the hard oak door. "And you're sure she knew when you were taking her out for breakfast?"

"Yeah, I told her we had to leave around eight because I have a meeting in Manchester later today. Did you two have coffee this morning? I thought you went outside."

"I did, and she... she texted me she was going to sleep some more. All that lack of sleep must have finally caught up to her."

"Weird, she didn't text me—I'm just going to make sure she's okay." Aulie's doorknob turns.

"Gus. No, she deserves her privacy."

"And I'm giving it to her. I'm just making sure she didn't have one of her damn fainting spells and knocked herself out on her desk or something."

Fainting spells? My brow furrows, glancing at Aulie burrowed against my chest. Her caramel locks flow onto the pillow, glittering in the beams of the streaming light.

I should escape out the window, but there's a certain peacefulness that's settled on Aulie's face and like hell am I going to mess that up.

My eyes trace the curve of her lips, remembering how soft and welcoming they felt against mine last night. Her surrender to my touch was a welcome surprise, like the pulling tension I've always felt between us wasn't the one-way street I thought. Whatever ass-kicking Gus will give me for this, I'll take it. She's worth every fist to the face or yelling match I'm about to endure.

"No, Gus, I'm serious. I'm sure she's—"

A sliver of light leaks in the room before it becomes a vast chasm, and doom floods the room in a seventy-five-watt, table-lamp hue.

"Alouette? Are you in here?" Gus peeks in, his gaze landing on Aulie's empty desk first and then slicing to her bed.

I only have half a second to decide how to play this without waking her—and I decide not to move. So my bare chest is on full display in the bed, my hand perched behind my head, and Aulie's plastered on me with nothing but a thin lace camisole covering her top half.

I try my best to flash Gus an apologetic smile as a scowl slowly takes residence on his face. "Heyyyy, buddy."

"The fuck, Parker?" he whispers.

I open my mouth to issue an explanation like, *So, funny story, I've been in love with your sister for years, and I finally told her.* But Aulie nuzzles deeper into me, my heart somersaults, and I get distracted, a cheesy grin creeping across my face as I watch her.

"Gus, don't you dare wake her up." Emy, standing slightly out of frame, tugs on his hand.

The death glare fashioned on me softens as his eyes fall on Aulie for a second time. Unclenching his jaw, he asks, "How long has she been asleep?"

"Since around eleven," I say, a grin curling my lips as I peek at her again. I hold her close, savoring the feel of her body against mine, and I stroke her arm in a slow, steady rhythm. "I don't think she's stirred since."

"Do whatever you can to keep her sleeping. That's all we care about, right, Gus?" Emy asks in a sharp tone.

"Right." I hear my giant best friend exhale. "We'll talk about this later," he says in the doorframe before the light from the hallway dims and the door softly closes.

Aulie stirs at the sound, and I rub small circles into her back until her breathing settles into its heavy cadence again.

Once more, that content, happy feeling blooms in my chest. This whole thing should freak me out, but...it doesn't.

Since yesterday morning, when I looked into Aulie's eyes and saw everything I've felt for the past five years mirrored in them—the yearning, the want, the heavy weight of carrying around unrequited feelings—my mind has been clear and focused.

It was finally time to tell Aulie how I felt, but since words failed me the first time, I opted to show her. That's why I bolted out of the house—the sound of her breath hitching as I neared, playing in a loop in my mind.

After that, I texted Emy and asked her to keep Aulie distracted for the day so that I could set up the backyard with the twinkling lights she'd mentioned and grabbed Lucy to help me with the porch. Luce mentioned an antique shop where Aulie sometimes takes her, and we picked out the table settings, then walked downtown, grabbing all her favorite foods.

With each passing moment, the weight on my chest increased in eager anticipation. The dynamic between Aulie and me was going to change tonight—although I suppose it had been changing for a while now and rather than getting my heart stomped on when I gave it to her, I was starting to believe it would be gently received.

I wasn't wrong—last night, the few kisses we shared, our first without any pretenses—filled my hollow chest cavity. Instead of taking my heart, Aulie gave it back to me.

Here, her lips whispered against my mouth. *I found this for you. I know you've been looking for it for a while now.*

With every pass of her lips, she built me back up until I fell asleep beside her, satiated and whole for the first time in ten years.

My fingers stroke her back, and I smile at the serene look on her face. *My little sorceress, do you know the magic you hold within you?*

Sometime later, Aulie stirs, swiping at a lock of hair that's fallen over her face in the past half hour or so. She peeks at me, still huddled against my chest, and flashes me a shy smile. "Morning."

"Morning."

"What time is it?" she asks, peeling away.

I grab my phone from the nightstand and clear off the daily countdown text from Grady. "Two."

"In the afternoon?" Aulie sits up straight.

"Yeah, you were *out*," I chuckle, tucking a fallen piece of her hair behind her ear. Pink dusts her cheeks following the swipe of my hand, and I relish the knowledge that I brought some color to her face. "But I'm glad. You needed it."

"Oh my goodness. How could I have overslept like that? I was supposed to have breakfast with Gus this morning. He's probably worried something happened."

"He knows you were sleeping...on me."

Aulie freezes. "He didn't come in here, did he?"

"Sure did." I grimace. "But I think he's okay?"

"Well, that's unlikely. He's probably outside digging your grave now."

I grab her hand, and press a kiss to the top. "You're worth it." My eyes flit to her lips, and she runs her teeth over them in response. "I like waking up to you, Dessy."

"Mmm, I like waking up to you, too." She drops her gaze to our hands, tracing the ink that swirls and spirals at the base of my wrist into a quote from Rousseau. "I just can't believe I slept that long. You poor thing, you must be starving."

"I am. Come here." Cupping her cheek, I lean in and kiss her.

Her lips part and meet mine in a savory kiss.

Slowly, I lay her back on the bed, caging her with my body. My heart beats wildly against my chest. If she only knew the power she wielded over me. How much effort it takes to tether myself to reality when she's like this, the effort it takes not to lose control.

"Is this still okay?" I whisper against her neck.

"No. I need to feed you. I feel terrible." She giggles, writhing underneath me.

"Yeah, food isn't going to satiate what I'm hungry for, Dessy. Even if I love yours." She shifts again, and I grunt at the friction. "Especially when you do that."

"What? This?" She moves her hips again in a slow, teasing manner. "Does that do something to you?"

I press my forehead to hers. "I'm trying to be a gentleman here, woman. Help me out."

"Jack?" She looks up at me, and the stars reflected in her eyes that I've desperately missed sucker-punch me with their reappearance. "What if I don't want a gentleman?"

Chapter Twenty-Seven

Aulie Desfleurs

Play: You've Really Got a Hold on Me by the Miracles

Slipping out from under Jack's looming figure to use the restroom was a mistake. Sure, it was the best call for the integrity of my bladder, having somehow made it through the entire night without waking, but now, as I sheepishly drag my feet back to my bedroom, the minuscule voice of reason I still possess is telling me to run.

Last night, Jack Parker kissed me. For real. With no character to mask the purpose of his lips. No pretense. It was just me, cardigan-wearing Aulie, and the man I've had a crush on since I was five—kissing. What's more, he cuddled with me, and instead of my body sparking alive with electricity, all I felt was a delicious serenity that lulled me into the deepest sleep I've had in months.

Maybe years.

And now, here I am, wandering slowly back to my bedroom, where that same man is waiting for me. If the intensity burning in his eyes this morning is any indication, when I pass through that threshold, if I want it, something more than cuddling will transpire between us.

And I do want that.

But I'm also terrified because I haven't moved beyond the boundary of kissing anyone since Tyler. Not just because I was safe-guarding my heart, but also because, with Tyler, intimacy hurt, like hell.

Like hell.

I don't know if it was a Tyler-and-me thing or a just me thing, but I've been anxious to find out if it'll be the same with someone else/Jack.

For the last ten years, that part of my body has been a perpetual letdown. For a hopeless romantic like me, I don't know if I can stomach a reality where intimacy—something glorified by rom-coms and romance novels alike as the pinnacle of a successful relationship—is something I can't do. I don't know if I'm ready to accept the fact that I'm broken and there doesn't seem to be a fix.

Finally, my feet bring me to my bedroom door, and I take a deep breath. At least for today, living in the present and saving my worries for another time might be my best way forward.

The hinges creak as I push the door open. Jack's shirtless silhouette dominates the space in front of my bookcase, his focus fixed on the pages of a mass paperback. My pulse skitters, drumming loudly in my ears at his figure illuminated in the morning sun.

I love him, rather hopelessly, and broken or not. Whatever he wants to do today, I want to do, too. It's been too long since I've had these sensations spiraling through me, and now that they're back, I'm addicted.

Being in love, as painful as the outcome might be—and let's be honest, with Jack, there's little chance this won't end badly—is better than having never felt at all.

I was a fool to think depriving my heart would save it. What's the point of trying to protect something if I never let it live?

"Whatchu'reading?" I smile, coming closer to my destruction.

He glances up, smiling as he rakes a seductive gaze over my body. "A very informational guide, it seems."

I blush. His stare kickstarts an electric storm that tumbles through my limbs. A wave of excitement crashes into me as a shiver grips my spine.

Thunder snow on the beach.

How is it fair that a single look can overwhelm me with a flood of sensations?

He snaps the book shut and puts it back in my historical collection. "You seem to have a thing for what the back of these books calls the 'reformed rake.' Although, I guess you told me that once, so I shouldn't be surprised."

My mind flashes back to a soggy version of myself, splashing around a fountain, trying to find a ring I didn't care for, and rambling at a man who always made my pulse race at dangerous speeds. *What can I say? I have a thing for reformed rakes?*

"They're a weakness of mine."

He cocks his head to the side. "Why do you think that is?"

I've pondered this question plenty. I think there's safety in the reformed rake. People who were supposed to be the pillars of my support system have left me my entire life, but with a rake, the promise that they're going to leave is in the premise. Fictional or not, that's what they're *supposed to do*. The fictional reformation is an added treat I don't expect to happen in reality.

I'm not tempting enough to convince anyone to stay, especially someone with numerous alternatives.

But that's not the answer Jack is searching for, if the deep smolder pinned to my face is any indication.

Rising on my tiptoes, I slowly drag his glasses off, glancing at him beneath lowered lashes. This close, our breaths synchronize. "Well, for one, they know what they're doing, and they take care of their—" My cheeks heat. How can I expect to do anything with Jack when I can't even talk about this stuff in a fictional sense? "I've just never—" Oh god, am I going to tell him that—"I've never had an orgasm."

Jack's left eyebrow rises a fraction. "Even by yourself?"

"Uhm, no. That's why, uhm. That was why Emy bought me the...vibrator."

"And the magazine of me." Jack smirks far too smugly. It's maddening how arrogant his face looks in this light. The friend side of me wants to put his ego in place, but the other part, the one that's grown far stronger, wants to kiss him senselessly until he forgets his name, and all he can think about is mine.

I roll my eyes. "And that."

"And that's all you like about these rakes? That they know what they're doing?"

"Maybe not the *only* reason. I think it might also have to do with the princess effect. Everyone around me thinks I'm this soft, dainty petal of a woman, and I probably am. But there's something alluring about being the woman can bring a man without scruples to his knees."

His hand wraps around the small of my back and brings me tight against his chest. He drops his mouth to my ear, sending my stomach into a freefall. "Do you want me on my knees for you, kitten? Because I can show you how badly you've brought me there."

Lingering wisps of electricity lick my nerve endings to life at the desperate tone in Jack's voice, like I really could be the type of woman to bring someone like him to his knees, however ridiculous that reality would have been to me a few days ago.

"I don't want to be a kitten," I whisper, stuck in a spell that only being this close to his lips can cast. "I feel powerless and silly most of the time, and I don't want that here."

He traces my jawline with his thumb. "How do you want to feel? Because fuck, Aulie, I want to give you whatever you want."

It's silly, really, what I want, and verbalizing it will only make it sound more pathetic, but there's a certain sincerity about the way Jack is looking at me that suggests however I want to feel in here, he's going to do his best to make it so. "I want to feel like a goddess."

"Then come here and let me worship you."

Rough stubble dusting Jack's cheeks scratches against my skin as his mouth crashes into mine with a sense of urgency. I gasp at the hungry, fiery possession he takes.

"Where did you put Emy's gift?" he asks.

I laugh against his lips. "I know you have a massive ego, but I'm not having a threesome with a magazine. No matter how hot that picture makes me." I lift my leg, and Jack picks me up, walking me toward the bed.

"Good to know you like the picture, but I meant the vibrator, smartass."

"Oh!" I pull away, studying his face. Jack's hair is standing on end like he was caught out in a storm. His lips are swollen, his eyelids hanging heavy with desire. "Why would you want that?"

He cups my cheek. "Just tell me where it is."

I nod to the drawer by my nightstand, and he walks over with me still latched to him like a monkey and pulls out a discreet case.

He groans as my tongue teases his earlobe, and I drag my teeth along the base.

With a gentleness that defies the fiery possession Jack's had on me, he places me on the bed. Leaning over, he continues pressing a series of small kisses along my jawline. My whole being is filled with waiting for his soft caresses to explode into something more. I hungrily grab at his pajama pants.

"Patience, love," he laughs. "Let me take care of you. Can I take your shirt off?"

I nod, and he slowly peels it off over my head.

Baring myself in front of him should set my stomach ablaze with nervous fluttering, but Jack's look of want over my body incinerates any self-conscious feelings I have. He lays me down, putting the vibrator in my hand. For what reason, I haven't quite figured out.

"Fuck, you're perfect." He grips my breast, and a captivating heat explodes out of my chest. Want pools between my thighs. "Aulie, I need my mouth here. Is that okay?"

I nod because what am I supposed to say if Jack *needs* his mouth there?

He palms my left breast with one hand, bringing his mouth to my right. His tongue caresses my nipple, already hard just from his touch. His tongue lashes against it, and I gasp with surprise at the sensation that pulses between my thighs with every pass.

"Use the vibrator when you're ready. It'll be torture not to touch you there; you have no idea, but you deserve to give yourself your first orgasm. I'm just here to do whatever it is you need. Boss me around, Aulie. Tell me what you want."

"I uhm—I fuck—can you bite me there?" I ask, need holding my body hostage.

Slowly, Jack trails a finger around my nipple and then brings his mouth hot against it, grazing it with his teeth. "Whatever you want. I'm yours," he says, continue to whisper incantations over my body. "I'm telling you now, Aulie, you can have your first, but I want to be responsible for your second, third, and so on. Forever. Tomorrow, I want you laid out on this bed begging for me like I'm the only key to your relief."

"Oh fuck—" I press the on switch to the vibrator. The tiny, hand held mechanism buzzes in my hand. It has a circle at the top that looks like it pulls in air, but I'm not sure what to do with it.

"That's it. Slide it under your pants," he rasps.

"I don't know what to do with it."

"Do you want me to show you?"

"Yes, please."

Slowly, Jack peels off my pants and takes my hand. He slides my finger over my seam, already slick and sensitive. I jolt.

"See there?" He rubs my finger against my bud.

"Mhm."

"Does it feel good when I touch you there?" he asks, on a tortured, shallow, intake of air.

"God, yes."

"Fuck. You feel so good. I don't want to stop." His eyes shutter closed like the thought of pulling away physically hurts.

"Then don't."

He circles my sensitive area again with our fingers. His eyes grow heavy with want, and I relish the effort he's putting in to stay composed. "No, not today." He exhales. "Put your toy there, slowly, and find your rhythm."

His hand falls to the swell of my hips. I bring the vibrator over my clit and hiss at the intensity.

"Go slow," he says, pressing kisses into my stomach. The muscles in my abdomen contract. A moan escapes my lips as Jack nips my navel.

I move the vibrator around my clit in slow, methodical circles.

Something long and hard presses against my thigh and I gasp, clutching the sheets with my free hand.

"Do you like how hard I am for you, Aulie?"

"Yes," I breathe out.

"God, I want you so bad." He returns his mouth to my nipples, sucking on the left one. "You're so perfect. So gorgeous."

Want coils deep in my bones and my blood. My nerve endings lick alive with a blaze that incinerates anything negative inside. The tensions grows unbearable, pulling tighter, tighter, tighter. My toes curl, my back arches, and in a flash of ecstasy the tension releases as a loud cry passes between my lips, and Jack captures it with his mouth.

As I catch my breath, Jack trails his finger down my sternum, tracing my center with his finger as aftershocks send ripples of pleasure through my body. "How do you feel?"

"Really fucking good." I shiver in the bed, the sheets a crumpled mess. My pants are hanging around my ankles, and my shirt is laying to the right of my head. Euphoria floods my veins, like sunbursts flaring incandescently in the sky. "But now it's your turn." I reach for him, and his eyes widen.

Chapter Twenty-Eight

Aulie Desfleurs

Play: *Lollipop by the Chordettes*

"Aulie." A soft, raspy voice beckons me from dreamland, where I've spent the past two days being thoroughly wooed by Jack Parker.

It had to be a dream. There's no way that the man I know and love as a friend has been harboring a secret, sweet and romantic side. The real Jack Parker would never set up an elaborate birthday dinner to tell me he liked me, right?

Soft phantom lips graze my forehead like a whisper.

I haven't slept this well—maybe ever—which would explain the detailed dreams.

My limbs, still heavy with slumber, fall across my body pillow, and I pull it tighter against me.

"Jesus, Dessy." A low rumble vibrates against my chest.

"Mmm?" I hum. So maybe I'm closer to dreamland than I thought if I'm imagining my pillow is Jack.

"I have to get up today." Fingers trail the nape of my neck, moving my hair over my shoulder and continuing slowly down my back.

With each light touch, I accept that this is real and better than any dream I could have imagined. Jack is here, in my bed.

"Why?" I murmur. Tilting my chin, I let my eyes flicker open. A soft-lopsided grin greets me as my eyes focus on Jack, highlighted in the soft glow of my reading lamp. He's lounging rather sinfully with his hand propped behind his head. His bicep flexes, and I follow the curve to his shoulders and dip down to his chest, where the messy lines of...something...lay across his chest. My fingers graze along the ink, following the curves of the letters. "Can't we just lie in bed for the rest of the day?"

True, after not working on my birthday and spending all of yesterday indisposed in here with him, I *should* work today, but this little bubble has been impossibly glorious, and I don't want to risk facing reality and losing it all.

"Trust me, I wish I could, but I have to get to skate, or Coach will have my ass more than he already does."

"Boo. Don't you already know how to skate? Isn't that enough?"

"I vaguely remember being a professional athlete or something, so no," he says, leaning forward and kissing the tip of my nose.

"I couldn't have someone like that for a bed guest. Seems fake," I say, dropping my head back down to his bare chest and exploring the ridges of his abdomen with my fingers. "What time is it, anyway?"

Jack hums, shifting in the bed like he's savoring my touch. "Five-thirty. Seriously, temptress. I gotta get to the rink."

The nickname elicits a smirk from me. *Temptress.* Yes, I could be wicked.

I play with the hem of his waistband, and he gently grabs my hand.

With a huff, I fall onto my back. "Why do you have to go so early?"

"Really?" he asks, climbing over me and caging me with his body. I'm not sure how he plans to exit the bed this way, but I won't complain about it.

"Well. Let's see." He dips down and engulfs me with his warmth. "Some beautiful," he kisses the column of my throat. "Kind." Another word. Another kiss. "Overly punctual woman—" His tongue swirls over my exposed skin as he presses his mouth above my breast. My back arches, and he groans slightly, slowly peeling my camisole down and exposing my right breast to the chilly morning air. Instantly, my nipple pebbles, and he runs his finger over it. "Gave me shit about getting to the fair on time. So here we are."

"But your time at the fair is over."

"I booked everything for the same time for consistency when I got here."

Wait, has he been getting up this early every morning just to make sure he made it to his one week of the fair on time?

"Okay, and I thank you, but now the beautiful, kind, overly punctual woman wants snuggles," I whine, writhing underneath him. Temptresses probably use sexier words, but I'm still a work in progress. Princesses don't change their tiaras overnight. "And maybe some other things. Don't you think other things are just as important for your game?" I reach for Jack, trying to pull him closer, desperate for a kiss on the lips.

"If you want to explain that to Coach, I'd welcome the phone call. But unfortunately, darling, I have to be an adult this morning." He kisses me with a finality I don't appreciate, and well, boo.

"You're so boring and responsible." I pout as he withdraws himself and stands.

"And you're scaring me."

"Please? Come here?" I beckon him with a crooked finger, glancing at him beneath lowered lashes. A look I'm learning might be Jack's kryptonite.

I'm not proud that I'm this clingy in the morning, but no one's touched me this way in years, maybe ever.

His eyes connect with mine, and he crawls back on the bed, seemingly unable to break free from the spell I've cast. "Seriously? You're like a cute fucking siren. I have to go."

"But I'm going to miss you." I smile, a little gleeful to see he's just as weak as me.

"Yeah?" He quirks a brow. "And why is that?" His finger trails the hem of my shirt and works its way under my fabric, grazing along my naval.

"Because—" His touch fries my brain circuit. *Because I'm madly in love with you.*

"You okay?" He smirks. He slowly strokes along my waistband. "You were so chatty a few seconds ago. I'm a little concerned."

"I'm—" Again, I start, but my voice quivers when he hooks into my underwear and pulls them down with my pants. What the hell kind of magic does this man have over me? I sit up, eager to catch my lips with his. He leaves his a whisper away, his warm breath falling on mine, but he never lets them touch, stripping my camisole off and slowly lowering back down on the bed.

Hungrily, Jack's gaze works over my body. Whenever he looks at me like this, I feel like the most beautiful person on earth—I feel powerful. I feel like a queen.

"I guess I can be a few minutes late. I can't leave you when I'm not sure your vocal cords are working." He pulls my legs, so I'm straddling the edge of the bed and then drops to his knees. "Is this okay?"

My heart somersaults in my chest as understanding of his intentions crash over me. I've read about what he's about to do enough times that I feel I've had secondhand...erm...ladyboners... as Emy would call them. But I've never...

"Oh, fuck yes," I say breathlessly.

A simple yes would have sufficed, Aulie.

Jack blinks at my uncharacteristic cursing. It's a problem in the bedroom, apparently. "Yup. I broke you. Looking forward to you becoming a regular sodomite after this morning."

"You'll have to reform me of my wicked—"

Jack slips a finger in, splitting my seam, and banter who.

"I'm sorry, Dessy, you were saying something?"

My teeth rake over my bottom lip. "Of course you'd be a tease."

"I told you your second would be mine, love."

His tongue follows, lashing against my bud. I writhe under him after a few punishing strokes. He changes to soft, even ones. A moan passes over my lips, eliciting a satisfied grunt from him.

My fingers thread through his messy hair, already ruffled from yesterday's day spent in bed. After the past twenty-four hours, I suspected Jack had somehow rewired my body's chemistry, so I only responded to him like this. Now, when everything in me seems to heed his command, I'm sure he's done something sinister. The pressure inside intensifies, but there's a hollowness between my thighs I can't explain, and I'm desperate for *something*. My back arches, and I reach for him.

Jack slams my hips down with a hand on my stomach, pressing me back into the bed.

"Jack—I need."

"Shh. I know what you need, Dessy. Just trust me."

I whimper, and he glances up from the floor.

"Oh, now how can I say no to that? So needy so soon, my goodness," he tsks. With a wicked grin and a devilish glint in his eye, he puts two of his fingers in his mouth before slowly dragging them out. "Someday, I will make you wait until you're a writhing, begging mess. But I will have to work up an immunity to that face first."

Slowly, he kisses the inside of my thigh.

"Do you know what you do to me, Aulie?"

He moves over to the other thigh, teasing the seam to my entrance with his fingers. When I don't gather enough air for a response, he continues.

"No? Well, I'll have to show you."

His finger pumps in and out as his mouth sucks against my clit.

My toes curl, and an intense heat spirals through me.

With each pump of his fingers, my body tightens until the tension breaks and release washes over me. A loud cry escapes my lips. Quickly, I clamp a hand over my mouth—hopefully Emy and Gus are in a deep enough sleep that neither of them heard that.

Jack regards me with pride, swiping at his mouth. "Yup, vocal cords seem to work fine." He chuckles.

I lay there, trying to catch my breath and debating if "please sir, can I have some more?" is an appropriate question given the situation.

I haven't talked to Jack about what he wants from any of this, but if he wants any form of friendship that doesn't include him doing that with his mouth for all of eternity, then I'm doomed.

What the heck am I doing?

I know about Jack's no-date rule.

I know his suspension will end soon.

I know he's used me as a distraction before.

And yet, here I am, diving headfirst into a dangerous territory without a parachute and hoping, however foolishly, that he'll catch me.

"Aulie?" Jack's grin falls. "Hey, you okay?"

"Fine," I breathe out.

"I've got to go to skate, okay? But I'll be back soon."

I have to talk to Harold, the rink owner, about the ice he lays for me in December at the estate, and I'm not ready to face Gus or Emy yet. "Would you mind terribly if I came?"

Jack meets my eye, and I spy a twinkle I thought he'd lost years ago. He looks younger, somehow. "Didn't you just?"

"Oh god, I regret you already!" I throw a pillow at his head, and he giggles. It's like our friendship is still the root of everything, and we've just added cunnilingus and kisses to the dynamic.

"No, you don't." Jack pulls me up from the bed and brushes his lips to mine. He kisses me as though he's been waiting years for this moment, savoring every inch of my mouth. My legs wobble, still unstable from what he just did, and he chuckles, holding me close. "I've got you, Dessy. Always have."

Reality crashes down around me with those four simple words, he's right—I've always been his.

~

THE COOL OF THE STEEL BLEACHER SEEPS IN THROUGH MY thin set of leggings I pulled on after attempting to wear jeans and being unable to button them without cutting off circulation to my legs. Whoever thought hard pants were a good idea was sorely mistaken.

After talking to Harold and confirming our plan to prepare the ice rink, I planned on using the empty bleachers to catch up on the work I've been neglecting over the past few days.

But here's the thing. Jack has a hockey butt—my weakness—and I've... I've touched the butt. And how can I think about Fanny Price and *Mansfield Park* Weekend when that's slicing along the rink?

Suddenly, ice sprays in my direction, and I blink, prepared for a freezing onslaught, forgetting about the protection the boards provide me. Jack stands on the other side with a smirk.

I used to think Jack's playfulness was a reminder that he wasn't interested in me romantically. But now, seeing him with other women, I think it might be a compliment. Like he's comfortable with me and I shouldn't take that for granted.

I always had a thing for Mr. Tilney's teasing smiles in *Northanger Abbey*, anyway.

Jack leans his arm on the plexiglass, and the images that have haunted me the past few weeks of him in the penalty box call forward, but I don't push them down or blush. "Hey, Dessy. I'm all done if you want me to grab some skates from Harold and join me."

I squirm on the bench. I've never admitted this to Jack, but I'm a miserable skater. Since I'm from New Hampshire, it's assumed that I was born with the skill, but I never learned how. Gus and my Memere were always too worried about my safety. Couple that with a terrible pain that's been spasming down my side and through my leg for the better part of the last hour, and skating doesn't sound like something I want to do today. "Please don't judge me, but I don't know how, and I don't feel like falling today."

"Huh, I wonder if you know anyone particularly skilled and willing to have an excuse to put his hands all over you to keep you safe."

Nervously, I swallow, recalling where those hands were last night...where they were this morning. Heat rises to my cheeks, despite the chill of the arena air.

Jack's smirk grows into a full-bodied grin.

How can I say no to a face like that?

"While that's a tempting offer, maybe I don't want to risk making him fall."

"Too late for that." He winks.

My heart somersaults in my chest, and warmth blooms through the acrobatics.

When Jack says sweet stuff like that, it's so easy for me to give in to my foolish side and think that we could be on the precipice of one of those great love stories I've only ever read or dreamed about.

But hope has never been my friend, and I don't know how to get myself to a place where I can trust it even if there's a certainty in my chest that says I should.

"I'm sorry. What was that impossibly corny line?" I laugh, deflecting the battle between my head and heart into humor.

"Forget I asked." He rolls his eyes like he's annoyed. But the blush coloring his cheeks betrays him.

Dang it, I should have let the part of me that was swooning out instead.

"I'm an eight," I say, trying to make amends for my poorly timed ribbing. "But I'm worried I'll pull you down."

I don't know if I'm talking about on the ice or something grander here. Jack doesn't belong in Chawton Falls forever, and when he's back in the world of professional sports, he isn't going to want a small-town nobody holding him back.

"You never would," he says, almost like he knows I need the reassurance and skates away.

At that moment, the pain shooting on and off through my right side intensifies. I gasp as cold sweat beads on my forehead. My lower half seizes, and I close my eyes and shift on the bench, hoping to find a position to ease the pain.

Nothing helps, and I sit there for what seems like an eternity in agony without an escape.

"Dessy. You okay?"

My eyes flutter open. Jack greets me with his signature furrowed eyebrow look.

"Yeah, fine." My eyes travel to the white skates draped over his shoulder, and I groan. "If I fall, please just release me. I won't be responsible for re-injuring the star player of the Brawling Badgers." The sharp pang continues in my side. Maybe standing will help since sitting clearly isn't the answer.

"I have two hundred and thirty-pound men hurling themselves at me regularly. You're not going to take me down. It'll be fine," Jack says, offering me his hand as I rise.

A rush of nausea overwhelms me.

"I just need to use the restroom before I put my skates on," I say, steadying my legs as the world around me swirls. *Play it cool. Please don't make him worry for nothing. You're fine.*

After I clear the corner and find myself out of Jack's line of vision, I hurry and bust through the bathroom door, grateful the arena is empty and I don't have to worry about breaking someone's nose in my haste.

I don't even bother closing the stall before my head is in the toilet and release the contents of my stomach.

My overdramatic body is getting old.

I grab the toothbrush I keep in my purse for these situations. Emy thinks it's weird I need one, but it's happened enough that I wouldn't dare go anywhere without it.

Something is wrong if you're vomiting that much in public,

Aulie, she would argue while I'd wave her off. My doctors were confident that my constipation was causing severe acid reflux, and who am I to question them?

I splash water on my face before another pain comes through, and I brace both hands on the counter, breathing through the overwhelming stabs.

Keep pushing. It's all in your head. You're fine. Just skate it off. What choice do you have, anyway? I try to give myself a pep talk, but the pain seems immune to the power of positive thought.

How annoying.

Holding my head high, I gather myself as best I can and march back to the bleachers. Jack hands me the skates, and I slip my feet out of my shoes and into the rentals, quickly tying them up. Jack shakes his head as I go to stand. "First lesson, you need to make sure your skates are laced tighter than that." He kneels on the concrete floor and pulls my laces taut.

"Good?" he asks, peering at me beneath his thick eyelashes.

My heart flips in my chest at his care to ensure my skates are snug. I've always known that Jack wasn't the gruff asshole he wanted the rest of the world to think he was, but I didn't know he could be...this.

I clear my throat as a million butterflies flutter in the pit of my stomach. I can be clingy and want snuggles, that's fine, but it's too soon to let Jack know just how much of myself he has in the palm of his hand, not when I don't fully understand it yet.

Jack holds out his hand, and I take it, wobbling as I try my first step with the skates. The minute my feet find the ice, I feel like Bambi learning how to walk for the first time.

My arms flail as I fail to find my footing, and Jack's muscular arms wrap around me.

"Jesus, Dessy," he laughs, hooking his hand around my waist and skating along my side. "You weren't kidding about being bad at this."

"How the heck are you so steady? They're like wearing stilts on a slippery surface." Another lightning bolt shoots down my side. "Fuck," I whisper, trying not to show how much pain I'm actually in.

"I've had a lot of practice." Jack shrugs, swinging me into him so we're chest to chest. "And I also have an incredible motivation not to fall and crush the potty mouth threatening to sully my virgin ears, so that helps."

"You poor angel, how you ever got tangled up with a scoundrel such as myself, I'll never understand."

"Simone warned me not to get involved. But the heart wants what it wants, and I've always had a thing for reformation projects." He winks, and I'm instantly transported to that girl in the fountain, aimlessly searching for the ring she flung in a furry, rambling incoherently because, of course, this is how the guy she'd been in love with since she was little would find her.

"I hate you so much."

"Didn't seem like it this morning," Jack says, pressing his hand on the small of my back and pulling me tighter against him. His eyes drop to my lips, and my breath hitches. With all the times we've embraced in the past few days, this action should be old news, but the anticipation of feeling his lips against mine still steals my breath away.

Pain hits me, more potent than it has all day, and the force almost knocks me to the ice.

I try to hide my wince, but this one is too great to keep from Jack.

My vision blurs.

My head swirls.

Black dots spot what little of the world I can see.

Oh no, no, no, no. Not here, not in front of Jack.

When I pass out, I try not to do it in front of people. They always make a big deal out of nothing. I get it; for most people, fainting isn't common, and usually, it's a symptom of something greater happening. But for me? I guess I'm just a weenie and can't handle regular pain levels because I black out regularly, and not a single doctor I've mentioned the symptom to has been concerned.

Black creeps in.

I'm not in pain. Everything is fine. Pull yourself together.

"Aulie, are you okay?" Jack's question sounds distant, but I know he's here, holding me firm.

I need to reassure him. I need to tell him not to worry about what's happening, so he doesn't overreact. Everything is okay. "I'm fine. I'm just going to pass out."

Chapter Twenty-Nine

Jack Parker

Play: *You're On Your Own, Kid by Taylor Swift*

"Aulie?" Oh. Fuck. Aulie's body falls heavy and unresponsive in my arms. I clutch her tightly, my heart pounding in my chest.

"Charlie!" I yell for the trainer I hired for my time up here—who's unlacing his skates on a bench. He was a freshman when I was a senior in high school and loaded with potential, but an injury in college ended his chances of turning pro. When he graduated, he returned to Chawton Falls to help train the next generation of hockey players.

And suspended professional ones, apparently.

"Charlie. I need my sweatshirt on the bleacher." Typically, I'm as stable on skates as I am on my own two feet, but I'm in the middle of the rink and don't want to risk moving her too far.

He glances up and his eyes fall on Aulie. In a hurry, he grabs my sweatshirt and rushes to my side of the rink, laying it down on the ice. I lay her gently down, supporting her head and trying not to shake too much.

"She used to do this every once in a while in high school," Charlie says. "Gave the teachers a wicked good fright, but she'd always come out of it okay. She's probably fine—"

"We should call an ambulance," I cut him off, so tired of everyone saying whatever is going on with Aulie is *fine*. For fuck's sake, she said those words herself before she fainted.

People don't just lose consciousness for fun.

Charlie runs a hand through his sandy blond hair with a grimace. "She's going to hate us making a big deal of it."

"I don't care if she's going to hate it. Just go do it." The words come out with more bite than I intend, and I immediately regret it.

He shoots his hands up in surrender. "I'm going. I'm going."

Sitting down next to Aulie on the ice, I scrub two hands down my face as Charlie's skates glide further away.

Fuck. How did I miss the signs that she wasn't feeling well?

I glance down at her paling skin. Was she like this this morning?

Her eyes slowly flicker open. "Hey," she says hoarsely.

I exhale. "Fuck's sake, Dessy. Are you trying to give me a heart attack?"

"I'm so sorry." She rests a palm on her stomach, and a small cry of pain passes over her lips before it grows into a louder wail.

I rub circles into her hand, my heart still running a thousand miles a minute. "No, I'm sorry. I'll try to be nicer—"

"Oh no, am I dying?"

My racing heart leaps in my chest, running hurdles. "Why would you think that?"

"Because you said you're going to be nice to me." She tries to laugh, but I'm not in the mood for playing.

"No more kidding, Dessy. Charlie's getting an ambulance, but I need you to tell me what's happening."

"Nothing's going on. This happens sometimes. Please don't make a fuss. I'm—" She tries to pick her herself up but stops. "I'm laying back down. But I'm fine, okay?"

It's not okay. Aulie's keeping something from me, and considering my history with my dad, I'm the last person emotionally stable enough to handle that.

It's hitting too fucking close to home.

I can't let it capsize me like it usually does. I need to stay strong because Aulie needs that, needs me—no more sulking.

She grabs her right side, breathing sharply.

"Is that where the pain is coming from?" I ask, bringing my hand over hers.

"Mmhmm."

"Looks like it's your appendix."

"It's being an appen-dick. But that might be why I vomited."

I refuse to acknowledge her pun. We're built from the same cloth the way we use humor to deflect away from heavier topics. "When did you vomit? *The bathroom*," I sigh, pinching the bridge of my nose. "You're so fucking stubborn, it's ridiculous."

"Don't be mad at me. I'm sick." She cracks an eye open and peeks at me with a soft smirk.

The storm swelling inside of me quiets. I can thunder and brood later. Right now, I need to be soft for her. I lean over and plant a gentle kiss on her forehead. Salty beads of sweat coat my lips with the contact despite the chill in the air. "Fine. But expect a firm scolding later when you're feeling better."

"Do firm scoldings include spankings?"

Lying next to her, I shake my head and take her hand, feeling the warmth spread from our intertwined fingers to my chest. "One day. I broke you in one freaking day."

"To be fair, it was a perfect day."

"Yeah, it was," I sigh. "But I'd like more than just one with you, Dessy. The paramedics are going to be here soon, okay? Just let me know if you need something before then."

I focus on my breathing and the sound of Aulie's, letting it lull me into a sense of calm. Each rise and fall is a reassurance that she's here still, with me. I trace her almost peaceful profile. The pinched corners of her mouth are the only visible sign that she's in pain.

If I didn't know her face like I do, all the soft curves and the usual upward tilt of her lips, she'd have me fooled.

I hate she didn't tell me she wasn't feeling well, but I hate even more that I missed all her subtle signs. I learned not to trust everything Aulie presented to the world a long time ago, but I thought we were past that. I thought we were being honest with each other.

Another tiny cry of pain passes over her lips—the sound serves as a dagger to my heart.

What other darkness is she hiding from me?

"I DON'T UNDERSTAND WHY YOU CAN'T TELL ME ANYTHING. Seriously, you saw me come in with her," I say, rubbing my temple with my forefingers. A tension headache is brewing, along with the storm inside. I've never been a patient man, and after the past two hours, I'm running on fumes. I'm going to break soon.

They brought Aulie to the hospital half an hour ago, and no one has given me an update or allowed me to see her.

The nurse behind the counter purses her lips but doesn't glance in my direction. She hasn't met my eyes since she refused to provide me with anything the first time. "And I told you, honey, it doesn't matter that I saw you with her. I can't release information to a non-family member."

Screw it. I'm not proud, but sometimes being Jack Parker—a star hockey player—comes with its perks, and I'm hoping now is one of those times.

I lean my elbows on the counter, flashing her my broadest grin. "But, Doris, I'm her fiancé. That has to count for something, right?

Gus is on his way, but he was in a meeting two hours south and won't be here for another hour.

There's no way my nerves can wait that long.

Doris glances up from her clipboard. "I know who you are, sweetheart, and I haven't heard of any engagement."

"My fiancée is very private, so she wanted to keep it quiet."

"Mmhmm, and that actress this summer?"

A muscle in my jaw jumps. Dammit, I didn't have Doris pegged to be such a busybody, considering she's giving me absolutely nothing. "She was a cover for the press."

"I don't see a ring on that girl's finger."

No, but there will be one day if I ever get my shit together.

"Aulie doesn't wear her ring when she goes skating," a soft female voice says from behind. I let out a sigh of relief, and my shoulders drop from their raised position under my ears. Emy. "She scratched him once while she was falling and could never live with herself for harming the love of her life. But here, she sent me a picture of the ring. He did good, huh?" She flashes the nurse a picture of Aulie's grandmother's ring that Gus and I refinished for her birthday. The pit in my stomach grows. Since we've been barricaded in her room, Gus hasn't had a chance to give it to her yet.

"You should have seen her when she got the ring," Emy keeps going. "He lit the gazebo with fairy lights and did it at sunset along King's Pond, and boy, did she bawl—her brother and I couldn't be happier for—"

"Is her brother here?" Doris interrupts Emy's convincing tale.

"He's on his way."

Sighing, the nurse regards me skeptically, but eventually, she nods. "I have some questions that need to be answered."

She pushes a clipboard into my hands, and I swallow, reading over the sheet. Address and phone number I can handle, but I know nothing about Aulie's family or personal medical history.

"I think I've got this," Emy whispers, sliding the clipboard out of my hand. "Poor guy is rattled, you know, Doris. She has been the object of his affection since he was a young boy, and it breaks his heart to see the love of his life in agony." She places a palm on her hand like she's swooning before meeting my eye with a spark of mischief.

Well, she has me pegged, huh?

I blush, letting my eyes roam around the room and try to find something to center myself on. A picture of a long-lost but not-forgotten rock formation snags my attention. The Old Man of the Mountain, a natural collection of rocks that vaguely resembled a man's profile, was a huge tourist attraction in New Hampshire until it collapsed. Locals woke up one morning to see it'd fallen in the night. Aulie's family crowded around the TV, watching in horror at the coverage, and her Memere even shed a tear.

Now, a monument stands at the base. It's a collection of poles with little cutouts hanging off each bar. If you stand at a certain distance and squint, it looks like the Old Man is still there.

But it isn't. It's a hollow space and an homage to something that *was*.

Standing here now, I can't help but feel that's what happened to me when my dad passed. I just crumbled, and I've been that collection of pieces that resemble the original if you didn't look too close ever since.

But after everything that's happened the past two days, it felt like Aulie was building me back up, rock by rock—I was becoming the real thing again, not a recreation.

And now, she's here, in a hospital bed, and just like my dad, something was wrong, and she didn't tell me.

I feel a tug on my arm. "Thank you again, Doris. We appreciate you," Emy says, moving me into the waiting room and out of earshot. "That woman has the bedside manner of a wet fart."

"Thank you." I huff, lowering myself into the chair and resting my forearms on the top of my legs. Now's not the time to sulk about how the people I love don't trust me enough to open up about what's happening in their lives. When Aulie is safe and home, maybe I can try to work through that, but not now.

"I'm a little hurt that I missed the engagement, but you know I've always got your back, Parker."

"The nurse wasn't giving me anything, and I was desperate."

"The words every woman wants associated with her happy day."

I snort, and a fraction of the tension coiled inside relaxes.

Since we were little, Emy's never feared my grumpy natural disposition.

"Gus should be here soon," she says, checking her phone. "I told him not to speed, but I wouldn't be surprised if he didn't listen."

My stomach becomes a ball of nerves and anxiety. I was eager for Gus to get here initially, but now—well, I'll have to face him, eventually, anyway, so I might as well get it over with. I stepped over a line, not telling him about Aulie and me, and now she's in the hospital. That's not exactly the track record I hoped to have during this discussion. "Is he..." I stumble, failing to find the right words.

"Pissed? Oh yeah, but he won't make a show here. Give him time to get used to the idea, and he'll be fine," she says, an unspoken *or else* implied in her tone.

The automatic swinging doors to where they're holding Aulie part, and a man in a white coat and a stethoscope around his neck, pushes his way through. Doris points at me, and I stand to greet him—a million thoughts still spiraling inside.

I force myself to focus, catching enough to gather that they're going to run a few more tests, but that I was probably right—they think Aulie has appendicitis. She's doing okay, awake and alert enough to agree to what she needs, which is good because otherwise, we'd have to wait for Gus to get here. The sooner she's sedated, the better. Her pain level still isn't under control, and it's causing her blood pressure to spike too high.

"I'll let you know more when we get out," he says, placing a hand on my arm and returning the way he came.

Rubbing the back of my neck, I pace the room. Aulie will be okay. She has to be.

Fuck, I hate hospitals. You'd think given most people are here for stressful situations, they'd make the damn waiting room cozier, but the sterile walls, pleather chairs, and dim lighting somehow add to the discomfort.

With each passing second, anxiety tightens its grip on my chest.

Aulie is fine. Everything is fine.

The tension builds and builds until my heart rests compressed into an impossibly tiny box.

I don't fight to release it.

The entrance to the emergency room slams open, and Gus storms in. He searches for Emy, not sparing me a second glance.

An act of mercy.

"She's okay," Emy whispers into Gus's slumped figure. Her arms encircle him, rubbing his back as his head falls to her shoulder. For all the time I've spent watching him protect and enforce, Gus looks impossibly small in this moment. "She's okay. You're okay. Let it out. I've got you."

They stand there together for a few minutes. Gus's shoulders shudder, and I feel that burrowed in Emy's shoulder he's probably crying.

Gus. He's the most stoic, dependable guy I've ever met.

And he's crying over his sister being in the hospital.

And it's...okay?

Emy's encouraging it.

I sit down. My leg shakes. I need a distraction.

I peruse the magazines littered on the table next to me.

Veronica's face engulfs the cover of *Happening*, a celebrity gossip magazine with the headline: *Veronica Burke on What She Learned Dating Jack Parker: Why she ignored the red flags and got her heart broken by a f***boy.*

And...looking at magazines is not going to help. Noted.

Emy and Gus chose two seats not too far away.

I glance briefly, catching the tears rimming Gus's eyes. He meets my stare, and a scowl grows in place of his worry.

With a nod, I accept his ire. I should have told him. I shouldn't have holed up in Aulie's room with her for a day and paid better attention to her this morning. One day with me, and she's already in the hospital. How must that look to him?

After about thirty minutes of nothing, a nurse comes out from behind the swinging doors and approaches us. "So, it's not appendicitis. The doctor is ordering an ultrasound, but there's room for someone in there with her." She looks directly at me, but I'm not the one who should go join her.

I glance at Gus and Emy. Gus nudges Emy with his knee. "You should go. You know how to comfort her."

Emy nods, whispering something in Gus's ear and pressing a kiss before bending down to say something to me. "He's not good at verbalizing stuff, but he hates hospitals, too. He needs his best friend, okay?"

"Got it." I swallow. She's right. I'm sitting here a wreck because I've already lost one person who meant something to me. Gus has lost fifteen in five years. I can't fathom what that's done to him.

I need to be a good friend even if I get my ass handed to me.

"Keep us updated. Okay?" I say before standing and taking Emy's vacated seat next to Gus.

He doesn't look up, but he also doesn't growl, so I will take the win.

"She's going to be okay," I say—as much to reassure myself and Gus.

Gus groans, leaning back in his chair. "This place sucks ass."

"Yeah, it does."

"I should get a punch card or something with the number of visits I've made to it in the past few years."

"I don't know how you guys handled it."

"Not well." He chuckles, swiping at some tears. "Shit, I thought I had this under control."

A nervous energy hums through me while Gus lets a few more fall. I hate that's my reaction to his emotions, but isn't there a manual we got as children about not crying as New Englanders?

"Do you remember when we had to bring Grady in for stitches?" I ask, deflecting to a funny story because that's my only strategy for navigating this situation.

"Which time?"

"The time he tried to smash the glass beer bottle on his head."

"Is that what he did? I walked in on the scene late, and he had glass shards sticking out of his forehead."

"Yup." I laugh, recalling the situation. Gus walked out of his room right after it happened. With a sigh, he got Grady in the car with a towel held to his head, and we did laps around the hospital in the bitter cold while I sobered up, preferring that to going inside. That night, Gus had been happy to accompany me in silence. He never acknowledged my issues with hospitals or brought up my dad.

I hate he has something similar weighing on him now.

With a chuckle, Gus shakes his head and crosses his arms. "He was always an adventure, that's for sure. How's he doing?"

"Fine." I shrug. "Better than me in some ways, I guess, where he's not suspended and exiled from the city we play in."

Slowly, Gus's stare turns on me. The heat of his eyes burns into the side of my face, and I swallow. "What's your plan with Aulie when you go back? You know she gets wicked attached to people, and you don't date during the season, so if I'm going to be okay with this, I have to know there's a plan."

I meet his stare. I don't know what happens to us, but I owe Gus the truth.

"There isn't one yet. We haven't had a chance to talk, but I promise, I'm attached, too."

"So, no stereotypical Asshole Jack stuff?"

"Not if I can help it."

"Cool." Gus shrugs, returning his attention to the empty grey chair before us.

Wait. What? "That's it?" I blurt, immediately regretting it.

I should be grateful Gus is being this chill. But after five years of torment, his laissez-faire attitude is unsettling.

Did I seriously have perpetual blue balls for years for nothing?

"I mean, I can kick your ass if you want me to," Gus snorts. "But yeah, that's it. She hasn't slept in months, and from what I can tell from her lack of rustling around the house she's slept like the dead the past few days. I won't block her from whatever is helping her finally move on from things."

Okay, rational and valid.

But I'm not buying it. Gus's tendency to overprotect Aulie

doesn't align with his calm demeanor. I'd expect at least a little pushback.

"Did Emy talk to you?" I smirk.

His eyes widen, and he nods. "Yeah, and she scares me. But she had a point. I'd be a hypocrite to date her and bar Aulie from you. You're my best friend for a reason. If you're showing that side to her, too, then we're cool. I want her to be with a guy that deserves her."

I nod. "I'm trying."

"As long as you do that every day, we're good." He lightly punches my leg. "But the minute you act up—trust me—"

"I'll be ready for the dropped gloves."

The swinging doors open wide, and Gus and I gaze in their direction.

Emy marches through them. A soft smile plays on her lips when she sees us together. "They just wheeled her into surgery. She has a cyst twisting her ovary and blocking blood flow, so they need to operate immediately."

Ice floods my veins at the shock of the news, and I sink back in my chair, seeking something to tether me to reality.

Fuck. Surgery?

After they ruled out appendicitis, I was hopeful Aulie would get out of this visit without a drastic procedure, but I guess I was wrong about that, too.

"Is this something that just happened, or does it have to do with why she's been going to the doctor so much?" I ask. As oblivious as I have been about certain things, I know something has been bothering Aulie for a while, and I hate that every time she goes to the doctors for help, they shrug it off.

If this surgery will help that, it sucks she needs to have it, but at least something good would come out of today.

"I think it might have something to do with the asshole doctors —her passing out today. She's so in her head about her pain because of their dismissal that she keeps trying to push through it, so hopefully, this will help set her straight. She shouldn't lose her ovary, but yeah, I'm over dickhead doctors. Especially the one that dismissed her a few weeks ago because they said the cyst was already there, though it wasn't fully twisted. They said she should be out in a few hours, but one of us should set up her room for when they release her later today. Are you guys okay to stay here and keep me in the loop?"

Emy exhales, and her shoulders sag. She cares for Aulie just as much as us, but she's had to be stronger than us today. Gus seems to realize this, too, and stands, rubbing her back and swallowing her with his arms.

"Go home and make sure you get some rest, too. We've got everything under control here."

"Thank you. I have a list from the nurse of stuff we should buy to make her comfy." Emy hands me the paper. "Maybe you can do a little online shopping while you wait?"

I nod, taking the list and pulling out my phone.

My daily text from Grady waits on my locked screen.

Twenty days until your suspension is over.

I swallow. Since my first week here, I haven't thought about how much longer I'll be in Chawton Falls. I've been too distracted with Aulie, coming through for her with the fair, and the sparks flying between us. But now I'm halfway through the suspension, and while I was itching for it to be over at the beginning, I don't know what I want.

I don't date during the season. I've had that rule for over ten years for a reason.

I have zero interest in following the rules when it comes to Aulie, though. Especially after today, especially after having to entertain, however shortly and overdramatically, the thought of a world existing without her.

No, I'll figure something out. That is if she wants something more than the fuckboy. After today, and her not telling me about her pain, I'm not sure how deep her side of the connection goes. When it came down to something important, she didn't trust me.

I'm not going to be able to shake that off so easily.

Chapter Thirty

Aulie Desfleurs

Play: *Hey Jude by the Beatles*

Two large hands firmly grip my calves. They squeeze—squeeze—squeeze. That's too tight. I open my mouth to let them know they're cutting off circulation to my legs, but my throat is hoarse and dry—currently muffled by some mask.

Where am I?

Slowly, I register a beep here, a comment there, until everything floods like a symphony of machines and hurried nurses.

Right. Surgery. I just had surgery.

I blink my eyes open, finding the heavy fluorescent light shining too brightly overhead. Okay, maybe I could keep my eyes shut for a few more minutes. I fade in and out of consciousness, vaguely registering a heavy pressure on my abdomen.

And oh, my sweet Peter Noone, a swell of pain follows. Something on my arm clamps down, tightening until I panic it will burst on my arm. But again, at that moment, it releases. A cacophony of beeps follows.

"She's still in too much pain," a soft voice whispers close by. "Should we give her another dose of the fentanyl?"

"Yeah, we should. But she's going to be nauseous when she wakes up."

At this, I open my eyes. I'd rather be in pain than nauseous. Pink scrubs and a name tag hang over me. *Vi.*

"Excuse me?" I try, the mask muffling most of my question.

"Oh, hi. Are you awake then?" The nurse smiles softly at me. "Are you ready for this to come off?" she asks, gesturing to the oxygen mask on my face.

I nod, and she unclips it.

Slowly, my pain subsides as a cool drip floods my bloodstream. I'm probably too late to stop her from injecting whatever it was into my IV.

"Scale of one to ten. Can you rate your pain for me?" the other nurse I've heard in the room asks. She's donning a similar pair of pink scrubs and an ornate candy corn headband.

A dizzying wave swallows my head whole, and I try to gather my wits about me enough to answer the question.

I've always hated the pain scale question because I don't know what a normal level is supposed to be. One time, during an awful episode, I told the doctor I thought my pain was something close to a six or seven most days, and he shook his head and said if it were a six or seven, I would be on the floor curled up in a ball unable to function so I must have been mistaken.

But I didn't feel like I was. I wanted to curl up in a ball. I just couldn't because the feeling and intensity was so constant, and I had a life to live.

Currently, my pain is more under control than that episode. And if that wasn't a six or seven, it was probably a five. So this is a three?

"Maybe a two or three?" I answer.

The nurse's brow furrows like she doesn't believe me. She presses a button on the machine and again the blood pressure cuff on my arm tightens.

The pressure releases, and the machine next to me beeps

wildly. "Mmhmm. Let's forget the scale question for now." She smiles, noting my blood pressure. "Usually, we can't let you go until you're under a five, but you're obviously a tough cookie considering how much disease they found, so we'll use your blood pressure number as a marker instead. We want to get it under 140 before we release you."

Tough cookie? Has anyone ever called me that? And disease? What is she talking about?

My head swirls, and the wall that I swear was plain and white morphs into a dancing print. I need to close my eyes again.

"How long was I in surgery for?" I ask, letting the darkness shroud my vision.

"Six hours. Do you want me to get your fiancé? He's been anxious to see you."

"It's been super cute," Vi says. "He kept double-checking with the nurses the stuff he was buying for you and pacing around the room. Your brother even had to put a hand on his knee at some point. We were all talking about how cute they were together."

Fiancé? Okay, so I'm not with it. I probably misheard her saying I had a disease, too, because a doctor would have invariably caught that over the years, right?

How common is temporary amnesia after surgery? I feel like I would have remembered agreeing to marry someone...and yet I'm drawing a blank.

"I'm anxious to see him, too."

"I'll go get him."

Both nurses leave the curtained room. What do I remember? I remember skating with Jack. I remember the pain getting worse. I remember them saying something about my ovary and putting something in an IV that made the world good. I remember being wheeled into a room and then nothing.

"Here she is." Vi's cheery voice washes over me, and I open my eyes again. The room still spins around me, but the nausea has calmed slightly. "She's doing pretty good. She said her pain is fine, but her blood pressure suggests otherwise."

A derisive snort comes from the other side of the curtain. "Of course, she said that." The voice is deep and grumpy, and my heart flips knowing exactly who it belongs to.

Jack.

"We're going to work on getting that number down, and then all she has to do is use the bathroom before we discharge her."

"And we're comfortable discharging her today?" he asks. "It sounds like they did a lot. I mean, I stayed a few nights just for a knee surgery."

"Unfortunately, that's not my call. The surgery they did is technically outpatient. I have opinions on the matter, but I cannot go against hospital orders. I'll send you home with phone numbers to call if something goes wrong, but this is the standard procedure."

"It wouldn't matter if I was willing to pay?"

Oh, Jack Parker, don't you freaking dare.

"Don't even think about it. I'm fine," I holler.

The curtain shoots open, and a worn-out man I love desperately sighs. A frown tugs at the corners of his mouth, and his eyebrows knit together in a scowl. "You're not allowed to use that phrase ever again. I'm banning it from your fucking vocabulary."

Vi bites her lip. The corner of her mouth twitches like she's trying not to laugh.

"I feel better than I did before surgery, honest." I cower, slightly, at the stern gaze I'm on the receiving end of.

No wonder the man is a force on the ice.

"Which only points to how fucked up you were before," he grumbles.

"Was I really fucked up?" I ask, my gaze waffling between Jack and Vi. Because I still don't understand what they did in that surgery or why it took six hours.

Vi flashes a sympathetic smile. "Where you're still waking up, it's not the best time to talk about everything, but yes, honey. You had quite a bit going on, and maybe your honey can explain it more to you tomorrow when you're more with it, okay? And you be patient with your love," she says, turning to Jack. "It's very common for people with her disease to carry medical trauma.

Because we can only diagnose it through surgery, most people we deal with who have it as aggressively as she has warp themselves mentally to cope and function continuously. It'll take time for that to shake out of her."

I try my best to listen and process the nurse's words. There it is again, that word, *disease*.

Jack regards me sympathetically, and something twists in the pit of my bruised abdomen.

Something was actually wrong, wasn't it?

I don't know how to process that. I want to cry while simultaneously laughing bitterly at the ten-plus years I've gone to appointments only to be dismissed.

"Alright, you go snuggle with your love. She could use it, and I'll get her some apple juice and crackers."

"Thank you." Jack slides his hands into his pockets, coming to my side at the bed.

"Hey." I smile softly. "Fiancé? Don't take this the wrong way, but did I miss something?"

He blushes and rubs the back of his head. "Yeah, I had to tell a little white lie because Gus wasn't in the area, and they wouldn't tell me anything."

"Should I play along? I mean, will you get thrown in hospital jail if you're found out?"

"I don't know that it matters now." He shrugs. "I might just get my ass handed to me by the check-in nurse."

"Well, we wouldn't want that."

"She does look like a bruiser."

"Guess we'll have to pretend we're madly in love then. However, do we keep finding ourselves in this situation?" I smirk. My heart somersaults in my chest. If Jack peered at the machine over my right shoulder, he'd see my heart rate spike.

I don't mind pretending that we've promised each other forever. The idea of drifting off to sleep with the steady beat of his heart beneath my ear and waking up in the warmth of his arms is far too tempting. So is the idea of being with someone who cares for me, who balances me out with how he advocates for me, and burrowing myself in the smiles he reserves for me. If he was mine, I'd slowly peel away the layers to what he's hiding, learning more about the soft, sweet, romantic side he's shown me lately without fear that he'll run away.

No, that doesn't sound so bad at all.

It sounds heavenly.

Jack brushes my hair behind my shoulder. A soft smile spreads across his face, making me feel safe for the first time today. "How are you really feeling, Dessy?"

"Honestly?"

"That would be my preference from now on, yes."

"Everything hurts, and I feel like I'm dying, but at least something's actually wrong with me. I don't know if that makes sense."

"After what Vi said, it's starting to."

I try to laugh the situation away, but my shoulders deflate as the realization slams into me.

Something was wrong with me.

And no one listened.

I was at the doctor's not too long ago, and he told me to see a therapist and take probiotics. I almost lost an ovary.

What the fuck?

There's no way I'll get my blood pressure under control if I keep focusing on this, and while Jack would like to keep me here, I'd much rather sleep in my bed tonight, thanks.

"Are Gus and Emy here?" I ask, hoping I can get my brain to stop cycling over the new reality I woke up to.

"Emy went home to set everything up for you, and Gus is in the waiting room. He didn't think he could handle seeing you in a hospital bed."

"He's such a roll." I snort. "I swear sometimes he's the baby brother. You didn't have to wait here, though. I know you don't like hospitals, and six hours must have been terrible."

My fingers intertwine with his.

"Of course, I needed to stay here, Dessy. You scared the shit out of me. I wish you had told me you weren't feeling well." His harsh tone betrays how frustrated he is.

A minor part of me secretly revels in the fact that he's frustrated with me instead of the other way around. This summer, he was a horrible patient, constantly pushing too much when he needed rest.

"I'm sorry. I didn't know something was wrong. I just thought —" Tears rim my eyes.

I thought my pain wasn't valid, whatever it was—it was just a me thing.

Jack tugs my hand tighter and rubs small circles into my palm. "Hey, I know. I know. Sorry, I don't mean to be a grump."

Vi sneaks into the room with apple juice and saltines. I demolish both of them, and it helps settle my nausea.

About thirty minutes later, my blood pressure is down, my pain is settling okay after another round of meds, and I'm able to use the bathroom. However, I lost a bit of dignity there since I had to show my urination skills to Vi, which was a first for me.

Jack, thankfully, moved his car closer to the exit during that one.

After wheeling me out to the Escalade, they handed Gus a list of things to pick up at the pharmacy, and he kissed me on the cheek and left to grab...whatever.

Settled in the passenger seat, Jack reaches over and buckles me in. Flashing him a hesitant smile, I am engulfed by his smell, setting off a rash of tingles that shoot through me and curl my toes.

"Are you comfortable enough?" he asks.

"Oh yeah, fi—"

Jack clears his throat harshly and fixes me with a piercing stare.

"I'm, uhm. I can make it home like this." I bashfully meet his eyes before looking down at my hands. "I'm sorry, it's going to take a while for me not to autopilot with that answer, but I'm going to try."

In the car, reality settles around me more. Jack's driving me home from emergency surgery.

I should want to cry, but a strange relief settles on my shoulders.

Whatever is going on, it's real. It's not some fictional malady that I made up.

Something's actually wrong.

My pain...is...valid?

Jack grabs my hand and presses a kiss to it. "We'll get there together. I'm sorry. I think some of the shit that happened with my dad is bubbling up too, but that's not on you. Let's get you home and comfy. Okay?"

"Yeah. That sounds good. Thank you for being here," I whisper, mist slowly clouding my vision.

"Of course." Leaning in, Jack's lips meet my cheek, tenderly kissing away a tear rolling down it. "I've got you, Dessy."

I sway a little as a wave of dizziness overwhelms me, unsure if it's the medication taking effect or my reaction to his gesture.

"I love you." The words come out before I can register that I'm saying them, and I don't know that I care that they're out there. They're the truth. I'm one hundred percent head over heels in love with Jack Parker, the man who frantically paces in the waiting room for me, wears breeches for me, and seems to care for me in a way that rivals some of the most important people in my life.

I catch Jack staring at me, his eyes blinking in disbelief. His hand grips the steering wheel, and then he laughs softly. "You're on a lot of drugs." He puts the car in drive and runs over my heart.

Chapter Thirty-One

Aulie Desfleurs

Play: *Here Comes the Sun by the Beatles*

Day two after surgery may be more painful than the first day.

The intense pain in my bloated abdomen is preventing me from doing anything, and I can't help but groan in agony. The nurse, Vi, warned me that if I fell behind on my painkiller schedule, I would regret it, and here I am—behind and filled with regret.

And gas.

I reach for my phone and text Emy.

AULIE

I need help.

EMY

I'm getting you groceries, but Jack is in the guest room.

My heart would be in my stomach if it could squeeze in there with all that mess. Jack, the man I professed my love to under the haze of way too many drugs. The man who laughed in return and slept in another room last night, even though he'd stayed with me the previous two. No, I won't be bothering him today.

AULIE

> Cool. It can wait until you're back.

My phone vibrates with a call in my hand, and Emy's name lights up on the screen.

"Hello?"

"Are you seriously not going to text him, even though he's two rooms down and staying home to take care of you?"

Emy's reading too much into this. Jack moved over to our house a good week ago, and there's not much to do in Chawton Falls. He's not here to care for me. He's just stuck. I know Jack. He's secretly way nicer than anyone knows, and it's part of the reason he's stolen my heart away from me, but he's also not exactly the caretaker/nurturing type.

"I can wait until you or Gus are back home. It's fine."

"Aulie," Emy says, her frustration escaping in a long sigh after she says my name.

"Emy."

"Aulie."

"Hi, I'm Patrick." Oh, I wonder if SpongeBob is streaming on anything. Maybe I can sneak out and watch some TV on the couch or something.

Or maybe I should stay and work on fair stuff in bed. Yes, there are a lot of things that still need to be done. Frivolous things like SpongeBob can wait.

"I hate you sometimes," Emy says. I can see her pinching the bridge of her nose in the grocery aisle, an action she usually inspires in me. "Why aren't you asking Jack for help?"

"I, uhm—I may have told him I love him when I was out of it yesterday, and I don't feel like dealing with that can of worms. Side note—would I ever feel like dealing with a can of worms?" I shift in bed, wiggling my toes and feeling restless. Between the

317

constant pain in my body, the one in my heart from yesterday, and the one mentally from dealing with the shock of needing surgery, I'm an enormous ball of itchy, fidgety, blech.

"Unlikely, but worms aside—"

"Aww, don't do that to the worms. I may not want to deal with them, but they—"

"Tu m'emmerdes," Emy mumbles under her breath. Again, the "you're annoying me" phrase is usually reserved for my lips only.

"When am I not?"

"Fair. But back to the loving Jack bit, did you mean it?"

I sigh, shifting in bed and trying another position to get comfortable. Nothing seems to ease the tension hanging in my shoulders and pelvic area. I may have to accept that comfort isn't possible. "Probably? I mean, you know me. Once I love someone, that's game over for me." It's the Desfleurs Family Curse. Platonic or romantic, it's physically impossible for me not to love with a deep, fiery intensity—despite my wishes to be more frigid. "But it doesn't matter whether I meant it. It freaked him out, and you know what Jack does when he's freaked out. He avoids things." Another sharp pain causes me to inhale sharply and hiss through clenched teeth.

"Was that a wince?"

"No," I lie through tightened vocal cords.

"Aulie, why haven't you handled your pain this morning?"

"I may have overslept, so my meds are overdue, and I can't bring myself to sit up more or walk to the kitchen to get some food."

"Call Jack. That's why he's here."

"Yeah, but the 'I love you' thing, it's—"

"Look, you told Jack you love him, drugs or not, and he canceled his morning skate and stayed home to take care of you, even though no one asked. So read into that what you like, but I don't think he's going to find it a bother."

"He canceled his morning skate for me?" Hockey always comes first for Jack. It's his one true love. I know he missed it the day after my birthday, but that day was filled with complications, such as a sleeping body holding him hostage and a big brother prowling the hallways. Today, none of those existed. He could have gone.

"Yes, because he cares for you, pumpkin. I don't know what happened yesterday, but I know that much."

"I'll text him."

"Thank you," Emy says on an exhale. "Oh, you want those little French yogurts in the glass jars? You like those, right?"

"Yeah, but they're expensive. Just get the store brand."

"What was that? I can't hear you. I think I'm going through a tunnel. Did you say to get the French yogurt? Sounds great. Okay. Bye."

Deadened silence follows, and I pull the phone away from my ear,

giving myself a few seconds to collect myself before texting Jack.

AULIE

Emy said you're here. If you're not otherwise occupied, I could use some help.

AULIE

Please.

Mere seconds pass before there's a soft rap on my door. Jack enters with a backward hat, a crewneck sweater with the sleeves pushed up, and his hands stuffed inside a pair of grey sweatpants.

My pulse races, confirming what I said yesterday was true.

I love this man rather hopelessly.

"How are you doing?" he asks.

"I'm fi—"

With a harsh clearing of his throat, Jack's stare narrows on me as if to say *try again*.

Lowering my eyes to my hands, I pull at my fingertips. I get why the phrase "I'm fine" bothers Jack. I know his history, and I can't imagine yesterday was easy for him, but I don't know if he understands from my perspective how hard a habit it will be to kill. That phrase has been more than a mask for the past ten years. It's been my mental savior because nothing has been fine, actually. I've been in constant pain with no one believing me, so instead of convincing them I was in pain, I tried to convince myself I wasn't. And it mostly worked until it didn't. Until I got to a point where I needed surgery to fix whatever was happening. "I'm in a significant amount of pain."

"I'm sorry to hear that. What can I do to help?"

"Can you help me up? I need to go to the restroom."

"Yeah, of course." He steps toward my bed, wrapping an arm under my back and offering the other to pull me up. I wince, planting my feet on the ground and taking a second once I'm standing to let everything settle.

I hope this intense pain isn't planning to stick around for too long because there are still three more weekends of the fair to get through, and I don't know how I'm planning on navigating those hills like this.

With a supporting arm, Jack guides me to the bathroom.

One glance in the mirror is enough to make me cringe. I try to brush through my tangled knots, but it's useless. I look like a raccoon who just had a fight with a balloon, with the dark circles under my eyes and my frizzy hair sticking up every which way.

And the guy I love is standing outside this door.

Awesome.

I sigh, resigning myself to my messy fate.

Jack's lips quirk up when he sees me, and I feel a wave of embarrassment wash over me. I hate everything he's seen of me the last few days, the way I passed out on the ice. The dramatics of the surgery. Looking like this now, I don't know why I'm bothering being upset he didn't say he loved me back. Who would expect him to?

"Good?" he asks, and I nod.

Suddenly, he places his forearm on the doorframe and brushes a piece of my gnarly hair behind my ear. His hand palms the back of my head before he leans and places a soft but impactful kiss on my lips. The touch is subtle, but it leaves a lingering heat that makes my toes curl.

"What was that for?" I ask as he pulls away.

"You just looked really pretty," he says, a tiny smile tugging his mouth into a crooked smirk. "And I like that I can kiss you now."

I blink at him, my mouth opening and closing as I try to find the right words to say. I thought after yesterday, he'd be freaked out and itching to run, but canceling morning skate and telling me I look pretty when I know for a decided fact I do not send the opposite message.

Jack puts his hand on my back, guiding me toward my bedroom, but I deviate from our trek heading to the kitchen.

"What are you doing?" he asks.

Bending, I immediately regret folding in half and hastily reach for a frying pan. "I'm making breakfast so I can take my pills." I open the fridge and pull out the eggs. Holy heck, moving hurts.

"Just a thought, Rapunzel." Gently, Jack uncurls my fingers, wrapped around the frying pan, and slips it out of my grip. "But do you think maybe I could do that, and you sit your ass back in bed?"

"You have been watching too many movies with Luce." I snort. "But, no, I can make my breakfast, not a problem."

Reaching into the silverware drawer, I pull out a knife. Quickly, it slips from my grasp and falls to a clatter on the floor. Darn. I blink, staring at the elongated silver utensil taunting me on the floor. There's no way I can bend down and pick it up with my bloated abdomen.

I glance up at Jack, wincing at the smug look on his face. "Okay. Come on." He wraps a hand around my elbow and leads me back into the bedroom. I drag my feet along, defeated by a damn butter knife.

"But I need food," I whimper.

"Yes. And I'm going to make it for you," he grumbles.

"How are your culinary skills? I was unaware you had any."

"Not fantastic." He shakes his head. "But Lucy thinks I make a mean peanut butter and jelly."

"Oh, that sounds lovely." I grin, settling back into bed. "Can you bring me the folder on my desk labeled invoices? I have a few phone calls to make before *Sense and Sensibility* weekend. Oh, and my agenda book too, please."

Crossing his arms, Jack shakes his head and directs a stern gaze toward me. "You aren't working today."

"Yeah, okay. Like heck, I'm not."

"Whatever you need to do, Emy, Gus, or I can handle it. You're resting. In bed."

"I've rested all morning," I groan, trying to push myself back up. "I swear I'm fi—I'm, uhm, I'm doing okay, honest." On my second attempt to push myself up, a sharp knife stabs me in the gut, and I wince, accepting my fate. I'm stuck here, as much as I hate it.

"Let us take care of you for once, Dessy," Jack says, fluffing my pillow and motioning me to lie back on my new wedge pillow that magically appeared when I got home. "Gus wanted to know when you were awake so he could set up the TV we bought you in here. I know it will be tough, but they said you'll probably need to be in bed for at least two or three weeks with all the disease they removed."

There it was again, that word I never thought I'd be associated with. The word that, weirdly, I had been desperate to hear.

"I'm going to go make you a PB&J, okay? Do you need anything else?"

"Just a glass of milk." I twiddle my thumbs, letting that word spiral in my mind. "Do you think we could talk about whatever happened yesterday, too? The nurses weren't very informative with me, and I understand I wasn't really in the headspace, but I think I could handle it now."

"Yeah, of course. I'll get the packet they gave me, and we can talk over everything once we get your pain under control. Promise."

"Thank you." I wince through another stab.

A few minutes later, Jack returns to the bedroom with a teal-colored packet tucked under his armpit, a plate with a PB&J, a glass of milk, and…his thick-rimmed glasses.

I stare unabashedly. As if his outfit wasn't dangerous enough. Those glasses are going to be the death of me.

A proud smile tugs at Jack's lips as he shakes his head. "I hope you know you look at me in glasses the same way you do when I'm in a towel, and it's bruising my ego."

"Imagine how I would look at you if you wore those *and* a towel."

"I'll keep that in mind," he snorts.

He puts my plate on a side table, leaving and returning with a wooden lap tray he must have also bought yesterday. So far, I have him to thank for a new wedge pillow, which has been a lifesaver, apparently a TV, and this desk. He opens the legs and puts it over my lap before placing the plate and glass of milk on top.

"Jack Parker, you spoil me." I flutter my eyelashes.

"Good, you deserve to be spoiled after all the things you've done for me." He leans down, pressing a kiss on my forehead, and I scrunch my nose at the affection. Moonbeams threaten to shoot out of my face at any moment, with the incandescent feeling spiraling instead. His lips may be stronger than any of the painkillers they prescribed.

My brother bows under the doorframe while Jack's lips leave my forehead. I wait for a scowl to be flashed in Jack's direction, the typical expression he reserves for people I'm involved with, but he smiles—a bit. "Help me with this." He nods to the box he's carrying. My desk in front of my bed is covered with folders and notebooks needed for the fair, and Jack gathers them, heading toward the door.

"Where are you going with those?" I ask.

"Guest room. You won't need them." He grins at me, a bit of a challenge in his eyes because I can't do a damn thing to stop him.

"As long as you bring them back tomorrow."

"Told you she'd be a pain in the ass with the bedrest order." Gus shakes his head.

"Rude. And I'm not being a pain in the ass; I have responsibilities." I huff.

"Eat your sandwich, Alouette. We can fight about what you're going to do and not do for the next week later." He takes out a box knife and slashes through the tape on the box. When Jack said they bought me a TV, I expected a small twenty-four-inch thing or something, but the thing Gus is trying to set up barely fits on my large mahogany desk.

I think about what Aunt Camille said, about people showing they love me through actions rather than words, and I try to hug that to my chest and bury the awkward feelings I've had bubbling all night after my "I love you" wasn't returned.

I grab one half of my sandwich, which I'm happy to see Jack cut diagonally. I don't know why PB&Js taste better when they're cut that way, but it's a truth universally acknowledged that they do.

Gus hooks up the TV and every streaming service known to humanity, while I finish my sandwich. After, Jack sits beside me on the bed with the folder he brought in earlier. "Are you ready to go over everything?"

I swallow. Yes, and no. I've been so relieved to find something was wrong with me, but now, staring at the *what* that terrifies me. What if it's going to get worse? What if there's no cure? What if it's still not that big of a deal, and I'm still a total softie?

"Ready as I'll ever be." I flash him a hesitant smile. He pulls out four or five sheets of glossy picture paper. Graphic pictures of the inside of my body sit in a two-by-two grid on every page. I skipped Anatomy and Physiology in college, so I don't have a clue what I'm looking at, but whatever they are, they aren't pretty. "They showed you these?"

I feel like seeing pictures of my organs should be something we reserved for later down in the relationship, not the first freaking week.

"God, I'm lucky you're still talking to me," I groan. "I'm sorry for putting all of this on you."

Jack tucks his finger under my chin. My gaze meets his.

Through his thick frames, he narrows his stare with a ferocious intensity, and I squirm, overwhelmed with his undivided attention. "Aurelie Desfleurs, you are not a burden, and you're not getting rid of me that easily," he says in a low, reverent hush. "I want to be there to share things like this with you. I want to be the biggest fan on your team. Understood? I'd be mad if you kept this from me, not vice versa."

I nod, losing a breath as he lowers his head to capture my lips in a slow, empowering kiss like he's claiming me in a way that can never be undone.

He presses his forehead against mine, his eyes drawing close. "I'm not going anywhere, Dessy. I know you well enough to know that has to be at the back of your mind, but tell that panic to quiet." We rest like that together for a beat until any thought that dares whisper he's going to leave me is incinerated by the warmth of his touch. "Now, let's get back to the photos so I can show you how much of a badass you are."

"I can honestly say that no one has ever described me in that way."

"They should." He shrugs. "See this?" Jack points to a large brownish mass hovering near a white mass. "That's the chocolate cyst that was twisting your ovary. So, they took that out. But they said they found—see these dark red splotches everywhere?" His finger traces over some filmy white stretchy stuff with red splotches. "The doctor said those are adhesions for something." He flips through the folder and pulls out an information brochure.

"Endometriosis" sits in big letters on the top.

"She called it endo, so I think we can, too. So that's all this endo stuff. She said, judging by how much you had and what some of it looked like—like those adhesions I showed you, you've had it for a long time, and that it's a bitch and you're a tough cookie."

My mind is buzzing, trying to process everything Jack's relaying to me. Those red splotches and stretchy film are on every photo. My body was loaded with them. And he's telling me it's some disease I've had awhile? How can that be? I've been to the doctors and begged to be listened to. How did they miss all of this? How can I be seeing the word "endometriosis" for the first time now?

"She said bitch and tough cookie in the same sentence?"

"I think those were her scientific words." He gently pulls me in and lays a soft kiss on the top of my head. "And you are. They were able to get most of it out, so they're hopeful you'll feel some relief soon."

I pull the info pamphlet out, nodding in a trance. I don't know how to process any of this; it's the answer to my prayers, and if I hadn't passed out, if Jack hadn't reacted and sent me to the hospital, I may still be waiting for it.

A list of symptoms sits on the second page of the brochure and I devour it, curious to find what of my mystery symptoms it's responsible for.

Everything—it's responsible for everything—how is that possible? How have they missed this diagnosis for so long when it seems so obvious? Painful periods, chronic fatigue, digestion issues, severe pain passing bowel movements, rectal bleeding, shoulder pain, pelvic pain, painful intercourse, and severe bloating.

None of my symptoms have been left uncovered after looking at this list.

With his arm still wrapped around me, Jack whispers into my hair. "Where's your mind?"

"It's—" Tears rip out of me in an uncontrollable sob. "It's everything I've ever complained about, and they told me it was in my head—even the damn shoulder pain."

Jack's arms encompass me in a warm embrace as I heave. The heaviness in my abdomen strengthens. I need to get these sobs under control before I flare my pain more. "I need to stop crying."

"No, it's okay, let it out. They were assholes."

"I know—but this fucking hurts."

"Oh. Right. What can we do to distract you?"

I wipe at my tears, chest heaving and pain pricking with every slight hiccup. I don't know if anything can get my mind off of this.

After ten years, this revelation might be too much too soon. I'm angry at the doctors who made me feel silly when I was right. How dare they? How dare they dismiss me when it seems like the answer was there all along.

"Do you think Gus would lend us his Nintendo so we can play Mario Kart?"

"Sure, we can do that."

When he disappears, my eyes return to the pamphlet in front of me. The big complicated word sits on the top of a glossy picture of an abdomen with barbed wire wrapped around it —endometriosis.

Ten fucking years of horrible pain, buckets of tears shed, and more shitty doctors than I care to remember.

And there'd been a name for it all along.

Chapter Thirty-Two

Jack Parker

Play: *R U Mine by Arctic Monkeys*

Papers rustling in the dead of night wake me from an otherwise peaceful sleep. Every sleep next to Aulie has been tranquil.

I reach over to her with a grunt, and my hand comes up empty. Blinking my eyes open, the commotion continues. A small desk light illuminates a hunched-over figure.

"Aurelie Lunette Desfleurs. What the hell are you doing up?" I groan. Aulie's shoulders raise with tension at the sound of my voice, and she freezes, shuffling through—wait, is that her planner? Oh, hell no, I hid that in the guest room.

I know I was a near-impossible patient this summer, constantly pushing the boundaries of what I could and couldn't do for the sake of rehabbing for the season. Still, since her surgery one week ago, Aulie has been ten times worse than I ever was.

She never asks for help and always tries to do everything herself.

Constantly saying in her sweet honey voice, "*I don't want to be a burden.*" Like that will assuage my irritation with the situation.

It's frustrating as hell that she doesn't understand how much I enjoy taking care of her. None of this is a chore to me. I want to be the one who makes her PB&Js, settles her into bed, and makes her cozy.

"I couldn't sleep, so I figured I'd try to catch up on stuff for the Emy's Halloween Birthday Party this weekend, because I'm wicked behind."

Pushing up from the mattress, I stand, motioning for her to hand me her planner.

She bites her lip, hugging her prized possession tight to her chest.

I'm too tired to be patient, and I flash her an overly stern look usually reserved for my misbehaving nephews.

The look only inspires her to tighten her grip. "I don't know where you got the idea that you can boss me around, but I'm sorry to report, surgery or not, I still have personal autonomy."

"Seriously, Aulie—" I sigh, scrubbing a hand over my face.

"It's annoying when the patient doesn't listen, isn't it?" She quirks a brow, her renewed sparkle glimmering in her irises.

It is. But there were times this summer when Aulie got me to do what she wanted, no matter how opposed I was. If only I knew the trick...

Flashes of when I complied come to me in painkiller-hazed moments. Aulie's bare arms and a silk tank top with lace scream through clear as day. Her lips contorted into a beautiful pout she always wore when frustrated with me.

Ah. So that's what it was.

The whole, I'd do anything for you, lovesick puppy thing.

I glance down at Aulie, whose fingers are running over her lips, her stare narrowed on my mouth.

Aulie said she loved me in the car a few days ago, but there's no way she meant it. She was just on a lot of drugs and had a harrowing day, that's all. Because someone like her doesn't fall for a guy like me. She's too good.

But maybe we're not as far off in the feelings department as I always thought—if she feels half of what I do, this may work. Might as well test the theory, anyway.

"I'll have to resort to more powerful measures,' I say with a slight upward tug on my lips and a shrug. "Just remember you made me bring out the big guns."

"I can handle the big guns."

God, I hope not.

"Suit yourself," I say, walking back to the bed. I bend down, slowly peeling off my pants, making a show of it and ensuring Aulie gets an unobstructed view of my ass in my boxer briefs. Stretching up, I grab the folds of my shirt, like they've had me do so many times in the soap ads, before getting into the shower. Deliberately, I pull the shirt over my head, feeling my muscles stretch and contract with the movement.

"What—what—are you—" The quiver in Aulie's voice gives me hope her feelings may be stronger than I ever dared to hope.

After five years of thinking everything was unrequited and only recently realizing she had some attachment to me, this—god, this feels good.

Reaching over, I grab my glasses from the nightstand and put them on before pivoting back to her. Narrowed on her face and intent on my mission.

"Oh, come on, that's not bringing out the big guns. That's just playing plain dirty!" she squeals as I prowl closer to her.

"You know I don't play clean, kitten."

Her back hits the bookcase. Her agenda book is still clutched tightly to her chest.

I lean in, caging her with my body, careful not to bump against her still-bloated stomach.

"Hey, beautiful," I say, my tone suggestive and alluring. Raking a hand through my hair, I peer at her beneath my lashes, hoping that the look and charm I've perfected for photos and other PR-related things works here, too.

Her mouth slackens.

With a glacial pace, I inch toward her lips, reveling in the way her breathing quickens as I get closer.

Finally, our lips brush, and Aulie relaxes into the kiss like my touch holds the key to her relief.

I wonder if she knows I feel the same way. If she can tell that I'm always one swipe of the tongue away from getting on my knees for her, that worshipping her is as natural to me as breathing.

Her body falls limp against mine, and I have my in, slowly plucking the agenda book out of her grasp.

A few seconds later, I search for the strength to pull away from the kiss. Fantasies of taking her against these books have tortured me for far too long, but not tonight. She's stood long enough, and I need to get her back to bed somehow.

I nip at her bottom lip, finally letting go.

"You're actually evil," she whispers as I withdraw. "You better not use that power too often, or we'll have to talk."

I flash her a cheeky grin. If she thinks I'm going to let that reaction to me slide... "Just glad to see the feeling is mutual for a change."

She crosses her arms with a scowl on her face. "Oh, please, when have I ever had you wrapped around my finger like *that*?"

Every second of every day for the past five years. Thank you very much.

No, we're probably not at the I've-been-in-love-with-you-since-the-moment-I-saw-you-again stage.

"You remember that silk camisole you wore in the summer?" I trace my finger over her shoulder, blanketed in a thick layer of flannel. She closes her eyes as I slowly trail down her arm. "Payback's a bitch, sweetheart."

"Really?" she asks, her eyes wide with innocence.

I brush a piece of hair out of her face. "You were absolute torture."

"But I didn't even know what I was doing. How is that fair?"

"Not my fault that you didn't realize I'm a mess around you most of the time." I shrug.

"It kind of is since I thought you're a mess in general." She smirks, bringing her hand to my chest and placing her palm over my ink. "How about we strike a deal? Tell me what this tattoo says, and I promise to be the perfect patient."

Ice floods my veins at this request, but I keep my expression neutral, careful not to show how much that request terrifies me.

For now, I'm eager to have her keep thinking it's just a nothing burger tattoo I got as a college kid, not living proof she's had my heart for years.

"How perfect?"

"I'll let you boss me around for however long this recovery is. Hide my planner, whatever you want."

I hide a shiver as she follows the curve of the ink with her fingertip. "Why do you want to know what it says so badly?"

"Because whatever it is, it meant enough for you to put it on your persona, and I want to know every inch of you, including this."

I chew on the inside of my cheek. Having Aulie resting and listening is tempting, but I can't tell her, not yet. I'll tell her someday, like when we're old, and we've been married for fifty years, but not yet. "I'll take my chances with my powers of seduction." I lean in for another kiss but am less eagerly received.

"Oh. Right. Well, that's just as well because I wanted to work, so now I can." She pivots back to the desk, and I gently guide my hand to her hip and steer her to the bed.

"Aulie, you need to rest. Please leave all of this to Bridget, Emy, and me. We can handle it without you, I promise."

"Oh right, you're right, you'll all have it under control, no need for me." Her face falls, and I sense that maybe this runs deeper than a stubbornness to keep working. Dragging her feet, she returns to bed, and her sullen figure rips my heart to shreds. "Night."

With a sigh, I tuck her in, flick the light off by her desk, and crawl back into bed beside her.

Clearing my throat, I do the only thing I can think to lift her spirits, even if it gives away more of myself than I'm ready to give.

"It's a poem from Bryon." My voice floats, unsure in the dark, landing between us.

"What's it about?"

You.

"It's a poem about stars, nothing more."

"Oh. Why are you so embarrassed about it?"

"Not a part of my public image to have a nineteenth-century poem tattooed on me. But I was a weird college kid anyway, so whatever." I lean over and lay a kiss on Aulie's forehead. "I look forward to seeing your interpretation of a perfect patient and bossing you around." The smirk plastered on my face clear in my tone.

"Worth it," she says, in a way that suggests we're both grinning through the darkness.

I could get through even the bleakest nights with her by my side.

Chapter Thirty-Three

Aulie Desfleurs

Play: *Will You Love Me Tomorrow by the Shirelles*

The light cascades through the picture window. I soak in the glowing warmth sitting in an armchair that Jack and Gus moved in from the living room earlier in the week.

Ten days after my surgery, all I'm managing is a three-minute lap around the house before I have to sit down again.

Which is getting wicked frustrating.

With every day, my mind is growing more restless and housebound.

Every morning, I'm taken aback by Jack's unwavering determination to care for me. It feels inevitable that he'll grow sick of this, but it hasn't happened yet. He's just as eager to ensure my comfort and nourishment as he was on the first day. In turn, I'm doing my best to be the perfect patient. I owe him that. Today, however, the excitement and energy of the crew setting up for a Halloween party outside makes it harder for me to rest. I feel useless.

Expendable.

And I hate it.

Emy and Jack went with a nineties-themed Halloween party —an idea that I'm not fun enough to have thought up on my own, and while I'm super excited that the cast is going to have a blast tonight, there's a part of me that can't help but feel rather glum that I didn't contribute to that fun.

Two men in overalls lay out a large fabric roll, and I watch as they turn on a machine, and slowly but surely, a cheeseburger bounce house takes form. "Gus!" I holler. "Do you know if Emy or Jack thought to make a Goodburger sign for the bounce house?"

"Like I would forget to make a Goodburger sign. That's the whole reason it's a cheeseburger." Jack's teasing voice comes from behind, and I don't jump. I'm finally used to his sneaky shenanigans. I'm glad he's back. He was out running errands, and I didn't expect him for another hour. Unfortunately, I'm attached and missed him even in that short time of separation.

What will I do when he returns to the team and I don't see him for weeks?

Or months if he keeps up with his non-dating during the season pattern.

"That was quick." I muse, watching another few crew members Jack hired to set up outside create a photo drop that looks like they ripped it right out of *Clarissa Explains it All*.

"Quick where it matters and slow where it counts." He winks, placing a kiss on my forehead. "I couldn't let my baby's poutine get cold."

To hell with *"You have bewitched me body and soul, and I love, I love, I love you. I never wish to be parted from you from this day forward."* Has a more romantic sentence ever been uttered?

Doubtful, but Jane Austen was at a disadvantage since I don't believe poutine was a thing in her time.

Jack slides a Styrofoam container in my hand, and I pop it open, my mouth watering at the site of Chez LaBranche's brown gravy and cheese curds smothering their crispy fries.

God bless poutine, everyone.

"How's the *Northanger Abbey* stuff going? It looks like it's a nice day, at least." I ask, stuffing a fry into my mouth.

Before grabbing my poutine, Jack ran over to the fairgrounds to ensure everything was going smoothly and to make sure that neither Emy nor Bridget was overwhelmed. I might not be able to walk much yet, but I was sure I could wobble over to the player's tent and manage things from there if things were going to hell.

"They're doing fine."

"Has Bridget made anyone cry?"

"Not that I'm aware of, no. But she asked how you were doing. She's excited to see you tonight."

"I'm excited, too." I glance away, hesitantly munching on another fry.

The fair is going fine. That should be a great thing, and it is. I'm mostly thankful for that, but again, it's another place where I'm growing to be expendable. Maybe even a burden. If I didn't have this disease, people wouldn't have to step up. They would have had someone else take care of everything who wouldn't bail last minute.

"I don't know how long I'll last outside, but I'll do my best," I add after a few seconds of silence. I don't want to let on that this bothers me because it's ridiculous to be upset that people are filling in for me and doing a good job. I just—I need to be needed because otherwise, how can I guarantee people will stay?

"Gus and I are going to move the old couch in the basement outside so you can sit near the fire. I'm hoping that will help. But don't push it."

"Yes, sir." My lips quirk at his authoritative tone. I thought I was going to hate it. Instead, I've grown to love how much Jack seems to care for me. Me. Not my face, my body, or any other things that might make me alluring, but when he's acting like this —a doting boyfriend (even if we haven't labeled it)—it's like he cares about my soul, too.

"I should go help him with that while you eat." He checks his watch. "You're due for your painkillers soon. The doctor said we should start weening you off them tomorrow, so I don't want to mess up today. After, do you want to take a break from sitting and nap with me?"

Over the past few days, napping with Jack has become my favorite hobby. There's a moment when he falls asleep before I do, where I sit and listen to his heavy breathing and flicker over his peaceful face, reveling in how his thick eyelashes rest against his cheek.

It doesn't matter if I'm still in a drug-filled haze. I'm in love with him, that much is clear. What's more, I don't think I've stopped loving him since I was five and became aware of his existence. I just learned to ignore the feeling like I've ignored so many other pains in my life.

Letting that sensation bubble to the surface once more has been liberating. There's a constant lightness in my chest and a swirling giddiness in my veins. Even when I know Jack will report back to his team soon and all of this could end very poorly for me.

~

"No way, you're napping? It's like four in the afternoon."

An unfamiliar booming voice rattles the bookshelves in my bedroom.

Eyes still closed, I question if I'm dreaming, because why would another guy be in my bedroom? One is weird enough.

"Grady, what the hell are you doing here?" Jack groans, his voice harsh and hushed, like he's trying not to wake me. "And why do you have a pumpkin?"

"I got it at a stand on the way up here. I thought we could make pumpkin beer."

At this, I blink my eyes open. Over the years, Grady's antics have been one of my favorite pastimes. True, he's toned down as he's matured, but there's a chaotic aura about him that's uniquely Grady.

His colossal figure looms in my doorway. His broad shoulders...and chest...and legs...are exposed, clad solely in a loincloth.

He's got a pumpkin tucked under his arm and a six-pack in the other. "Did I overdo it with the drugs, or is Grady in my bedroom dressed like George of the Jungle?" I whisper.

"If you're hallucinating, so am I, and I don't want to unpack what that would mean. But you're due for ibuprofen anyway, so I'll make you a sandwich." Jack pushes himself off the bed, pressing a quick kiss to my lips, which sends my heart a flutter. He's always sure to kiss me *somewhere* whenever we're about to be separated, even if its for a few seconds and one room over. Grady raises an eyebrow in surprise, but says nothing. Jack drags his tired hand through his messy bedhead and directs Grady toward the exit. "How are you planning on making pumpkin beer?" he asks as they disappear down the hallway.

"I don't know. I just figured we'd carve the pumpkin out, pour the beer in, and the juices would soak into it, right?"

"Dude. No, that's not—"

After being locked up in my bedroom for ten days, there's no way Jack will ruin this for me.

"That's exactly how it's made!" I holler, wincing as I get up and stroll out of my bedroom and toward the kitchen.

A hint of disapproval flickers across Jack's face as he glances in my direction. He's probably irritated that I got out of bed without him standing near me, and well, fair, considering I'm not as sure on my feet with all these meds. "Grab a towel out of the closet in the hallway, Grady, and I'll get you a knife," I say.

I shuffle to the silverware drawer and pull out a sharp knife as Jack dances around me, grabbing bread, deli meat, and mayo from the fridge. "What are you doing? Why are you encouraging this?"

"I'm bored out of my mind, dude. Let me have this. Please." I flash him some puppy dog eyes, and he nods. "I'll drag your recliner out to the porch so you have another space to use tonight, and I'll set him up on the floor so you can watch. I've gotta go pick up the tie-dye shirts Lucy made us for our Clarissa and Sam costumes, anyway, so it'll be a good way to keep you out of trouble."

"Trouble? Me?" I put my hand on my heart, the picture of innocence.

"Don't think I didn't notice you coming out here alone. The doctor said you're not supposed to be doing that."

"That doctor is a thief of joy," I grumble. "But I guess you'll just have to add it to the spank bank." I shrug.

I invented the spank bank in my itchy-to-move, bored-as-hell descent into madness the last few days. A national institution dedicated to appropriate butt taps in the bedroom that I'm determined to cash in on when I'm allowed to do things with Jack again.

Which is, unfortunately, a good six weeks away, according to my follow-up five days ago.

Jack has yet to agree to the existence of the spank bank, but I'm sure I'll be able to convince him to withdraw when the time comes.

With a final diagonal cut I've grown far too used to in the past week, Jack rinses the knife, twists the bread back up, and puts all the ingredients away in the fridge. The way he effortlessly maneuvers around the kitchen is mesmerizing, his shirt revealing the tension in his shoulder blades and his biceps showcasing a fluid grace.

"Got a towel," Grady says.

"Great. Help me move Aulie's recliner to the porch, and you two can supervise each other while I run an errand."

Guilt pricks my chest, and I try not to let it rot too much. Jack's been running errand after errand since my surgery, and I appreciate it, but making sandwiches, taking midday naps, and running around town can't be the lifestyle he enjoys. Considering he's used to going to clubs and parties in Boston and bar hopping at away games with whatever woman he's found in that town, domesticity must feel like a noose to him. This current situation certainly isn't forever, but if he keeps our relationship going when he returns (which isn't a guarantee), his life will be softer just because I'm in it, and I don't love that for him.

Fluorescent green backward hats shouldn't be a killer look on anyone. Annoyingly, Jack can pull off just about anything, including a bright tie-dyed shirt with blues, greens, oranges, yellows, pink, and lime green shorts and a pair of sunglasses hanging down the front of his chest. The silent confidence that's oozing off of him in his outfit is just...

"You liking what you see there, kitten?" Jack's lips tip into a smug grin. "Should I be concerned that you're eye fucking me in this?"

"I really liked *Clarissa Explains it All.*" I clear my throat. He motions for me to sit on the bed and rolls up a pair of sunflower leggings with a soft stomach for me to slide into. "I may also just really like you, and like that we're doing our first couples costume. You're sweet, you know that?" I kiss his cheek as his brow furrows, concentrating on the leggings.

"Meds still making you overly emotional, huh?" he asks, grabbing a folded yellow tie-dyed tunic Lucy made from me from the top of the dresser.

"I haven't been that bad."

Jack quirks a judgemental brow at me, and well, fair, I've probably been a little more emotional than usual. And maybe I burst into tears when I was scrolling on the internet and saw a pattern for a tiny crocheted kitten couch with a small blanket. Everything was little, and Willoughby needs one, and oh no, if I keep thinking about that darn couch, I'll start crying again.

"Kitten couch?" Jack asks, gesturing for me to put my arms up.

"It's a miniature version of a normal-sized thing, and it's so cute, I need to make one."

"We can go yarn shopping online tonight."

"You're a ray of sunshine, you know that." Tears fall and Jack's shoulders raise as if he's on guard. "Why can't you just accept that you're sweet and I like you?"

He shakes his head. "Not possible, princesses don't feel that way for asses," he says, smiling softly at me, trying to mask it like he's teasing me, but he means some of what he's saying.

"Well, good thing I'm a fucking queen then," I say, chin high.

Jack snorts. "You are, but that only makes me lowlier." Gently, he slides a headband on over my head. His palm cups my cheek. He narrows a penetrating, heated gaze on my face. When he stares at me like this, I can't help but wonder if he might love me after all, even if he hasn't verbalized it yet.

Of course, I've misread situations like this before, and I'm on a lot of meds, so it's hard for me to say any of that with certainty.

"What the fuck?" A loud shriek from the hallway shakes Jack out of his hold on my cheek.

"I'm so sorry." Grady's voice follows.

Jack's forehead presses against mine. "I've got to go put a Grady fire out," he says.

"Take me with you." I offer out my hand.

Jack supports me as I stand, lowering his mouth to my ear. "Please don't push it tonight. When you're done with the party, we can watch some TV in bed or something."

"I want you to have fun, too. You haven't gotten out like you usually do," I say as we shuffle out of the bedroom.

"Seriously, what the actual fuck." A voice that sounds suspiciously like Bridget's bellows down the corridor, and I'm suddenly very concerned for the integrity of Grady's spleen.

"I don't need to go out as long as staying in involves you." A feather-light smack hits my tush and skitters my pulse. "There, you can subtract one from the spank bank. Can you make it the rest of the hallway by yourself? I'm worried Grady'll lose an organ if I don't go save him."

"Go save your buddy."

I've tried my hardest not to think about my time alone with Grady on the porch. While Jack was gone, Grady asked me a bunch of questions about Jack and my relationship while he carved a pumpkin with his tongue out. I didn't have an answer for most of his questions. Which he seemed to shrug off. I don't think he meant anything by it, but he told me I was a good distraction for Jack while he was up here—and that? Well, I haven't been able to shake that off as easily.

It might be closer to a truth I've feared than I want to acknowledge.

A pumpkin and beer-covered crime scene greets me as I round the corner into the kitchen. Bridget, dressed like Evelyn from The Mummy, with her auburn hair pinned into a chic chignon and a white blouse dripping beige with beer, stands holding a basket and directing a scowl in Grady's direction.

Beer trickles out of Grady's pumpkin as he blinks back at her, a look of decimation I've never seen the golden retriever of a man wear.

"Does he say words?" Bridget asks Jack, whose head is swiveling back and forth between them.

"I'm—" Grady's voice quivers. He's retreated into himself, looking far more like a teenager being scolded and less like the man who lays men out on the ice on the regular. "I'm so sorry."

"Right," Bridget pushes a pair of round glasses up the bridge of her nose and sighs. "I believe we already established that. If you'll excuse me—" She waves for him to move out of her path, slamming her basket down with a huff. "Aulie, I'm sorry, this was for you, but I fear most of it is useless now."

"I'll rebuy everything in there." Grady's shoulders stand prouder with this proclamation. "Least I can do."

With a pause, Bridget meets Grady's gaze and signals her approval with a nod. "I'll send you the order. Have Jack give you my number, and we can square it away."

"I'll get you some baking soda and vinegar." I finally snap into action.

Grady's face is still crestfallen when I walk by him. "It's alright, we'll get the stain out," I say, patting his arm.

"I'm taking my shirt off if it's going to offend anyone's sensibilities," Bridget announces, undoing her buttons and revealing a black lace bra.

Damn. Bridget is—

Grady makes a strangled sound next to me.

"Let's go get some towels," Jack says putting his hand reassuringly on Grady's shoulder, and cringing. "God, you're sticky. We should clean you up, too."

"I overfilled it," Grady whispers as they walk down the hallway. "And then—she—Evelyn—Brendan Fraser—I couldn't."

"I know, bud. I know," Jack says like Grady pouring a six-pack of beer out of a pumpkin all over somebody is a typical, tragic day.

Bridget peels the rest of her shirt off and I grab the baking soda and a spray bottle, handing her a washcloth for her stomach.

"Thank you." She huffs, letting the water run and bringing the cloth over her abdomen. "How are you feeling? They did a laparoscopy procedure, right? You didn't need a laparotomy?"

Her hand brushes over two identical scars on her abdomen, old and healed, right where my fresh ones are.

Has she had a similar surgery as me? Those can't be a coincidence.

"Just a laparoscopy," I say, puzzling over what I know of Bridget, which is not as much as I'd like.

"I wouldn't say *just*." She shakes her head. "The scars may be tiny, but I'm sure they did a lot internally. Did they tell you if they had to operate on any adhesions on your organs or ligaments?"

"I think Jack said some of my ligaments were covered and stuck together—I'm sorry—how do you know to ask these kinds of questions?" Since my diagnosis, most people have been clueless about... everything. From the excitement that I'm finally cured, which, from my understanding, is a misconception, to it being a menstrual disease that will go away if I stay on the pill.

The surgery is only meant to manage my symptoms, not cure me. Nothing can, not fully.

Bridget grabs the spray bottle out of my hand with a sigh. "I'm sorry. I got so flustered when I came in, but Emy told me they found endometriosis during your surgery, which I also have. That's why I came with a basket. I thought you might not know everything you need, and I've had the surgery a few times."

"That was really thoughtful, Bridge." I sniff back a few tears, careful not to show Bridget and freak her out. While love has surrounded me for the past ten days, there's been an undercurrent of loneliness too.

While I would never wish this disease on anyone, knowing that Bridget understands is a comfort I won't take for granted.

"And look where thoughtfulness got me." Bridget shakes her head, scrubbing at the stain on her shirt.

"I'm sure the stain will come out where we got to it fast enough, but we'll need to let it dry. Come on, I can see if I have a white blouse you can borrow, so your costume isn't ruined," I say, motioning for her to follow me to my bedroom.

Rummaging through my closet, I try to wrap my head around the fact that I've had a kindred spirit in Bridget all along. What if I hadn't tried to hide my symptoms from everyone? Would she have caught on and been able to help me sooner? It seems like hiding, hiding my pain, hiding my feelings, hasn't been the lifesaving coping mechanism I thought it was.

"So you and me having the same thing, that's crazy, right? Like, what are the odds?" I ask, buried in my dresses and cardigans.

"Pretty good. It's more common than you probably knew, considering most people have never heard of it. One in ten people assigned female at birth have the disease. Considering there are over twenty of us at the fair, if you count the vendors, the odds were good there'd be at least two of us. I guess we were the lucky ones."

"Okay, so answer me this: I read about that statistic in the brochure they gave me, too, and what I don't get is, if it's so common, why was it so hard for me to get a diagnosis?"

"Ah well, that, my dear, is simple. The answer's a dick."

I stick my head out of the closet to see Bridget's lips curved upward. "Was that a joke?"

"I make one once a century or so."

"I like Joking Bridget," I say, handing her a white blouse nearly identical to the one Grady destroyed with his pumpkin. His pouting puppy dog face still pulls on my heartstrings. "Hey, when we go out there, can you do me a favor and try to take it easy on Grady? I know he suffers from Resting Bro Face, but he's secretly a giant softie."

"He spilled a gallon of beer and pumpkin guts on me."

"Yes, and I recognize that was a giant misstep on his part, but I think he might have done it because he was stunned by you. I don't know if you noticed, but you're freaking hot in that costume."

Bridget snorts. "Oh yeah, like a professional hockey player with rock-hard abs would like a small-town Janeite like me. Now that's realistic." Bridget reaches for the door and winces. "Sorry, I didn't mean—you and Jack are different—you're sweet and funny, and warm, and anyone would be lucky—"

"Bridget, it's totally fine." I hold up my hands to stop her. "We should get back." I motion to the door.

And it is fine. Bridget's not saying something I haven't already been thinking. That joke hasn't quieted since Jack first kissed me on my birthday. But if I'd listened to it, I'd have missed all the quiet, special moments Jack and I have had in the past two weeks. All the tiny smiles reserved for me. The sweet phrases he's uttered against my ear. The feel of his palm on my arm as we sleep at night, like he just needs to make sure I'm there. They way he always looks like he's the one in pain when I wince. They're all moments I'm going to hug tight to my chest and take with me to the grave.

All I can do is keep living in the now and hope that my shattered heart won't be punchline someday.

Chapter Thirty-Four

Jack Parker

Play: *Tighten Up by the Black Keys*

"Okay, so why are you here?" I ask Grady, leaning against a tree illuminated in the night sky. Aulie is sitting outside near the crackling fire, on the couch, which Gus and I took out of the basement earlier. She reclines with her legs elevated on a fluffy pillow, surrounded by the fair crew—none the wiser that I've sworn them all to secrecy about how stressful everything is at the fair without her. The last thing she needs is to feel guilty about taking the time she needs to rest. Lucas, donning frosted spikes and a silver jacket, chuckles, and I can't help but feel a pang of jealousy that he's seated beside her while I'm stuck with George of the Pumpkin Bungle.

In the past two weeks, Aulie's grinned softly often, but tonight, she's wearing her soul-crushing smile. The one that I've come close to dropping to my knees and begging for so many times this year.

Given the circumstances, the death, and the illness, the stars in her eyes shine with an extra defiance tonight.

With my head tipped back, I drink my beer and wait for Grady's response. It won't come. He's equally distracted with the woman to Aulie's right in a fold up chair. Of course, a woman dressed as Evelyn would be his undoing.

Grady and *The Mummy?*

Brendan Fraser?

That's his jam.

With his easily excitable rom-com brain, it doesn't help that he's dressed like another Brendan Fraser character.

I should tell him entertaining his infatuation will only lead to his destruction. Bridget would kill him in his sleep if he ever tried to make a move—or maybe she'd do it while he was awake. Either way, it wouldn't be a good way to go for the man.

"Grady—" I poke him.

He blinks. "Sorry, what did you ask?"

"Why are you here?"

"Oh. Gus invited me."

"Mmhmm, and small-town bonfires are your things, so obviously, you had to drive the two and a half hours up here."

He sighs. "Coach is worried that your time away has made you soft and wants you to return early. He was hoping I could talk you into returning tomorrow."

Tomorrow? What? Aulie's a good week from being able to care for herself, and I have eight days left on my suspension. Hell no, I'm not giving her up early.

I know that's not the right reaction to Coach asking me to do my job. The team is my career. It's my priority.

Or it was... before I thought I could have something with Aulie.

"Why is coach worried I'm getting soft?"

"TMZ may have posted articles about you playing some dude in tights."

"They're breeches." I correct, burying my bottle in my mouth. I wouldn't blame Coach for being concerned about those pictures without the proper context. "Just tell him not to worry. That whole thing was for charity. I needed to do something after all of Veronica's videos online."

"Right, had nothing to do with the fact that Aulie was playing —whoever that was—"

"Lydia."

He shakes his head and laughs. "According to TMZ, she's your fiancée too. I didn't believe that one, but after seeing you look at her tonight, I have to ask is there any truth to it?"

The fire cracks near Aulie, sparks fly spiraling their way to the dark night above.

"Wait, what? How did they get there from me volunteering at a fair?"

"Someone up here was in the hospital's waiting room when you rushed in and told the nurse that she was your fiancée."

I groan. Rumors happen, and I rarely let them get to me, but this one doesn't include just me. Aulie hasn't had to deal with stuff like this before.

"And then a jeweler in Boston confirmed you picked up an engagement ring a few weeks ago."

I scrub a hand over my face. "I picked up her grandmother's ring. Gus had it restored for her birthday."

"I'm surprised your publicist hasn't called you about it."

"I've been ignoring her calls."

"Of course you have. Well, that's a relief. For a second, I was worried you were ignoring our no dating during the season pact."

I laugh nervously, avoiding Grady's eyes. "Yeah. So..."

"Seriously! Un-fucking-believable," he exclaims, running a hand through his mess of blond curls.

"What?"

"Dude. We're two games back from a playoff spot. Thanksgiving is right around the corner. We need you. And you're going soft."

"Relax." I force my voice into a teasing lilt, hoping to appease Grady's present concerns. "I'm not going soft, and I get it. I'll be focused when I return, and we'll get over the hump. It's not like the Thanksgiving standings are permanent, anyway."

"Seventy-five percent of the time, the teams that are in playoff spots at Thanksgiving are the ones who make the playoffs."

"I know the stat, but we could be part of that twenty-five."

"Uh-huh."

"I don't get you. Everyone wanted me to figure out my shit, and I did. My head's never been clearer than it is now. Why aren't you happy about that?"

"As your friend, I'm ecstatic. You've been drooling over Aulie for way too long. But as your teammate, I'm worried. Coach said you've been missing skate time."

I sigh. I have been less dedicated since Aulie's surgery, not wanting to leave her side longer than necessary.

"I needed a break after all the off-season rehab, but I'll be all in now."

"Great." Grady mumbles. "But you should have been all-in this month."

"Just stay in the guest room tonight and come to morning skate with me tomorrow, asshole. And then you can stop worrying that I've gone soft."

Like I could lose my edge after a month.

～

THERE IS A SLIGHT POSSIBILITY THAT I'VE LOST MY EDGE. I can't remember being laid on my ass more or missing more wide-open shots than I have today.

"Your ass take enough of a beating?" Grady asks, looming over me as I lay splayed out on the ice for the fifty-millionth time.

"Yeah." I moan, the chill of the ice seeping into my spine.

He extends his hand and helps me get up. "Is there a weight room in here?"

"No, I haven't been doing that, just some bodyweight exercises at home."

"Explains why I could move you so easily."

Unfortunately, all the work I poured into the off-season to

gain a few pounds of muscle has gone to waste. I'm like a freaking leaf blowing in the wind out here.

"I'm sorry, but you've gotta come back early, bud. If you step into a game and play like this, you'll get destroyed—on and off the ice."

I nod, skating toward the bench and wincing as my MCL screams in my leg. It would probably be best if I were near my trainers and they could massage that out.

Unfortunately, that means tearing myself from Aulie—a thought I don't want to entertain.

Maybe when the fair is over and she's feeling better, she could stay with me in Boston for a while.

She did it over the summer when we were just friends, so it's not too soon for me to ask now...I think...I don't want to look like I'm coming on too strong too soon. Even if this doesn't feel new to me, it feels like I'm five years in.

"Do you want to grab breakfast across the street? That café looked decent," Grady asks.

I shake my head. One of the weirder things about being in Chawton Falls for a month is you learn more about other people and their habits than you want to. On Mondays, for example, because Aulie and Bridget usually meet at Cup of Joe's, she's still sent me in there for a pain au chocolat (sent, I beg her to tell me what she wants for breakfast as a treat, same thing). Bridget, another creature of habit, still works in the café, even though Aulie can't join her. We should find another place to eat for Grady's protection since she kept shooting daggers his way after what Grady referred to as their meet-disaster last night.

"Not a good idea. Bridget gets coffee there on Mondays. I doubt she's over you pouring a massive amount of beer and pumpkin guts on her last night."

Grady scrubs his hand over his face. "Don't remind me. Seeing her again—and like that, god, she was like a wet fucking dream."

"What do you mean again?"

"She graduated with us at Wentworth College." Grady

shrugs. "I was in the same English class with her, but your paths probably never crossed. No big deal."

Grady glances to the side, and his Adam's apple bobs with a nervous swallow. He's not telling me the whole truth, which is weird—he's usually an open book.

I've also never seen a woman fluster him quite like Bridget's managed to. I thought he was about to have a heart attack when she unbuttoned her shirt. It was like the man had never seen boobs before.

"Let's try Anne's. It's a little further down the road, but Aulie likes their coffee just as much."

Grady flicks his wrist, making a whip-cracking sound as I untie my skates.

"Yeah, yeah." I wave him off. I don't care what he thinks about Aulie and me. As long as Aulie is happy with us, whatever, that's all that matters.

Although, it'd be nice not to suck at hockey too.

"You need your edge. You're too fucking soft," Grady says, standing.

"You annoying me can be my new edge."

"I'm serious. You need to come back."

"I know, I know. I'll gather my shit and drive back tomorrow. But I'm not giving Aulie up. She's my dream."

"Dude, seriously? The cup should be your dream."

I shake my head. The cup is still important to me; it's the pinnacle of my career aspirations, and I don't want to let the guys down. But my obsession with winning the cup was always about doing something that would make my dad proud, and if my time away from the team in this town has taught me anything, it's that his legacy in my life was never about a championship. It was the quiet moments before the games when we'd sit in the parking lot and talk about anything that wasn't hockey. It was the way he softly danced with my mom when she was upset. Or wore a purple polka-dotted bow tie to a Sporting Award ceremony because I bought it for him with my money.

That was my dad. That was his legacy.

The fact that he won the cup multiple times doesn't even crack my top ten for why he's my hero.

And if I want a long-lasting legacy, the cup won't be mine either. It will be something I create with the woman I love instead.

~

A WAVE OF CLOVES, NUTMEG, AND CINNAMON GREETS ME, entering Gus and Aulie's. My mouth waters, even though I just ate way too many donuts.

A new tablecloth and a smattering of plates and cups sit on the dining room table. A growl works in the back of my throat. What the hell? She should be in bed, resting—not cooking and setting tables.

Fuck, and she probably used her cast iron pan, and that thing is heavy as shit.

My traitorous stomach pulls to the table with excitement. It's missed Aulie's cooking something terrible over the past few weeks.

"Shit, something smells good." Grady inhales next to me.

"Thank you!" Aulie peeks her head out of the kitchen. "Have a seat. I'm almost done in here."

Walking over creaky floorboards, I enter the maple cabineted kitchen and hand Aulie her coffee. "What are you doing up? You should be resting." I grump, laying a kiss on her cheek.

"Oh, what a nice treat! Thank you! And I felt decent and figured you'd be hungry." She scrunches her nose as I pull away. "You stink."

"So does his hockey," Grady laughs in the doorway. "Which is why his ass is shipping off to Boston tomorrow."

Wow. Way to hang me out to dry, bud.

Aulie's lips quiver like she's fighting a frown, and I shoot a scowl in Grady's direction.

"Tomorrow? Really?" she says, not meeting my eyes. "Did you already tell me, and I just forgot?"

"Unfortunately, no. It's—uhm—a sudden change of plans. I

was a little rustier than I expected this morning, and my legs could use some love from the trainers, too."

"Right. Well, that makes sense. It is your job, after all." She flashes me a weak smile and turns to the stove, stirring something in a large pot.

Tell me to stay. A ridiculous part of me nearly begs. *Sure, it's my job, but you're my everything.* The words I want to let slip past my mouth follow.

But I can't let the guys down.

"I'm going to rinse off," Grady says, stepping on his heels. His knack for setting a fire and then leaving is impressive...and annoying.

I approach Aulie at the stove, wrapping my hands around her hips and turning her to me. Again, her eyes don't reach mine, and I tuck a finger under her chin, lifting it. "Hey. Just because I have to return to Boston doesn't mean I'm leaving you."

With her history of abandonment, I imagine this sudden departure is freaking her out. Even if she'd never show or say it.

"I know. I get it and I'm going to miss you. But you have a job, responsibilities, and a team of guys that rely on you—and you have to do what's right by them. I'll count down the days until you visit again at Thanksgiving and be fine. Promise."

I swallow. I don't know if staying this ridiculously happy is doing right by my teammates, but hopefully, returning to the city and being in my routine will help me get the fire back I didn't have this morning.

"So actually—" I rub my neck. Heat rises to my cheeks. It's probably too soon to have this talk, but maybe where she's bummed it isn't. "I wanted to talk to you—"

Aulie pulls at her fingertips as her face falls. "Oh yeah, of course, but I promise, whatever you need, I'm cool with."

I suppress a chuckle, because her flustered appearance looks anything but cool. "Okay, great, because what I need is you. So when the fair is over, and we have a home stretch—would you maybe want to come to Boston and stay with me? I can set up a little desk in the living room so you can still work."

"Really? You'd want me there?" Aulie's face radiates with a brightness that no longer brings stars to mind. No, she's the whole freakin' sun, and I am a planet that revolves around her, basking in her glow.

"Of course I do. I'd sling you over my shoulder and take you with me tomorrow if I thought the drive wouldn't hurt." I cup her cheek and relish the warm comfort of her velvet skin. *I'm still considering it, even if I'd be an ass to move you in your condition.*

"What about your no-dating rule during the season?"

I swallow. Today on the ice, instead of the fiery music of Dropkick Murphys, a cheerful oldies song about rainbows, sunshine, and lollipops played in a loop in my mind. There's an unsettling feeling deep in my bones that choosing Aulie means I'm picking her above my edge, above being the best I can be for my team.

But how could I not? How could I let this brilliant, unique, beautiful woman go?

"There was always an asterisk to that rule." I shrug.

She quirks a brow at me.

"No dating during the season—" I lower my mouth to her cheek and press a kiss there. "Unless the woman that—" *I love.* The words dance on my tongue, but I don't say them. She has to know. I've shown her enough—what's the point of declaring them? It'll just make everything overly mushy, and no one wants that. "I've been desperate to kiss for years finally notices me."

She snorts. "Oh, well, that's silly, Jack. You've been well and noticed for twenty years, didn't you know?"

Chapter Thirty-Five

Aulie Desfleurs

Play: *Stay by Maurice Williams and the Zodiacs*

Jack Parker reported back to the Badgers last week. *According to inside sources, certain members of the training staff have expressed concern over his lack of commitment to his fitness regimen while away from the team, stating that he isn't in optimal shape for the season.*

Are you surprised, Jeremy? The man has never committed himself to anything. They've got to trade that guy's ass. Yeah, he's talented, but he'll never be the guy—it's time to move on and let him be someone else's problem.

"And that's enough of that." I turn down the speaker in my car and push away the guilt gnawing at my chest. If Jack is out of shape, it's my fault. Since my surgery, he cut his time at the rink in half, sometimes not going at all. In hindsight, I should have pushed him to go instead of reveling in all the flannel blanket snuggles and early morning conversations about nothing.

I drive down the road near the baseball field and put the car into park. A blast of November wind greets my cheeks as I open the door and step out to my family's plot. Winter in Chawton Falls is almost here. I'll have to stop visiting soon, but after being unable to come this past month, I'll need a few more trips before I'm ready to let go.

After a quick brush of the dried crust of leaves off the granite markers, I grab my Seven Novels book and blanket, rolling it out in front of my Memere's marker. "Salut," I say to her, placing a coffee on her grave. "Gosh, I've missed you." A shiver works down my spine, and I sip my coffee, hoping to warm my insides a fraction.

"I know, it's getting colder." I shrug off her concerned look shining down on me from above. She'd hate that I came out here when it's this chilly and I'm recovering from surgery, but tough. "We'll finish *Persuasion* today, and I'll be content to visit in the car after this." My fingers wrap tighter around my coffee mug and find comfort in its warmth. The metal sphere around my finger that Gus gave me yesterday as a belated birthday gift presses against my skin. "Oh! You'll never guess, but Gus surprised me with your ring for my birthday; he had it restored, and now I'll be able to take you everywhere. You would love what he did, and I guess Jack too, with the band. It's absolutely gorgeous."

I twiddle with it, moving the small sphere around my ring finger. A ghost of a smile curls my lips. Gus couldn't afford to do this on his own. The stones on the band were definitely from Jack, but we hadn't acknowledged our feelings for each other yet when he did this. And he hasn't tried to claim any credit now that we're...something.

I don't know what to call what we are since neither of us took the extra step to define the relationship before he left.

How long has he been quietly doing these small, thoughtful things?

"You remember Jack, right? Well, he and I are...seeing each other. Although he had to go back to Boston."

I'm unsure what his departure means for us, either, but I'm remaining optimistic. Despite his track record, I believe he meant it when he said he wanted to keep exploring our relationship.

Though, it's unclear how long that intention will last under the weight of the season's pressures.

"Can you believe that? Me, dating a hockey player! How ridiculous is that? But he's so thoughtful, sweet, and funny." I shrug, taking a sip of my coffee.

"You know how Captain Wentworth's half agony, half hope? I feel like that's me. It's like I've never let somewhere this far in. Because it hurts when they leave. None of you meant to abandon me, I get that, but heck, it still shattered something inside of me. Sometimes, I want to be angry at you all. You taught me to love with this deep passion and never taught me how to cope when I have all this love to give, and the person isn't there anymore. I'm terrified that I'm there with him, that he's as deep as Emy or Gus, and I don't know that I trust him yet not to demolish me.

"But I guess if Mr. Wentworth could let Anne go for eight years on a boat, then I could learn to do that, too. What am I saying? He just went to Boston. It's not like he's a world away." I shift. "Just a feeling—I don't know—" Stretching my legs out, I lean back on my palms to relieve some pressure off my pelvic area. The sun streams through the barren branches above, and I soak in the pale warmth.

"I know. I know. Worry about the future when it becomes the present because it's undecided until it becomes so. You're right.

"I'm going back to the fair in a few days for *Persuasion* weekend, so that will do nicely. Oh yes, let's finish our read."

Opening the page to where the silk bookmark lies, a little prick of hope sparks in my chest. Anne and Mr. Wentworth are about to confess their love to one another and embark on their journey of a happily ever after. It's an ending I usually revel in fictionally.

But today, despite all my misgivings and fears surrounding my current situation, there's an undeniable voice whispering that maybe a happily ever after in my life is possible after all.

~

AFTER TWO TERRIBLE GAMES BACK, YOU HAVE TO WONDER IF *Jack Parker has it this year or if the injury and suspension were too much to overcome.*

If you're Coach Tidwell, you can't be happy about him running around in those tights during his suspension. You'd want him training or watching game tape or something.

Do you think his sudden engagement has anything to do with it? The girl's cute, but when you have Veronica Burke as an option, I don't know how you could let that go.

Be honest, do you think a guy like Jack Parker can't have both? He probably has his cake and is eating it too.

Whatever's going on, he needs to figure his shit out soon, or the team isn't even going to make the playoffs this year.

"THEY AREN'T TIGHTS! THEY'RE BREECHES! AND WE'RE NOT engaged!" My head falls to the steering wheel with a dramatic sigh. I need to stop listening to this stuff. I thought it would help me stay connected to Jack while he's away, but I was mistaken.

All I feel is a continued well of guilt. His job performance is suffering because of me.

This is why he doesn't date during the season. Because the Cup is and should be his priority, not some soft girl from a small town in New Hampshire.

A little voice that's never been kind to me scolds. I turn the off radio and cut the engine, making my way into the house with takeout from Chez LaBranche.

Since my surgery, I've had issues with anemia, so this burger isn't just a want. It's a need.

After listening to way too much sports radio, so is a beer.

I dip into the fridge, grab a bottle of pumpkin beer that Jack left for me, and pop the cap. Wisps of cold air spiral from the top, and I bring the bottle to my lips, savoring the cinnamon and nutmeg mixed with the hops.

"Game out back?" Gus peeks out of his office, the sound of a beer opening apparently his call to arms.

"That sounds perfect!" I happily sigh. "I'm just going to change into my game day sweater, but I'll meet you out there?"

"Sure, I'll go start the fire."

"I got you both food in here, too." I motion to the giant bag of stuff.

Emy stretches her arms, walking down the stairs from a mid-afternoon nap. "Oh, is that Chez LaBranche I smell?"

"Mmmhmm."

"Yes!" she says, shooting her fist in the air. "Have I told you how much I love you lately!"

"Not nearly enough." I bat my eyelashes and feign a wounded countenance.

"You're right. Five times a day isn't enough. I'll work on getting it up to the twenty you deserve." Emy pulls plates down from the cabinet. "I'll plate. You go change into your cute Parker jersey—"

"Sweater." I correct. My Uncle Claude was very particular about me using the correct terminology when referring to parts of the hockey uniform.

Emy waves me off. "Yes, yes. You're a dying breed, my dear. I hate to tell you, but I've even heard the hockey players refer to it as a jersey online."

The fire is already roaring when I meet Emy and Gus out back in my green and gold *sweater*.

Nervously, I settle into my seat, pull a blanket over my lap and sip my beer. Jack hasn't just played poorly his last few games. He's been nearly killed in each of them. Every time he's slammed against the glass, the impact reverberates through my body.

"He's going to have a better game tonight. All the rust will be knocked off. I can feel it," Emy says as if she can sense the nervous energy humming along my skin.

"He better, or Coach is going to have to drop him down the line soon," Gus says in his signature matter-of-fact manner, making me want to throw something at him.

I toss him a look instead. "No way, he's better than anyone on that line, even on one foot."

"Aww, such a good fiancée," Emy teases, wiping at a glob of ketchup on her cheek.

"Ha. Ha." I roll my eyes. Jack warned me that some celebrity gossip sites had run with a story about us being engaged before he left. I shrugged it off, like anyone would believe him to be that smitten with me. But for whatever reason, the town is living for the rumor. Moulton's Farm, for example, started an "Apple of the Eye, Jack and Aulie Dating Package." I'd be tempted to ask them not to use my name, but since one of their sheep is still on the... lam, I'm scared to ask anything of them. "But seriously, he's just getting back into the swing of things. He's still Jack. Still the best in the league. Even when he's not his best."

I sit back, confident that Jack will overcome this slump soon. But when the game starts and the puck drops, it's hard for me to remain biased enough in his talents.

Jack's not just in a slump—he's in something more profound than that. And if he doesn't figure it out soon, he will either get benched or die.

During his third shift, Jack gets slammed against the boards with an extra force. I cringe and cover my eyes, desperately wishing to block out the scene. When I crack them open again, the broadcast is replaying him skating back to the bench in slow motion. With slumped shoulders and a defeated expression, he's carrying himself like a man who's lost all hope.

"It's like his heart is somewhere else," I say. My chest constricts, almost as if it were stuck in my throat.

"It is, pumpkin," Emy says quietly. "It's still here."

Emy's words fall like ice water in my veins. I know Jack cares about me, but hockey has always been the most important thing in his life. He may have given me a fraction of his heart this past month, but if he keeps playing like this, it won't be long before he asks for it back.

Chapter Thirty-Six

Jack Parker

Play: *Faithfully by Journey*

Another bad game for Jack Parker. Tidwell needs to move him off the first line.

Screw the first line, I want him off the damn team. He's not the guy, Mike. He's done—and I don't know if it's for the season or for good, but I'd rather another team figure that out. Trade his ass or ship him back up to New Hampshire so he can run around with those weird pants.

God, New Hampshire, can you imagine wanting to go there?

Good fireworks and cheap liquor, though.

True. Maybe they can light one under his ass.

"Okay. That's enough radio for today." With a nervous chuckle, Grady shuts off the stereo in my car. My knuckles tighten on the steering wheel as we approach the practice arena. I weave in and out of traffic as tourists, and regular Massholes make a mess of the road in front of us.

"God, there's so much traffic today," I grunt.

"Seems normal to me." Grady shrugs. "Chawton Falls made you—"

"Don't. Say. It." My jaw clenches. Maybe I was too happy my first few games back, but now, with my shoulders tense and annoyance clinging to my muscles like a second skin, the fierce grump is back—it's only a matter of time before I shake the rust off and get back into the zone.

Parking the car, Grady is quick to get out. We're not *Parker Late*. But we're not exactly *Grady Early,* either. Not when I've been playing like shit, and his anxiety is taking a hit.

It's not fair that my performance affects him, but it does, and I owe him to get my shit together on the ice.

I grab my phone, opening a string of texts from Aulie as I walk into the building.

A picture of Willoughby laying on a crocheted couch sits in my messages.

KITTEN

Best idea ever.

JACK

He's going to hump the hell out of that.

KITTEN

Hey, whatever keeps Quackers safe.

Oh. Oh dear god, I should probably leave him and the couch alone now.

A huge grin spreads wide across my face. Just like that, all the tension from the car ride over melts away.

"Game face, Parker." Coach Tidwell yells, passing me.

"Yes, Coach." I swallow, stuffing my phone into my pocket.

Right.

I am fierce.

Grumpy.

Think of things you hate, like...cows...and bare feet......

Images of Aulie giggling in bed, our feet tangled in the sheets, push all the negative images away.

Warmth spreads in my chest.

I'm too happy.

Fuck.

~

I DON'T KNOW IF I'VE EVER BEEN BOARDED MORE IN MY LIFE. Groaning, I drop my body on the bench and start untying my skates.

"You coming out tonight?" Grady asks.

I shake my bed. How could I? I'm one giant fucking bruise. "Nah, I'm going back to the apartment and ice...everything. I can hardly walk."

"Wouldn't have to worry about that if you had your head in the game." Grady shakes his head and crashes down next to me.

"He's right, Parker," Coach says, hovering over me. "You know where we are in the standings?"

"I do, sir. Three games back."

"The climb to a playoff spot will be hard, but it's not impossible as long as you step up and play the way you're expected. We need you all in."

"I understand, sir."

"I don't think you do. When I said no more distractions, I didn't mean to find a different one. For the next few months, hockey needs to be your sole focus—I don't care what that means in your personal life. Look around. Your teammates need you."

My eyes roam over the locker room with a swallow. Grady, Wes, Coop, and Big Ed have been carrying the team on their shoulders for too long because of a mistake I made at the beginning of the season, and they're starting to show the wear and tear of my actions.

I owe them.

Even if it means jeopardizing my happiness. That's what a good teammate would do, anyway.

"Hey, Jack." A security officer sticks his head in the locker room. "Your girlfriend is waiting out in the hallway for you."

Aulie's here?

The anticipation to see her fills me with excitement, humming along my skin like a buzzing electric current. I should feel frustrated that she came when she hasn't reached her recovery window yet. Instead, I'm a plant about to receive a well of sunshine after many days of cloudy skies.

"Shut it down, Parker." Coach Tidwell grumps, walking away and shaking his head.

Shit yeah, waxing poetic about being a plant isn't the type of stuff I should think about. When I was away from the team, I was so confident in my decision to keep things going with Aulie that no other choice seemed possible. But now, there's an inkling of doubt that's telling me I'm being a selfish-ass staying this happy.

With a little less pep in my step, I toss on a shirt and go out to see Aulie. I don't know where we're headed, but I need to figure my stuff out for my team and her. I need to choose once and for all.

Aulie's figure stands shrouded in the hallway. Her caramel hair is bound in curls that look...different than she usually wears. She's draped in my sweater, leggings underneath, and...heels. Okay. That's weird.

She's FaceTiming someone with her back to me. Probably Gus, so he can say "hi," too.

"Hey, there's my girl. This is the best surprise." I go up behind her and wrap my arms around her waist. "I missed you," I murmur into the top of her head, a hint of vulnerability in my voice.

The moment my eyes snag on the person's reflection in the camera, the smell of an expensive perfume tickles my nose. Raven-black hair shows on the screen, even though I swear it's caramel in reality. They blow a kiss into the camera and hit end on the recording.

This isn't Aulie. And that wasn't a FaceTime. It was a livestream.

"Veronica." Startled, I instinctively jerk back, as though stung by an invisible force. "What the hell are you doing here?"

"Aww, it's so nice to see you, too. Do you like my hair? I told the hairdresser I wanted quaint fall vibes, and I think they nailed it." She runs her manicured fingers through her caramel tresses that look far too much like Aulie's natural color to be a coincidence.

"What the fuck do you think you're doing? I told you our arrangement was over."

"Doesn't look like it's over from the live we just did. Boy, did you look like a man in love." Her signature red lips tip into an evil smirk, and I bite back a growl.

"I thought you were someone else."

"Oh, yes, your fiancée, right? There's no way you want people thinking you're engaged to that *thing* from the North. That's why I've come to save you. I have a proposal of my own." Her fingers creep up my chest and I take hold of her hand and push it aside.

"Her name is Aulie, and considering I intend to propose to her someday, I don't mind people thinking it's true now."

"I thought Jack Parker didn't date during the season. Isn't that your personal rule?"

"Aulie was always going to be the exception."

A flash of hurt briefly flickers across Veronica's polished features. "And I wasn't? What makes her so special?"

God, that's a loaded question, isn't it?

I think about the soft feel of her hair tangled in my fingers. Her velvet skin, lightly scented with rosewater and lilacs, flowers that she's somehow more delicate and lovely then. How is that even possible?

And then I think about the paradoxes within her. How can she be that soft, delicate flower and a complete badass, overcoming so much grief and pain and never letting it fully destroy her?

Fuck, that woman is a queen.

How did I briefly entertain the thought that I would give that up? Even for a room full of guys who mean the world to me?

Aulie is the infinite night sky, littered with sparkling stars. She's the sun. She's—

"Everything. She's the love of my life, and there isn't one ounce of her that isn't extraordinary," I say.

"Well, hopefully, she's understanding, too. Because, boy, that video looks like our bad boy is two-timing us both. She watches my lives sometimes, you know. Hopefully, that wasn't one of them for your sake." She grimaces

My mouth drops as Veronica rises to my cheek, presses a kiss, and snaps a quick selfie before I can register...anything.

I knew Veronica was fake, but I didn't realize she was evil, too.

Aulie trusts me. Everything will be fine.

Veronica saunters away, and I slide my phone out of my pocket, dialing Aulie.

The phone doesn't even ring once before I'm sent to voicemail.

Chapter Thirty-Seven

Aulie Desfleurs

Play: *End of the World by Hermans Hermits*

A dull ache fills my abdomen. Dragging my body out of bed, I raise my arms, hoping to stretch the ache out in the wink of early morning light. It doesn't help. It's rather rude that this pain insists on persisting six weeks after my surgery.

Maybe it shouldn't—perhaps I have a disease, and I'm still a weakling.

The thought itches at me until I don't want to be in the same room with it anymore. I need to prove that I can rise above all of this. That I'm capable of taking my life back. Yes, a run should do that.

Grabbing a pair of leggings and a long-sleeved workout shirt, I put both on and lace up my sneakers. Slowly, I move toward the front porch. Emy and Gus are probably still sleeping, and I don't want to wake them up.

"You're up early." A figure illuminated in the halo of a blue light says as I pass through the living room.

"And you're up...late?" I cock my head to the side. Sometimes, Gus gets into his coding and will clack away without any reference to time.

"Almost done," he mumbles, sipping his energy drink. His beverage of choice irks me to no end. Gus literally takes negative care of his body, pumping it with chemicals, and ignores his sleeping schedule—and he's fine. Yet when I misstep and eat or drink something "wrong," it's game over. I'm caught in a flare of pain for days. How is that fair? "Where are you going, Alouette?"

"Out for a run."

"You think that's a good idea? You're barely walking."

"I'm fine." I wave off his concerns. I'm too itchy to get out of my head to care about the practicality of this idea. "I'm just going to the do the loop around the pond, no big deal.

"That's two miles."

"And I usually do five. See? Taking it easy."

His lips press into a hard slash. "Bring your phone."

"Yes, papa." I roll my eyes, but Gus, consumed by his coding, misses my obvious annoyance with his helicopter brother's antics.

"Don't be freaked out, though. I shut it off yesterday afternoon because I needed a social media break, and that was the only way to stop myself from doom-scrolling." While recovering from surgery and grappling with my diagnosis, I've learned some days are better than others mentally.

I've been mourning the loss of the people I love for so long that I'm painfully aware of how grief hangs on me and this time, that familiar feeling isn't for someone lost, but a life not lived. Mine.

When I was younger, I had all these plans. I wanted to travel the country or abroad to England. I wanted to see Jane Austen's house. See a performance at Shakespeare's Globe. I wanted to make something of myself. I didn't know what—I just wanted to be impressive—extraordinary, even.

But as time passed, I became stuck in a war over my body. One that I'm still not done fighting, and all the while, my friends who've been unencumbered have gone on to big and glamorous lives. At least that's what I see on social media, and I can't help but compare that my—albeit cozy—existence is significantly stilted compared to theirs.

I need to get over it. I need to overcome the fact that I'll never be as impressive as someone like Veronica Burke. And I need to be okay with who I am now. No more mourning who I could have been if I didn't have this disease.

Brisk air kisses my cheeks when I exit the house. Dragging the fresh air through my lungs, I focus on putting one foot in front of the other and shaking the cobwebs off my muscles, which have grown stiff and weak over the last few months. "Just keep running," I tell myself as cramps settle on the tops of my thighs. "You're not in pain. You're fine."

My feet carry me around a corner and down a slope. Dead leaves crunch under my feet. Barren branches sway over head as the grey light of dawn slowly cracks the sky open.

The dull ache doesn't recede as I hoped, and I try to focus on the rhythm of my feet on the path and my breathing.

Left. Right.

Inhale. Exhale.

Lightning shoots from the crook of my thigh down the back of my leg. Gasping on an inhale, I focus on getting my leg to land safely on the ground. It doesn't comply, and I collapse.

Catching myself with my palms, gravel rips up my hands.

With a groan, I roll over on my back, tracing the stars still faintly glimmering in the sky. A loon wails hauntingly in the pond as I lie there, palms stinging.

I give up.

There is precious little in my life that I have control of.

People leave.

Relationships end.

Even my body is against me.

And yet, the world still spins on its axis.

Life goes on.

The chill of the ground seeps through my shirt and chills my spine.

I'm not doing my body any favors still lying here.

I pick myself up and drag my overly spasming-body back to my house. Gus briefly glances away from his computer as I enter. "That was fa—" he blinks, taking in my sullen figure. I don't have the strength to hide how defeated I am. "I'll start the fire."

"You want some coffee?" I ask, limping into the kitchen and using the counter for balance.

"I'll get it. Come on. Let's get you out near the fire and sitting on a cushion." He grabs me by the crook of my elbow and guides me outside.

"I can get the coffee," I say—but my heart and feet following Gus otherwise. Why am I still such a wimp?

~

WHILE THE WHITE, STERILE WALLS OF THE DOCTOR'S ROOM hold little comfort for me, an odd sense of calm settles into my chest as I roll off my leggings and climb back onto the table. Paper ruffles as I slide further up. Resting on my palms, I wince at the pressure of my scrapes, only a few hours old.

I still feel imprisoned by my limitations, but there's a certain freedom in understanding the reasons behind it. However paradoxical that may sound.

I was right. Something was wrong. And while assertiveness isn't a part of my nature, at the very least, there's a sliver of confidence to advocate for my health that didn't exist before.

The OBGYN who performed the emergency surgery on me, Dr. Smith, enters the room in yellow scrubs, her hair clipped up high with a claw. She narrows her gaze on me, peering through thin, gold-framed glasses.

Does she know how much of a hero she is in my eyes?

The woman who saw my endo when she was in there to fix my ovary torsion.

The one who removed it from my appendix, my rectum, under my ribcage, and sidewall. No matter how much pain I'm still in, it's nothing like before. And I owe her that.

"Aurelie. Let's see—" Dr. Smith smirks, flipping through the pages on her clipboard. "Well, that was a cute unintentional rhyme. How are you doing today?"

Not great. I fell this morning because the pain is still intense, and I'm frustrated I haven't recovered fully yet.

"Alright." I shift on the table, and the sheet over my lap falls away a smidge.

"Can you lay back for me?" She runs her fingers over my incision scars. "They look good. But seriously, if we were to omit the phrases, fine and alright from your vocabulary. How are you feeling?"

I pull at my fingertips. Way to call me out, doc. "Better. But I don't think I've reached the place where most people function. Does that make sense?"

"It does." Dr. Smith sits in a swivel chair in front of the computer. Her fingers fly over the keyboard as she assesses something on the screen. "Unfortunately, I don't have the perfect solution to get you to that place. Endo can be a demoralizing disease but you're a tough woman."

I swallow a laugh because Dr. Smith is serious, but I doubt if she knew me, she'd think I was tough.

"I have a few things," Dr. Smith continues. "That we can try to help manage some of your symptoms. Everyone's journey with this disease is different, so I can't make any guarantees, but these strategies should help give you a better quality of life: take what works, leave what doesn't. That being said, although I removed a good portion of it, it's next to impossible to excise the entire disease, so you're always going to have endo to some capacity."

My heart sinks. In my research since my diagnosis, I had stumbled upon that truth, but hoped however weakly, that the select few who claimed they had cures were actually correct instead.

But as always, I was a fool to hope.

For someone with abandonment issues, I guess it serves me right I developed a disease that will never leave.

That being said, Dr. Smith's offer for strategies and the ability to give myself some control here is exciting. So, I'll focus on the positives today and leave the negatives for a drearier day.

"I'm going to be frank with you, Aulie." She reaches out and grabs my hand. "After talking with your fiancé at the hospital, you need to hear this. There will be days and things you cannot control. For some people, that's hard to accept, especially at first, while you're adjusting to your new life post-diagnosis. You've had this disease for a while, but it didn't have a name. A lot of things mentally are shifting for you. I would recommend seeing a therapist to talk through this transition."

The recommendation to consider therapy feels like a slap in the face. I should be beyond that here, right? It wasn't in my head.

A tear rolls down my cheek, and another one falls because I'm incredibly overwhelmed. Oh, shoot. No. No. For the first time in forever, I'm being listened to in a doctor's office, and I'm about to ruin it by crying.

"I'm sorry. I don't know why I'm crying, but—"

"No apologies needed. Your medical history and summary visits show you've had some shitty doctors before this. Everything you're feeling is valid. I'm sorry if they've made you feel otherwise. You wouldn't be the first patient I've had sitting here feeling like that, and unfortunately, you won't be my last."

I pick my gaze up, meeting Dr. Smith's. Tears rim her lower lid as she flashes me a sympathetic smile. A smile that wraps me up in a blanket of validation I didn't know my hollow chest had been so desperate for.

I wipe at a tear and nod.

Rolling across the room, Dr. Smith grabs a box of tissues and offers them to me. "I wish I could offer more than a few strategies because this disease will interfere with your life. That's reality. Still, it doesn't have to ruin anything more than it already has. You might have more detours ahead of you than expected, or things will take longer to accomplish. Look for the positives in the detours, and the endo won't own you. Now, let's talk about your stupid super high pain tolerance that was getting you in trouble."

"High?" My chest shudders as I hold back a sob. As much as

Dr. Smith seems okay with my blubbering, I am determined to remain composed in this room. I don't want to give her a chance to dismiss me. There has to be a limit to her compassion. There always is.

"From the stories I heard, you push through a lot."

"Oh, that. I mean, I wouldn't say I push through anything. I'm just doing what needs to be done."

"I need you to stop. That's why you black out so much."

I purse my lips. Dr. Smith has a degree, but she doesn't have the pain association. She can't understand how impossible her request is. There's always pain. I'd get nothing accomplished if I didn't push through it.

"Hopefully, once you're fully healed, you won't have pain as frequently as you did, so this isn't the big ask you think it is. But I'm serious about learning to take it easy. Your body is shutting down because you aren't listening to it. Start listening. You've done a great job caring for it, but you must give it grace, too. Even when you don't feel like it, it's doing a lot just trying to heal itself and fighting the disease."

I wipe at a tear. My mind's heavy and full with Dr. Smith's words. They're everything I've needed to hear from a medical professional, but never thought I would. "Thank you. For everything."

"I'm sorry so many doctors were assholes to you, Aurelie, I really am. We have a long way to go in the medical community, and a lot of educating needs to be done." She gives me one last small smile, pivots in her chair facing the computer, and clacks away on the keyboard. Those key clacks sound like hope for the first time instead of the derision for disappointed hopes they usually inspire.

A very unfamiliar prick of anger burns furiously inside, churning my stomach into a white-hot molten mess.

How many times have I sat in a room like this, and the people wearing the white coat made me feel weak? Mentally unstable, even.

And all the while, my pain was real.

Everything I've felt in the last ten years was real.

Sitting on the bed, waves of validation wash over me, giving way to anger and fatigue. It's like I just finished running a marathon, and now I'm being told there's another race to run. A lifelong one. But this time, I have support. I have someone who believes in me. And I have faith that this leg of the race will be so much easier because of it.

Chapter Thirty-Eight

Aulie Desfleurs

Play: *Make Your Own Kind of Music by Cass Elliot*

"How did your appointment go today?" Bridget asks, setting a table in the crew tent with the props needed for the day. She pauses, placing the umbrella down, and smiles.

A heavy sigh shudders my chest. Today chose violence when it came for my emotions.

"That good? Huh?" She eyes me sympathetically. "I was hoping this doctor would be better."

"Oh, she was great," I say. "I'm just—it was a lot to process, but it was good. She validated me and listened to my concerns, which is more than I could ask."

Bridget shakes her head. "It's the bare minimum you should expect. But I'm happy you finally found one of the good ones."

"Hey, Aulie? Roger." Emy's voice sounds over the walkie-talkie.

"Here. Rabbit."

"Uhm—have you been on Instagram or TikTok today? Roger."

"No, my phone is off. Did someone else elope? Oh god. Who could—"

"No, no one eloped. It's fine, everything is fine… just…I…I'll be right there. Roger Rabbit over and out."

Well, that sounds oddly ominous.

The spasm from earlier hasn't quit, and I look at my watch to see if it's time for more ibuprofen. Thank god it is.

I grab my purse, where I'm always sporting a bottle now (and pads), and settle on the couch while I wait for Emy.

"Did she say what she wanted?" Bridget asks.

"No, but she sounded…panicked."

"Of course, the fair from hell would end with a problem."

A wrinkle forms between my brows. While I haven't been able to get to the fair, all the reports were that everything was fine. It's part of the reason I've felt so expendable and unaccomplished lately. "What do you mean, the fair from hell?"

Bridget's stoic expression breaks. Her eyes widen, and her throat bobs nervously. "Nothing. Everything has been great."

"Bridget, you're a terrible liar," I say, looking suspiciously at her. "How has the fair been going?"

She takes a deep breath, collapsing on the couch across from me. "If you were a fair-goer, it's been fine. But we fucking missed you—it's been miserable on the planning side. I don't know how you've shouldered most of this the past few years. I've already applied for a student worker grant for next year because I refuse to let it fall all on you again. Why haven't you spoken up about how much there is to do? Seriously, you were doing the work of like four freaking people."

"I—uhm. I don't know if I ever really thought about how much there was to do. I just did it." If I'm being honest, for the longest time, productivity and results were so ingrained in my self-worth. That's the only thing that I was focused on. "Was it that much?"

Leaning in conspiratorially, Bridget peers at me through the glasses falling on the slope of her nose. "Colonel Brandon married Marianne in his street clothes because I didn't have the will to tell him to change into his uniform."

"No." I gasp.

"I'm serious. He wore a brown waistcoat! And I didn't care!"

I place my hand on my heart like I'd been shot, and we both break into a fit of giggles.

Emy bursts through the tent flaps, pausing as she enters and putting her hands on her knees. "Lord, I'm so grateful this is the last fucking weekend. This has sucked." Her eyes widen, meeting mine.

"I know everything was a mess, and you need me." I wave her off, my chest warming.

"Great, because we need to discuss how much you did yourself. What the hell were you thinking?"

I think Dr. Smith might be right about that therapy thing.

"I need to get through Christmas at Pemberley season, and then we can revisit how much I've taken on." I smile.

"Right." Emy slides the clipboard with the checklist out from my hands and writes *ask Bridget and Emy to help with Christmas at Pemberley stuff* on the list. "Okay, but tabling your overworking issue for now. I—" She takes a deep breath. "You need to see this."

She places her phone in my hand, and I look at her skeptically. "You realize that most of the problems in my life start because *you* checked Instagram, right? I'm considering banning you from the platform."

"I don't think this is a problem—I just—I think you need to see it from the source rather than through the rumor circulating. Sabrina is already discussing it with some of the other cast members in the house, so I can't keep it from you today."

A video from Veronica's page is pulled up. The caption reads, "Visiting bae after the game. It's a good thing I'm confident enough to share. There is no way he won't choose me in the end. #MayTheBestGirlWin"

"Hey, there's my girl. This is the best surprise." Jack's face lights up in the background of Veronica's shot. Ecstatic. Decimated. *Hers.* He wraps his arms around her like she's the most precious thing in the world. "I missed you." He kisses the top of her raven-black head and stays there while Veronica blows a kiss to the camera and shuts it down.

If there were a way for my stomach to sink through the ground and into the middle of the earth, it would.

"Now, I know it looks bad," Emy says, "—but there must be a logical explanation. That man doesn't do what he did the past few weeks and then this. It doesn't match who we know he is."

"He would if it'd help him get his game back. He needs to be an asshole to play well. You and I have seen that the past few weeks." I shake my head. I don't want to think about this today when I'm already dealing with a million and one other things to let my heart be demolished. I can cry and break down later because I'm tough, just like Dr. Smith said. "Whatever, it's fine. It's not like we defined our relationship or anything before he left." Bury the pain. Move on. It's the one thing I'm good at in this life. "I should get working on this checklist."

"Oh bullshit, you're such a Jane." Bridget scoffs, halting my rise.

"I don't see how me being like the oldest Bennet sister has anything to do with this." I press my lips into a thin line. The warmth that had been building inside me for the past two months is wilting away.

"No. OUR Jane...you know, the reason we live and breathe? Jane Austen? Hello. You sound just like her letters. Take the ones after the love of her life died, for example. There's hardly any evidence in the letters that his death ruined her, but she wrote— hardly anything during that time despite her being prolific. It had to get to her somehow, even if it was all internal. But that was her calling card; she joked sorrow off way more than she should have, and when her illness was wreaking havoc on her life in her late thirties and early forties—the illness that would eventually kill her, she even freaking wrote that she didn't think she had the right to complain.

And I'm sorry, but fuck that. What she had, was different, but her illness, our disease, it's all shit. You have every right to complain as much as you want about it, and you have every right to feel however you want about Jack, too. Because feeling something is what colors the world in poetry and art, otherwise all that's left is science and observation—important, yes? But does it sing and leave us fulfilled? Not typically."

Emy and I blink at our usually robotic friend. "I'm sorry...but who broke you?" Emy whispers.

"I uhm—it takes me a while to warm up to people. I can go back to being—"

"No, we like you—like this or anyway, you want to be. We like Bridget Funk, just as she is." I smile. "It was just unexpected."

Bridget rakes her hands through her auburn curls. "We're a team now."

And she's right, we're bonded now, her and I, forever. Emy is my platonic soulmate, but she'll never understand the quirks of this illness. Of what it's like to feel good and that turning on a dime of the intensity of the pains or the cramps that black us out. She'll never understand writhing on the bathroom floor begging for mercy, and I'm so glad for her for that.

But it's also lovely, however much it sucks that Bridget has it too, to have someone who knows how this thing messes with me mentally.

Bridget endured all these things, yet she's still a badass literature professor. She's hope that this disease won't dominate every facet of my life someday.

A blonde head sticks her through the tent flaps, wearing a smug expression. Whatever news Sabrina has, I don't want to hear it. "Hey, Aulie, Veronica Burke is here...to see you."

In a panic, I glance at Bridget and then back to Emy. "What the hell could she want all the way up here?"

"Oh, she's totally going to De Bourgh your ass," Bridget says with a look that empowers me to think, *Bring it on.*

~

A MAN WITH A BACKWARD CAP AND SUNGLASSES ANGLES A phone on Veronica as I trudge up the hill toward Wentworth

Mansion, with Bridget and Emy flanking both of my sides. In the late-fall sun, her hair appears lighter than the raven-black hair on her video.

Is it usually like this, and she uses a filter?

I have limited knowledge of how all that social media influencer stuff works.

She doesn't move as I approach her. Instead, she adjusts her champagne sequined mini skirt, lace camisole, and feathery mess of a jacket on her top half.

I swallow. Jack told me they really weren't originally dating, but after seeing how he looked at her yesterday, I...I don't know what to believe.

"Wow," Emy whispers, gathering closer. "With her hair that color, she looks like the Evil Barbie version of you."

"I can see that." Bridget nods. "Enough that a certain someone might have mistaken you two from behind."

"Oh please, she's gorgeous, there's no way—besides, did you see how he was looking at her? That was a man gone."

"Yeah, pumpkin, that's the face he's been flashing you forever when you aren't looking," Emy says before we're too close to Veronica to have this conversation any longer.

Veronica's harsh gaze rakes over my body, a look of disgust contorting her face. "Are you Owlie?" She asks, butchering my name and running her fingers through her curls.

"Yes, can I help you with something?"

"Oh, please—don't pretend like you don't know who I am. You follow me on Instagram." She pivots back to the camera, giving it her undivided attention. "She follows me on Insta. Someone screenshot that before she can unfollow and deny it, okay? Love you."

A wrinkle creases my brows. So what if I follow her? She's a public figure. That's not what I was asking.

God, I'm so tired today; forgive me, Memere, I don't have the strength to be kind.

"That's not what I said. Of course, I know who you are. What I don't understand is what you're doing here."

"That baby-doe-eyed look won't work on me, sweetheart. You know why I'm here."

Emy's fists clench beside me, and she steps forward. Lightly, I put my hand on her arm. For the first time in maybe ever, I've got this.

"I believe I already stated this, but I'm sorry. I'm really clueless about the reason for your presence here."

"There's a rumor circulating in the tabloids that you and *my* boyfriend, Jack Parker, are engaged."

Something feral claws its way to the surface inside me at Veronica referring to Jack as *her* boyfriend. While we haven't defined the relationship, I can't help but think *mine, mine, mine* in response. "That sounds like a ridiculous rumor to be circulating if he was yours."

"Are you seriously pretending that you haven't heard of it?"

I cross my arms. "I've heard of the rumor, but I haven't heard of any confirmation on his end that he's dating you again. And Jack tells me *everything*." I don't want Jack to get in trouble for breaking an NDA, so I keep my answer vaguely threatening, hoping Veronica picks up on the subtle context hidden within.

Slowly, her mouth pulls into a grin. "Oh, so obviously, you haven't seen the video from last night. Let me show you." She slides another phone out of her jacket, and I raise my hand to stop her.

"I've seen the video."

"And you still don't think that we're together?"

My chest tightens. The rational mind I've tried to keep through this conversation clouds. I don't think Jack would do something like this to me. I trust him—what I don't trust is my ability to read his feelings for me correctly because while I've grown, I still have that headfirst tendency that's more likely to burn me than be correct. And yes, Veronica is gorgeous. But seeing her in the light of day without the benefits of a filter, I'm also seeing something else.

This woman is incredibly insecure. And if Veronica, the woman I've held as the pinnacle of womanhood for the past year, isn't confident in herself. Who's to say that my feelings of inadequacy aren't just a normal feeling that everyone deals with and overcomes? Who's to say we all aren't carrying some hidden weight or pain and have to cover it up in the world? And who's to say it's a healthy burden we're all silently carrying?

No. Screw that.

"Do you think he'd choose someone like you when he has me as an option? I mean, seriously." She laughs, running her hand through her hair again. Emy's words about it are oddly looking like mine flash through. And I can't deny it now that Veronica's lost her miracle wash.

Her hair is exactly the same shade as mine—a dirty blonde, light brunette that no celebrity would randomly get.

Could she have set Jack up? Why would she feel threatened by someone like me?

And if she set Jack up... that look on camera was for me.

He might not have said the words, but his face said everything: he loves me.

Maybe.

I'm getting ahead of myself, and there's an angry celebrity still live-streaming a conversation with me—and oh my god, when did my life get so weird?

"I'm not going to speak for Jack or pretend I know his true feelings for me. He may pursue whatever relationships he'd like. I don't claim him to be mine exclusively or at all. But I have a feeling that you're unable to claim him as well since, for whatever reason, you drove up to Chawton Falls, New Hampshire, to have a meaningless conversation with a small-town nobody. And you know what? I pity you for that, Veronica. I'm sorry for whatever is going on in your life that makes you feel so incomplete that you've taken these actions. But I'm not a rung to be stepped on in your ladder to healing. Now, if you'll excuse me, I have a fair to coordinate, and you've taken up enough of my time."

Veronica's eyes widen as a harsh scowl cuts across her once cheery façade. "I've taken up—"

A maa from behind interrupts her as she jumps and turns to

see Gio. He sticks out his tongue and lets out a blaring bleat.

"He's never going to choose you!" Veronica shrieks, keeping her oversized purse as a shield between her and Gio. "What makes you think that your folklore ass is going to keep someone like Jack Parker if I couldn't? Hockey is the love of his life, it always will be. You're a fool if you think otherwise."

"So I'm a fool in love." I shrug. "And yeah, he might destroy me, but at least I'll have felt something real for a change. Can you say the same?"

Gio takes a step forward, and it backs Veronica on her heels. A mud pile behind her catches her foot, and she slips, falling on her ass. "Cut the live! Cut the live."

Gio walks over, licking her face.

"Are you kidding me?" The man recording asks. "This shit is gold."

"Not for me!"

He shrugs.

"Can someone get the goat off me, please?"

Emy walks over and pulls Gio away. "While today is the last weekend for the Annual Chawton Falls in Love with Jane Austen Festival, there's still time to buy your tickets for Christmas at Pemberley, a fun recreation of a regency Christmas at Wentworth Mansion. Tickets available online!"

Behind her, Veronica tries to get up but manages another slip.

Feeling merciful, I walk over to the guy recording and put my hand on his. "I think that's enough," I whisper. He shrugs and finally ends the recording.

By the time I turn back to Veronica, she's covered in mud and on the verge of tears. I sigh. I know what my Memere would want me to do in this situation, and I'm realizing it's not a weakness. It's a strength.

"Come on, I have some dry clothes in the tent." I lend her my arm, and she grabs it. "Do you like tea? You must be freezing in that."

"Tea sounds amazing. Thank you," she whispers, wiping back a tear. "He was right. You really are extraordinary."

Chapter Thirty-Nine

Jack Parker

Play: *Slow Show by the National*

"Glad to have you back, Parker." Coach Tidwell slaps my back in the Philly Away Team locker room. "Hell of a game out there."

"Thanks. It felt good." I lie. After the last week I've had, a two-goal game *should* feel like a relief, but—there's a hollowness in my chest that hockey isn't touching. I haven't been able to contact Aulie since Veronica's video posted last night. Her messages are undelivered, and I'm being sent to voicemail when I call. I can't tell if she blocked me that fast...or what. But something in my gut tells me she wouldn't do that to me without giving me a chance to explain myself.

Either way, it lit a fire of frustration in my chest that made it so I could finally play out of my freaking night tonight. So if she is mad at me, at least I've got that going for me.

Not that I want it.

Powering on my phone, I tell myself not to read too much into it if she hasn't texted me back. We have two days off starting tomorrow that I was planning on spending at home with an ice bag before a long road trip, but maybe I can drive up and see her instead.

A few texts populate. One is from Aulie, and I let out a sigh of relief.

KITTEN

> Hey, SO sorry. I should have told you I was powering my phone down for the day. Feel free to call me when you get home. Good luck tonight! I hope you kick butt.

The timestamp says it was sent five hours ago, and the text doesn't super read like she wants to hurt me, so ...this is good.

We don't have WiFi on our plane where I can text her, but luckily, Philly isn't that far of a flight. We had an afternoon game, and we're leaving immediately so that we can sleep in our beds.

JACK

> Sounds excellent. I'll talk to you soon.

A shrill voice screeches in the locker room. God, I've heard enough of Veronica's voice to last a lifetime. I'll never forgive her if she ruined what I have with Aulie. "Yo, Parker, you need to get a look at your girl." Wes laughs.

"She's not—" I turn to correct Wes because there's no way I'm letting this rumor spread.

He shoves a video of Veronica in my face, but the immediate background takes me off guard.

Familiar rolling hills sit in the back, with a crowd and a backdrop of Wentworth Mansion, that I know well.

Aulie's figure comes into focus, and I squint in confusion at the video.

"Can I?" I ask, reaching for the phone. "Where did you find this? That's not Veronica's handle."

"It's a live-stream from Instagram. Apparently, Veronica posted it originally; she took it down, but enough people were watching that there are already thousands of reposts. It went viral after Veronica said she would expose the golddigger who was after her man, but it didn't go well for her."

"Thousands?" I croak. Oh, Aulie would freaking hate that.

Like a car accident, I can't look away from, I watch Veronica attack Aulie, throwing last night's video in her face. She confirms that she's seen it, but her reaction to the video isn't bitter. To her credit, Aulie doesn't back down from Veronica's accusations, and a swell of pride burns in my chest. She's standing up for herself.

That's my girl.

"Do you really think he'd choose someone like you when he has me as an option?" Veronica asks, her voice cruel.

Say yes, Dessy. You know I would.

"I'm going to speak for Jack or pretend I know his true feelings for me."

Oh, come on, you know I love you, Aulie. Right? It's obvious.

My heart sinks as Aulie continues, making it obvious she's not as confident in her relationship with me as I thought. I thought I had made it clear how I felt about her when I left. I thought it was obvious in how I took care of her, in how I kissed her. And yet, she's standing there, having completely missed the mark.

A maa on screen sends a shiver down my spine, and I take a beat to remind myself that Gio is on screen in a recording. He can't hurt me here.

"Hockey is the love of his life. It always will be. You're a fool if you think otherwise!"

"So I'm a fool in love. And yeah, he might destroy me in the end, but at least I'll have felt something real for a change."

Opposing feelings spiral inside. Without her narcotics, Aulie's still saying she loves me—but she doesn't trust that I'd choose her over hockey, and that's a real fucking problem.

I hand Wes his phone back. I don't have to see any more. Aulie isn't mad at me, and I'm thankful for that, but I need to figure out how to communicate how I feel better. She can't be with me feeling like that. I won't allow it. She deserves to know how devoted I am—she deserves to know how fucking much I love her.

~

I SIT SILENTLY FOR THE PLANE RIDE HOME AS THE TEAM fills the planes with whoops and chatter after our first good win. A win that happened because I was wrecked. Something I intend to fix when we get home.

Fuck. I hate that I have to let these guys down. It's a terrible casualty, but I love her too fucking much, not too.

"Hey, Parkey." Grady punches my leg. "Any reason you played out of your fucking mind tonight, and there's a video of you with Veronica Burke."

"Unrelated." I shake my head, staring out the window and watching the clouds float beneath us.

"Because I love you, man, and you're playing well. But Aulie doesn't deserve that. Find a different way to let her down."

"Do you think I'd be that much of an ass?" I growl.

Grady sticks his palms up in defense. "No. No. I just—fuck, dude, I meant nothing by it, unclench the jaw, draw in the claws. We're good."

"Sorry. I'm just frustrated about that video—I thought it was fucking Aulie last night." With a sigh, I rake my hand through my hair.

"Ah. That makes more sense."

"So what I don't understand—" Coop climbs on his seat in front of us and turns around.

I groan. Is everyone going to get in on this conversation?

"Is why she said in *her* video today that she wasn't your girl-friend and didn't know where you stood. When you returned to the team, you seemed confident about your relationship."

"I didn't get that either." I shake my head. "I thought I was pretty obvious while I was up there. You saw me, Grady. It was clear as day how I felt, right?"

Grady rubs the back of his head. "Yeah, I mean, I thought it was...but..."

"But what?"

"When I was carving that pumpkin with her, I kind of got the sense that she was less sure about you than you thought like some-thing was holding her back from thinking you weren't going to leave for real the minute you had the chance."

"That makes no fucking sense. I did everything I could to show her I was all in."

"You keep saying that, but did you *tell* her you were all in?" Coop asks. "Because no offense, Jack, but you're hard to read on a good day and don't communicate as much as you should."

Jesus, that was blunt.

But Coop's wrong; Aulie doesn't need the words to know how I feel—she has to know that everything I did was for her. That I loved her through my actions.

That's how Darcy showed himself to Lizzie.

Captain Wentworth to Anne.

Mr. Knightley to Emma.

Shit, sure they showed it. *But they also had some poetic decla-rations of love too.*

The combination of the two gave what they said weight and what they did a deeper purpose, didn't it?

Fuck.

"I might not have said it out loud." I rub my heels in my eyes. "But she might have. Shit. Yeah, no, I know where I messed up.

"**What the hell are you guys doing here?**" I blink, staring at Wes, Grady, Big Ed, Coop, and his baby Carson huddled in the doorway of my apartment. "And why does Coop have his baby?"

"I promised Mandy she could have the night off." Coop shrugs like that answers both parts of my question.

"Let us in, it's chilly." Grady pushes past me with five different pizza boxes. He goes to the kitchen, and the other guys bustle in. "We're here to talk about you and Aulie."

Oh.

"I'm sorry. I don't know why I suck when I'm happy, but I'm not giving her up."

"Why would you think we want you to do that? Asshat." Grady opens the cabinets where my plates usually are. "Are they seriously all dirty?"

"We had a road game. I was busy."

"Box it up, boys," he says.

"And I thought you'd want that because you told me you did— you kept reminding me about the no-dating pact."

"I was a man jilted by love." Grady waves me off.

"I wouldn't call what happened gilting, but sure." Grady hands me a box loaded with every topping imaginable, and I accept my fate, going to the couch with the rest of the gang.

"If I need to play better to pick up your slack, I will. But as your friend, I can't let you accidentally fuck this up—and you are."

"Can you play better, Grady?" Coop asks, taking Carson with him to the couch in his carrier. "Because if you can, you probably should do that."

Big Ed sits next to me, his pizza loaded with meats. "I don't think you're playing poorly because you're happy. You were just rusty and in your head. Your dad always played best when he was happy. You know, the last thing he did before he got on the ice was look at a picture of you and your family. He said it helped him remember no matter what happened on the ice, he had everything he wanted waiting for him at home. It took the pressure off to play loose and hard. I think you could play like that, too."

"And if you suck, you suck." Wes shrugs. "But at least you'll be happy. This shit could end tomorrow, you know."

"And hockey isn't everything. Your dad could have played more at the end." Big Ed says his mouth is full of pizza. Grady walks around placing an open beer on a coaster for everyone, and I want to joke about how comfortable he is in my house. But also— Grady's fucking awesome, and I don't feel like ragging on him tonight. "I wanted him to, of course, but he shook his head and said he wanted to spend more time with his family. Because he knew he'd regret the time he didn't spend with you when he was old, but he'd never wish he'd played more hockey."

"He prioritized what he wanted." I nod. "Fuck I miss him."

"He was one of the best." Big Ed picks up his beer and clinks it against mine, sitting on the table.

"Okay," Grady settles in a leather armchair nearby. "Now that we've got the mushy stuff out of the way let's strategize telling Aulie how we feel."

"We?"

"Like we're letting you figure this out on your own."

"I'm fine." I wave him off. "I appreciate all of your concerns, but I've got this. Why don't we watch something mindless that blows up on TV and chill?"

"I like documentaries personally." Wes burps.

Loading up my streaming device, I wince when I see it littered with regency romance stuff and hope the guys don't rag on me too much.

"No offense, Jack— "Coop starts.

"I used my account on Aulie's TV so she could watch whatever after surgery. She's wicked into this regency stuff."

Grady's lips curve, mouth full of pizza. "You don't say."

"So, is there one we're supposed to start with?" Coop asks. "Like, is it a series or something?"

"We're not watching Jane Austen movies." I groan.

"Oh, no. We are," Grady says. "Hold him down and take the remote, Big Ed."

~

THE MORNING SUN SHEDS ITS WARM RAYS IN MY APARTMENT. I rub my temple with a groan. I haven't slept on the couch or pulled an all-nighter since college, and my body is officially too old for this.

Grady picks up his head, wiping drool from his lips. "So, what do we think? Should we write a letter like Captain Wentworth?"

Why the hell does he keep using "we"? This is a me and Aulie thing.

I shake my head. "I'm a worse writer than a verbal communicator."

The boys collectively wince.

"Wouldn't want to risk that then," Coop says, checking his phone. At some point, he set up a portable monitor and laid Carson down in my bed . "Can somebody tell Mandy this is really what we did? I think she will think it's a cover for something."

"Maybe we take the Mr. Knightley approach then. His confession about riding through the rain was very romantic." Big Ed picked up his phone. "I'm going to call Maria and then order us some hangover food." He rubs at his temple. "I shouldn't have tried to keep up with you last night."

Aulie, oh shit.

"Fuck." I exclaim, shooting up and checking my phone. It's dead and I groan. "I was supposed to call Aulie last night, and—fuck—should I plug this in and call her now? Should I blurt it out on the phone? If one you finds the monologue, I'll read it to her."

"No fucking way. We're going up to Chawton Falls. Do it in person," Grady says. "But I think what you say has to come from the heart—vulnerability from a big strong man, that's the key."

I shake my head. "You like romance way too much."

"And yet, romance has never loved me."

Chapter Forty

Jack Parker

Play: *Here Comes Your Man by the Pixies*

I sincerely regret this big gesture.

Two beady eyes stare into my soul, chewing their cud and standing in front of the Wentworth house. I'd rather slay a dragon to get to the princess than deal with this. Why couldn't overcoming my anxiety and confessing my true feelings to Aulie be enough for today? Did I seriously have to confront this damn goat, too?

Grady's shoulder brushes against mine. "He's—"

"Creepy as fuck," I say.

"Does he do anything else?" Grady whispers.

"No. This is it." I rub the back of my head. The embroidered waistcoat I'm sporting pulls taut as I raise my hand. Shit, I'm going to have to get closer to Gio than I ever have if I'm going to pull off this big gesture.

A shadow creeps over Grady and me. "Why are we standing here?" Big Ed asks.

I cross my arms and nod toward the wether. Who's currently

looking at me like *where are my balls, Jack? They took them, and I want them back.* "Goat."

Tiny giggles follow. Coop bounces his way to us with his little one in the carrier. "Oh, he's so cute. Can we pet him?"

"You think *that's* cute?"

"I mean, he is a very nice-looking animal. Here, I'll get him for Baby Carson." Big Ed walks over to Gio and tucks him under his arm in one swift motion. Stunned, Gio lets out one tiny maa but seems content to be in the arms of the defenseman.

He shuffles back over the rolling hill, scratching Gio's chin. "See? He's a good little goaty."

I shudder down the fear Gio's casting a curse this close to me. Maybe it's his fault I'm in this ridiculous costume, dressed like a duke, absolutely demolished by a woman instead of running around Boston with the freedom I used to enjoy.

"Right. I guess I should—I should go in now."

"You've got this, bud." Grady pats my back. "Just remember, no more keeping how you feel inside... any instinct you have, do the opposite."

"Opposite, right? Tell her the truth. But where should I start?"

"Tell her about the tattoo that shit made me weepy," Wes says.

"And obviously, tell her about your sweater number, too." Coop adds. "Look, Carson, Uncle Ed got a goat for you to pet."

A poot emits from someone in the group. Followed by a disastrous odor.

Coop wrinkles his nose in disgust while Grady gags nearby.

I'm blaming the goat. There is no way a human could produce that smell.

"Jack?" A delicate voice wafts through the haze of our stink bomb. I gaze to where the sound initially came and see Aulie with her head out the window, brow furrowed.

My heart thumps, this close to its other half. I haven't seen her in two weeks, only talking to her on the phone, and being here now makes me realize how hollow I am when she's not around.

"Oh, hey, Aulie." I wave at her, unsure how being dressed like a duke, surrounded by my teammates, one of whom is currently holding a goat, is being perceived by her from up high.

"What are you doing here?'

"I'm big gesturing you." I shrug.

Her face scrunches in confusion. "I don't understand."

"I'm not particularly good at it."

"Yes. I believe we established that once before, but you rallied beautifully the last time, if I remember correctly." She smiles at me. It's radiant and blinding. The sun's rays seem frigid compared to the warmth that radiates from seeing her with that expression.

"Would it be okay with you? If I did it again? I don't want to bother you if you're busy."

"By all means, big gesture away. Should I—meet you down there?"

I glance at the guys, their eyes all directed at me with solemn pleas, like lonely puppy dogs that desperately need a good scratch behind their ears.

While I appreciate all their help, there's no way I'm doing all this in front of them.

"I think it'd be best if I meet you inside." I holler.

Wes's shoulders slump.

"Killjoy," Grady mutters.

"Who is a good goaty?" Big Ed coos.

Coop plugs his nose, backing away from Gio. "Dude, what the heck did you eat? It's rank."

"Well, I'll be in here." Aulie smiles, her cheeks coloring pink.

With a deep breath, I leave the guys on the grass in front of Wentworth Mansion and make my way up to the parlor room, where we danced, following the soft sounds of Aulie playing "Yellow" on the piano. Apparently that moment meant something to her too.

With every note that brings me closer to her, my heart pounds. After I admit my feelings for her, there's no going back. She'll know exactly how bad I've had it for her for years, and I can only hope that she'll still want to be with me after and that I won't come across as too emotional for her.

The wooden floorboards creak as I step into the parlor, and Aulie pauses her playing and turns to me. "Hi," she says bashfully. Slowly, her eyes rake over the tight vest and breeches I purchased for this.

A smile tugs the corner of my mouth up as she rakes her teeth over her lower lip.

"You know, I saw an interesting video yesterday."

"Did you?"

"Mmhmm." I step forward, standing further into the room, with my hands tucked behind my back. Too anxious for stillness, I pace over the blue and white area rug in the middle of the room. "Curious thing, I left for Boston thinking I had a girlfriend who understood my feelings for her, but I guess I wasn't clear. So, if you'll allow me, I'd like to make a few things expressively clear to you."

"I suppose I would be open to listening to that."

"Good." I turn sharp on my heel and pin my stare on her. On an inhale, I ready to give her my heart on a silver platter, the one she's always owned. After I admit this truth, there will be no questioning how I feel. "The truth is, Aulie—the tattoo, the one right here—" I gesture to my heart. "It's about you."

"What?" Aulie's head shoots up.

I clear my throat and start reciting the lines of prose inked on me since the summer we were reintroduced.

"She walks in beauty, like the night
Of cloudless climes and starry skies;
And all that's best of dark and bright
Meet in her aspect and her eyes.
Those lines, they're about you."

"But you've had it for years," she whispers incredulously.

"I've been yours for years. I'm sorry I haven't been clearer about that, but that's the god's honest truth, Dessy. And I want to make sure you know that. I thought there would be nothing harder than baring my soul to someone. I was wrong. Watching a video of you where you doubted the depths of my affection and thinking I valued something more than you was far worse. So here I am, telling you who I am—a man that is hopelessly and utterly yours—a man who always has been."

"I'm sorry. I'm not fully comprehending all of this." Her lips wobble like she doesn't know whether to smile or cry. "Hockey's always been the number one priority in your life. How could I possibly be higher than that to you?"

"Actually Dessy, it never has been. Since the day I started my professional career, I've you carried you with me everywhere. What's my sweater number?"

"Forty-seven." She shakes her head, a tear rolling down her cheek. I take a few short steps to the piano bench and gently wipe them away.

"April Seventh, that's the day I found you in the fountain and you stole my heart away. I tried to fight my feelings for so long because I thought they would freak you out, but I'm done hiding them. I'm in love with you, Aulie. Desperately, hopelessly in love."

"Why did you think that I would be freaked out by that? I told you I loved you—you had a chance to say it back, and you laughed it off."

"I wanted to say it so bad, but I thought you'd have to be on drugs to think that."

"That I love you? Why wouldn't you believe I meant what I said?"

"Because you see the real me." I shrug.

"And it's a thousand times better than whatever shit you try to show the public! You foolish, foolish man." She scowls at me, and I'm tempted to lean and brush my lips against her to see if it'll soften. "Listen to me. Jack Parker, you are the kindest, sweetest gentleman I have ever met. And I love you, I've always loved you, and I don't see that changing anytime soon...

Especially if that outfit isn't a rental." She tugs on my lapels and brings me tighter. "Understand?"

I nod with a swallow. Unsure if my lips should be curving up with joy, brushing hers, or trembling from the overwhelming feelings churning inside.

Ah, fuck it, who am I kidding? Kissing her is going to win every damn time.

Leaning, I brush my lips against hers, and she savors the feeling. "I missed you." She hums against my mouth.

"I missed you more." I pick her up from the bench, and she wraps her legs around me.

"Oh, is this going to be the new game? One-upping each other's affections?"

"I've got to stay competitive somewhere, kitten." I tease the seam of her lip, and she parts for me, hungrily devouring my mouth with hers.

"You're going to have your work cut out for you, us Desfleurses are known for giving our whole hearts away."

"Woman, I'm here in dukes costume, what makes you think you don't already have that entire organ in your hand?"

"I guess we can both be fools in love, then."

I don't know if she knows what she's given me, that holding her like this and hearing she loves me, feeling it in the way she kisses me, is the greatest thing I could ever possibly win in this world, but I plan on showing and telling her that for the rest of my life.

Starting now.

My forehead drops against hers. "Where can we go that isn't full of two-hundred-year-old breakable stuff? I have some more confessions to make."

Epilogue

Aulie Desfleurs

Play: Rose of Sharon by Mumford and Sons

"Where are we going? Blindfolding me was so not the vibe," I say, as Jack's hands gripped fully on my shoulders steers me...somewhere. It's ridiculous that man thought I could let go enough to be guided like this anywhere...

"Can you just trust me for once and let this happen?" Jack says in a frustrated tone. He's not really that annoyed. How could he be after winning the Stanley Cup a week ago? Besides, after nine months of dating, I know he knows how much I trust him, which is why I'm comfortable answering with...

"No. Have you met me?"

"Yeah, I didn't think this part through."

Suddenly, my walk in darkness halts. Two arms wrap around my waist, and I'm hoisted over Jack's shoulder in one fluid motion.

"Jack Parker. Put me down!" I screech.

"Sorry, kitten. We've got places to be." A smile laces his words, like he's relishing the control he has that I regret granting him thirty minutes ago.

To be fair, I thought I was granting him some kinky bedroom thing...not this...

"Don't think you can be cheeky out in public. That's a bedroom thing."

Coughing and choking follow my rebuke. "Fuck, I didn't need to hear that," another low voice says.

"Why is Gus here?" I ask.

"You're the worst." This time, the voice is soft and feminine.

"Emy, too?"

Jack sighs and slowly puts me back on the ground. "You can take your blindfold off now. We're here anyway."

Pushing the piece of fabric off my eyes, I slowly blink in the warm June sun. Green leaves dance against a clear blue sky, hanging over a familiar place full of people I love. "We're at the cemetery?" I glance down and see my Memere's marker by my feet, a coffee from Anne's already sitting there.

Red and white picnic blankets are laid in between the Desfleurs' family markers. Jack's mother, sisters, Lucy, Blake, Bridget, Grady, Emy, and Gus sit on them with plates full of food for a regency picnic. Finger sandwiches, fruit, delicate cakes, and tea are scattered along the finely dressed blankets. Flowers, fine china, and pillows, it's precisely how I imagined the picnic in *Emma* to pass.

Hopefully, minus the cruel barb hurled at Mrs. Bates.

I scrunch my nose, trying to figure out why this collection of people I adore is here. It's not my birthday, or as far as I know, some holiday...

Oh my god.

The reason behind this gathering dons on me. Jack reaches into his pocket, sliding a small wooden box out, then drops to one knee.

He breathes out. "I'm not going to be very good at this, but I hope I can at least do this better than Mr. Darcy's first try."

"Boo. Insult her family," Bridget yells from her blanket.

"I wouldn't. Gus scares me. Mrs. Bennet wasn't much of a fight," Grady says, leaning on his hand in a way that brings his shoulder closer to Bridget's than necessary.

"Shows what you know, Mrs. Bennet would have thrown down!" Bridget crosses her arms, almost like a taunt, and instead of backing down, Grady faces her, narrowing an intense stare on her face.

"She had fragile nerves."

Bridget opens her mouth to respond, but a strangled sound comes out instead of her usual eloquence.

Grady's lips tip in a smug grin.

Jack sighs. "If you guys don't mind, I'm trying to propose over here."

I lean in with a conspiratorial smile on my face. "I think Grady was flirting with her."

"He flirts with everybody."

"So this proposal!" Emy yells.

"Right!" Jack straightens. Delicately, he grabs my hand, holding it in his. "Aurelie Lunette Desfleurs. Since the first day I saw you, you've been it for me—the minute your eyes landed on me, I've been utterly and completely yours. There's nothing more I could want in this world than to start this next part of my life with you. So without further ado—"

He opens the box.

"I love you. Most ardently"

is engraved on the top of the inside lid, and below that, on an emerald velvet pillow, sits an Edwardian-era ring with a diamond in the center and intricate filigree engravings along the band. "Would you make my world and be my wife?"

"Jack, it's gorgeous." I gasp. We haven't talked about rings, but if I were to show him what my dream one would look like, it wouldn't even come close to this. He knows me better than anyone has ever gotten to. Down to my slight grimaces when I'm in pain (which is happening far less frequently), my fears, and the weight of grief I still carry (which hasn't gotten lighter, as much as I have another hand helping me carry it)—and he's still here. He's choosing to make a commitment of forever with me. "Yes. A thousand times, yes." I cover my mouth to hide the blubbering and then laugh because I'm re-enacting Jane's reaction to Bingley's proposal without intention.

Whoops, hollers, and clapping surround us as Jack picks me up and twirls me around. Placing me down, his forehead falls against mine. Moisture collects on my cheeks. I go to swipe the tears away but come up dry.

Glancing up, I catch Jack crying. "I love you," he whispers, grabbing my hand and tugging me forward. "We'll be right back," he hollers over my shoulder. "I need to go introduce Dad to my future wife."

Acknowledgments

One day after my 27th birthday, on February 1, 2019, during the showcase showdown of the Price is Right – the woman whose title of "Memere" was the first word out of my mouth, passed away. For months I didn't sleep, nightmares plagued me, and I started going to therapy twice a week. After her passing, I was determined for a while to keep my heart closed off, determined not to let anyone get that deep again, determined not to deal with loss in such a magnitude again.

But one day, I realized my Memere loved many people who left with the same intensity I held for her, and she never let their sudden loss harden her. She loved as strongly and fiercely as ever before carrying that with her. Memere, thank you for teaching me what true strength looks like. Thank you for keeping me as one of your own, forever and always. I'll never know a stronger earthly love than the one you showered on me every day. I miss you every freakin day so much. I miss your cooking, your singing, your fingers flying over your electric organ, and the little screeches and Frangloisms that would fly out of your mouth. Je vous aime beaucoup.

To the aunts and uncles that raised me along with my Memere, thank you for all your patience and care you took with me. Thank you for letting me tag along to French Club, and giving me the keys for the treasure chest at Yokens. Thank you for the ice cream adventures, stories, lessons, card nights, and terrible jokes (I'm looking at you Aunt Gemma). I'm thankful every day for the time we were able to spend together, I hope you're all behaving around that big card table you've gathered at. Although, I know the answer to that—Uncle Jerome, don't get Aunt Cecile worked up like that, be nice to your sisters—I'm sorry, my Memere's beans were always better.

To the Instagram Writing and Bookstagram communities, thank you for supporting and believing in me. I wouldn't have gotten to this point without your unbridled enthusiasm. Thank you to everyone who has screamed about my books, shared it in their stories, and passed their existences along to friends.

To my dear husband, I fear I've reached my thank you quota as a good New England wife in my previous two acknowledgments. But please know, there isn't a day that I don't wake up thankful that you're on the other side of the bed. Thank you for always believing in me, and continuing to stoke my wild belief in soulmates. You'll be my book boyfriend always and forever. I can't wait to start this new lifelong journey with you.

To my little JoeyBean, Mama wrote this book while you were in my stomach. Thank you for not judging my puns too harshly and kicking me when I needed to cut a line, you were right. Now, please never read this.

To my sisters Anne and Kate, thank you for being my rocks as we navigated all of this loss together and thank you for being the best big sisters I could ask for.

To my parents, thank you for supporting my dreams, and Dad, thanks for answering my questions about NH history and bicorne hats.

Jax, thank you for being the best editor and cheerleader I could ask for. This book wouldn't be the novel I'm proud of it becoming without your critical eye, and brilliant communication skills. I appreciate having you as a daily remote co-worker.

Jo, thank you for reading and encouraging me along when the self-doubt hit me hard. I love you to the moon and back.

Sonja, thank you for your critical eye and all your encouragement.

Allison, thank you for always knowing what to say to push me to the final line.

Sara, Sara, Sara—what can I say to the person who has kept

me going this year, and made finishing this book with some sanity intact possible? Just thank you for everything, thank you for all your hard work and support. I appreciate you tremendously.

Anna, thank you for giving me a gorgeous cover, it came out better than my wildest dreams could imagine.

Dr. Vyas, Dr. Guan, & Dr. Carla—as always thank you for giving me a second chance at life and being the doctors that listened.

To Alison and Maria at EFHOU, thank you for all the support of my works, I'm so happy endo gave me you.

To my friends, Rae, Zoe, Kayla, Cassie, Rebecca, Morgan, TL, Alex, Jonny, Laurie, Emma, Caitlin, Kayleigh, Antwan, Sinehan, Cathy and Blue Willow Bookshop, and anyone else my pregnant brain may have forgotten. I appreciate and love you all. Thank you for being understanding when I disappear for weeks at a time.

And to anyone who picked up this book and took a chance on me, thank you, thank you, thank you!

About the Author

Torie Jean is a granite stater sweating it out in Texas. She is married to her high school sweetheart who reaffirms her belief that the magic of romance is in the tiny everyday things. She has had endometriosis for over half of her life, and hopes to raise more awareness of the disease with her writing, while providing the happily ever afters people with endo deserve.

 instagram.com/authortoriejean

Also by Torie Jean

Finding Gene Kelly

Love Letter to Old Movies | It's Always Been You

Fake Dating | Cinnamon Roll Hero

"A heartwarming novel of love triumphing over life's struggles." – Kirkus Reviews

Love at Frost Sight, A Holiday Novella

A Meddling Faerie | The Soulmate Bond

Enemies-to-Lovers | College Romance